We think of history as a list of dates, a highlighted page in a text book, a crumb trail of footnotes. But sometimes history is personal, as tangible as the touch of lips or the clench of a fist.

Susan Streeter Carpenter takes us back in *Riders on the Storm*, her novel of the sixties, and of 1968 in particular. It's a year that makes us think—flower power, groovy, love beads— all the trappings of the counterculture, something to make fun of, to dress up a movie, the tie-dyed T-shirt as faded and dated as a flapper's beaded dress. But in *Riders on the Storm* you'll know 1968 as a year in the life of people who wanted to do right, to do better, who wanted to take the world with them to that better place. Ivy Barcelona, a college student in Cleveland, puts all of herself on the line for those aims.

But it's not just about politics—it's about love (for had not the Summer of Love just passed?), about hard truths, about the conflicts that arise when the personal and the political collide. Ivy begins as a political naïf, burning with undifferentiated idealism, and we follow her on the journey to a more tempered humanism. The novel takes us and these friends into the shabby, ill-lit rooms where revolution is embraced, to the marches in Chicago during the Democratic Convention, to the tunnels under the city where something dangerous is plotted. Ivy is our guide, an unknowing one whose political and sentimental education are emblematic of a generation of searchers. The explosive ending is like a fire that illuminates the thirty odd years since then, the story we have to know to understand who we are now.

Before 1968 shrinks away to a word in an old font on a dusty page, open *Riders on the Storm* and take the trip back to the era that shoved us into the future.

—Mary Grimm, author of *Left to Themselves*

National Guardsmen arrive at the scene in Hough area
(*The Cleveland Press*, photo by Bernie Noble)

To Bill Schermbrucker — with thanks for visiting and encouraging my class and me, too. Best wishes Susan Streeter Carpenter 11/16/10

Riders on the Storm

A Novel

Susan Streeter Carpenter

Working Lives Fiction Series
Bottom Dog Press
Huron, Ohio

© 2010 Bottom Dog Press, Inc.
Susan Streeter Carpenter
ISBN 978-1-933964-35-5
Bottom Dog Press
PO Box 425/ Huron, 44839
http://smithdocs.net
Credits
Cover Photo by Pete Dell
Cover Design and Artwork by Susanna Sharp-Schwacke
Larry Smith, senior editor
Editing Assistants: Catherine Gabe & Danielle Nuzum

This is a work of fiction.

Acknowledgments

For the journey that was the making of this novel, I had support, advice, fellowship, and good counsel all along the way.

Tremendous gratitude to Michael Griffith for his guidance through the first two drafts. Thanks also to Brock Clarke, Amy Elder and Stan Corkin for their help and to the University of Cincinnati for the fellowships that made the work possible. Thanks to the Cleveland people who talked with me at length, gave me their memories, and confirmed my own, especially Carol Close, Bill Anderson, Lewis G. Robinson, Harllel Jones, and Roldo Bartimole.

At the Vermont Studio Center, Chris Abani, Rodger Kamenetz, and Joanna Scott offered key insights. Thanks to Bluffton University for a research grant and a fellowship that supported the continuation of the work—and also for giving me a home.

Ten thousand thanks to my readers and friends. There are more than I can name. The Yellow Springs writers and the Kelley's Island writers listened patiently to long messy chapters. Thanks to Erin McGraw for her unflagging encouragement. Special thanks to those who read the emerging book and told me what worked and what did not: Liz Kaplan, Ed Davis, Mary Grimm, Rachel Moulton, Ailish Hopper, Jackie St. Joan, Linda Ziegahn, Chris Morgan Sumner, Stephanie Wells, Karen Joy Fowler, and Jeff Gundy. Thanks to Larry Smith and Catherine Gabe of Bottom Dog Press, and thanks forever to Berch Carpenter who provided time and space and turned the car around at the last minute to visit the German Cultural Garden off the road that used to be Liberty Boulevard.

(Continued on page 400)

Contents

To the people around the supper table
in Glenville, the night
in April 1968
when the students took over Columbia.

PART ONE

I came to the cities in a time of disorder
When hunger ruled.
I came among men in a time of uprising
And I revolted with them.
                from "To Posterity" by Bertolt Brecht

1968: Some of us wince.Some of us bristle.Our memories are orange and gray, the colors of asphalt and flame and darkness, the open mouth of a napalmed child, Lyndon Johnson's ponderous earlobes, a helmeted man in the jungle, another climbing the shoulders of a bronze statue in Chicago. King shot down. RFK shot down. Priests pouring blood on Selective Service files. Helicopters everywhere. For some of us, the only way to stop the earthquake-rumble in our gut is to put together the story.

We lived in Cleveland. Carl Stokes was the first Black mayor. There was a fire-fight in a Glenville neighborhood and a lone Black Nationalist charged with killing police. We thought the war had come home.

Some of us were students desperate to stop the military industrial machine. Revolution seemed the only way to save the world from disaster. The Movement throbbed under our feet and in our collective bloodstreams. As children of the nuclear bomb, we never believed we'd get old. We hurled our breaking hearts into the void of the future.

This is a story of three people who might have been us. Beginning with the King assassination (or was it Johnson's refusal to campaign? Or was it that modest supper in a Glenville apartment), they worked full-time to torque the world. In the process they became strangers to themselves and each other.

Jane Revard had been a Mississippi Summer volunteer. Then she was a Peace Delegate to North Vietnam. She organized Cleveland welfare mothers into a nearly-integrated grass-roots force and became a liberator of women. At the end of 1968 she would leave Cleveland.

Chuck Leggit, who didn't know he would be Jane's last male lover, began the year by renting a one-room apartment to be near Ivy Barcelona whom he thought he might marry when they'd stopped the war and ended the draft. They failed to stop the draft, and to end the war, and to get married. Chuck did, however, learn to write. By the time he was released from draft-resisters' prison, 1968 was a slow-healing wound he would try to forget.

Ivy Barcelona ended the year with a bomb in her hands. Her beginning was April 23rd, the night she and Chuck became lovers, the night she fled a party in the Heights for another in the ghetto, the night she got to know Jane Revard. She called it The Night Students Took Over Columbia and titled events for the rest of the year: The Balloon Drop, The Glenville Shoot-out, Chicago, the Hour's Late Split. All those events fell into a jumbled pile in the back of her mind's dark closet. 30 years later when she opened the closet, she almost forgot what the titles stood for and could not be sure she'd ever known.

Chapter 1

April 23, 1968
The Heights & The Inner City

Setting her shoulders straight so no one in the room would notice what she'd done, Ivy Barcelona looked down at the picture lying where she'd knocked it on the floor. The glass had broken in jagged lines, and the gilt frame had come apart. One glass shard stuck up, a menacing arrow pointing at her. The print—Moreau's *Phaeton*—seemed to have survived the crash intact.

"We better get out of here," said Chuck, Ivy's boyfriend (lover, as of that afternoon). He'd left the cluster of people around Gilligan, the Candidate for whom they'd all come to this mansion in the Heights. Gilligan had said triumphantly, "America must not be policeman to the world!"

"What the hell is that?" Chuck looked at the broken gold sticks, the shattered glass. "Oh, shit." Phaeton's small white body slipped away from the tumbling chariot, flanked by a roaring lion and a huge serpent about to strike. The white disk of the sun filled the picture with its rays.

Ivy took his hand, watching the well-dressed suburbanites uncluster and head for the drinks. "They'll be passing the hat soon," Chuck said. "Time for us to leave."

Months from now, in the dead of winter, holding a homemade bomb in her hands, Ivy would remember that she had once stood aghast because she'd accidentally knocked a framed picture—a print, not an original—off the wall. That night pegged the beginning of a path that led to the fuse uncoiled, ready to be lit.

"You can't just stand here feeling sorry." Chuck leaned over, picked up the broken *Phaeton* by its edges, and tucked the whole mess under a chair. He put his arm around Ivy's shoulders. "I promised Marvin we'd be at his place for dinner. These people can afford to replace that frame. C'mon." The crowd milled around them.

Ivy's lungs felt stiff. She needed air, as Chuck, who loved her, must have guessed. The shaving-nick on his jaw still showed, a dark pink scrape, but he looked good in his only sport jacket. Ivy let him steer her toward the foyer. Across the hall in the dining room, her Aunt Peg stood next to a loaf of rye bread the size of a bed-pillow surrounded by various cheeses, cold meats, and both kinds of olives. Peg's hair exactly matched her beige silk dress. She was listening to the host, a bald man in a turtleneck and blazer, enthuse about Gilligan's courage: "At last!" he beamed, "A candidate for U.S. Senate has come out against the Vietnam War."

Ivy smiled and riffled her fingers at Aunt Peg across the expanse of food. "Gotta go," she said cheerfully. "So sorry; we're expected at dinner with friends. Can't be late." If she came close, Peg might notice something new about her niece, a softness around the hips, maybe, or a scent. Ivy hadn't been able to shower after they'd made love.

"We're due in Glenville in fifteen minutes," Chuck added, nodding to Peg as he grasped the heavy brass handle of the front door and hauled it open. "Nice to've met you."

Guilty, gasping cold air, Ivy held Chuck's arm on the front walk, their heels resounding on the slate. "Shouldn't have said 'Glenville,'" she said. "Aunt Peg'll tell my folks. They'll freak out, think *ghetto*." Her breath was too short to speak more than three words at once, then too short to speak at all (She'd be fine in a minute; she often felt stifled at parties; the outdoor air had helped, hadn't it? This couldn't be an asthma attack.) They found Chuck's old Pontiac in the line of cars along the curb.

Sitting still, she could indeed breathe a bit easier. They drove through curving darkened streets of the Heights and then down Cedar Hill, the last foothill of the great Allegheny mountain range, down under the Rapid Transit tracks, down into the circle of lights around the bus terminal, past the Case Campus, past the Art Museum lagoon and the church that students called the Holy Oil Can.

"Those people had too much house," Chuck said. "Did you see the giraffe? A giant Steiff thing that filled a whole corner of...was that a drawing room?" He took off his nametag and stuck it to the plastic visor.

"We're not late, are we?" Ivy held herself straight on the seat clutching the door handle. Fear had returned. She didn't want to use her inhaler in front of Chuck, didn't want him to know about the damned vise clamped around her breathing tubes.

"Thanks to that picture-crash, we're in plenty of time," he said, his head cocked, probably listening to the engine. He swiped the ginger hair off his forehead and turned the steering wheel with careful, long-fingered hands. They drove down Liberty Boulevard, the winding road through Rockefeller Park. Once it had been a shady place for well-off Clevelanders to promenade or picnic. Now the homes nearby were carved into low-rent apartments: the inner city. The lights were dull yellow and sparse. They were about to meet people who lived in one of those apartments and worked full-time on the Revolution. Ivy tore off her tag and held her breath as she pasted it next to Chuck's, so their names partly overlapped. The car smelled of oil, old vinyl, and the cigarettes they had smoked earlier. "Love you," she whispered, as he turned a corner and climbed the hill. "Best of all." The whisper was faint—no air.

They stopped for a light. Chuck hugged her and kissed the top of her head. She resisted his pressure on her chest: Her lungs felt like balloons blown to near-bursting and knotted tightly. She couldn't wait any longer. "Back in a sec," she gasped and pushed open the passenger door with her shoulder.

The neighborhood had grated store windows and Black voices in the shadows between buildings. Someone laughed, loud and high, almost a scream. Ivy pressed the inhaler and sucked the medicine in. She coughed, inhaled, then exhaled all the way. A door swung open, and a woman's dark face appeared, "You need something?"

"No thanks." Ivy met the woman's curious eyes and dropped her head. She inhaled another dose and coughed again. Now she could breathe—and if she was careful, her breaths would come clear for the next hour, at least. She'd have to wait another two to use the inhaler again. If she used the inhaler more than once every three hours, it would backfire, making her lungs even tighter.

Chuck rounded the front of the car, his face contorted. "Ivy—Jesus, what's wrong? Are you okay?"

She let the inhaler slip back into her coat pocket. "I needed air," she said. "Let's go."

He grasped her upper arms and looked down at her. It was too dark to see his eyes. "You know, this isn't a friendly neighborhood for honkies like us." He jerked his head toward the corner, where young men in narrow dark pants argued, their voices sharp and fierce. Then he put his arms around her. "You sure you're okay?" She kissed him and he stepped back. "When you need your thing," he said, "just use it. Don't run away into the dark."

He wasn't supposed to know. "It's private," she said. "I was..." She couldn't say *ashamed*. Asthma had caught her again. Four hours ago, smoking one of Chuck's unfiltered Camels, she'd been sure the attacks were over. "I didn't want you to know."

"I can smell the stuff on your breath, Doofy," he said. "I'll take you back to the dorm. Your aunt's probably still at the party; if you want, I'll take you there."

"No!" She rushed him, burying her nose in the sweet collarbone hollow at the base of his throat, blotting tears on his shirt. She would not abandon him. Asthma was a nuisance, but it would not keep Ivy from doing her part in the great change underway, making sure it happened soon, happened right. She was "part of the solution, not part of the problem." She would "seize the time," no matter what. The Black Panther slogans steadied her.

"Don't cry," Chuck cupped her cheek and kissed her medicine-mouth. "Please don't. Okay? Let's get in the car and go to Marvin's. I'm hungry." He held her elbow and opened the door for her.

That afternoon lying next to her, close, close, he'd asked, "Are you okay?" because she was weeping as well as bleeding. "Are you sure?"

"I'm happy," she'd said, and that was true. *I've taken a lover,* she told herself, avoiding the ugly *I've had sexual intercourse,* the fearful *I've lost my virginity.* Thrilling, to be completely naked with a man for the first time, hard and soft and melting and burning, all at once. The sheets slid deliciously over her body. And she would sleep in his bed tonight. "I hate the Heights," she told him, as the Pontiac nosed back into the street.

The Heights crowd had been suffocating, groomed with a suburban sheen that Ivy could never quite manage. The *Phaeton* was only the most recent crash; all her life she'd been breaking things. The first was her mother's Wedgwood platter, an heirloom brought on the boat from England and still mourned. Then other dishes, the toaster, a window. With the first dangerous asthma attack in ninth grade, Ivy had broken her excellent-health record. And she'd smashed a headlight on the car. Her parents had allowed her to leave home in Bloomington for Western Reserve only because Aunt Peg lived in Cleveland Heights and would keep an eye on her. This afternoon with Chuck she'd broken nothing. The soreness between her legs was temporary.

For her freshman and sophomore years, Ivy had avoided Aunt Peg as much as possible. Tonight's party with Peg's anti-war Democrats was a concession. Before the speech, Ivy and Chuck had been introduced to Gilligan, tall and strawberry-blond, by a woman wearing a mini-skirt and white lipstick. When Chuck said he was a student at Cleveland State, the woman's lips pursed, disapproving. "Even snobs oppose the war now," Ivy said. "Since Tet, I guess."

"You don't just *jump out of the car* like that," Chuck said. "Christ! I thought..."

He frowned with his thick eyebrows.

"What did you think?"

"Never mind. Just don't *do* that. I'm looking for—there it is." He turned onto a small street. "Are you feeling better?"

"Yes." She leaned against him, breathing all the way in, all the way out, again herself: Ivy Barcelona, campus activist, traveling with her lover to the people who knew how the Vietnam war was only one symptom of the whole late-capitalist sickness. How the universities were complicit, turning students into skilled workers for the odious machine.

"Gilligan was standing on an antique coal hod," Chuck said. "Did you notice? Expensive, a hundred bucks, I bet, and no coal in sight. The Democrats were serving imported lager to all those people. Marvin and his roommate live on five dollars a week each. They're feeding us dinner out of that."

"Do they think we can organize campus protests on the scale of Columbia?" At Reserve, protests were confused and disorganized. The loudest faction was demanding "parietal hours" (the Deans' term) so boys could visit girls in their dorm rooms. At Cleveland State, Chuck had started a chapter of Students for a Democratic Society; the meetings were small and quiet. Meanwhile, at Columbia, the SDS chairman had shoved a pie in the face of the Selective Service director.

"Marvin just said they've decided to connect with the Cleveland campuses." Chuck slowed the car, peering at narrow houses, looking for numbers. Ivy combed her hair with her fingers and regretted her clothes. She'd been under-dressed among the suburbanites but was over-dressed for this group. Beneath her coat, the madras skirt and navy-blue shell would be fine for tomorrow, however. She could go straight to class, no run-in with the housemother. Chuck stopped the car. "Here we are," he said.

He reached for her, but she trotted ahead of him into the dark, following the broken-cement path around to the side. The door was stuck shut, not locked; Chuck shouldered it open and led the way upstairs. At the landing he felt Ivy's hand come into his and he squeezed, thinking of her in his bed this afternoon—the heat under her arms and behind her knees, the silkiness of her breasts, the lovely unbroken sweep of skin to that soft secret space between her legs. Her long hair, almost black, falling over his arms and between his fingers. He was her first. Never before had he been the first. Cherish the experience, he told himself. Cherish her. The tune came into his head, and he wondered if he'd have used that word if the radio weren't playing "Cherish" twenty times a day.

He'd asked if it hurt. She'd said "Not much" and turned away from him. Then she'd fled to the bathroom clutching her clothes in one hand, a Kotex in the other, and she'd returned fully dressed. He told her he loved her, he respected her—and he did love her, more than any girl he'd ever screwed—*made love with.* When she leapt out of the car his first thought had been that she loathed him for what he'd done this afternoon.

But no, she was being "private" about the asthma medicine. Private and impulsive. Sometimes her fearlessness took Chuck's breath away. The first time he saw her—last October, at the Pentagon—she stood on tiptoe in knee-high boots and a short skirt talking to a soldier. Other demonstrators kept their distance, though a few had stuck flowers in gun barrels. Ivy's hair blew across her flushed round cheeks; her earnest lips were an inch from the soldier's ear, her naked fingers on his shoulder. Chuck saw sweat on the boy's forehead and thought what the girl must be saying: *You're a fool, clutching your gun, working for a government that will send you to kill or be killed.*

Chuck had regretted leaving before the draft-card burnings, the tearing-down of the fence, and the mass arrests. He'd settled into a window seat halfway to the back of the bus, telling himself he wasn't a coward, just had to get a paper written. Then Ivy appeared across the aisle in a group singing Dylan's

"Hard Rain's Gonna Fall," and she was the only one who knew all the words to that long, bewildering song. By three in the morning, when they pulled into Cleveland's Greyhound station, she was sitting next to Chuck, her head on his shoulder, and he was glad he'd left early.

Now he felt sorry again. His draft card was still deep in his wallet, right there in the back pocket of his good slacks as they climbed the dingy stairway toward Marvin, who'd been at the Pentagon holding the other end of the Cleveland banner. Marvin's roommate, Bert Augustin, had been there too, leading a draft-resistance contingent. Chuck had written that history paper instead of making history itself, he thought, putting his arm around Ivy now as he knocked. On Bert and Marvin's door was a large clenched fist in black paint. Tonight they would challenge him again. To do what?

Marvin opened the door, said, "Come in, I'll be a minute," and turned to the oven door, which lay open. He lifted out a roast chicken, golden brown, then set the pan tenderly on the counter. "The others are in there," he said, removing his quilted mittens and pointing to the next room. Chuck watched, fascinated, as Marvin pulled a rope attached to the oven door's handle and held the door closed with one knee, looping the rope around a large hook in the wall above the stove, fastening it with two slip-knots. He and Bert lived close to the edge. "Go on in," Marvin said. "Jane's not here yet, but we can start the wine."

Bert was pacing behind the sofa: "What'd I tell you? At the Stop & Shop, beans are up seven cents a can—seven cents!" He was lecturing a woman who sat cross-legged in the stuffed chair opposite him, her skirt stretched like a drumhead over her thighs, her mouth twisted skeptically to one side. "They can excuse price-hikes on fruit and vegetables and meat," Bert went on, "but Van Camp's Pork and Beans do not spoil; they do not grow scarce and increase in value. The rulers are getting audacious when they raise *beans* on Welfare Check Day."

"They're only showing their hand," she said. "They're scared the city's gonna blow, and they've gotta cut their losses."

Chuck yanked his eyes from the cave formed by the woman's thighs and the skirt across the top. He looked at Ivy, who stood watching Bert with her hands in her coat pockets. It was a tan raincoat, a London Fog she wore everywhere. Rather than carry a purse, she kept her stuff in the pockets.

"Well, why the fuck *hasn't* the city blown? All the other cities are smoldering from the riots after King's death," Bert demanded. "Why not Cleveland? Tell me!" A tall man with hair to his shoulders, he loomed over his listener as if he were accusing her personally of something.

Marvin came between them, gathering the newspapers from the coffee table. "Mayor Stokes phoned the Black Nationalist leaders, that's why not," he said, adding the papers to a stack in the corner. "Told 'em to keep their people quiet. So they did." He went back to the kitchen.

The girl stood up, unfolding her bare legs, and her skirt stopped at the middle of her thighs. "I'm Tessa Buchanan," she said, her hand extended. Chuck shook it.

Marvin returned with an assortment of cups and glasses. "What did you and Tessa do with the Chianti?"

Tessa Buchanan was a med student at Case Western Reserve, Marvin explained, finishing the introductions. Tessa brought the raffia-strung bottle in from another room and demanded to know how Stokes had gotten in good with Black Nationalist revolutionaries at the same time he was tight with the Governor, a law 'n order Republican. "Stokes is basically a hustler," Bert said, and suddenly they were all talking at once, spouting names Chuck didn't recognize. Tessa pointed for emphasis, hatcheting her arm from the elbow, the finger a blade. Bert declaimed loudly, and Marvin rumbled. They seemed to be performing for Ivy, who sipped her wine, her blue-green eyes growing larger and darker as she listened.

Chuck took his teacup full of Chianti to the round table spread with mismatched dishes and looked out the window. He had to screen his eyes with his hands against the glass to see. A single streetlight glowed at the end of the block; the only car on this part of the street was his Pontiac waiting below. Any minute one of them would ask the membership of his SDS (four or five), his position on draft resistance (he wasn't sure), or what he knew about defense contracts at Cleveland State (nothing). He wished he could think of some action that would stop the gears of the military-industrial complex, right here—right now. This would be the week for it: a student strike at Ivy's campus, an anti-war rally at his, mass protests scheduled across the country.

Marvin appeared, peering out the window next to Chuck. "Yep, still there," he said. "See that Ford down the block?" Marvin had a long nose with little glasses perched halfway down. He looked over the glasses at Chuck. "Belongs to the Subversive Squad of the Cleveland Police. They're keeping an eye on us."

"Oh." Chuck felt his guts tighten.

"Where the hell is Jane Revard?" Bert called as though Marvin were far away, rather than across the room.

Ivy looked startled. She'd removed her coat and was holding it over her arm. Chuck put his hand on her sleeveless shoulder and she moved away, toward Bert. "I've met Jane Revard," she said. "She borrowed my student ID so she could fly standby to New York last September."

"Last September, Jane flew to Bratislava," said Tessa, the woman in the tight skirt. "To meet with the North Vietnamese. Guess she didn't tell you."

"She went all the way to Hanoi," Bert said. "The North Vietnamese wanted to meet American women."

"And she's coming *here!*" Ivy's eyes brightened.

Chuck had never met anyone who'd been to Hanoi. He wondered if Jane Revard knew the Subversive Squad was watching the apartment; maybe they would keep her away.

"She'll be here. She had to take care of something with welfare rights." Marvin emptied the bottle of wine into the last glass—a jelly jar. "That's for Jane," he announced. "Don't anybody touch it."

Chapter 2
April 23, 1968
Glenville

Jane Revard didn't care that she was late; she had nothing particular to say to students, had tried to beg off. But Bert Augustin had insisted, "The campus is where it's at." He'd been to New York, talking with the action faction of Columbia SDS.

"This is Cleveland," she'd said.

"Yeah, I know," Bert said. "Armpit of the nation. Mistake on the lake."

I guess the point is that people do things humbly here, Jane thought, as she drove down Euclid Avenue where Cleveland State University held class in Quonset huts. Western Reserve and Case had been united for half a year before each institution discovered that the other didn't have the money they both needed.

Jane had liked being a student herself; she still wore the same clothes she'd worn at Ann Arbor, though she'd cut and hemmed all the skirts. But three years' work in Glenville, Hough, and the near West Side had made her impatient with students' cushioned idealism; they couldn't see their own privilege. After the Hough riots in '66, the city had set aside money for housing and then spent most of it in University Circle for dorms, rather than for houses in the Black neighborhoods. Students hadn't noticed.

She would be late to dinner because she'd promised a ride to Dora Williams, keeper of the East Side Welfare Rights group. Jane hadn't seen Dora for three weeks. She'd tried to call, but Dora's phone wasn't hooked up. Now guilt made sure she'd keep her promise and take Dora to the West Side.

Interracial Movement of the Poor: that had been the goal. Radicals finished or fed up with college had come to organize welfare mothers and unemployed men. Jane had found Dora in the laundromat. While most poor people wouldn't listen to white kids so dumb as to live in the worst neighborhood in the city on five dollars a week, Dora had responded. Yes, she'd said, in effect. Welfare mothers need to stand up for their rights. Help us figure out what those rights are.

The door was half-opened by a tall man who blocked the light, Dora's latest boyfriend. Jane didn't trust him. Stephen was a skittish fast talker, good-looking, with smooth brown skin and sharp cheekbones. He'd put the rattan-throne poster of Huey P. Newton over Dora's bed, and whenever he felt like pumping up his own manhood he roared "Power to the People!"

"Where is Dora?" Jane demanded. "We're on our way to the West Side."

"She not goin," Stephen said. "Dora's done with that shit. You go on without her." He spread his long arms across the doorway; his hair, too soft for a crisp Afro, stuck out in tufts, like dark flames around his head.

"Come on in, Janie." Dora's voice came from the kitchen. She was the only person in Cleveland permitted to use *Janie*. Jane ducked under Stephen's elbow and forced her way in. There was a blank spot over the sofa where Dora had kept a framed photograph of herself with Martin Luther King, Jr.

"Don't get all conversational," Stephen said. "You don't owe a thing to those welfare people, or to this white b—"

"Stop right there," Jane said. "I fully understand that this city's full of nasty racist white people, but that doesn't mean you can call *me* names." In the light, she noticed that one of his front teeth was chipped.

He leered at Jane. "If Dora wasn't here," he said. "I'd *show* you somethin nasty."

"You *quit* that talk." Dora came in, baby on one hip. She wore pedal pushers, white sneakers, and full make-up. "Hi,

Janie. I'm-a go to a Soul Power meeting tonight, so I can't go to the West Side. That's all." She did not sit down, did not nod toward a chair for Jane.

"Stephen's group?" Jane asked. Dora nodded. "I hope you're not..." Jane stopped the next words: *leaving me*. Black power groups were good for young men like Stephen. But they dominated the women, went around quoting Stokely: "The only position for women in SNCC is prone."

"Manhood is *such* a big deal," Dora had said once, to explain why she'd bought a black leather jacket for the man then in her life while her children went without apples. Jane had seen Dora confront middle-aged white men in suits, but she'd also seen her cave in to the whims of several boyfriends.

"I been figuring stuff out," Dora said now, rocking side to side to settle the baby, not looking at Jane. "When I'm all busy with Welfare Rights, I'm still accepting the authority of the colonizers, continuing the oppression. I'm saying it's okay for white people to control the jobs, the property, *and* the Welfare System. You know what I mean?" Jane saw Stephen nod approval. He stood in one corner of the room, arms crossed on his chest, Black Panther style; Dora stood in the center. Jane stayed near the entrance, with the back of a stuffed chair between her and them. Cheerful white voices came from Dora's bedroom where the older children were watching TV.

"I know," Jane said. "Stokes can't fix all the racism." The police and some city councilmen hated having a Black mayor; they thwarted him at every turn, even as Stokes himself sucked up to the governor and the business community.

"I mean I'm sick and tired of white *people*." Dora hoisted the baby to her shoulder. Her eyes blazed weariness and anger.

Jane backed toward the door. "I wasn't planning to go to the meeting," she said. "I promised you a ride. I keep promises."

"That's settled, then," Dora said. "Paid the phone bill yesterday, so I can call Lillian." She resettled the baby on her hip and turned to the phone on the counter that divided the kitchen from the living room. Lillian was the West Side keeper, a white welfare mother, smart, aggressive—and more than once a good friend to Dora. Jane had thought *she* was Dora's friend, too.

"But you and Lillian and I were writing a Welfare Rights Handbook," Jane said. Quite inappropriately, she felt like crying.

"You can still do that." The baby fussed, and Dora put down the phone to run her finger along the new gums. "Yeah yeah yeah, those teeth'll be in soon," she sang. "White ladies," she spat the words. "They either ashamed of that welfare check, or they gonna push the rest of us out the way. Except Lillian. Maybe."

Jane held up the underside of her arm, frog-belly white. "If I could take a pill that would turn my skin dark brown tomorrow," she told Dora, "I'd do it."

"I know you would," Dora said. "That's *your* thing. *Mine's* with the brothers and sisters."

Stephen looked irritated. "When's your mama coming? We gotta move."

Jane would have said, go ahead, I'll stay with the kids, but that would support Dora's being a pushover for her boyfriend-of-the-month. Anyway, she was too upset to be around children. "I gotta move on," she said. "I'm already late." She left quickly, defeated and feeling somehow at fault.

Jane had been close to Dora—closer than she was to her Black friends during Mississippi Summer. Three of them worked that county with Jane and some white Freedom Riders, registering voters, careful to keep the police from seeing them share the seats of the old Packard. At the end of each brutally hot day, they'd stand in a circle, arms around each other singing. *Black and White together*, they sang, sometimes with tears running down their faces. *We are not afraid.* But they couldn't be together, not in public, and after the three bodies were found in the dam, the songs couldn't drive away the fear or express the anger. By the end of August, Jane had lost touch with all of them.

How wonderful, two years later, to be with the Cleveland mothers. East Side Black and West Side White together, they'd taken over the Welfare Department for a day and a night, Dora changing her baby boy on the director's desk, asking what to do with the dirty diaper. Lillian had said, "Put it in the director's wastebasket. Give *him* some shit. Better, put it in his desk drawer." They were all in jail together for six hours, came out singing *His eye is on the sparrow*. Late nights talking in the kitchen, drinking cheap red wine.

She'd rounded the corner of Bert and Marvin's street when she saw the Subversive Squad's pale-blue unmarked car. Sgt. Ungvary would recognize the car she was driving, a white Valiant with a red passenger door. Several Movement people used it. She thought of driving to the end of the street and parking around the corner, on Auburndale.

No. The thought of giving Ungvary that much power over where she parked made her angry. Let them report that Jane Revard was having dinner with her friends Bert, Marvin, and Tessa. Let them try to make something of it. Except for a handful of peanuts this morning, she hadn't eaten since yesterday. No wonder she was hungry.

She parked behind an old car she didn't recognize and sprinted up the stairs, wondering how things would go with Tessa and Bert at the same dinner table. Until the Pentagon, they'd been unable to keep their hands off each other during meetings; afterwards they shot hostile comments across the room. But Tessa had said they were getting along okay now. Jane sighed. Late tonight she would go home to Norman, her own private boyfriend, who could at least keep her from thinking for a little while.

She'd forgotten about the students until she saw them at the table on either side of Bert. The dark-haired girl with turquoise eyes looked familiar. The other was a boy with a mustache. Bert was banging a fork against a glass for emphasis. Tessa and Marvin shared the sofa and a copy of *New Left Notes*. They both stood to greet Jane, and the paper fell from their laps. "At last we can eat," Tessa said. "That's yours." She pointed to a jelly glass full of red wine.

At the table Bert had his fist in the air over a big bowl of rice. "Columbia sits on this bluff," he was saying. "Here's Morningside Park, which belongs to Harlem. Steep slope, trees and shit." He put a napkin against the bowl. "And here's where they're putting the gym." He tapped the bowl with the fork. "A fucking fortress, off limits to Harlem citizens."

"Let's start that rice around the table," Marvin said. "Ivy—dark meat or white?" He peered at the chicken through his glasses, poked with a knife, and the leg dropped to the platter.

With a pang, Jane remembered the student's name: Ivy Barcelona. The ID. Probably it was still in her purse. She'd look right after supper. The mustached boy passed her the rice bowl and said his name was Chuck. Jane heaped rice onto her plate, loaded her fork, and filled her mouth with gratitude.

"The salad bowl's empty already," Tessa said. "Bert, you should have used the whole head of lettuce." She curled her upper lip. So that's how it was now.

"Don't you appropriate my salad-making," Bert said, picking up the salad bowl, studying the shreds of lettuce and carrot-scraping inside. He carried it out to the kitchen, stoop-shouldered, making a show of penance.

Jane could at least be polite to the students. Next to her, Chuck frowned, his reddish-brown eyebrows pushing together over his nose—a handsome guy worried about something. He wore a yellow oxford-cloth shirt with the sleeves neatly rolled to just below his elbows. "So you're Chuck...what?" she asked.

"Leggit," he said. "When my dad sold used cars, his slogan was 'Leggit's legit.'" He chuckled, but his forehead didn't relax. Maybe he wanted to talk about his father.

"What does he do now?" Jane asked. She thought about sneaking another piece of chicken while no one was looking, but gave up on the idea as Tessa sat down to her left and began filling her own plate. Tessa had bitten her fingernails shorter than usual.

"Sells Chryslers," Chuck said. "In Cincinnati." He seemed about to tell a story of the generation gap. Or maybe about capitalism: its benefits or its inherent oppressiveness. Jane didn't want to hear either one. Chuck was a junior at Cleveland State, according to Bert. Should she ask about Cleveland State's buying up land, destroying neighborhoods near Thirtieth and Chester? Not yet.

Bert returned with more salad and for a few minutes they ate without talking, all six of them at the round table, a little too close for comfort. Between Marvin and Bert, Ivy Barcelona ate primly, elbows close to her sides. Marvin looked around, his glance darting from plate to plate. When his eyes met Jane's, he smiled and looked anxious. He'd called them all together, and they had come. Now—what would they do? Jane tried to reassure him by smiling back. She trusted Marvin, but she had no expectations of these students. There was enough chicken left for one mouthful, maybe. Tessa was chewing on a drumstick-bone.

"I heard you made a trip to Hanoi?" Chuck asked. Jane speared a chunk of lettuce as Vietnam loomed into her mind, a bright-green place where soft rain washed blood into the earth. She had bowed and said *I am with you* to Thi Dinh and Thanh Van; they had wept and returned the bow. Since then, what had Jane done? During the Tet offensive—more than 40,000 Vietnamese dead in a few weeks' time—she had not even gone to the silent peace vigils. Fuck the trip to Hanoi, she thought. "Sorry," she said to Chuck. "I can't be social right now. I'm sure you're a good person, but this is my first meal in two days, and I just want to eat for a while."

Ivy had forgotten how short and thin Jane was. Seven months ago her hair had been loose; now it was braided, hanging over one shoulder, dipping its end in French dressing. Ivy watched Jane spoon rice onto her salad, mix it with lettuce and dressing, and chew with her mouth closed into a smile; she made messy eating look wonderful. Ivy's cheeks and ears were hot from wine; her bare left arm brushed Bert's blue work shirt as he turned toward Chuck. Bert's hair was the exact color of the molasses taffy Ivy and her mother pulled at Christmas time, smooth warm brown with a gold shine.

"Resistance!" Bert was saying. "Draft counseling's not enough. Burning draft cards is not enough. We need to screw up the system." Chuck nodded, stroking his mustache: his non-committal gesture. He'd been waiting, Ivy knew, for the perfect moment to burn his draft card, when the act wouldn't be mistaken for showing off, on the one hand, or going along with the crowd, on the other. She pictured Bert screwing up the system, pouring sand in a gas tank, ramming a screwdriver between shiny brass gears.

Next to her plate, Marvin's forearm glinted with pale hairs. He was listening to Tessa talk about Regis Debray. Ivy wondered what *Revolution in the Revolution* meant and noticed how Marvin's blond hair curled thick in back and wisped thin on the top of his head. His bare scalp had a few freckles. Time seemed to jerk, ratcheting her forward into an utterly new time and place; impossible to go back to where she'd been even an hour ago. Bert was telling Chuck about some guy who'd been sending stuff to his draft board—newspaper clippings, then whole magazine articles, then a subscription to the *New York Times*—all to clog up their file cabinets. "Next thing," Bert said, "he sent a rubber raft, the kind that inflates as soon as you open the box. By law, they had to keep it."

The sense of being stuck in the future before she'd become used to the past made Ivy queasy. She rose for a little walk around the apartment. In the kitchen, a large poster of Karl Marx (black eyebrows, bushy gray beard) faced a poster of Shirley Temple (ringlets, polka-dot dress, baby-toothed smile). She kept close to the walls, nearing the table as Jane said "Soul Power" to Tessa, and Tessa responded, "Right on," raising her clenched fist. Someone had drawn the Terminal Tower on brown paper and stuck it with thumbtacks over the couch. Inside the outline of the building, two cartoon-men who looked like millionaires in the Monopoly game waved sheaves of paper with dollar signs. Their hands dripped red-ink blood. Underneath, spiky letters cried, "Let the people decide!"

Along the wall behind the sofa, three doors opened into two small bedrooms and a dirty bathroom. Ivy settled on the toilet to replace her Kotex pad with one from her coat pocket. Not too much blood. She carefully fingered her sore vagina, vulva, labia—uncomfortable words!—and marveled at what she now knew of herself.

The telephone rang. Someone thudded across the floor to answer. One of the bedroom doors clicked shut. Her lungs were still open. In the cracked bathroom mirror her eyes looked unusually dark, her cheeks unusually red. She combed her hair and thought how at noon she'd been a virgin co-ed, studying German vocabulary. At four she'd become Chuck's lover. At 6:30 she'd met a liberal anti-war candidate for senate. Now she was eating at a table with revolutionaries in the inner city. These were her people. She wanted to settle down here.

Outside the bathroom she stepped on the long phone cord. Bert's voice squawked, "Far fuckin *out!*" from behind the door. At the table, Tessa and Jane sat talking among dishes flecked with bits of food. Tessa picked up a grain of rice and tucked it into her mouth. Chuck leaned against the wall in the kitchen, telling Marvin about his summer in Nicaragua, when he was seventeen.

Marvin smiled at Ivy over his wire-rimmed glasses. "There'll be coffee in a minute," he said. What had Chuck told Marvin about her? She glanced at Chuck's face, but he was concentrating on his hand, ticking off a finger for each bit of evidence that the U.S. supported the dictator Somoza.

"Sit with us," Tessa said. She had a blurry exhausted look around her eyes and mouth. "I wish we had some more wine, but it's gone."

"Not quite," Jane said, and drank the last of hers. "Now it's gone. Ivy, you know what? I'm gonna return your ID." She tilted her chair back to retrieve her purse from the floor. It was a scuffed brown-leather shoulder bag, its strap broken and knotted. Jane brought out a fistful of newspaper, dittoed sheets, candy bar wrappers. A Polaroid photograph of a man with dark curly hair. Ivy leaned forward to see, curious about Jane, who so plainly did not care about the look of purses or wine glasses. She was burrowing again, bringing up Band-Aids, a pack of Clove gum, a hairbrush with rubber bands around the handle, and a small spiral-bound notebook. "I guess I should clean out my purse," Jane said, adding a broken pencil and Kleenex wads to the mess on the table. "Oh, here it is. Good thing it was laminated." She put the ID into Ivy's hand.

The door banged against the wall as Bert came out with the phone in his hands. "It's happened," he said. He set the phone on the end table next to the sofa, stood straight, then raised both fists and whooped. "They did it!" He did a Flamenco stomp and whooped. "Ai yi yiee!" Marvin and Chuck appeared in the archway between kitchen and dining room.

"Who was that on the phone?" Marvin asked.

"Rudd, at Columbia. They're in Low Library."

"They're sitting in at *the library*?" Jane said.

"It's the administration building. They've taken over the president's office." Bert looked straight at Tessa, who looked stunned. "They're sitting at Grayson Kirk's desk, using his phone. Smoking his cigars!" Two steps across the room and a reach: he by-passed Tessa to pull Jane out of her chair. "Dance with me, honey!" She stumbled up, laughing, and they twirled with their arms around each other's waists, Bert crooning "Up against the wall, Muthafucka..." If Ivy hadn't heard the laughter, she would have guessed Jane was crying.

She grasped hold of Chuck around the waist, and everyone stood, six people bunched in the middle of the room. Then Marvin began to sing. "Paul and Silas begin to shout. Jail doors open..." His voice climbed like steps out of a stone cellar, each note true. "...and they walked out," Tessa chimed in. Then Jane sang high and sweet. "Keep your eyes on the prize, hold on!" A civil rights song. They sang it like a hymn, Bert's arms over Jane's and Tessa's shoulders, tightening the circle. "Hold on—hold on." Even Chuck joined, his uncertain voice carried by Marvin, who sang with his head tilted up, as if drinking rain. "The moment we thought we was lost, Dungeon shook and the chains fell off." Then all of them, loud and full, "Keep your eyes on the prize..." rocking side to side. Ivy felt the floor grow thin under her feet, the walls tremble, about to come down now all over the land. They pulled each other close, Chuck's arms around Ivy's waist, Marvin's across her shoulders, Tessa holding Ivy's hand across Chuck's back.

At the end they hesitated. To keep them going, Ivy started singing "We shall overcome," but Bert cut her off with the first ponderous lines of "Masters of War." Not a good group-singing song, Ivy thought, and Marvin must have agreed: as Bert paused, he began "Will the circle be unbroken..." and their little circle drew in again as the singing filled the room. Ivy's lungs were beginning to thicken, but songs helped the air escape, and the others carried what she missed. But before they were "in the sky, Lord, in the sky" they had to sing the "hearse come rolling," and the voices faltered there. Chuck stopped singing, then Tessa, then the rest.

"How about coffee?" Marvin took off his glasses and wiped them with his handkerchief, looking around with pale, unfocused eyes.

"We should be drinking brandy," Bert said. "Or champagne."

Chuck bent to Ivy's ear. "One coffee; then let's go home," he whispered. Bert, Tessa, and Jane had regrouped around the table, talking about people they knew at Columbia.

"Are you kidding? We can't go," Ivy said. She sipped her coffee thinking what it must be like, barricaded inside Grayson Kirk's office. Students would touch everything, look through the files and the bookcases, maybe dance on tabletops. Make love on a huge soft leather couch.

She felt Chuck's lips on her cheek, then her ear. She heard the soft whistle of her breath forced out too slowly through too-small tubes. She didn't want to go. She wanted to stay at this table talking all night with Bert and Marvin, Tessa and Jane, stay until they'd figured out how to make a successful student strike, cover campus with raised fists, puncture the apathy students wore with their angora sweaters. She wanted to know at least when she'd see these people again. They were all smiling as she put down her empty coffee cup, picked up her ID from the table. She thought, There's dirt from Hanoi on this card. She would keep it forever.

Chapter 3

May 1, 1968
Case Western Reserve

Canadian winds came across Lake Erie into Cleveland, bone-chilling, locked under clouds solid as asbestos, and pushed against Ivy, who clutched a Styrofoam cup of coffee topped with a plain doughnut to keep it hot. Wrapped in her London Fog, she climbed the Art Museum steps and stopped to catch her breath under the statue of The Thinker.

She was fond of The Thinker, his hair swiped in a blob to one side, his forehead knotted in perpetual worry, his outsized knees and elbows ready to shift position. He was completely naked; no drapery pinned him to an era. He could be a caveman or some guy she knew, stripped for a draft physical. His big knobby feet toed in like Ivy's did. She inhaled coffee steam to loosen her lungs.

Her mother's call had wakened her at seven this morning. Thank goodness she had left Chuck's at five. "But you said you had a German Lit paper to write," Mum said.

"I got a bit sidetracked," Ivy said. Not quite true. These days, the Movement was the main track; German Lit was the path to nowhere. "But I am working on the paper." That was true: She'd taken her Thomas Mann book to Chuck's and read long after he slept. "Why are you calling? I just talked with Dad on Sunday."

"Yes. He said you were quite hoarse. You sound better now."

"I'm fine, Mum." She'd been hoarse from chanting all Saturday afternoon. President Morse had refused to act on any of the students' demands. The request for parietal hours had "to go through proper channels." And the university's official repudiation of the war? He'd "give it considered thought." Hundreds of students picketed. *What do we want?* The gray-suit administrators seemed to have stopped their ears and closed their hearts. *Peace!* She had shrieked for hours, begged with her whole soul. No defense contracts! Call for an end to the war! Listen to your students! *Now!*

Barely able to talk, she'd promised her father she'd keep up her grades—which she could not do unless she turned her attention to German Lit. She'd been given an extension with an ultimatum: *Turn in the paper by Friday noon (pünktlich!) or fail the course.* She didn't even have a topic.

"Your aunt has been trying to reach you," her mother had said, as Ivy rubbed sleep out of her eyes and wished she'd brought her inhaler to the phone. "Will you ring her up, please? I don't enjoy delivering her messages this early in the morning any more than you do. But she's taken an interest. You ought to respond." Her English voice crisped the "t" and the "d."

"Okay. Okay." If Ivy had stayed on the phone another second, she'd have had to tell her mother she was wheezing. "I'll do it."

She was still wheezing now, but ever so slightly, and savoring the last bite of doughnut as she trudged up the rest of the stairs to the museum. She wanted a Movement job this summer; maybe Jane would help her find one. Then she wouldn't have to be on two tracks at once.

In the great hall a life-size horse in armor carried a knight among tapestries, ancient figures frozen in place for centuries. Past the horse was the Guelph treasure, encased in glass. An anonymous artist beat gold thin and fashioned a reliquary around a shard of bone, supposedly some saint's. Serfs mined and smelted that gold. The armor, the bone, the gold—all vestiges of brutality. Think of the man (a slave, probably somewhere in the Middle East) whose hands chiseled these red stone gryphons, then polished the granite for days. Ivy stroked the smooth head of a gryphon, entered the lecture hall, and slid into a blue plush seat near the back.

Sherman Lee was at the podium, showing slides of Chinese paintings. On the screen, clouds and mountains swirled together, gray, brown, with tinges of green. "Streams and Mountains Without End," Lee said in his easy dry monotone. Ivy wrote as he talked: "Sung Dynasty. *Lu Shan. Chu Jan. Tung Yuan.*" She could barely see her notebook because of the dim light, and her eyes kept closing.

She'd spent most of the night drinking instant coffee and listening to Chuck's soft, slow breaths as she read Thomas Mann. *Unordnung und Frühes Leid.* The words turned in her mind: "Disorder and Early Sorrow." Chinese painters used a wet-brush technique, Sherman Lee was explaining; they dipped their brushes in sorrow and mixed blood with wax for the signature stamps, which hurt pressing into the skin. Ivy felt sharp edges on the backs of her hands, on her neck, felt sorrow drip into her lap...Coffee was spilling into her skirt. She jerked awake. "Stones were essential to Chinese painting," Lee was saying, "rubbed smooth." She had promised to place stones on the path ahead, but she couldn't see the path at all.

Sherman Lee turned up the lights and explained the exam on Monday. She'd have to read the textbook to pass. First she would write her paper. Shivering in her coffee-damp skirt, Ivy made her way back to the dorm. Four flights to her room: she clung to the bannister, waiting on each landing for the breath to catch up; too soon to use the inhaler again. In her room she'd take a tab of aminophyllin and sleep for a little while.

It was a good room with a carpet, a dormer window, and a walk-in closet. Ivy kept milk outside the window and Raisin Bran inside. When the milk soured in the sunshine, she added a little fake-maple syrup to make it drinkable. She would eat after she'd rested. She kicked off her shoes and propped herself, half-lying, on the bed. Behind her closed eyes, thoughts jabbered, stabbed, and wailed. She struggled to make sense of them, but sleep came, swirling and muffling every word and image.

Hours later she woke mouthing words in German. She was good at German, had spoken it almost fluently in Stuttgart during the summer after high school. Her father had sent her, thinking she'd major in biochemistry, and every well-trained scientist had to know German. But in Stuttgart she'd found cathedrals and museums. And she'd met people who proved to her that the Vietnam War was a heinous disaster.

Now it was almost dark. In the lavatory, she heard the sound of vomiting in the stall next to hers and watched the girl emerge. It was Gail, who lived in the room across the hall from Ivy's. Gail's face was pasty, her eyes glazed. "You're sick," Ivy said. "What can I do?"

"You don't have to do anything," Gail said, dabbing at her mouth with a washcloth, filling her cup with water. "I've just had...hm. Call it a surprise. Joe's back from Vietnam."

"Home for good? Is he—is everything okay?" Ivy had never seen Joe, only his picture on Gail's dresser. He'd been the boyfriend since high school.

"He's on leave," Gail said. "Says he's fine. Big hugs. But." She sipped water, swished, and spit it out. "I don't know. He *acts* like nothing's changed." Her face crumpled. Ivy stood still, clutching her cup, toothbrush, and Colgate. "He says, 'Here's a present from Vietnam,' and hands me a little box," Gail went on. "I think, Oh nice, a pin or a bracelet, you know, smile, untie the ribbon. Inside," she whispered, "an ear." She stared at the frosted-glass window as though any second something huge might crash through it.

"A human ear?" Ivy had heard of cut-off Vietnamese ears, fingers, other body parts. Nightmare stories; she had not believed them, not really.

Gail soaped her hands, her palms, her wrists, each finger, each knuckle. "Joe says, 'It's a trophy, get it?' I say, 'Was this some dead guy?' He says, 'He's dead now.' Grins."

"Do you have it here?" Ivy looked at Gail's make-up bag squatting on the ledge in front of the mirror.

"Are you kidding? I threw the thing in the bin outside the back door."

"What's it look like?"

Gail shook her head. "I closed the box right away, didn't touch it." She soaped her washcloth and began to wash her face. "He's in the lounge, waiting for me to dress pretty and go drinking with him. I'd rather not put anything in my mouth for a while." She was wearing a sweatshirt and jeans. Her short hair stuck out in odd directions; ratting snarled the back of her head. Four flights down was a man who'd sliced off another man's perfectly good ear.

"Want me to go tell him you're sick and you need to stay in tonight?" Men were not allowed past the front hall and the two lounges. Whenever she heard a male voice, Mrs. Cartwright, the housemother, would emerge from her private apartment, rocking from side to side as she walked, peering from under her eyebrows rather than raising her head.

Gail leaned over the sink, scrubbing her teeth as Ivy insisted it would be no trouble to take a message to Joe. "No," said Gail. She spat into the sink. "I'll go down in a few minutes." She rinsed her mouth, spat again, and frowned at herself in the mirror. "I won't be squeamish. Okay, I'll get drunk. First I'll get pretty; then I'll get really drunk."

"I'm sorry," Ivy said.

"For what?" Gail asked, attacking her hair with a wet brush. She went to work with comb and hairspray as Ivy brushed her own teeth, feeling with her tongue the backs of the lower front incisors, the stony canines. She splashed water on her face and neck, touching an earlobe—a blob of flesh, slightly disgusting. What kind of monster had the war made of Joe, that he'd imagine Gail—an honor student, a double major in psych and English—would enjoy his ear-in-a-box? Why had Gail allowed him to wait in the lounge? Why dress up for this man?

Ivy trotted downstairs and out to the trash bin. She wouldn't reach inside if it was covered with wet garbage or slime. But there was the gift box, perched on a dry empty pizza carton. She had to know.

It was brown, a little shriveled. Like a dried peach-half left out too long to be edible, but with bits of dark blood along the edge that had been—yes, you could see it had been an ear, and had been cut. Ivy closed the little box and held it in her hand. She could use it to show people what the war had done to one Vietnamese man (and so many more) and to Joe (and so many others). She'd put it in the drawer with her underpants. It would rot. The stink of old garbage rose out of the bin, permeating the air near the back door. She tossed the box into darkness under the pizza carton, closed the bin and returned to her room.

All the German prose had flattened into meaningless words. Thomas Mann had been dead for thirteen years; these stories had been written before the First World War. What a joke, to call this literature "contemporary." Ivy had nothing useful to say about it. Her thoughts were for Gail, trying to go through the evening as if Joe had not done what Joe had done. The war was a sewer, sucking down young men.

She heard the phone ringing in the stairwell and ran to answer.

"Gotcha," Aunt Peg said. "At last."

"I've been busy. I was just..." *about to call*, she would have said, but Peg was talking about her own hectic life.

"Politics along with a full-time job can really keep a girl running," she said. "Anyway." She was working hard on the Gilligan campaign, wanted to reach out to students, and could Ivy come to supper on Sunday? "I'd like to pick your brain. And bring along your friend Chuck."

"I'll ask him," Ivy said. "But...um, advice?" Aunt Peg would not want to hear what Ivy knew: that Gilligan was owned by wealthy liberals who wanted the war to end so they could continue in comfort their privileged lives in the big houses on the boulevards of the Heights.

"Doesn't really matter, my dear. We haven't chatted in ages, so I thought...and now that we're both so involved..."

"My mother said she'd talked with you," Ivy said. Silence on the line.

"And...?" Peg said cautiously. "Does it bother you, that I might converse with your parents?"

"I don't like them spying on me," Ivy said. "Why are they worried all of a sudden? They seem to think I'm about to jump out a five-story window. I'm not."

"I know that. Hem." Aunt Peg cleared her throat. "I think your parents know, too. You're not the self-destructive type." She was choosing her words. "But, my dear, you do go awfully close to the edge sometimes. And you might not notice when the window frame is about to give way."

"So I should come to supper and bring along my window frame?"

"That's the trouble with metaphors, isn't it? I wasn't thinking of him—although I suppose he could be one. But we don't have to talk about all those things. Let's simply have a pleasant time, shall we?"

Ivy had to say yes. Then she could excuse herself, "German Lit paper to finish," and hang up. The Vietnamese ear stuck in her mind, its bloody edge insistent. She was loaded with promises—this one to Peg, on top of the commitments to her father and her German professor (*pünktlich*, noon, Friday). She still could not write. Nor could she rest.

She needed to act: start a draft resistance group at Reserve, maybe, raise funds to fly boys to Toronto. She phoned Bert Augustin. "I want to help with draft resistance," she told him. "When's the next meeting?" She'd promise to come to the meeting; then her mind would clear so she could return to Thomas Mann.

"Half an hour," Bert said. "You and me in the Student Union. Glad you called."

She told herself she needed coffee anyway and went. The Union was pungent with cigarette smoke, loud with the Mamas and the Papas complaining that the sky was gray. "Your phone has an echo," Bert said. "Not safe to talk on." A yellow button was pinned to his workshirt. *Children are only newer people*, it said.

"It's in a stairwell, that's all. Voices travel down four floors," Ivy said. "Cool button."

"I work at the community day care center." A molasses-taffy lock of hair dropped over Bert's brown eyes. He shook the hair away.

Ivy tried to imagine Bert holding a child: his arms could be sturdy and cradling, but the rest of him would be impatient to get away. "I saw a cut-off Vietnamese ear this evening," she said, and told him about Gail and Joe. "He must've been close enough to see the man's eyes—must've heard him scream," she said. "What kind of person can do that?"

Bert's coffee turned beige as he stirred in cream. "Crazy-mad, I guess," he said. "Maybe Joe's best friend was killed that same day. Maybe tortured. And he didn't necessarily have to look the man in the eye. They often blindfold and gag Vietnamese prisoners." He shrugged and looked sad. "America's a violent country. We started by slaughtering Indians and importing slaves. Then we went on from there." He swiped his hair off his forehead and glared as if he'd pulled the curtain off a horror too enormous for words. *See how big this beast is?*

"I just want to keep men away from the war," Ivy said, thinking of Chuck—and of Glen, her brother, who'd lost his grad-student deferment when the law changed last summer. He'd applied to join the Peace Corps. He was waiting to hear from them.

"Yeah, yeah. Keep 'em safe with draft evasion tactics." *Crack!* Bert hit the table with the flat of his hand. The coffee cups jumped and clattered. "I'm *done* helping middle class guys avoid the draft so they can be *peaceful* (crack!) while the system keeps on making soldiers of men who aren't so lucky, or smart, or who are *sadists* (crack!) and love to kill." He splayed his hand on the dark wood. One of the pinky fingers was mangled, with a wrinkled stump of a nail—so ugly, Ivy squeezed her eyes shut.

Bert noticed. "I was trying to disable myself," he said. "I'd just dropped out of school, had to give up that student deferment, got scared. Went freaky." He tapped the finger on the table, show-and-tell. "First I froze it; then I smashed it with a hammer. No good: Got re-classified 1-A."

Bert could be inducted any time. His finger had survived torture. "What will you do if you're called up?"

"Join and raise hell." He rubbed the back of his neck. "I'm determined to raise as much hell as I can." He leaned until his face nearly touched hers, his long torso crossing the table. Then he wrapped her wrist in his mangled hand. "Ready to join me?" His lips were parted, his eyes impossibly wide and dark. He knew the truth.

Children *are* only newer people, and the System thinks they're mindless and malleable, Ivy thought. She bobbed her head. "What do you have planned?"

He let go of her wrist. "In Baltimore they poured blood on selective service files." She flicked her eyes shut. "Animal blood," he added. Ivy wondered if she could train herself to do such a thing. "If there were blood poured on the files in Cleveland..." Bert was saying. "All across the country, draft files bloody—or burned." The idea blazed in her mind, a perfect response to the machine which was crippling a whole generation.

"I'm with you," she said.

"Good. Now get beyond the fucking draft," Bert said. "Look at your own university. Students hammer out fourteen reasonable demands—some aren't so reasonable, but who am I to quibble?—and the administration says, no dice. They got something more important to do: Move Claude Foster Hall half a block." Work crews had already begun jacking up the dorm, slowly separating it from its foundation. Ivy knew students hadn't much liked to live there, called the rooms "incubators" or "gerbil cages." But the Development Corporation wouldn't tear it down because of Claude Foster's money. His building had to keep standing, and it had to front Euclid Avenue. "They'll trundle that sucker down Euclid and turn it, so one end still faces the street." Bert made an invisible dorm with his hands and mimed the slow lift, the gradual turn. "What's the priority here? A rich man's ego."

Ivy began to laugh. "What an engineering feat," Bert said, his voice nasal, impersonal, administrative. "We know these movers can do it because they once moved a six-story prison *with all the inmates inside.*" He was quoting from the newspaper, Ivy knew. The Development Corporation president hadn't known how he'd revealed himself. She laughed harder, pulling a crumpled Kleenex from her coat pocket to wipe her eyes.

"See why I want to fuck up the System?" Bert returned to his normal voice. "I wish I'd been with Hoffman dumping dollar bills on the floor of the New York Stock exchange. We ought to be able to do something wicked like that. With balloons, maybe."

"What?" She couldn't keep up; his mind had veered into someplace else.

He shrugged. "Don't know yet." Suddenly he reached with his battered hand and stroked her cheek. "Let's go somewhere." He winked.

"What?" Ivy was startled, then disappointed. She didn't want to fool around with Bert. She wanted to help fuck up the draft. Why had she suddenly noticed his lips? Maybe she'd led him on without knowing. "I'm sorry," she said. "Got a paper to write." She rose to leave.

He stood up too. "Wait," he said. "You want to work with me, right?"

"I think so." He was far ahead of Chuck. "I want to stop that war," she added. "And fuck up the System."

"The Revolution," Bert said, "starts on Saturday, in the Public Auditorium."

"With the Reserve Officer's Training Corps?" Ivy knew there was an ROTC event in the auditorium, and some anti-war groups were planning to protest outside.

"Maybe not the whole Revolution." He shrugged again. "Maybe just something with balloons. I'll let you know."

"Fine," Ivy said. She did not have to plan beyond Saturday, nor do anything before Saturday. She could put Bert out of her mind for a while.

Ten minutes later, sitting cross-legged on the floor of her room, she bent over her notes on Thomas Mann and saw a theme: teeth. "In Mann's short stories, teeth are harbingers of death," she wrote at the top of a new page in her notebook. She leafed through the stories. Yes, it would work. Teeth. *Zähne.* They gleamed in the characters' mouths; they rotted. Even where Mann didn't mention teeth, she could see glimpses and hints. She settled at the desk with her notes and books, Mann in German and in English, a dictionary. It was easy now to post in her mind a skull, hairless, lipless, earless, grinning through every scene, every story. The pressure of time forced her fingers down on the typewriter keys.

Chapter 4

May 2, 1968
Euclid Avenue & The Monmouth

Chuck shut the mailbox, put the letter back in his pocket, and turned to walk home. Euclid Avenue was silent except for neon hissing above a door, the sharp tap of heels as a couple walked past holding hands. His feet were freezing in wet sneakers and no socks. No time for laundry. No time for anything but politics—meetings, a rally, and more meetings—until this evening.

He could have gone to the laundromat. He should be reading Kant. But he'd written to his draft board, finally, this letter he'd meant to write since January and now couldn't send. "Dear Uncle Sam," it began. "Since you've ordered me to report all 'changes in status resulting from circumstances over which I have no control,' I guess I better tell you what's new. Too many changes to enumerate them all, though. I'll just give you the highlights. Okay? Here goes." Chuck liked the idea of the Selective Service as an inquisitive uncle; he wanted to believe at least one person in that bureaucracy would appreciate his writing as he'd want to be spoken to, more or less.

"First, I've got a new residence, on the third floor of a building with *The Monmouth* carved in marble over the door. I live in one room with three big windows full of sky, mottled pearl at the moment, with pink edges—a circumstance over which I have no control. I moved here because I've fallen in love with a girl, another such circumstance." He tried not to be too much of a smart-ass.

"One thing has not changed: I'm still a student." His father had reluctantly paid the semester's tuition, insisting that Chuck sign an agreement to pay it back and not ask for more. So far he hadn't been able to save enough money. His shelving job at the library should have made it possible to scrape together some kind of repayment, but he couldn't work enough hours. Couldn't or didn't? He crossed two four-lane streets against traffic, interrogating himself. He'd stopped buying lunch, subsisting on free crackers and pickles in the cafeteria. He'd stopped driving to save gasoline.

He'd written, "The Tet offensive and related circumstances since then, none of which I can control (who can? Think about it), have changed my status significantly: I am now a full-time anti-war activist, as well as a son at odds with his father."

According to Father, the war was necessary to defeat Communists, who were evil, and all men in government office had been made wise with secret knowledge. Conscientious objectors were just draft dodgers in Charley Leggit's mind: cowards who let others do their dirty work. "You could say the same thing about students who accept a 2-S deferment," Chuck had argued. "And CO's do alternative service—real work; students don't." He should've mentioned the guys on the front lines were mostly poor folks with no other choice, while middle class kids in college or the National Guard got to stay safe in America. But his father had thrown his linen napkin onto his plate and walked away from the table, leaving Chuck to face his mother's tears, his sister Bonnie's disgusted voice, low: "Ruined another dinner, didn't you, boy?"

"Because my status as a student is financially at risk," Chuck told the draft board, "I'm considering alternatives. Please send me an application for Conscientious Objector Status. Thank you very much. Your loving nephew, Charles Leggit, Jr."

Chickenshit. He should have just sent the letter. No one would go over to Leggit's Chrysler dealership and say *Hey*

Charley, your son wants to be a CO. They'd just stick the application into an envelope and send it. His father would find out only after Chuck had applied—which he had not quite decided to do.

Service? Yes. Chuck had wanted to serve his country ever since watching Kennedy's inaugural speech. He'd won the prize for the best seventh grade essay on the theme, "Ask What You Can Do For Your Country." He'd spent happy weekends with his church youth group taking meals to old people, painting stairwells in run-down apartment buildings, tutoring in settlement houses. Service came easily to Chuck.

His father's approval did not. Chuck's boyhood was punctuated with baseballs doggedly thrown and caught on long Saturday afternoons, listening to his father talk about the importance of winning. When Chuck dropped the ball, Charley would say, "Never let yourself do that, boy, if you're gonna succeed in life." Even when Chuck won the essay prize, he felt like a loser around his father.

Charley Leggit had been a Nixon supporter. After Kennedy won, he stayed gloomy. Long after everyone else seemed glad about JFK and Jackie, Father hid out in his den, snapping at Mom and Bonnie, neglecting the cocker spaniel. Chuck still wanted to please his father, so one Saturday night he proposed a game of checkers. Charley grew cheerful, setting up the board on the ottoman in the den. It so happened that Chuck played well, taking several of his father's men, and then five lovely jumps in one move. Charley puffed, "I'll get you for that," jumped twice and said, "King me." Chuck did, and then got two kings of his own.

When Chuck won, Father was not pleased. "You should've been in bed," he said. "Pretty sneaky, to trick me into a game so you could stay up an extra hour."

Bonnie heard Chuck's curses and sniffles and came into his room. "You know it's all competition with Father," she said. "He's in a funk, and it's not because you beat him in checkers. It's not because Nixon lost, either. It's because

Oldsmobile sold more cars than Chrysler last month. He'll be a jerk till he wins something, that's all."

"If I let him beat me in checkers..." Chuck began.

"Oh, don't do that," Bonnie said. "Keep your self-respect."

Father didn't cut off tuition because of political differences. Chuck had lied to the draft board about that. The lie was the real reason he couldn't send the letter. Father had decided his son should transfer to the University of Cincinnati, live at home, and work at the dealership, sweeping, washing windows, and when he'd proved himself (this was supposed to be the prize), helping to sell Chryslers on weekends. Chuck refused. The circumstance of his father's decision he could not control, but he could have done what his father had asked; then his letter would say that he was working for Chrysler so he could hold onto his student deferment. He wondered if anyone on the draft board could see how loathsome that idea was.

Now Chuck was edging the Western Reserve Campus, passing the Church of the Covenant, a short walk from Ivy's dorm. She'd refused to see him till tomorrow afternoon, after she'd turned in her paper. They'd be together Saturday at the protest march, and they'd eat supper (a full supper!) at her Aunt Peg's on Sunday. He wished men were allowed in the girls' dorms, so he could look into Ivy's room, watch her poke away on her portable typewriter. She'd be smoking; she said she couldn't write without smoking. He was out of cigarettes; they could share one. He would hold her in his arms and sniff the smoke-and-Prell scent of her hair.

He could walk around the tennis courts and look up at her window. But what if the light wasn't on? She might be asleep. She might be out. He'd be too worried to leave the tennis courts till he knew, and finding out could take all night. He started again toward The Monmouth, jogging to warm his feet.

Footsteps thudded behind him; then came a shout: "Leggit!" Greg Lambert caught up with Chuck near the

Commodore Deli. Greg was big, a high school linebacker growing pudgy, with thick glasses and an eager pink face. At the anti-war rally on Friday he'd grabbed an *America: Love it or Leave it!* sign out of a Young Republican's hands and torn it in half. Three conservatives jumped him, several Movement people stepped in, and the brawl had to be stopped by campus security.

Too eager, that's how Greg was. He was trying to become Chuck's pal; now he thrust a McDonald's bag into Chuck's hands. The hot salty fragrance rose out of the paper. "Three hamburgers," Greg beamed, "one for each of us and one to split. I would've bought four, but I didn't have enough cash, so I got fries."

"You shouldn't have done this," Chuck said.

"Why aren't you driving?"

"My car's at The Monmouth, waiting for me to have enough money to give it a tank of gas. Very patient, that car is." Chuck began walking again.

"You should get a job that pays better," Greg said, walking too.

"Easier said than done," said Chuck. Greg's elbow touched his, and he moved away without slowing down.

"I need your help," Greg said. "I bombed the philosophy mid-term, so I have to do well on this next project, but I don't understand it. You're doing good in that class..."

Not if he didn't catch up with the reading. "I get it," Chuck sighed. "This is how I earn my supper." They stumped upstairs to the apartment; Chuck put his key in the lock, pushed open the door, and saw Bert Augustin stretched out on the bed. Next to him, a girl struggled to cover her breasts.

"Did you have to put your boots on my bedspread?" Chuck said.

"Woops." Bert raised one blue-jeaned leg toward the ceiling, almost over his head. The sole and heel were worn, but not dirty. He swung the leg over the edge of the bed and rose to his feet. "I wish you had some beer in the fridge. This," she sat up, buttoning her sweater, "is Shelly." She had frizzy hair and big silver hoop earrings.

"Hi, Shelly," Chuck said. She nodded hello, then fished a cigarette out of her purse. "How'd you get in?" he asked Bert.

Bert held up a plastic American Express card. "Easy." He grinned.

"Couldn't you use your own bed?"

"Ah, but Shelly was dating Marvin last month." Bert flushed. "We decided it was better not to cross paths."

Greg leaned over Bert and Shelly. "Chuck and I have work to do, so unless you know a hell of a lot about philosophy, you should leave." He seemed to be staring mesmerized at the skin between Shelly's breasts, visible through a gap in the sweater's button line. She blew smoke in his face, and Greg made a show of inhaling it.

"This is Greg Lambert," Chuck said. "He and I were about to eat a couple of hamburgers and discuss Immanuel Kant, and we're too hungry to share. There are a few peanuts left in the cupboard, if you're desperate."

Bert shook his head. "We ate at the Crystal. Full meal for a dollar each. Guess we'd better..." He reached for Shelly's hand.

"Make like a bomb," Greg said, "and go off. Ha!" His laugh was a short solo bark. Chuck took the envelope of French fries out of the McDonald's bag and opened the refrigerator, wishing for a beer instead of this Koolaid. He rinsed two glasses and set them on the table. Then he saw the poster leaning against the wall.

Girls say yes to boys who say no. Under the words, three women sat on a couch wearing big hats and serious faces. These women would not be pushed around. Two of them were barefoot, with smooth tan calves and long Californian toes, the kind of legs you'd want to stroke, but you'd ask first, and these two women might laugh at you. The third wore shoes and stockings and a white blouse with a high neck. Chuck suddenly recognized Joan Baez, leveling her gaze at the camera, her *yes* a challenge. He thought of his letter and felt like a dumb-ass. Baez's eyes said, *Don't mess with that Uncle-Sam good-nephew shit; just refuse. Go to jail if you have to.*

"This poster yours?" Chuck asked Bert, who was halfway out the door.

"Mine. Almost forgot," Shelly said. "It's for Saturday's anti-war march."

Bert heaved a breath. "Another boring anti-war march. Piss on it. Let's go." He pulled her by the hand. "These guys have to study long-dead white philosophy."

"I'm taking my sign," Shelly said. "I put in some *time* with that staple-gun." The poster had been mounted on a flattened cardboard box. She hoisted it gingerly.

"Wait a sec." Chuck wasn't about to let Bert put down the demonstration. The Movement had a duty to welcome students in the Reserve Officers Training Corps coming from all over the state for a marching competition. "You can't just quit protesting," he told Bert. "We've done it fifty times, but the ROTC guys will think, if we're not there..."

"I'll be there," Bert said. "I plan to stage a balloon-bombing."

"Bomb the ROTC guys with balloons?" Greg looked up from his hamburger.

Bert smiled. "Shitload of balloons dropped over the balcony, onto the floor where the ROTC squads are marching. The balloons represent napalm."

"That's cool," said Greg. "I like that."

"How will they know the balloons are supposed to be napalm?" Chuck asked. He pictured balloons drifting down, bobbing along starched, gold-braided shoulders, bouncing among polished ROTC shoes as the students tried to maintain formation.

"Write 'If this were napalm, you'd be dead now' on the balloon," Shelly said. She'd lit another cigarette and settled herself back on the bed, leaning against pillows.

"I have an idea." Bert lifted Chuck's notebook from the top of a pile of books next to the armchair, opened it to a blank page, and sat down to write.

"Aren't you Ivy Barcelona's Chuck?" asked Shelly.

Nice way to be known? He wasn't sure. "How do you know Ivy?"

"I'm in the Reserve SDS. Also Ivy's in my art history class. Heard about you. Don't think I've ever seen you."

"No," Chuck agreed. If he'd seen Shelly's fuzzy red-gold mane and slender legs, he'd have remembered. And Marvin had dated her, too. Well, well. "I'm in SDS at Cleveland State."

"Sho am I," Greg said, his mouth full.

"Listen to this." Bert pushed hair out of his eyes to read what he'd written: "If this were napalm, you might not be dead now, but you'd wish you were. Your skin would have burned off, and your flesh would still be roasting. Third-degree burns cause the most excruciating pain known to humans. Recovery is never complete. Stop bombing Vietnam."

"Aughh!" groaned Shelly. "It's fabulous, Bert."

"You can't write that on a hundred balloons," Chuck said.

"Put it on paper, roll it up and stick it inside," said Shelly.

"But you'd have to make tight little rolls," Chuck said. "People would have to break the balloon to read the message."

"The curious ones would rip the balloon to shreds, pick out the paper. They're the ones we want to reach." Bert's mouth curved up at the corners. "Might work."

"They'd have to be extremely curious," Chuck said. "Put the message on little squares of paper and tie each one on with string."

"Okay!" Bert joined the idea. "The paper pulls the balloons down, makes them more like bombs. Now, who gets to buy balloons, blow 'em up, print the little papers?"

"Tie the strings, too," Shelly said. "Not me. Classes all day tomorrow."

"I gotta work," Chuck said. Four precious hours among the library shelves. Plus Immanuel Kant. And this was Bert's stunt, not his.

Bert turned to Greg, who was quietly staring at something. "How about you? What the fuck are you doing?"

Greg had picked up Shelly's cigarette and was holding the lit end to his wrist. "Just a tad of the most excruciating pain known to humans." He smiled wanly, looking at Bert, then at Chuck, then at Shelly, then back to Chuck.

"Give me that." Chuck held out his hand, and Greg put the cigarette into it. Chuck took it to the sink, doused it in water, and dumped the soggy remnant in the trash. "Now show me," he ordered. The burn was a small dark hole on the pale underside of Greg's wrist. In his bathroom Chuck looked through the cabinet under the sink. He had a bottle of peroxide, which would clean the ash out of the hole, and a few Band-Aids.

He brought out these supplies thinking warily of Bert's idea. If the balloons didn't fall just right, they'd all look like fools. They could be arrested for disruption. Not much sympathy in Cleveland for almost-military march disrupters. He poured peroxide into the hole in Greg's wrist. It fizzed and foamed. "*This* is the excruciating part," Greg said. His voice was calm, but his face turned red, then pale. Chuck laid a Band-Aid carefully over the sizzling wound and pressed it down.

"Okay, we're done for tonight," Bert said. "You can edit what I wrote, make the little papers and all that in plenty of time."

"Who can?" Chuck looked sternly at Bert.

"Okay," Bert said. "I'll do it. Greg'll help me, and we'll get Ivy and some of her girlfriends to do the typing."

Greg only grunted through his teeth. Maybe the peroxide was a bad idea, Chuck thought. There would be no discussion of Kant.

"You think that wrist'll be okay?" Bert asked kindly.

"Of course, it will," Greg said. But when Shelly and Bert had gone, he sighed and lay on the bed. "If we fastened lead sinkers to those balloon strings, they'd really be noticed," he said.

"Shall we go to the Emergency Room?" Chuck asked.

"No thanks." Greg rolled his head side to side, his jaw set in refusal and pain. "I'll be all right. Eat your hamburgers. Eat two—I've lost my appetite."

The hamburgers were lukewarm, but Chuck ate gratefully, and when he'd swallowed the last bite, Greg was on his feet, swaying. "You shouldn't drive," Chuck said. "Where's your car? I'm taking you home."

Before they got to his Volkswagen in the Church of the Covenant lot, Greg was leaning against Chuck. He kept his eyes closed as Chuck drove down Euclid (good car, nice tight gears—terribly small, though) and he wobbled as they walked to his basement apartment. He leaned against the doorjamb, working his key.

"Better lie down," Chuck said. "Get some sleep. Is that a grenade-case?" Greg's desk stood in the center of the room with a baseball-shaped metal thing on top of a pile of papers.

"Not a case," Greg said. "It's fully loaded. If I pull the pin on it we'll be blown to bits in four seconds. I like having it there, waiting."

Live grenade on his desk, Chuck thought. Dear God, protect me from Greg Lambert. "Okay if I borrow a quarter?" he asked. Greg was already flat on his bed, eyes closed, but there were some coins on the floor. Chuck's feet would freeze if he had to walk two miles home. With Greg's quarter he had bus fare.

He'd get the letter in the mail to the Cincinnati draft board early tomorrow morning. Rewrite the part about his father. When the CO application came, he'd decide what to do. Rain was falling, so he waited in the bus shelter, wondering if God had sent Greg Lambert on purpose to plague Chuck Leggit. The hamburgers and fries made a greasy knot in his stomach. He would skip the balloon drop to be with Ivy; for her the protest march would be festive, a celebration after finishing her German paper.

Five Black people rode the bus with him, two of them noisy and probably drunk, the rest quiet. Chuck looked out at the rainy night and saw the whole competition, clear as a game of checkers: hamburgers (point for Greg), philosophy (point for Chuck), Shelly (big points for Bert; Chuck hadn't ogled her breasts, as Greg had, but he'd thought about them). With the balloons they'd managed a tie, but Greg had trumped them all with the burn. Or had he? Bert had gone off with Shelly and a risky plan for civil disobedience (more points) on Saturday.

Charley Leggit staked his manhood on Chrysler sales and Republican candidates. Chuck played a comparable game with different pieces: guts, sex appeal, radical acuteness, other things he couldn't quite name. And what about that loaded grenade? He added up tonight's score again. Then he did it again, until he'd won two out of three times. He wondered how to stop the game. Say no? To whom?

He would phone Ivy as soon as he got home. He'd have to let the phone ring ten or fifteen times in the stairwell, and then wait while another girl fetched her. She'd be upset because he'd interrupted her work on the paper. He didn't care. He needed her voice.

Chapter 5

May 3, 1968
East Cleveland

Still nothing in the cupboard. Jane teased out a glass from under the egg-crusted frying pan, turned on the tap, and waited for the water to get hot so she could wash out the orange pulp. She wished her boyfriend would do the dishes when he said he'd do the dishes. Two days ago Norman had said, "I'll take care of the kitchen." Tonight, when she couldn't find enough counter space to make a sandwich, he'd said, "I agreed to take care of the kitchen and I *will*. Don't go pushing your schedule on me."

The water was hot. Jane scrubbed the glass, rinsed, filled it with milk, and drank. The hot glass made the cold milk taste sour. Norman was typing, sitting at what should have been the dining table with his reporter's notebook propped against a stack of books so he could flip through his notes without slowing down. He typed astonishingly fast, pausing between pages only long enough to run his fingers through the dark curls on top of his head. Jane could talk to him during one of those pauses if she spoke quickly. She sipped her milk and waited. It was like playing jumprope, waiting for the right instant to leap without being caught around the ankles.

There. He pressed the carriage return three times, took out the typed page, raked his hair, and Jane said, "I've got to go to the West Side. I'll need your car." She had to meet Lillian. Since Dora had left Welfare Rights for Soul Power, the handbook project had moved to the West Side.

Jane hated to ask, hated having to fit her work around Norman's car. Just this afternoon she'd been in a meeting with Ivy and five other SDS girls when he arrived, double-parking next to the dorm, trotting up to the porch where they sat, telling her to hurry. She'd had to break off in mid-sentence, sorry but, of course, she had to leave. Now the abruptness of that leaving bothered her.

They'd been talking about pockets. The question was Ivy's: "How come men's clothes have pockets but women's don't?" None of the others had thought such a thing into words, but they'd all wondered. Men reached into their back pockets for wallets, into their front pockets for change. Their jackets had deep inner pockets for checkbooks. Men were supposed to carry money and one folded handkerchief to loan a woman who cried at the end of a movie. (Men never cried at movies.) Women's skirts and pants had zippers at the hips, but not pockets. A woman carried a purse with a strap over one shoulder, or a little strap held in one hand, or no strap at all, under one arm. She never had both hands, so she was easy to rob.

"Pocketlessness is another form of women's oppression," Jane realized out loud. Several of the girls on the porch had been startled by the phrase "women's oppression"— that's why the conversation should have continued. But Norman had agreed to pick Jane up at 5:30, and there he was, with something urgent to do next, as usual.

Now he picked up a clean sheet of paper and rolled it onto the typewriter. But instead of typing, he turned to her. "I thought you had the Valiant."

"Bert's taken it to Kent State for the night."

"I don't like being stuck here without a car," Norman said.

Come to think of it, why had Jane allowed Bert's need for the Valiant to take precedence over hers? *Fine*, she'd told Bert; she'd use Norman's car. "You're not exactly stuck," Jane said to Norman. Their apartment was in East Cleveland, near plenty of shops and bus stops. "I'd take the bus, but I don't like to walk alone at night." Street lamps on the near West Side sputtered; she'd walked there arm-in-arm with Tessa, slinking past dark silent doorways, scurrying across light-speckled sidewalks from the bars, hearing catcalls every time they passed a cluster of men.

"You're right." Norman turned to his typewriter and sat still, hands on the keys. Then he twisted in his chair to watch her swallow the last of her milk. "I don't *like* you driving my car," he said. "Especially to the near West Side."

"Well, *I* don't like..." If she mentioned the dishes again, or scolded about the towels in a damp heap on the filthy bathroom floor, he'd accuse her of nagging. Jane put her glass down, far from Norman's notebook and typewriter. "Just for tonight?" she said, hating the way her voice came out small and pleading.

"I don't see why you can't deal with Lillian over the phone. But if I must drive you, wait till I finish this story. And you'll have to get a ride home from someone else."

"Okay," said Jane, but she seethed, pacing. She didn't know how to explain to Norman the importance of being at the table with Lillian, telling experiences and thinking out loud together, coming up with points they both wanted to make, watching as an outline evolved on paper that both could touch. Breathing together, you could feel changes happen. Norman did all his writing absolutely solo, with such certainty that Jane couldn't even say to him, "Don't be silly; you don't have to go anywhere tonight." Nor could she simply take the bus to the West Side and walk a couple of blocks. That was part of the problem, wasn't it? A man could walk alone anywhere, but women had better avoid Lillian's neighborhood at night.

She picked up Norman's typed pages. He'd been to the official kick-off for Carl Stokes' Cleveland: Now! fund-raising campaign. Jane read the unbelievable numbers aloud: "one billion, five hundred million dollars over the next ten years." Norman rolled the next sheet out of his typewriter. "Stokes is trying to get corporations to pay for quiet in the inner city," she said.

"He's succeeding," Norman said. "Cleveland: Now! is extremely popular. No one else on the planet could pull this off."

"He's got support from the Governor," Jane said, "so he must have convinced big business there's profit to be made."

Governor Rhodes's slogan was *Profit is not a dirty word in Ohio.* There was a rumor he was having the sentence carved in marble around the capitol rotunda. "He's implicitly raised the status," Marvin Kaminsky liked to point out, "of the Marxist-Leninists who think profit *is* a dirty word."

"Business loves Stokes," Norman said, "but so does the Black community."

"He won't be able to keep both," Jane said. She knew that what the Black community thought Stokes was promising—what they needed—wouldn't profit big business. "The men named in this article aren't going to give up control of their money."

"Go ahead, be cynical." Norman liked Jane to be interested in a story he was writing, enjoyed sharpening his wits against her disagreement. He balanced on the back legs of his chair; it nearly tipped over and he rescued himself by catching the edge of the table as the front legs hit the floor. "The money is real. What the hell is it you want?"

"Shouldn't you be asking the Black community what *they* want?" She could have said houses, jobs, businesses, and government positions. Power. But the debate would have spiraled into empty speculation, for the question wasn't hers to answer. As for the question he'd actually asked, she didn't know where to start.

Jane and Norman had met during the Cuban Missile Crisis, when they were students at Ann Arbor. The very air that week seemed paralyzed, the maple leaves hysterically bright. No one would talk much beyond jokes about Khrushchev and his shoe-pounding or about the world ending any minute: *We'll all go together when we go.* The professors kept on teaching English Lit, Spanish II, and Physical Chemistry (Jane was getting through her required courses) while terror and curiosity rose to flood-level. The world waited to be rescued.

Norman was the one who would talk to Jane. They began over ham sandwiches in the cafeteria. When it got dark they went to his dorm room, where a metal fallout shelter sign hung over the bed with its arrow pointing downward. Across the official yellow and black shelter symbol, a sticker said, "In case of a nuclear attack this shelter would be useless." They lay next to each other talking until deep in the night, when they began to kiss. At dawn they took off the rest of their clothes— maybe the last dawn for both of them; in case of a nuclear attack, Norman's bed would not save them. They rocked together softly, reverently; having sex seemed the right sacrament for two people who could not save the world, who might be bidding it farewell.

Then, as the world went on after all, they went on being lovers, together in Ann Arbor, apart when Jane was home in Minneapolis and Norman was working in New York. When people asked about their relationship, they said, We approach the world differently: Norman documents it; Jane changes it.

By then it was 1964. While Jane knocked on the doors of little weatherbeaten houses in Mississippi, drank cold well-water offered in hospitality, waded through miles of dust to register one voter—that same summer, Norman was in Washington, writing catalogue entries for the Library of Congress by day, conducting his own research by night; he was writing a book about the Wobblies which he still hoped to publish some day. When they finished college a year later, Norman took a job near his home, writing for a small newspaper in Staten Island. Jane came to Cleveland.

They'd tried sex with other people—Jane had done so, at least, and she assumed Norman had, too, though he hadn't told her in so many words. Experiments with sex seemed a natural part of social change, especially in the Civil Rights

Movement, especially when a Black man from New York confessed to her his loneliness and fear and listened to her confessions in return. His name was Roland. His chest was hairless, milk-chocolate smooth. They'd slept together only twice when the regional coordinator told them to quit. "You don't hold hands, you don't give each other those sweet looks, you don't ride in the same car," he'd said. "Not if you want Roland to live long enough to go home." In one heart-freezing moment Jane realized her supervisor wasn't threatening; he was simply telling the truth. For the rest of the summer she stayed with the other white women in an apartment where she slept on the couch. She did not regret having slept with Roland. But in Cleveland she saw how little she'd known Roland, how much he'd attracted her because he was vulnerable, and because of his beautiful chocolate body.

The phone rang; Jane had to step around Norman to answer it. He kept typing.

"I'm returning your call," Marvin said.

For a few seconds Jane couldn't remember why she'd phoned Marvin. Bert had answered and they'd talked about the Valiant and his trip to Kent. Then she remembered. "Ivy wants to work for the Movement as soon as she's done with school. I said I'd talk with you, see what the possibilities are."

"Not much, if she wants to be paid," Marvin said. "Our money goes for rent this summer. I just signed a lease for an office—June, July, August. If Ivy wants to volunteer? Well, sure. We'll need people to answer the phone and organize—raise consciousness and stuff. She seems awfully young, though, don't you think?"

"She's no younger than you and I were when we started." Jane thought of herself at twenty, before Mississippi, as shamefully naïve. Yet she liked Ivy, who'd declared she was a Feminist after the first hour of this afternoon's conversation. "She's a quick study. Have you heard from Tessa? Was she busted?" Tessa was visiting Columbia where the police had arrested 692 students.

"No," Marvin said. "I talked with her a little while ago; she said they're setting up some kind of liberated university curriculum. She sounds excited."

"Can't wait to see her," Jane said. She was acutely aware of standing between Marvin and Norman, as if Norman had some reason to be uncomfortable. She ended the conversation quickly.

Her sexual experiment with Marvin, before Norman got his job at *The Plain Dealer* and moved to Cleveland, had been disappointing. Marvin-as-lover was tentative and obsequious; there were no sparks, no thrilling ripples deep in her belly. She had quit sex with Marvin so she could keep on liking him—which she did, a lot. She adored his wit. She even liked his Roman nose, his blond hair thick over his collar and thin on top, his carpenter's hands, his long torso with a little belly. Norman was just plain handsome with big shoulders, dark curls, and expressive eyebrows.

He glanced up at her with one eyebrow cocked and the mouth-twitch that meant he was amused; then he returned to the story of Cleveland: Now! His brow furrowed, his lips moved, his fingers punched the keys. His fingers were powerful and tireless, typing or making love.

Something had come between them. Jane felt deeply unstable, as if a volcano had begun to boil, as if an earthquake were threatening to make a fissure that couldn't be closed or crossed. She and Norman had collapsed many distances— between Mississippi and Washington, between Minneapolis and New York. Yet these tremors were deeper than geography; they had begun, she recognized, well before Norman refused to loan his car.

When you don't know what else to do, run hot water and add soap. Her mother had said that many times. Jane turned to the sink and ran water over the mound of dishes, streaked and mottled with tomato sauce and cheese blobs. Mold floated up from below. She soaped the sponge, selected a cup, and began to wipe off the dark scum. The water was cold. Suddenly Jane threw the cup to the floor, where it smashed.

Norman stopped typing and turned around. "What was that?"

To show him, Jane threw a jar. It sailed over his head and shattered high on the wall. The sound was very satisfying. Jane picked up a china plate, but Norman had popped out of his chair and was reaching for her. He got the plate before she threw it.

"I don't need this, Jane," he said. His fingers vise-gripped her wrist. "I've got a deadline. I'm willing to schlep you over to the West Side, but I don't have time to deal with you trashing the kitchen for no reason."

She looked at his tight, expressionless face. He was absolutely sure he was right.

"Jane, I understand that sometimes you just get willful, but..."

She thought the inside of her throat might rupture. *Deadline. Schlep you. Trashing the kitchen. Willful.* She could feel tears under her eyes and blinked them away. He would misinterpret them.

"A minute ago," she said carefully, "you asked what I want. It is this: I want Stokes to put Dora and Lillian on the Commission for Economic Opportunity. And pay them well. I want to finish the Welfare Rights Handbook and have a copy for everyone who walks through the door of the County Welfare office. I want to go anywhere I want to at night—alone, on foot. I want you to write what you know perfectly well about the need for fundamental change in the way the city's governed." She held up her hand to stop him from interrupting. "*And* I want the right—not permission, but right, as a partner in this household—to drive your car sometimes." She avoided his eyes, looking down at her own dishwater-damp shirt.

"I thought you were a realist." Norman's voice had that familiar condescending tone: *I'm very disappointed in you*, said her father, her 10th-grade science teacher, her field hockey coach, her college advisor. All the men wanted her to be a good girl. She had tried. She felt sick from so much trying.

"I'm not," she said. "I've decided to stop being a realist. I'm sorry, Norman, that the decision came on the night when you had a double deadline, but I couldn't postpone it any longer." She fetched another plate with her free hand (he still gripped her wrist) and flung it across the room; it sailed over the table and smashed on the wall next to the door.

Norman grabbed her other wrist and pulled her close. His thick forearms locked hers to his chest, and he looked down into her eyes, where tears floated but did not fall. Her anger was turning them to steam. Norman's jaw was very still as he said softly, "Okay, Babe. I'm going to meet these deadlines and keep my job. In fact, I'm going to try for a promotion. I'm going to write about Carl Stokes and whatever assignments I can get about Cleveland: Now! which I find exciting, hopeful, and a hell of a lot better than the police beat. And I'm going to do those things away from flying dishes. Call me when you've come to your senses, okay?"

He began to pack his typewriter into its case and fill his briefcase. She stayed in the bathroom listening as he walked to the bedroom and back to the kitchen. He would pack underwear, socks, a clean shirt. He would go to his brother's in Beachwood. He would come into the bathroom for his toothbrush, and they would look at each other sadly, as they usually did after a quarrel. This time she would not say she was sorry.

She heard his steps outside the bathroom door. He stopped for less than a second, then kept going. The door slammed.

Now Jane allowed herself to cry, bending over the sink, running hot water and soaping the washcloth. She washed her face and her neck, her breasts—and then she decided what the hell and ran the bathtub full, adding in dishwashing liquid to make bubbles.

On the West Side, Lillian would be putting kids to bed, clearing the kitchen table, expecting Jane, who would phone eventually and explain. Lillian would laugh because she knew about men walking out. Jane wouldn't phone till she was ready to be laughed at—till she'd come to the senses that were not the kind Norman thought they should be. Tomorrow she'd take a suitcase and go to Tessa's apartment. When Tessa came home, they'd sit at the table and talk till dawn if need be, telling experiences and thinking out loud, watching a pattern evolve, breathing together, feeling the changes.

Oh, Norman! Already, she wanted him back. She clenched her teeth on the washcloth to stop herself from screaming.

What the hell *do* I want, she asked herself, sinking under dish-soap foam; her hair floated around her like seaweed. She wanted to go to the liberated university and talk with the 692 Columbia students out on bond. She wanted to go to Hanoi, where hatred for the invaders burned pure and clear, unpolluted by love or rage. She wanted to join the Black Panthers, to have dark brown skin and a badass mouth, to move to bongo drums and wave a rifle. Or perhaps to become a cloistered nun, renouncing activism, money, and men. When she sat up, her hair lay over her shoulders like a sodden shawl.

PART TWO

Ah, what an age it is
When to speak of trees is almost a crime
For it is a kind of silence about injustice!
    from "To Posterity" by Bertolt Brecht

The great songs were brain-morphing, blood-spinning, intensely personal. Now, plastic-coated, they fill soundtracks of movies that have nothing to do with how it felt when our records played in ratty apartments lit by candles dripping over wine bottles.

The Vietnam War raged like a distant furnace. In Catonsville, the Berrigan brothers, jailed for burning hundreds of draft files with homemade napalm, sent glowing messages from behind bars.

In Cleveland, segregationist George Wallace accumulated supporters from the Hungarian Freedom Fighters and the Fraternal Order of Police. The Democrats' almost-presidential-candidate Hubert Humphrey personally delivered two million dollars destined for Cleveland's small inner city businesses. One was an African culture curio shop owned by Ahmed Evans, an astrologer and Korean War veteran. Journalist Roldo Bartimole quit *The Plain Dealer* and published his own broadside, *Point of View*. The first issue called the Cleveland: Now! campaign "another gimmick" and "a pornographic answer to the city's ills." *Point of View* eventually gathered enough subscriptions to keep going for more than 35 years.

In the park out front of the Cleveland Museum of Art, ornamental cherry trees blossomed, and we tossed bread-bits to pigeons and to the orange carp in the lagoon. We pinned posters to boards, taped them to walls, and tied them with string around telephone polls: *Not with my life, you don't. Support Our Troops; bring them home. Victory to the NLF. Free Huey.* We imagined ourselves kin to revolutionary students in Paris, who wrote *A Poem is a Petition. The more I make revolution, the more I make love. Je suis Marxiste, tendance Groucho.*

During the first week of May 1968, more Americans were killed in Vietnam than in any other week of the war. We couldn't know that until much later. Twenty years would pass before we saw our faces reflected among the names of the dead on the black granite memorial in Washington.

Ivy Barcelona finished her last exam and left to visit her parents. Chuck Leggit drove her to the bus station, and while they waited in the coffee shop, he took his draft card out of his wallet. "Now's as good as ever," he said, striking a match. It burned neatly in the ashtray on the Formica table-top while Chuck lit cigarettes for both of them so as not to attract attention. He didn't tell Ivy he'd taken a job selling cameras door-to-door. Wait till he'd sold a few, he decided, as the bus left.

Bert Augustin was in the Cuyahoga County Jail. His napalm balloons at the demonstration had caused satisfactory havoc, but the marchers turned out to be Junior ROTC squads from local high schools. Parents were in the audience, and if the angriest had prevailed, Bert would have been beaten to a pulp. Instead, the judge settled on a three-week jail sentence.

Jane Revard and Marvin Kaminsky rented a storefront office on Euclid Avenue and equipped it with twelve metal folding chairs, a beat-up military-issue desk, and a stained couch that leaked stuffing. They installed a phone and argued with Movement people around the country about what Robert Kennedy's assassination meant for their plans to protest at the Democratic National Convention in Chicago. Jane now lived with Tessa on East 124th, only a block from Dora's. But she spent most of her time in the office, on the phone. It rang often, so when Norman called she was taken off guard. For a second she felt her heart rise into her throat, pounding, choking. But she managed to stay business-like, and all Norman really wanted was a story. She passed the phone to Marvin.

Chapter 6

June 10, 1968
Bloomington, Indiana

Ivy sat in a lawn chair next to her mother, gazing at the dark green lawn and the wooden fence lined with peonies, their pink round heads about to burst. Next to her the TV table held a pitcher of iced tea.

Along Euclid Avenue, she knew, the heat would be relentless; Chuck's apartment would be sweltering, though he would be out—job hunting, or maybe already on a job.

She shouldn't have come before visiting Bert in jail. She'd played scout for that balloon-drop, pattering around Public Auditorium in her good-girl Capezios and her Peter Pan collar. She'd opened the side door for Bert and Greg, dragged an enormous cloud of napalm-balloons by their strings up the staircase and into the balcony, and helped push them over the edge. Then she'd run to the Ladies' Room, and from there on she could have been an ROTC sister or girlfriend. Bert had taken the fall.

Chuck had been so busy marshalling the anti-war march that he didn't know Ivy had helped with the balloon stunt. She didn't tell him until they were in the Greyhound station. "You got guts," Chuck admitted. "But it sure was dumb not to know they were high school students." She hadn't told anyone else—

not Marvin, not Jane, certainly not her mother, now quietly pouring iced tea that would taste as sweet and lemony as always.

She lifted her bangs to let the sweat evaporate. This afternoon seemed wrapped in cellophane, preserved unchanged from last summer, and the summer before, and the one before that. What if she were to suggest to her mother that they drink beer instead? There were four bottles of Miller High Life in the Fridge. But she didn't want beer; she'd only just awakened. "I intended to make you some biscuits," Mum said now, "but it slipped my mind until this moment. Do you want some?"

"Sure," Ivy said. Her mother didn't move. The pear tree's speckled shadow lay across the blacktop driveway, making slow, gentle movements she'd always found comforting. There were no sirens here, no traffic sounds. No news.

The last month had been all news. Every day at their table in the Union, Movement people thrashed out the establishment's upheaval and the various uprisings. The National Mobilization Against the War, which everyone called "the Mobe," kept changing its plans. The table filled with arguments: The Mobe was too single-issued. The Mobe was doing necessary work. The Mobe was changing with the times or rolling with the punches. The Mobe was compromising way too much.

"The Bloomington campaign for McCarthy needs volunteers," Mum said. She had read Ivy's thoughts again, and misinterpreted, again. "He does seem the most promising candidate, since Bobby..." Her voice choked; she sipped iced tea. Hetty Barcelona talked about Kennedys as though they were her relatives, people who might like to join her in the garden for afternoon tea. If she'd stayed in England, she would have talked the same way about the Windsors. Ivy couldn't see the difference, except that the Windsors had less swagger than the Kennedys. She wasn't interested in volunteering for McCarthy, who wouldn't bother with the Cleveland Movement any more than the Kennedys would have had tea with Mum.

Four days ago, the morning after Bobby Kennedy was shot, a young Black man who called himself a Panther had come to the Movement table with news that a brother named Stephen had been gunned down. The Cleveland police were not even looking for the killer. Not even looking! For Ivy, that was the shame of this country—not another Kennedy's assassination, but Stephen's unnoticed death, unspeakably far from her mother's garden.

Instead of saying that, she tried to sympathize with her mother. "No one would think of assassinating the queen."

"England is not violent like America," Mum said. "They don't carry guns."

"They do if they're in the military," Ivy said. "And English people go shooting in the country, don't they?"

"Only the posh folk," Mum said. She came from Hexham, in the North, where everyone loved the working man and the queen but scorned the "posh folk." Mum's permanent was growing out; rather than poufing smoothly, her short dark hair grew flat on the top of her head and ribbled on the ends, wisping in odd directions below her ears.

Ivy felt sorry that her mother had such hopeless hair. "I'm going back to Cleveland Wednesday," she said. "If I dawdle too long, the summer jobs will be all snapped up."

Mum's eyes flashed blue-green. "But you have a job here," she said. "Didn't your father make that clear? His receptionist is quite pregnant; he wants you for her post. Volunteer for McCarthy on the side."

"I don't want to work for McCarthy," Ivy said. "He's still part of the System." Days in a sterile doctor's office, evenings and weekends licking envelopes with McCarthy Democrats, a succession of afternoons on the green lawn? A year ago she might have accepted such a life. Now? Impossible.

"Oh, you and your System," her mother said. "As if there were some giant machine in the clouds, operated by an evil cabal pushing mind-control buttons. This is not *1984*, you know."

"That's not what I think at all, Mum. The System is how power is rigged, and now, *right now*, it's being exposed. It must be stopped. We need to..."

"People can vote," her mother went on. "That's the democratic way. We have a political process you can *use*. It works. One step, then the next; you'll learn how to make things change."

As if Mum really didn't know that was a lie, as if she had no idea what Ivy had been learning for three years. Ivy bit her tongue so she wouldn't swear in frustration. "On my campus this spring, the students tried for months to get one little change—parietal hours, that was all."

"So you all wrote manifestos and held sit-ins over the right to have a cuddle in your dorm room? I must say, I don't know whether to laugh or cry at your generation of students."

"Actually, I didn't do anything but sign the petitions," Ivy admitted. "I was trying to get the university to repudiate the war."

"Oh, the administration must have loved that."

"Mother!" Mum's ignorant sarcasm grated like sand in the eyes. The point was to expose the System—the web of connections—between the war and everything else. Yes, parietal hours too. When men and women mingle freely, as equals, war becomes less possible. Why couldn't her mother see? Her own mother, the person from whom she'd learned to talk?

Hetty crossed the lawn and leaned over the rose bushes, tweaking a leaf here and there. Even now Ivy had the urge to follow, put her arms around the sturdy waist, lay her head against the flowered blouse, pet her mother's frizzy hair, promise to do whatever her parents wanted to make them happy with her. Love was such a trap.

She was hungry, but she didn't want to mention the biscuits that Mum had forgotten again. Ivy didn't belong here, in this fake-English garden, that was the thing. She belonged with Chuck, in his small apartment in the big seedy building.

Last Thursday the Black militant Jonas Bey had spoken in a soft voice: "Brother Stephen has been killed, just a few blocks from here." He straddled a chair, one arm resting on the chair's back, spinning his black beret around one finger. "I got to let y'all know."

"Who did the shooting?" Shelly asked.

"Some junkie working for the police—don't want us messing with his territory." By "us" he meant the Nationalists: the Afro set, the Republic of New Libya, the Soul Power, the Black Panthers. "We're allies against the white colonizer," said Jonas Bey. "Not everybody understands that."

They kept him talking, bought him a sausage sandwich and two Cokes as he told how the promises from the mayor's Cleveland: Now! campaign turned out empty: a shiny box with gold ribbon, open it up, here's ashes. "Stephen walking to the park with his baby sister when they got him, blood running down the brother's face, still holding his sister's hand, she crying, no police in sight. A sweet man, loved his mama, shot by a punk." After the ambulance carried away his friend's body, Jonas Bey said, he didn't know which way to turn. He started walking, ended up at the Student Union. What could the students do besides pay for his food?

Ivy had gone from the Union to the library to study Asian art, thinking *I no longer have the right to imagine I live in a nonviolent world*. In all the Chinese landscapes she examined, men with daggers lurked invisible behind the trees and in the crags of the mountains.

Stephen had been shot within a ten-minute walk of the Western Reserve Campus. A few months from now Ivy could reasonably expect that men with guns would be creeping behind the wooden fence and the peony bushes. She took a final swallow of her tea and joined her mother near the roses. "I want a job in the city," she said, "tutoring, playground supervising, something. The rest of my life will be about making social change. I should start in Cleveland."

"Like your brother Glen, wanting to help the less fortunate," her mother said.

"That's one way to put it." No point in mentioning the bloody hands of the more fortunate. No point in reminding Mum why Peace Corps was one of Glen's few choices. He was about to report for training. He might still have to go to war; a lot of candidates were rejected during training.

Hetty put one arm around Ivy and hugged. "I understand how you feel," she said. "Why do you suppose I went into nursing?" She retrieved the pitcher and carried it into the house. Tea time was over.

Ivy set the two glasses on the grass while she folded the tray flat against its legs. Her mother had been a girl her own age, with her very own war in England. A necessary, clear-cut war, citizens and the government and the military all working together. Also the war zone would have been more interesting than Hexham—an empty place with tiny roads and fields all closed in with dry-stone dikes. Ivy had seen it: no excitement at all.

Old photographs showed how her mother's hair had been braided or wrapped into a bun during the war. When Randy was a baby she'd had it cut to a pageboy curling on her shoulders. By the time Glen was born it just covered her neck, and in Ivy's baby pictures the sleek dark hair brushed Hetty's earlobes.

"But aren't you glad you did it?" Ivy found her mother rummaging through kitchen cupboards. "Worked in the war, I mean."

"I suppose so," Hetty said. "I met your father."

"But to be a nurse for the soldiers—didn't you feel like you were doing the one thing that made sense?"

Hetty set the Bisquick box on the counter. "Look," she said. "Here were all these blokes, healthy and strong, nineteen, twenty years old, fit to climb mountains, sail a boat single-handed to Spain, play rugby, anything they wanted to do, and when I met them they were in bed with no legs, or their intestines shredded, or half a brain. All in two seconds that happened to them. Same with Robert Kennedy: one moment he's the prime candidate and he'd be a fantastic president, you know he would. Next moment his brains are leaking onto a kitchen floor. And you're trying to make *sense* of things?" She opened the refrigerator door. "Do you want some eggs?"

"Don't bother, Mum. I'll eat later."

"But you haven't eaten since yesterday, and your father and I are going out for dinner—the Oliphants' garden party. Will you come along?"

"I have to stay here; Chuck's going to call." Ivy watched her mother return the eggs to the fridge and take the nested mixing bowls down from the cupboard. How much had Hetty changed in the past thirty years? Ivy couldn't know. She didn't often hear her mother's English accent, but she knew that tea and biscuits in Hexham would have been hot tea with milk and dry whole wheat cookies called digestive biscuits. In her great-aunt's chilly bungalow Ivy had eaten one. And a scone, her first. She'd felt like a visitor to a distant past.

Now she felt like a visitor to her own past, watching as her mother, in a skirt and blouse and sneakers with little ankle socks, poured Bisquick into a bowl, added milk. "I guess," said her mother, cradling the bowl and stirring with a fork, "you'll have to find out for yourself. Make your own mistakes. But you do understand, don't you?" She gave Ivy her I'm-looking-through-you stare and sighed, as though discouraged by what she'd seen. "I don't want you to be hurt."

"I've been in Cleveland three years, Mum. I know how to take care of myself."

"It's different when you're not in school. Whom will you live with? Peg's place is much too small."

"I'll live with Chuck." Ivy hadn't meant to blurt the news like that.

"Oh." Her mother stopped, a blob of dough in her left hand, wooden spoon in her right. "Are you telling me you plan to be married?"

"No," Ivy said. She cringed inwardly as her mother's face changed—lips pressed together, eyes traveling overhead, as if she were looking for something on the wall. "I guess I'll be living in sin," Ivy said. It was meant to be a joke. Her parents were liberals; they did not believe sex was a sin.

Hetty set the spoon on the counter, dipped her right hand in flour, and began with a teaspoon and her thumbs to shape the biscuit dough into a disc. Ivy had loved these biscuits when she was a little girl. "Let me help, Mum."

"Not now," Hetty said, jerking the bowl away. "You'll have your own cooking to do, soon enough." She tucked the round puck of biscuit carefully into the pan. "Cooking, cleaning, and doing his laundry. You get to handle his dirty socks; aren't you lucky. 'Living in sin' sounds romantic—and it will be, for about two days. Then you'll have to get groceries, and you'll not have the money for fresh fruit and lovely things from the bakery, and the romance is gone. Ta-ta!" Her voice rose, almost shouting.

"Oh geez, Mum, it's common for people to live together, these days."

"Common," her mother said, giving the word its dirty English connotation. "I suppose you've already had, eh, *relations* with this young man?"

"You *know* him, Mum, he's Chuck," Ivy said. She tore off a paper towel to wipe her nose and eyes. "Listen, most of the girls I know sleep with their boyfriends. And they lie to their parents. You answer the phone in Guilford Hall; you say *She's not here right now*, or *she's still asleep*, and then you call her up: *Hey Gail, phone your parents.* I will not lie, Mum, to you or to Dad. I won't."

"And what happens"—Hetty slammed the teaspoon on the counter—"when you get pregnant?"

"I won't get pregnant. I'll get birth control pills." Ivy had meant this discussion to go slowly, gradually, as her parents realized, of course, their daughter was doing what people do. At least Mum hadn't asked what the neighbors would think.

"Oh, you'll just go to the birth-control-pill store and buy a dozen or two? It's a bit more complicated than that, my girl." Mum's mouth was now a bitter gash across the bottom of her face. *My girl* meant she was angry.

"I know," Ivy said, miserable. She slunk to a chair at the kitchen table, kind of hoping her mother would sit across from her. "I guess I thought that Dad..."

"You're planning to ask your *father* to help you have illicit relations?" Hetty pushed the pan half-full of biscuits to the back of the counter, ran water over her hands, dried them with two swipes of a towel and crossed to the door. "Excuse me," she said, in her strained, most-English voice. "I feel a bit ill. I need air." She went out.

Then the tears came. Ivy bent forward till her hair closed over her face, *I'm sorry I'm sorry I'm sorry*. She'd handled it wrong, all wrong; no one should hurt her parents this way. She'd have to leave—maybe not forever, please God, not forever, but for a long time. She'd find a doctor in Cleveland to prescribe the pill; it would be hard, because she wasn't married, but it couldn't be that hard. She felt so stupid. Coming home in itself was a mistake—worse: a lie about her intentions. When Chuck phoned tonight she'd tell him she'd be on the first bus she could get.

She wiped her face with a paper towel. The kitchen was quiet except for the clock's ticking, the refrigerator's hum. The old Toby mugs in a row on their shelf, the pencil container she'd made in school out of a tin can, macaroni, and gold paint still in its place by the telephone, the fraying rag rug on the floor by the sink—everything was precious and about to vanish from her life.

She decided to finish the biscuits, taking care to shape the dough into perfect rounds. She was fitting the last one into the pan when her mother came back, closing the door tidily behind her. "Well, I've had a small think," Hetty said. "We'll not discuss your plans with your father. I gather you've not told Glen or Randy."

"I told Glen," Ivy said. She held out the pan. Glen had phoned last week, the night before the killings. He'd been in Bloomington picking up their father's old car, planned to go camping with a girlfriend, wanted Ivy's sleeping bag. What was she doing this summer? Moving in with Chuck, she'd said. Getting a job in the city.

"Oh," Glen had said. "Groovy."

Mum did not touch the biscuits. "Put them in the oven then," she said. "Set the timer for eight minutes. I trust Glen was...reasonable?"

"He didn't think it was a big deal." Ivy shoved the pan into the oven and set the timer.

"I mean," said her mother, "I hope he knows to keep quiet about it."

There it was, after all: *What will people think?*

"Well, then." Hetty sat in the chair Ivy had wept in; Ivy felt the tears return. "Here's what we'll do," Hetty said. "Before you return to your summer of glorious romance and filth, you'll have a proper gynecological exam. You'll see my gynecologist; he can fit you with a diaphragm."

"I was planning to go on the pill," Ivy said.

"I'm a bit wary of the pill; it's too new." Her mother was using her crisp, English-nurse voice. "There's no knowing what changes those things make in your body. But"—she took a deep breath—"you must decide for yourself. I see that now. Talk with the doctor about the pill. Mind he tells you everything, all the possible side effects."

Days would pass before the gynecologist could fit Ivy into his schedule. She'd be stuck under the cloud of her mother's disapproval. And her father's. "Dad will have to find out, eventually," Ivy said.

"I'll do the explanation after you've gone. Or Peg will. Somehow I think the news might come better from his sister. You've told her, I suppose."

"Not yet," Ivy confessed. She hadn't even phoned Aunt Peg to thank her for supper, weeks ago. "But I will. I guess she has to know how to get me by phone. Mum?" Her mother was staring out the window, her arm and shoulder blocking the rest of her body. "I'm sorry," Ivy said.

Her mother turned, and Ivy saw her eyes were wet. She'd seen her mother cry only once before, at the death of the great-aunt in Hexham. "I suppose it's to do with war," Hetty said, her voice as level as if she weren't crying at all. "When they might go off and get killed, you think differently about sex." She pulled a handkerchief from her pocket and pressed it to each eye, then blew her nose. "Your father will be irrational for a bit, but he'll settle down and help us minimize the damage."

"Minimize the damage! Mother, I'm fine. I'm in love with Chuck. He loves me better than—he loves me *so well*, Mummy..."

"That's what Peg thought. And she didn't have a diaphragm, much less the pill."

"Aunt Peg? She had a lover?" If she'd thought about it at all, Ivy realized, she would have guessed. Of course, Aunt Peg had once had a lover.

"She had a sweetheart and a baby," Hetty said. "The man vanished, and the baby was put up for adoption. Broke Peg's heart, of course. I didn't know her then, but I knew your father. He went into a rage, wanted to go to battle for his sister's honor. Lucky for Peg's man that we were in England." The timer went off. Hetty leapt to the oven.

"It does sound like a soap opera when I tell it that way," she said, returning to the table with the biscuits on a plate. "Peg's made a decent life for herself, but it's smaller and meaner than it should have been. And people haven't changed, not that much."

"I won't get pregnant," Ivy said. "If I did, I'd get an abortion."

"Oh dear Lord." Her mother dropped her forehead into her hand. "The things you think you can just go get: birth control pills. An abortion. It's not pretty, my girl. And it's damned expensive. You'd have to go to Mexico or Sweden."

"I know." Ivy pulled at a biscuit, burning her fingertips. Mexico and Sweden bloomed in her mind as colors—the first a hot rainbow of pink, mustard-yellow, and orange, the second a chilly palette of ice, pale green, dark ocean blue. Both countries seemed attractively far from her mother's flint-edged voice. Ivy pulled out her biscuit's soft center and tucked it onto her tongue. Her mother had as good as told her: not only Aunt Peg, but her parents had had sex before marriage. They hadn't had the pill. And they'd been trapped by *what people think*.

Her mother sighed. "How long have you known Chuck?"

"A long time." Ivy thought back to October 21, when she'd found Chuck on a bus in the middle of the night. "Eight months." She'd been drawn to his handsome bumpy face with the mustache, his quiet way of understating things. They'd told each other why they hadn't stayed for the civil disobedience, reassured each other there'd be other chances. His jacket had a faint pleasant scent of motor oil, and remembering that smell made her miss him with a visceral pang.

"Hmph," Mum said. "Your father and I were engaged after we'd known each other six weeks. But it was wartime."

"It's wartime now, Mum." How different, though, Hetty's ideas and hers. Getting engaged would be absurd. "Not the same kind of war, I guess." She wondered if her parents had had sex before or after their engagement.

"You'd be surprised how much is the same," her mother said.

But there had never before been an international youth Movement. How would Mum react if she knew about the balloon-drop? Ivy had looked over the balcony briefly as her balloons tumbled, and glimpsed a red astonished face looking up from below. Then shouts came from the audience and she'd skittered into shadow, crouching close to dust and floor-wax. There was a pom-pon, red and white; she'd brandished it casually on her way to the rest room, then flourished it while she walked quietly out the front doors to join Chuck in the line of demonstrators.

"Obviously we've a good deal to discuss," Mum said, wiping biscuit crumbs from the table with her napkin. "But your father's home—hear him?—and we must be off to the Oliphants'. I've still to bathe and dress." Ivy heard the crunch of her father's car door's closing. "Suit yourself for supper," her mother said, already on her way up the stairs. "There's ham salad in the fridge."

Ivy should run and greet him, *Hi, Daddy, big hug*, but then he would ask, "What have you and your mother been talking about?" And she'd have to lie. She closed her door carefully, making as little sound as possible. She listened to his footsteps tump-tump on the stairs, muffled by the new carpet, headed toward the bathroom. There was a new mirror on the table—an attempt to make her desk into a dressing-table. Her parents must have thought she'd want above all else to sit and put on makeup, primping to be Dad's receptionist. Maybe they thought she'd like to paint her nails, too. The obedient girl-daughter who wanted such things had vanished. Maybe she'd only pretended to exist at all. Standing, Ivy could see her torso reflected: the red T-shirt, the cutoff-jean shorts, arms and legs too white, too naked. She should reveal herself as the revolutionary woman, tell them her duffel bag was already at The Monmouth, along with her typewriter and a box of books. Not yet. Mum would be furious that Ivy had disobeyed her; Dad would be...she couldn't think how Dad would react.

Ivy heaved a breath and felt the squeeze that slowed her exhale. Damn. She'd take another aminophyllin when they were gone. Then she'd wash the clothes she'd brought home bundled in Chuck's bed sheets, now in the middle of her floor.

She rolled the laundry into a corner, smoothed the striped madras spread over her bed, plumped the pillow in its square-edged case, lined up the Navajo rug parallel to the floorboards and the wall-molding, and settled in the big soft chair with her bare feet on the ottoman. Her father rapped on the door. "Hey girl, you decent?"

"No," she said. She thought how her shirt clashed with the deep-rose fabric of the chair. She was an alien in this house, she needed aminophyllin, and she would not let him know.

"You were out cold this morning when I left," he said through the door, "and your mother tells me I have to hurry up and get casual for the garden party. See you later?"

"Yeah," Ivy said. "See you later, Daddy." Her eyes flooded with indecent tears.

Her bookshelf still held her childhood friends: *The Princess and the Goblin, Black Beauty, The Singing Tree, The Story of Davy Crockett* she'd bought with her own two dollars. She pulled out the Davy Crockett book. His slogan was *Be sure you're right, then go ahead.* Her parents' cheerful voices echoed on the stairs. The back door closed.

At 7:00 Ivy was nauseated by the two aminophyllin tablets, but she could breathe. Chuck hadn't called. Was he still job hunting at this hour? She put in the second load of laundry.

9:00 came. Chuck might have been mugged, might be all alone bleeding in an emergency room or in an alley. If his grandfather had taken ill, he'd rush to Cincinnati—but still he'd call, wouldn't he? Perhaps he'd gotten reclassified 1-A. Perhaps some of his Cleveland State friends had come along in a VW bus. *Hey Chuck, we're on the way to Canada, wanna come?* Sure, Chuck would say, climbing over the tents and fishing gear, curling up in the back, ready to duck down when they crossed the border. He wouldn't be able to call till sometime next week. If then. He'd never be able to come back to the States; she'd make her way to Cleveland and find his apartment rented to someone else. She'd sleep on the floor of the Movement office till she found a job and a place to live. She hoped Glen would return her sleeping bag soon.

Nausea gone, hollow with hunger, she pulled out the ham salad in its glass-covered dish and found three leftover biscuits. "Suit yourself," Mum had said. Ivy opened the fridge again and took out a bottle of Miller's High Life. Perhaps Chuck's old Cincinnati girlfriend had come to visit him. They'd be drinking wine. Ivy didn't know that Chuck had an old Cincinnati girlfriend, but now in the dark kitchen she was sure that he did. The fact that he hadn't told her meant they were still attached. She imagined Chuck and a blonde smoking grass, getting all turned on; he'd forget about Ivy.

She made sandwiches out of biscuits and ham salad and drank beer between bites. She needed to talk to Chuck so badly, now that she'd thrown over her parents for him; without Chuck on the phone she was completely alone, trapped in a place where nothing fit and everyone's assumptions about her were wrong.

Chuck would not abandon her. He was probably somewhere dull and ordinary. He'd explain, and she'd say, "Oh why didn't I think of that?"

She picked up the kitchen phone receiver and dialed zero. What if he didn't answer? What if he answered and refused to accept the charges? She put the receiver back on its cradle.

Mum would tell Dad tonight. Dad would ask, "What's wrong, Hetty?" He'd say, "Tell me. Out with it." That's what Dad said when he figured (and he usually did) you were bothered by something. He wouldn't let it rest, even at the dinner table when your brothers were there and the thing that bothered you was stupid—something your friend had told you a boy had said about you, or a bad grade on a quiz, or a pen you'd borrowed and lost.

She put the empty beer bottle in its box. Then she got out another bottle, opened it, and went back upstairs. When her parents came home, she would have to say that Chuck had not called, and all her plans would spill out and be ruined. Her father would force her to stay in Bloomington for the summer, working at a desk where he'd watch her all day long. She'd pretend to be their good girl; she'd have to sneak out to find the Movement at IU.

She went into her parents' dark bedroom for a Kleenex and crashed into her mother's night table. Thick curtains made the darkness total. Their phone jangled to the floor. Ivy pulled the switch and set the phone back in the circle of light under Mum's lamp with its blue pleated shade. Maybe Chuck was asleep. It could be that simple; he'd gotten a job and exhausted himself working. She picked up the phone and dialed direct. By the time the phone bill came, she'd have earned the money to reimburse her parents for the call.

No. If they found out she'd called Chuck long distance without permission, they'd know he'd failed to phone her. If she called collect, she'd at least hear his voice. But when the operator asked for Chuck's number, Ivy couldn't answer; she was sobbing. She glimpsed herself in her mother's mirror— swollen-eyed, blotchy-faced. She could not call Chuck this way. Grabbing a pillow, holding it close in both arms, she sank down into her mother's side of the big bed, a baby again, making little screaming cries without words, without thought. There was only the desolation of being borne away, as if she were on a raft headed for the empty sea.

Chapter 7

June 12, 1968
The Movement Office

Bunched among the Movement people, Chuck stood on the basement floor watching Tessa Buchanan, who stood on the stairs above them. The light was dim, but the room was cooler than upstairs. Tessa was talking about the Yankees and the Cowboys and eating pink yogurt, dipping her index finger into the cup and licking it off. Yankee capitalists in New York, Boston, and Europe were being overtaken by Cowboys (dip, lick), Texans and Californians whose money came from oil in the Middle East, fruit and coffee in Latin America. Also (dip) from the arms trade (lick).

Chuck thought about the family he'd stayed with in Nicaragua the summer he was sixteen. His father and the Managuan father had done business with automobiles, of course, but if Tessa was right, there must have been something else. Chuck hadn't seen the Guardinas' business, only their home, its courtyard filled with flowering trees, protected by a wall with broken glass along the top. Father admired people with multiple business connections; he would like to be as wealthy as the Guardinas.

"Domhoff laid it all out," Tessa said. "Cowboys get the big profits from the Vietnam War. Yankees don't." She twirled her finger in the yogurt.

"I hear you, honey," a man near Chuck muttered. Johnson was a Cowboy; Kennedys were Yankees. Nixon, a Cowboy. McCarthy, a Yankee. Tessa's finger came up dripping pink. In April at the supper party in Glenville, Chuck had only glimpsed her thighs under her tight skirt: now legs and thighs, summer-tan and muscular, were eye-level from where he stood. "What you're saying is, McCarthy can *afford* to oppose this war." The speaker, the only Black man of this group, was taller than Chuck, with light brown skin and close-cropped hair.

In Managua, Chuck had learned to speak basic Spanish and to drink fine Scotch. He spent most of his time with the Guardinas' son, Eduardo. One evening Chuck and Eduardo, cool and well-dressed, had walked along a city street. They were on their way to a bar; a woman sat against the wall in a narrow strip of shade. She had dark, smooth cheeks and penetrating eyes. Her bare legs and feet stretched in front of her; there would have been room, if Chuck had stepped left, but he didn't. He was staring at the woman, allowing her to stare back, and Eduardo kicked her leg without breaking stride, as though she were a piece of trash blocking the path. She cried out, surprised.

"Why did you do that?" Chuck asked.

"Her feet were in the way," Eduardo said. He was not even annoyed. "She should not be here; she should go to the plaza by the cathedral. That is where beggars belong."

"Why do you assume she's a beggar?" They spoke English to keep the conversation private. Eduardo had to search for words to explain what was obvious to him but never spoken about, even in Spanish.

"Because she looks like a beggar," he said slowly. "Because if she is not a beggar, she is in the market or in a bar. Because of the baby."

Chuck hadn't noticed a baby. In the woman's lap, maybe? All he'd seen was her interesting face, her calm stare.

"Surfacing of the contradictions," Tessa was saying. "Watch for those moments."

Chuck had begun right then in Managua to loathe the Thing—it seemed to be in the air—that allowed his friend to casually kick a woman's bare leg as though the path belonged only to him. He suggested Eduardo go back and apologize, and Eduardo laughed at the *loco* idea.

Had he stayed longer than ten weeks in Managua, Chuck knew he would have learned to kick, as he'd learned to avoid the eyes of the lower classes. Back home in Cincinnati he noticed for the first time the same Thing in the air. At bus stations and in the park by the river were people who lurked at the edges of downtown sidewalks and stayed away from Fountain Square, people whom he knew should be avoided. Instead, he began to meet their eyes.

"Class hostilities arise out of economic conflicts," Tessa said, scraping her finger around the inside of the cup and licking off the last of the yogurt. She stood in a shaft of light from upstairs, illuminating her beautiful legs, her tight T-shirt dress, her bare feet in sandals, her bare finger, her analysis. The Thing that made a nice guy like Eduardo behave brutally was somehow more than "class," Chuck thought. The Nicaraguan woman had challenged them, just by the way she sat, and yet she had not. Not like Tessa's combination of touch-me sexiness and keep-your-distance intellect.

Tessa finished and wiped her hand across her thigh. "Gotta do something." She sprinted ahead upstairs to the Movement office. The stairs creaked and rumbled as the Movement people followed.

It was 7:30, an hour till Ivy's bus came into the Greyhound station. At noon today Chuck had given up trying to sell cameras. At 2:00 he'd done the easy thing, the cheating thing: phoned Granddad. "I been expecting you to call," Granddad had said, not quite chuckling. "Two weeks ago, I would've been able to get you in somewhere good. You haven't learned yet how to be a go-getter, have you, Chucky?"

Granddad had made a contact, and tomorrow morning Chuck was expected to report at Lake Erie Savings & Loan, wearing his wingtips. He loved his grandfather too much to be anything but grateful. In twelve hours, he thought, he'd join the Yankees and Cowboys. He needed the Movement to rescue him.

Marvin and Bert were hammering plywood over the front window, shattered that morning by rocks. Bert had finished his jail sentence on Sunday. "How you doing?" Chuck asked him.

"What we need," Bert said, "is a fucking big fan."

"He's putting the word *fuck* into every sentence," Marvin said.

"Someone in the neighborhood must know the rock-thrower," Tessa said.

"They're not telling, though," Marvin said. "We haven't been here two weeks yet." Sweaty from hammering plywood, he faced Tessa with his thumbs hooked in his belt. Marvin had claimed this storefront because here Black neighborhoods met white neighborhoods, though they didn't exactly mingle. A sign saying "Movement for a Democratic Society" now stood against the wall behind the literature table. The Black man who'd stood beside Chuck in the basement was browsing, smoking a pipe. Cherry Blend tobacco-smoke gathered in the warm air over the pamphlets and magazines.

Chuck moved closer to Tessa. Her face was shiny, and she had a faint mustache. Damp patches spread around the neckline and under the arms of her dress, which clung to her breasts and hips. "That was good analysis-sharpening," Chuck said. "I'd like to know more about the banking." Up close, she was less of a challenge. "Savings and Loans," he added.

"Bloodsuckers," Tessa said. "They charge high interest to people who can't afford it; shareholders and investors make out like bandits." The thin skin under her eyes was dark; the eyes wouldn't focus on him. She must be exhausted. "Read Domhoff," she said. It was a sigh, and he hadn't the heart to say he was about to get sucked in by Capitalists. She turned and walked to the desk in back where Jane sat talking into the phone.

Bert hammered plywood as if he had a personal grudge against each nail. Marvin spoke close to Chuck's ear. "They seem to think we'll stay open all night." He beamed across the cement floor at the dozen people in clumps of two or three—all young, not one girl in stockings, not one boy in wingtips. Chuck recognized a few of them from rallies and picket lines. He knew he should get acquainted but didn't want to.

He needed to cool down after Tessa. Marvin would understand the conundrum about the banking job. But now Chuck noticed the young man with a reporter's notebook watching Marvin explain how revolution worked. He made a pyramid in the air with his hands, then pointed to the tip, where the few and powerful ruled, and layered downward, his arm dividing the layers. "Corporations, public administrators, bourgeoisie," Marvin said, naming each layer. "Middle classes, workers, and," both hands swirled the air at waist-level, "the large powerless mass of folks at the bottom. And we think it should be flipped." Marvin up-ended the pyramid with his arms: presidents and plant-owners at the bottom, masses on top. "Is that what you want to know?" he asked the reporter.

The reporter nodded once and began to scribble. Chuck's mind was having difficulty with the flipping pyramid: it came apart, bricks tumbling into disorganized heaps of rubble. Marvin meant people, not bricks, but how could a large mass of people stay on top like that? "Neat summary," he said, after the reporter had left. "But how will the masses make decisions? Don't say 'dictatorship of the proletariat,' either."

"All right, I won't," Marvin said with a little smile. He knew the phrase was a Marxist cop-out; that's one reason Chuck liked him. "Maybe if we talked tomorrow? No. Tomorrow's the Vietnam slides. Later this week. Right now, I'm dead on my feet." He rotated his shoulders, shook out his arms. "Time to quit," he called to Bert. "That plywood'll stay through earthquakes and hurricanes." Bert gave the wood one more thwack with the hammer and walked out the door onto Euclid Avenue.

"Vietnam slides?" The Black man had come close.

"Sheldon, meet Chuck," Marvin said.

Sheldon nodded toward Chuck. They said each other's names. "Slides?" Sheldon said again.

"Taken last spring. The photographer's a vet; he's been showing them around Cleveland to private groups."

Chuck said he'd be there. Now that they'd been introduced, he wanted to find out more about Sheldon. But it was time to pick up Ivy, who'd called in tears because he hadn't phoned her. He felt guilty. He hadn't wanted to phone Ivy till he'd sold a camera. But he'd had no sales and only two nibbles, which the supervisor had stolen immediately. Yesterday in Parma three houses had let him in and allowed him to take sample pictures to show them how the camera was "better than Polaroid"—the company's unwritten slogan. He didn't know that the camera *was* better than Polaroid, but it wasn't worse. The film was harder to get than Polaroid's and more expensive. Chuck had spent his own money on the film. Not one of the three households wanted a camera. He'd taken the last picture— a kid with his new bike. Then he'd driven back to the office (a small drab room above a liquor store), dropped the camera on the desk, and walked away, more in debt than when he'd begun. He'd told Ivy when she called with her bus information. And by then Granddad had already contacted the Savings & Loan.

The evening air was moist. The sky lowered, tensed for a thunderstorm, as he pulled to the curb in front of the bus station where Ivy waited. Her body reminded Chuck of a ripe apple. The image of Tessa's legs dissolved as he pulled Ivy into his arms, felt the back of her neck hot under his fingers, her cheek wet on his lips, her round softness under his hands. She talked lavishly as Chuck drove up Carnegie Avenue into rain and darkness. He kept one hand on her thigh and half-listened: her brother Glen was in Peace Corps training; she'd seen her mother's gynecologist.

"He's got his fingers on my cervix, asking me about school, of all things," Ivy said. "I tell him I love classical Indian sculpture—especially this one temple where the statues are having sex. He blushes. Then he asks if I like math." She had a prescription for the Pill, but the birth control wouldn't kick in for a couple of weeks. "So what's with your job?"

"Start tomorrow," Chuck said. The words "fingers on my cervix" flashed as if strobe-lit between "doctor" and "statues having sex." He tucked his hand between her thighs.

"That was quick," Ivy said. She moved away.

"Yup." He pulled her hand to his mouth, kissed her knuckles, held her hand against his lips while he navigated the maze of streets between Carnegie and Euclid. Rain had begun and he had to drop her hand and turn on the wipers. Ivy nestled into him.

They found a parking place at the curb in front of The Monmouth. "We'll get your suitcase later," he said, unlocking the front door, hurrying to get them out of the rain. She came close under his arm, and he didn't want to let her go, even as they climbed the stairs.

"I feel like I've crossed a big river or something," Ivy said as Chuck jiggled the key.

"Welcome home." He closed the door behind them and fumbled with her blouse buttons. He'd purchased a bottle of Almaden Blanc which he couldn't afford, planning to be suave and relaxed. But this was all he wanted: to unbutton Ivy's skirt and feel it fall, to unhook her bra.

The next day he sat at his desk in the Lake Erie Savings & Loan, in plain sight of prospective customers. That was the idea: they'd come to him thinking they were talking to a man who could help. He'd ask a page-full of questions, filling in the answers. If they fit one set of guidelines, he'd send them to the junior loan officer; if they got into the more exclusive group, they'd go to the senior. If they didn't qualify at all—that is, if they had no money and badly, badly needed some—he was supposed to escort them to the door with a line that went, "We'll consider your case, and someone will be in touch."

He was hoping to interview a Black person. The junior officer would say, *Are you sure this person qualifies?* And Chuck would respond, *Your institution wouldn't discriminate, would it?* Junior would say, *Oh, of course not.* When the applicant (Chuck pictured a Black man with an extremely white shirt, rather like Sheldon) was turned away for a bogus reason, he would publicly expose the Savings & Loan.

Maybe he could invite Sheldon to apply for a loan. He'd get to know Sheldon better, of course. He'd say it was a test. He wouldn't want Sheldon to think he'd actually get a loan to buy a house or a big car. If he wasn't careful, when the loan application got rejected, Sheldon could hold Chuck responsible. And Chuck would be guilty as hell.

A staple-end bit into his finger. What Chuck was actually doing, while he thought about Sheldon, was staple-removal. He had a stack of paper on his left, the toothed staple remover in his right hand, and a good view of the clock, brass and ebony, with Roman numerals on its white face. It was barely 9:30. Ivy was still asleep in his bed. When he'd finished removing staples, he'd check arithmetic on a stack of pages to his right. He wished someone would come in to be interviewed before he got to the arithmetic.

Three women—secretaries, he guessed—greeted him as they walked by, their heels clicking on the marble floor. He smiled and waved the staple remover at them. They knew he was a flunkie in a suit.

By noon he'd interviewed two young men who wanted to open a car wash, a woman in the midst of a divorce who wanted to buy her husband's half of the house, and a man who had debts to pay off. The car wash guys went to a senior loan officer; the divorcee went to the junior, and the man in debt would have gone to the junior, too, but one of the senior officers recognized the debtor and invited him to the top office.

At lunch time he had half an hour to roam the outsized doorways and towering sandstone walls of downtown Cleveland. In the Davis Bakery window was a tall, thin stranger in pin-stripes; he suddenly recognized his own reflection, his hair and mustache trimmed, wearing one of his grandfather's ties. A young man on the way up. He looked classier than his own father, who wore bright blue suits with white shoes in the summer. He didn't know whether he liked the man in the window. He fit in; that was evident.

In the Arcade the shops were small, grubby, and fragrant with leather, sandalwood and, a few steps further on, hair oil. He bought a French mint at Fanny Farmer for Ivy. She'd be out hunting jobs by now. Then he went to Western Union, where Granddad had wired fifty dollars to tide him over till payday. He had to get it together to be independent; that was all there was to it. He'd run out of time. Mom had sent all the money she could. If he didn't reimburse his father for last semester's tuition he might as well forget going home. Forget school. Prepare for induction?

Outside Higbee's Department Store stood a preacher, a short red-faced man above an eager crowd who pressed close, their bodies hiding whatever he was using as a platform. The preacher shrieked, raising his hand into the air, hammering his Bible with one finger, the words garbled by his Slavic accent. Chuck squeezed between coat-shoulders and shirtsleeves, trying to understand, drawn toward the preacher's passion. The whole crowd was riveted with the noise and fury of the man's belief.

Three businessmen walked past, swerving into the street to get around the preacher's crowd. They wore suit coats, yet they seemed cool and relaxed, as though they traveled in a cloud of their own chilled air. "A new Porsche," said one, a foot from Chuck's ear. He imagined them lingering in a restaurant with white tablecloths and cold drinks.

He was sweating when he got back to Lake Erie Savings & Loan. He ate his egg salad sandwich at his desk while he did arithmetic, careful to keep the egg away from the papers and his clothing. He'd save money by washing down lunch with water from the fountain—no coffee, no pop. By 4:00 he'd sent three more applicants (all white) to the junior officer.

Ivy was not at the apartment when he returned. Chuck hung his pinstriped suit in the closet, threw shirt and underwear onto the pile, and took a bath. Then he remade the bed. His dirty socks emerged from the bedcovers. So did Ivy's underpants—pink nylon, with a faint yellow streak. He rubbed the slick fabric between his fingers, smiling. This was living together. He shoved her underwear into a pillowcase along with his socks and T-shirts—white, with v-necks, meant to go under his work shirts. He was a white-collar worker—a wage-earner, though, not a bourgeois; a Savings & Loan employee, not a capitalist.

When Ivy buzzed, he was still naked, poking around the laundry, and he'd barely buttoned his jeans before she pounded on the door. "I need to make you a copy of my key," he said, letting her in.

"No shit, Shakespeare." She kicked off her flats. "I wandered around the Art Museum till I was sure you'd be home. That was after I got my job." Already, just like that! Her lips were buttoned over the secret of her job, her eyes wide and bright.

"What?" he demanded, hands on her waist, hoping she'd raise her arms.

She did, hugging him around the neck. "The Big Penny," she whispered in his ear. "I start tomorrow at eleven." The diner across the street: she could roll out of bed and go to work. Not a good place for tips; he'd never left more than a quarter. She'd probably get treated like dirt. But transportation was not a problem. She kept smiling, eager for his approval. "Aren't you pleased?"

"Sure," he said. "What happened to the city playground jobs?"

"Taken. I phoned at 9:00: all positions full. So I put my name on the waiting list, went across the street, and got hired. You and Jane and Bert have been telling me to get with the working class, the engine of the revolution, so I said, 'Yes, see you tomorrow.' Then I went to the Art Museum."

"I see," Chuck said. He hadn't expected her to settle for a waitress job.

Barefoot, she danced around the table, talking about her uniform with an apron and a little paper cap. For a month he'd looked forward to her moving in. Sex all the time, that's what he'd imagined. Now here she was and his thoughts surprised him: Money. Respectability.

The senior loan officer had said today, "Do the job right, Leggit, and you can keep working here. There'll be a position for you after graduation. A smart clean-cut fellow like you, with a college degree, can get into management quickly." In some dark corner of his mind Chuck had been pleased.

"If The Big Penny doesn't work out," he said, "you can quit without notice."

"I thought of that," Ivy said, throwing herself into the big chair by the window with her legs spread; he squelched his impulse to tell her to sit straight. "I'll try to find something else, too; they just want me three days a week for now. When does the Vietnam slide show start?"

The basement was filled with people sharing folding chairs, perched on crates, crowded onto a bench, cross-legged on the floor. A sheet had been tacked to the ceiling beams; a man—the veteran, to judge from his short haircut—fiddled with the projector. Chuck nibbled Ivy's earring, a little silver ball, and she smiled. A snarl of green and brown flashed on the screen and disappeared. A helicopter came on. "Wrong way around," said the vet. He pulled the helicopter off the screen and turned the slide. "I'm a photographer," he said, standing in a military at-ease posture in front of the sheet. "You can call me Rick. I worked for the Army, but this is stuff I took with my own camera. My tour's finished. I'm trying..." he pressed a button; jungle foliage filled the screen, "...to show you people how it is there. This is a village." A cluster of children grinning. Thatched roofs. "This is a medical team helping villagers." The medics were much larger than the villagers. "How it *is*," Rick said, "doesn't go into words." Green leaves, brown earth. The helicopter. Chuck had never seen Vietnam in color; even his parents' color TV showed the news in black and white.

"This is a guy in Charlie Company." A soldier walked toward them with a determined expression; the sheet rippled, making his body undulate. "They had a lot of casualties before they went up to this place they called Pinkville. It's pink on the map." The next slide showed a soldier pitching large flat baskets into a bonfire. Grain lay in heaps around his feet. The next slide showed a woman whose face looked as if she had seen a thing unimaginably dreadful. Someone's arms were around her middle as if to hold her back from attacking whoever was outside the frame. Chuck heard his own gasp with the rest— dozens of lungs sucking air at once.

"What happened in Pinkville, see," Rick's voice was flat, hesitant. "Charlie Company'd lost so many men, they wanted to get Cong. *Needed* to." The next slide showed a dead child in a ditch.

"Oh, no." Jane's voice. More slides filled the screen, mud and bodies and American men leveling guns in their arms. Soldiers' expressionless faces. In one photo a rifle puffed. A baby lay near a heap of clothes that might have been its mother.

Rick was silent now, working the projector. What was he thinking when he took those pictures? What did he think now? Chuck imagined confronting him: what is your *point*, man?

Then came a close-up of a woman, open-eyed, her conical straw hat covering her mouth. She wore a silver-ball earring. "What's that on her forehead?" a voice in the darkness asked.

"Brain," said Rick. "She got shot in the head." He changed the slide, and a pile of bodies loomed on the wavering sheet. "This is what's happening everywhere. Understand? The enemy could be anyone. A woman. I know a guy got his leg blown off when a little girl threw a grenade." A vet couldn't accuse his fellow soldiers, Chuck figured. You work for the Army, you put your sympathies with the soldiers. But then

Rick had come *here* with his photographs. Chuck felt his stomach hollow out, as if he stood over an abyss.

The sheet moved with the collective breath of the watchers. Elbows and knees, feet and hands showed at random among dark-clothed huddled bodies. Twenty or thirty people had been gunned down on a dirt path between tall green grasses. Several were babies with bare behinds.

"It's about pressure," Rick said. "What pressure will do to you, I mean. And what you'll do. You dig what I'm saying? You live with it."

"How many dead?" croaked a voice. Marvin's. "In that village, I mean."

"It was what you'd call a hamlet, not big enough to be a village. The number I heard was 300." He moved another slide onto the screen: two children on the ground, the bigger one on top of the smaller, looked at the camera. Trying to protect his brother, Chuck thought. He thought of how he'd photographed the kid on the bike in Parma. Doing a job, he'd told himself. He hadn't really looked at the kid.

"Did any of these people kill American soldiers?"

"Only one American casualty, that day," said Rick, "shot himself in the foot."

"How many of the villagers survived?" Jane asked.

"I don't know. No one can count the enemy. Those body counts you're hearing on the news? Made-up estimates."

"But what we're looking at," Marvin's voice, "is American soldiers against unarmed villagers."

"You could say that," Rick said. He switched to another slide—two American soldiers, lounging by the road, leaning against their packs. One had a straight-lipped smile. "I been showing these slides, so..."

"How could you just stand there and take pictures?" a voice called from the back. "Why didn't you try to stop them? They were killing babies!"

The soldiers' T-shirts shone white against their tan necks and arms, against the high greenery behind them. "I guess I wanted the pictures to speak for themselves."

"They're speaking, pal. Fucking loud and clear." Bert's voice.

The people in Pinkville seemed to be in the room, that was the awful part. And the Charlie Company guys—they looked like boys in Chuck's high school. Their T-shirts had vee necks.

When the show was over, someone flicked on the light. Marvin stood up and said, "Well, thanks for coming" to Rick and "Let's go upstairs" to everyone else.

Ivy had been silent the whole time, clutching Chuck's hand. She kept a tight hold as they mounted the stairs to the office. "Welp," he said. He swallowed the bitter stuff that had risen in his throat.

"Their bare feet," Ivy whispered. "Their feet are so...walked-on."

In the office people crowded the vet, asking questions. "These are great pictures; you got the war up close," Marvin said. "How do you plan to approach a wider audience?" Shorter than Rick, he looked up over the rims of his glasses, his blue eyes not quite focused. Good question, Chuck thought, but Rick looked baffled, as if the idea of publishing the slides was too much to take in.

"There's been a fucking massacre." Bert leaned between Marvin and the vet. "The public don't believe American soldiers commit atrocities. They need to know."

"Hey wait—you don't get what I'm saying." Rick's neck swelled and reddened as he backed up two steps to face Bert. "If you did, you wouldn't say 'atrocities.'"

"I believe my own eyes." Bert stepped forward, squinting. He had cleaned out the basement for the slideshow; dirt streaked his cheeks, his arms, his blue work shirt. The vet's fist clenched and rose toward Bert's jaw.

"Oh, you don't want to do that." A deep, soft voice: Sheldon's, Chuck was sure, but the Black man was lighting his pipe as if he were only a bystander.

Rick's hand relaxed and dropped. "I'm not interested in a fight," he said. "Any more questions?" He called to the crowd as he backed toward the door; if someone threw him a ball, he'd catch it. People filled the space with their voices: How long were you in Vietnam? What else did you see? Were there other massacres? Who all did you show these slides to? They clustered by the door, getting answers; Rick was doing better now.

Then Greg Lambert stepped up. "You should've stopped them," he said. "If you don't act, you're no better than the other butchers."

Chuck put a hand on Greg's arm. "Lay off!" he said.

A woman's voice interjected. "Lambert's right."

Rick's face went dark red, and he lunged for Greg. Marvin and Chuck grabbed his arms. His skin was hot, his triceps thick and hard. He shook them off.

"You heard him. He was making excuses for atrocities," Greg insisted, as the vet made for the door.

Chuck went out after him. "Greg doesn't speak for all of us," he called. Rick stopped on the sidewalk. "He doesn't speak for me," Chuck said.

"I don't need his attitude, you know what I'm saying?" The vet loomed against the night sky. "Marvin Kaminsky said you wanted to know the real stuff. He didn't tell me you'd already made up your minds." He turned his back on Chuck and, with the slides in their case under his arm, ran fast and steadily, the soles of his boots appearing and vanishing, smaller and smaller, going east.

"I don't think I was scared," said Ivy, as they walked west on Euclid. "I'm not scared now. I feel like I've been shaken hard; my legs are wobbly." She wobbled to demonstrate, like a fake drunk, and Chuck laughed, wondering how he could laugh.

He didn't want to talk. A sucking roar filled his head. If he could sit with the lights off, listening to the roar, words would come, and he'd understand something important. His request for the CO form had come back from the Selective Service with a checklist of mistakes. His mistake was "insufficient information." What the hell else did they need?

"The Vietnamese are beautiful," Ivy said. "In their pictures I mean. Tan, thin, with good cheekbones."

"Yeah, good cheekbones," Chuck said. "That's why they photograph so well."

"I don't mean that how it sounded," Ivy said, stung. "What I mean is, how could anyone kill children? I mean...I can't say what I mean."

"Then shut up," Chuck said. "I can't take superficiality." To say what he felt right now was to cut off thought; the word *shame* was insufficient. He loathed the sensations that made him aware of his body.

Ivy shut up. He wished he were alone. They climbed The Monmouth's stairs in silence and let themselves into the apartment. He sprawled on the bed fully dressed.

Ivy sat in the chair. "You're so goddamn profound," she said. "Tell me where to go so I don't trouble you with my superficial self."

"Just be quiet," Chuck said. "Sometimes I just need to think without talking, dig? Turn off the light and come to bed."

"Sometimes you just need to insult me, while you're at it," Ivy said. "Is that how it goes? I keep my mouth shut unless you decide you want to put up with my superfic..."

"Stop it," Chuck said. She had that wet sound in her voice that meant tears, and he didn't want to see her cry. "I don't think you're superficial."

"So what *do* you think? Are you sorry I came here?" She was crying, after all, and he couldn't stand how forlorn she looked sitting in the chair, dress bunched around her waist, hair in her face, hands twisting in her lap.

He patted the bed next to him. "C'mere," he said. She lay down, carefully not touching him. He took her hand and kissed it. "I love you."

"I'm sorry I..." Ivy's breath came in short gasps; she turned from him onto her stomach, "can't stop crying." The pillow muffled her words. Chuck felt his own eyes wet. He rubbed her back softly, and she didn't pull away from his hand. Next to his face, her earlobe cushioned its silver ball. He rolled away, trying to bury himself in darkness, but he couldn't stop seeing a T-shirt blazing white, the stare of a little boy who covered his brother with his body.

Finally he rose and went to the bathroom, where he pissed, then washed his hands and his whole head without looking at himself in the mirror. Then he brushed his teeth. When he came back, Ivy was naked under the covers. "Hi," he said, climbed in, kissed her briefly.

She almost whimpered. "The second I close my eyes I see the people in those pictures." She took his hand in both of hers and stroked his palm with her thumb, moving it round and round. It felt good, somehow. "They move; I can hear them talking, shouting to each other," her voice was high. "Like from a distance, you know? No words. I'm scared. I *was* scared, down in the basement. What I said earlier? That was stupid."

"I knew what you meant," said Chuck, though he hadn't known, till now. "I'm ashamed of my job," he whispered. "I'm working for a racist Savings & Loan corporation, wearing a tie and wingtips."

Ivy rolled onto her back. "You need the money," she said. "So it's just a hustle, not the real work. And you learn how the enemy thinks."

"I guess," Chuck said. Then he added, because he needed to come clean: "I got the job because my grandfather knows the manager."

Ivy propped herself on one elbow; her hair brushed his arm. "You've got two months," she said. "Then we'll go to the Chicago counter-convention, and then school will start." She rolled to the edge of the bed and reached for something on the floor. Her inhaler. She didn't use it, just stuck it under her pillow and lay back, eyes closed. "Hold me," she said. "I don't want to see those people."

He pulled her close and she tucked one leg between his thighs.

Chapter 8

June 27, 1968
The Movement Office

They were making revolution now; the office banged and sang. *Don't you wish*, Jane scolded herself. Bert was hammering and singing "Banks of Marble," that was all, building a table out of scrap lumber from the back alley, and Jimmy Fulero was helping him. Jane watched Jimmy's naked back bend and straighten as he sawed. She could be fond of him; he'd come to her bed last night, and she'd realized how much she missed having sex. His shoulders were golden brown, frosted with sawdust.

The saw blade broke through, and the board-end cracked as it hit the floor. "Off the pigs!" Jimmy shouted, stretching with the revolution-fist. He'd appeared at the office two weeks ago, home from Kalamazoo, full of questions, looking for action. He'd bought Jane a Baskin-Robbins blueberry cheese-cake ice cream cone, explained that he couldn't stand his parents, and moved into the apartment she shared with Tessa. It was flattering to have a beautiful man compliment your plain face, your straggly hair, and then take possession of your knobby, weary body. This morning Jimmy'd urged her to unbraid her hair and brushed it for half an hour, sitting behind her on the bed. He was only twenty-one, but that was part of his appeal. Tessa's comment: "So, Jane, I guess you're finally on the rebound from Norman."

Jimmy saw Jane looking at him and grinned. He had good teeth. She shouldn't let him sleep with her tonight; he might think he could have sex with her whenever he felt like it. She turned to Ivy, who twirled back and forth in the office chair, tap-dancing idly to stay in motion while she looked at *Redbook*. Ivy wore a new blue shirt that clung to her body and a short flowered skirt. Her stiff patent leather Mary Janes clicked against the cement floor.

"Got a job interview?" Jane guessed.

"Got a job," Ivy grinned. "I'm a fundraiser for the Poor People's Campaign."

"No kidding. They closed Resurrection City yesterday." If someone was still fundraising for Martin Luther King's encampment (muddy disaster on the Washington Mall, quarrelsome leaderless committee) Jane should know. "Who are you working for?"

"Guy named Shapiro; he had an ad in the paper." Ivy shrugged. "I start tomorrow morning, soliciting door-to-door. I came here for a copy of the Kerner report on poverty, so I could persuade people."

"Ah," Jane said. "Well, help yourself." She didn't recognize the name Shapiro, and she knew the names of all the Movement people in the city, even those on the West Side. She was about to tell Ivy to be wary, but Ivy was waving a page in the magazine and reading aloud: "*A good housewife knows how to be an expensive mistress.* It's an ad for Russian Crown Sable coats," she added. Her pigtails made her look extra innocent, but also fetching; one lay neatly on each breast. No wonder Shapiro (whoever he was) had hired her. "What I don't get is, why would anyone *want* to be an expensive mistress?"

Jane swallowed a laugh at Ivy's naiveté. "Better than being a housewife. A wealthy man pays for your room, board, and fur coat, and all you have to do in exchange is have sex with him. A housewife has a lot of work to do as well as sex."

"Yeah, but if you're married, then..."

"Then what? How's being a wife different from being a mistress, except that you've got a piece of paper that says you're legal?"

"What about being in love?"

"What about it?" For a second, Jane considered *love*: Norman came to mind, a sharp blow against a bruise she wished would hurry up and heal. "I don't even know what the word means anymore."

"It's past three. Gotta go be a waitress." Ivy sprang to her feet, and the chair rolled crashing against the big metal desk, startling Tessa who sat cross-legged on top; she jumped, but kept right on talking into the phone. "You know what?" Ivy said, stepping close to Jane. "Jimmy Fulero looks exactly like Verrocchio's *David*. Can I borrow this?" She waved *Redbook*. "And the Kerner report."

Jane pointed to a stack of books on the floor. Past 3:00; no wonder she was hungry. She needed to use the phone. Ivy found the book and scrambled out the door.

"The Black and Vietnamese brothers and sisters are under attack every minute!" Tessa hissed into the receiver. "We owe them. We've got to challenge that power structure in every way possible till we've *brought it down*." She emphasized the last three words by yanking a scab off her bare knee and flicking it into the wastebasket. Her knee developed a red patch, like a strawberry. "Yeah. I've thought that, too. Okay." She hung up, then picked up the receiver again and began dialing. Tessa had been calling all over the country for hours. "Yes, of course," she said to whoever answered, "the Cleveland Movement will go to the Democratic Convention. We have two months to figure out what to do there." She leapt off the desk and paced, waving her hand for emphasis. Blood ran down her leg.

Two months from now: the end of August. A long time. Tonight Jane would meet with Heights housewives eager to do something about poverty in Cleveland. If they didn't chicken out, she'd get them to think up an action. Something solid. She had to phone...oh, what was the woman's name? It was on a slip of paper in her purse. She began to rummage.

"...further than that," Tessa was saying. "We can stop the Convention." She paused. "Well, sure—we'll fill the jails to overflowing, dig it?"

"Revolution has co-ome (off the pig!) Time to pick up a gu-un (off the pig!)." Jimmy and Bert had quit building and were trying to dance like the Temptations, fingers clicking, feet synchronized. Bert twirled on the heel of his cowboy boot without missing the beat. The jerk of his shoulders and the cigarette smoking from between his lips made him look very unlike a Motown dancer. Jimmy was loose and shuffly. Jane wondered what Verrocchio's *David* looked like. In the apartment, she had supplies for a bologna sandwich with mustard. She'd make that one call; then she could go eat.

She looked out the new front window, still clean, at the kids sauntering past—four Black kids who could probably do a better Temptations act than Bert and Jimmy. She felt his body against her back, heard his voice, "Hi, Tiger," felt his lips on the back of her neck.

"Shouldn't you finish the table?" She stiffened her shoulders.

"Woah!" Jimmy held up his hands and backed away. "Wha'd I say?"

"Don't take it personally," Jane said. "I just thought you and Bert were going to have that table against the wall ready to use by 4:00."

"Break's over, Fulero." Bert waved a hammer. He understood. At 4:00 he and Tessa were meeting with a journalist. The office had to look good. Jane mouthed *Thanks* and Bert smirked. He'd seen the kiss.

Somewhere in that jail, Bert had acquired a deep coldness that showed through his eyes which made Jane think of gray-brown gun metal. He never talked about what had happened.

The phone rang. Tessa got it. "Oh sure," she said. "Jane!" She hopped off the desk as Jane took the receiver.

It was (of all people) her mother. "Just wanted to check signals," Mom said, chirping, the way she did when Jane was in Mississippi, and a year later when Dad had his heart attack.

"How's Dad?" Jane asked. "What's happened?"

"He's fine, still working out with his dumbbells every morning. I just called for fun." Mom would never call for fun.

"Oh." Jane would have said, *Cut the crap, what's wrong?* but her mother went on.

"There's a letter I want to read to you. Hey, you know what? I'm so silly, I left it in the car. Call me back, okay?"

"You should call *me*," Jane said. At her elbow, Tessa was blotting her knee with Kleenex, her foot propped on an open desk drawer. She frowned at Jane. She had more calls to make. "I don't want to run up long distance charges any higher than they..."

"So use a pay phone," Mom said. "Call collect." She hung up.

"Right." Jane clipped her purse shut and slung it over her shoulder. On the way to the phone booth she could get a candy bar at the drug store. Mom might be freaking out about something. All the more reason to eat—especially protein. A Snickers at least had peanuts.

By the time Jane had licked the chocolate from her fingers, she'd figured it out: Mom hadn't left a letter in the car. She believed the Movement phone was tapped. Was it? Jane didn't know what a phone tap looked like, hadn't heard the clicks they said would give it away. Tessa obviously didn't think there was a bug. Jane wedged herself into the phone booth and dialed.

"Oh, good, there you are," Mom said. The chirpiness was gone. "I had another phone call and thought I'd missed you. Here's the letter."

It felt odd, listening through the heavy receiver to her mother's voice reading a report of Jane's activity with "an increasingly subversive organization." A few yards from the booth stood a dressed-up young man, apparently waiting for the light. Then a man with gray hair came out of the photography shop and stared her in the face.

"Who sent that?" Jane demanded. The gray-haired man went back into the shop.

"The Chicago office of the FBI," Mom said. "Listen, you've got more than a bugged phone at that office; you've got an infiltrator. Someone was at the meeting where you talked about disrupting the Democratic Convention. Someone wrote down your words: 'Let's move in as close as we can to the convention site, whatever it takes.'" The light changed, and the young man crossed.

"It wasn't exactly a secret meeting," Jane said. "We were talking about a completely legal assembly, with permits. And we didn't reach any conclusions."

"*Whatever it takes?* I hope you're not using more subversive language than that."

"Oh, probably I am, Mom. I can't censor everything that comes out of my mouth, like..." She didn't say, "like you and Dad do." They were so careful that it was a shock to hear her mother use the word *infiltrator*, to realize Mom knew to bypass a tapped phone. This was a new side of her mother. No. Not new—rather, an old side.

Her parents had never told her, flat out, *We belonged*, never shown her their membership cards. But Jane's memory contained vivid fragments: "Union Maid" and "Joe Hill" sung around a campfire. The Lincoln Brigade. The living room full of laughter and smoke. A mustached man in a dark suit. He came often, bringing lollipops special for Jane; then one day she was told, "That man was not here, never. Do you understand?" She understood only that *Do you understand?* meant *Accept what I say, no questions.*

The change came with the Rosenbergs' execution: June 19, 1953. Jane would have been nine-and-a-half, just finished with fourth grade. What she remembered was sitting on the living room rug, working a puzzle, when her father suddenly exploded. "Damn them! *Damn* McCarthy and Cohn, damn Truman and Hoover! God damn them all to hell!" Her gentle Daddy, who said "Shhh!" when her mother swore after breaking a dish, now cursed deliberately, filling the room with rage, red in the face, shaking. Jane reached up for his hand; rather than unwrapping his fist and accepting her fingers, he rushed from the room.

Mom had sat at the dining room table with a handkerchief to her eyes; she stroked Jane's hair without looking up. "He'll be all right, Janie. Don't worry." Her voice was muffled by the hankie. "He'll be all right, and you'll be all right, and..." a breaking noise in her throat and a huge breath. "I'll be fine. I will. Shall I fix you a sandwich?" She pushed herself up from the table and went into the kitchen.

Jane had sat back down on the rug. Neither parent could calm her; she'd have to calm herself. She'd been putting together the pieces of thatched roof on a cottage surrounded by flowers. She decided to work on the people, now scattered in pieces. To make it interesting, she'd promised herself not to look at the picture again till the puzzle was finished. She'd made three faces and a blue skirt, and was hunting for the pieces that would connect the skirt to the face, when she realized her mother had been in the kitchen too long to make a sandwich, even tuna fish with pickles. Even if she were boiling eggs. There were no sounds in the kitchen—or in the bedroom.

Standing in the phone booth marveling at her memory of that afternoon's details (she could still see that silly puzzle coming together, bit by bit), Jane felt her own terror then and her mother's terror now as if they were the same moment. The sky seemed to darken; the gray clouds had a purplish tinge. From within the phone booth, the street noises seemed soft and far away.

In the silence then, nine-year-old Jane had crept down the hall to the bedroom and tapped on the door. No voice, no sound of footsteps. She wasn't supposed to go in without permission, but what if Daddy were dead? What if they were both dead? Jane stood in the dark carpeted hallway, seeing with X-ray eyes her father fallen backward onto the bed, his feet still on the floor; her mother slumped over the kitchen table. While they died, she'd been working a puzzle. She'd never forgive herself.

She had opened the bedroom door just a crack and peered through. Her father lay face down on the bed; she saw his back move as he breathed. Okay.

She tiptoed across the living room to the kitchen, wading into cold dread. Her mother stood at the counter, the jam jar in one hand, a spoon in the other. A knife stuck out of the open peanut butter jar; bread spilled from its wrapper. Jane touched the arm holding the spoon. "Mom?"

Her mother jumped. "Oh Janie! Don't *ever* sneak up on people!" Jane was short for her age; her mother towered over her. She shrank even smaller, backing out of the kitchen and watching from the doorway. "I was just making you a sandwich," Mom said. She took the knife and stroked peanut butter carefully to the edge of the bread, then dipped into the jar for more to spread to the other side and then swirl, making the half-sandwich look like an iced cake. "I completely forgot about supper," Mom said. "I don't know how I could have done that." She laid another slice of bread on the counter, spooned jam onto it, took a clean knife from the drawer and spread the jam—strawberry, made from berries they'd picked in a field and brought home in buckets. Jane had stirred the thickening jam—bubbling hot on a hot Sunday—hating the heat, wanting to be with her mother. "Can I have a glass of milk?" she asked.

She had to sit at the table to drink the milk and eat the sandwich while her mother went to talk to Daddy. Her parents' low voices rumbled and hummed wordlessly while evening filled the room with gray, and Jane slowly labored through her supper, knowing she had to finish every bite, every swallow: that was the rule. The time might well come again, her parents had warned her, when they would not have nice food.

Before she could sleep that night, Jane got Mom and Daddy to sit on her bed and explain again about Mr. and Mrs. Rosenberg, the electric chair, the Bomb. "As if there could be one single secret to the Bomb," her father spat out. No, he said, Jane had never met the Rosenbergs. Mom and Daddy had met them, a couple of times, in big meetings. No, they had not come to this house, had never come to Minneapolis, so far as her parents knew. They lived in New York, had regular jobs like Daddy's and Mom's. "Two boys," her mother wailed. "Ai yi, the children!" But if the Rosenbergs couldn't have been spies, Jane asked, then why did the government make such an awful mistake?

They must have explained, but Jane couldn't remember the words, only that afterward she knew: the government hated and feared Communists, because the government didn't understand Communism; they had it mixed up with Stalin, who was not a true Communist. No, Mom and Daddy were not Communists. No, the government would never come after Mom and Daddy. They were safe. Jane was safe. They could all continue to eat well and live a normal life.

But a normal life meant a hushed, cautious household. Her parents kept going to work and coming home, fixing food, mowing grass and washing the car on weekends. But they stopped seeing their old friends and didn't seem to have new friends. The mustached man in the dark suit might never have existed; indeed Jane believed for a time that he never had. Her parents got a TV and began to watch every evening. Jane grew accustomed to their dull talk about *The Honeymooners* and *I Love Lucy*, department store sales and Green Stamps. She joined a softball team and went canoeing in the lake country with the Campfire Girls. She was normal; Mom and Daddy were normal.

In eighth grade Jane decided to write a report: "Communism: What It Really Is," and her father tried to talk her into writing something else. Her mother said, "I don't know what Communism is, Janie. Why not write about some government close to home—like Minnesota's?" Jane did the best she could with the encyclopedia, a copy of Marx's *Capital*, and a *Life* magazine article; she got an A that did not satisfy her. She hadn't learned what she wanted to know.

By the time she was a sophomore at the University of Michigan, Jane thought she had a fairly complete picture of what happened to her parents when the Rosenbergs were executed. She understood which side she was on and what her work in the world would be. When her parents tried to stop her from going to Mississippi, she shouted at them. "I'm not *like* you—I won't cower, and I won't be silenced."

Now here was her mother getting her to use a pay phone and saying *infiltrator*, reading a letter from an FBI operative who knew what meetings Jane had attended. "You can't be too careful," Mom said.

What did the FBI know about her mother? What threat of danger to her parents was hidden between the lines of this letter about their daughter?

"Joe McCarthy's dead, but J. Edgar Hoover's not," Mom went on. "You should be thinking about your future. You don't want to be stopped from doing something you really want to do—taking a government-funded job, for instance, or going to law school."

"I don't want to go to law school," Jane said. *Who?* she thought. Who would feed *that* information to the FBI?

No one in the office really knew Jimmy. He'd shown up one day when they were installing the new window, and since then he'd been always around, everywhere. She almost stopped breathing. "I'll be careful," she said, making her voice steady. "I will, Mom. I'm glad you called."

Her mother sighed, a ragged, aging sigh that blew cold into the phone booth. "We hated getting that letter, Janie."

"Burn it," Jane said. "I'm fine. I'm not dumb."

"I know you're not. When will we see you?"

"I don't know; I'm awful busy. Thanksgiving, for sure."

"That's ages from now," Mom said. "Call collect, okay? Your father's constipated with worry."

"Give him popcorn," Jane said. "Sorry, Mom. I'll call."

"Once a week," her mother said, with a little hic-hic noise—a laugh about the popcorn, forced for her benefit, Jane realized. She twirled slowly in the phone booth to look out all four glass walls: no sign of the men she'd seen earlier. Whom could she ask about phone taps? Bert Augustin might know.

The journalist would be interviewing Tessa and Bert soon. All the "subversive" things they said would come out in the paper distorted and out of context. The FBI had much bigger Movement groups to infiltrate in New York and Chicago. Who would care about a few radicals in Cleveland, Ohio? Ungvary? He'd like to get J. Edgar Hoover's attention. Who would he recruit to infiltrate?

Jane walked east, fitting pieces together. The word "infiltrator" had first come up two weeks ago, at the SDS convention in East Lansing. Someone from the Chicago office put together a workshop on sabotage and explosives to attract infiltrators, Tom Hayden told Jane, so they wouldn't come to the important workshops. Apparently it worked. "Sabotage & Explosives" was full of strangers. Jane, with the women's caucus, had dismissed the incident as paranoia.

But paranoia was dangerous. Bert understandably had gun fantasies after his jail experience, and he hadn't been through nonviolence training. Jane had given up a month of weekends and a high grade point average to study nonviolence before she went to Mississippi. Don't freak out, she'd learned. She would not get distrustful and secretive, even though she could see something suspicious now about every Movement person she'd met in the last three months: Chuck's shiny Oxford wingtips, Ivy's new job with a fundraiser Jane had never heard of for an action that was ending, Jimmy hanging around, making love to her...no. No. Fuck it. She would not allow herself to think like this. She would go home—eat, take a nap, something—but she couldn't walk around distrusting everyone. She would have no secrets. "Time to pick up a gu-un." The Panthers needed to patrol the streets of their own neighborhoods. That was their business. But white kids had no reason to blow things up. The Subversive Squad's blue sedan drove past and turned the corner—not interested in her. Jane was on the familiar shady sidewalks of Glenville now. She thought of Stephen, whom she had last seen in his coffin.

She'd gone to the funeral to support a revolutionary brother. But except for about twenty young Nationalists in black berets with ANC colors, the program had no mention of the Revolution. There were Jesus songs, wailing family members, and refreshments in the church basement afterward. Dora was thinner, with a gray tinge to her skin, and she was glad to see Jane. "Stop by sometime," she'd said.

Jane turned the corner at a trot. Dora's house was only two blocks from here. The street was shady, lined with old maples and sycamores; the houses had wide heavy porches, steep roofs, dormer windows. The neighborhood resembled the Revards' in Minneapolis, except for some boarded windows and rows of doorbells on each house, showing how many apartments had been made out of that building. Dora's daughter and son never ran barefoot, as Jane had done every summer when she was a child: too much broken glass. Her sandals slapped on the slate sidewalk, and she slowed to a walk.

She pounded twenty times before Dora opened the door. "I got a fussy baby won't go to sleep," Dora said. "And here you come to disrupt my afternoon even more." But she smiled and held the door open for Jane.

The two older children were with Dora's mother for the afternoon. "Let me hold her." Jane reached for the fretful baby. "Leatha Jane," she murmured into the little round ear. When Dora was pregnant with this baby she'd been with Jane nearly every day.

"She gets these flusterations," Dora remarked. "The police sirens woke her up."

With Jane holding the baby, rocking side-to-side, petting the small back, Dora could enjoy a cigarette. She tapped the pack against her wrist, pulled out a long menthol Salem, lit it, breathed in, and blew smoke carefully toward the open window.

"How is your mother?" Jane asked.

Dora shook her head. "Got to have a hysterectomy. She don't want to, but I put my foot down. I told her, 'You can't die. I can't stand to lose another person.'"

Poor dead Stephen was on the wall in a gilt frame; an enlarged color snapshot showed him in his high school graduation robe, laughing against a background of leaves. Why couldn't she have tried to like him? Jane considered men they both admired: Stokely, Harllel, Huey. But when those militants spoke, you got the feeling they were bringing up the words from deep places in their hearts. Stephen was just reciting lines. Maybe he could have grown out of that.

Dora was worrying aloud about the cost of Mama's hysterectomy. Mama cleaned houses for a living. She wouldn't be able to work for a month, at least; she'd fall behind in rent and utilities. Dora could make the food stretch, as long as the welfare people didn't find out she was feeding Mama, along with the kids, but she couldn't figure out how to raise enough rent money. "After the Revolution, this won't be a problem," Jane said. She stroked Leatha Jane's soft, soft hair; the baby was quiet, breathing easy. Asleep?

"Yeah right, and we all go to heaven if we good enough." Dora stubbed out her cigarette and leaned to see her baby's face. "Let's put her down in the back where it's quiet," she said.

The back room was stuffy, windowless. Dora spread a little pink blanket on the African cloth, and Jane eased the sleeping bundle on to it, thinking how to tell the Heights ladies about this: hardworking woman has a necessary operation, spirals into poverty. "There's a new group of Heights ladies," she told Dora, who was filling two glasses with ice water. "Mothers Opposed to Poverty." She still had to make that phone call. "MOP for short."

A police car drove by; Dora went to the window to watch. "We got some business here, I tell you. Mm-hmm," she said.

Jane joined her. "Are the police doing more than usual?" She hadn't noticed.

"I don't spend all day spying," Dora said. "But I know some people been talking about *We gotta protect ourselves against the Cleveland police.*"

"Soul Power? I thought they disbanded."

"No one in Soul Power ever bought any guns; they just talked like they badder than Malcolm X. I mean Ahmed and his kids, that group."

"The Republic of New Libya." Jane had heard from Bert how Ahmed Evans's African cultural center was being harassed by police. Ahmed had been evicted, moved to a new shop, tried to fix it up, was in a fight with his landlord. The members of his "republic" were teenage boys. "They're buying guns?"

"Nothing illegal about buying guns," Dora said. "Remember that rifle club, when you first moved here? Black men doing target practice in the countryside just like white men? Police got *all* uptight. Evans and them not going to the country, not practicing. Someone talking too much, that's all."

"Over-reacting as usual," Jane said. She thought of Jimmy and Bert, doing the Black Power strut. *Hate the white man* rhetoric was hip. An infiltrator would want it to sound dangerous. She changed the subject. "I remember Kelvin when I first got here," she said. "He'd just started talking, said 'chicken' so cute, *tsiki!*"

"He loved to *eat* chicken, too," Dora said. "That was when his daddy was still around; he was a nice man, but too expensive." She clicked her tongue, tut-tut.

"Where is he now, Kelvin's daddy?" Jane had never met the expensive man.

"Chillicothe," Dora said. "Picked the wrong people to help him get his debts paid. I still talk to his mother sometimes. Want to see his picture?" She took her album from under the coffee table, then lit another cigarette and sat next to Jane on the couch to show the photographs of Tina and Kelvin as babies, of their fathers, and of Dora herself, a little girl in a plaid pleated skirt with a white blouse. The house on Cedar Avenue. The grandfather who died. The new dress worn to the junior prom, 1961. The date—a gangly, dark-skinned boy. "That's Tina's daddy."

Jane and Dora were the same age. Dora's prom was one of the best nights of her life, even though her date had gone to college in the South and forgotten he'd made a baby. He'd never come back to Cleveland. Jane's memory of her own junior prom featured uncomfortable high heels and silence. She and her date had nothing to say to each other.

Dora had aunts and uncles and cousins, nieces and nephews, dozens of people gathered in living rooms, around tables, in front of new cars, sprawled on the grass in the park along Liberty Boulevard. Each new page of the album introduced new people and their stories—this one has six children and lives over in Hough. This one died—heroin overdose. This one's in a wheelchair. Shot in the back.

Jane was not used to knowing her friends' relatives; she didn't know Tessa's family. Bert's parents shunned him. Marvin had a mother he occasionally visited somewhere. And Jane's own family? She'd never told anyone but Norman about her parents' history. Did anyone in the office even know her parents lived in Minneapolis? Had she left a letter lying around? It was possible. This afternoon's promise to call home once a week had been a big concession. And Jane didn't know other relatives; if there were any, her parents must have estranged themselves back in the thirties. Dora would be astonished at Jane's isolation. She looked at all those faces smiling at Dora, with Dora, for Dora, and felt suddenly impoverished.

After the Revolution...She'd assumed Dora was a Soul Power revolutionary. Had she been loyal to Stephen but not his politics? Why didn't Jane know? She and Dora used to discuss politics. Walking back to the office now, Jane shifted her thoughts, pulling out the scrap of paper with the phone number on it. *Peggy* was the name. Where would a phone ring in Peggy's house? Jane pictured a wall phone in a kitchen with big windows looking out to a backyard flower garden. Peggy would have a dishwasher and a lush green lawn. She might have a cleaning lady, might not know that the cash she paid was holding together three generations, might not think about what happened if a cleaning lady got sick. Jane wished she could put the Mothers Opposed to Poverty into Hough or Glenville, let them go hungry for more than a couple of hours, make them listen to rats in the walls.

Greg Lambert was sitting at the office desk, tossing tight-wadded newspaper toward the wastebasket. "Woops," he said, retrieved the paper ball, and threw it again. It landed in the basket this time. "One for me," he said, and sprang for the wastebasket so he could make another throw. Pudgy, with a blond butch haircut, he reminded Jane of an overgrown seven-year-old.

"How about letting me use the phone?" Jane said.

"Go ahead," Greg shrugged, and threw again. The paper wad landed on the floor. "Motherfuck," he said.

"I need to sit at the desk," she said. "Why not get yourself something to eat?"

"I guess I could," Greg said. "Maybe I'll throw better with food in me."

"Maybe," Jane said. "I've got to find a meeting."

"I can't come back," Greg said. "I'm staying at my mom's, you know." He lumbered out. Jane breathed relief that he was gone. The desk was littered with bits of wood: Greg had evidently tried to sharpen a pencil with his pocketknife and carved it down to a two-inch stub. Jane brushed Greg's pencil shreds into the torn newspaper he'd left on the floor and stuffed the whole mess into the wastebasket.

She phoned Peggy, who was brisk and friendly: the meeting was at 8:00, and not far from here. Then she phoned Marvin, who had the Valiant. "These folks bought our new window, right?" Marvin said. "Hm. Well, yes. How about I drive you?"

"Pick me up at the office by 7:30," Jane said.

"Have you thought at all about what you're going to *say* to these women?"

"I'm working on it," Jane said. *Think*, she told herself. If only one of those women tried to feed her family on a food stamp diet...And here was an idea. What if a well-known woman in Cleveland did it—Dorothy Fuldheim or Shirley Stokes or Frances Payne Bolton? The results could go in the paper, and the public might begin to see what poverty was like. Call it a voluntary Welfare Food Allowance month. Good idea. Jane could rest for a minute, enjoy the quiet of the empty office, cleaner than usual for the journalist. The new table stood against the wall; someone had swept the sawdust and wood-bits into a neat pile. Someone had made a tidy stack of Jane's papers, too. She paged through the stack, throwing away flyers and agenda for meetings that had already passed, keeping letters that needed an answer, writing notes in the margin with the pencil-stub; Greg had whittled a good point.

The screen door banged like a gun. Jane reared up from the desk and saw Jimmy with blood on his face, almost staggering, cradling his right arm with his left. He let her help him to the couch and sat, bent over the arm, broken (she could see the unnatural bend between wrist and elbow) and swelling, growing purple.

"Where's your car?" Jane bent to look into his eyes, glassy with pain and tears. "C'mon, Jimmy, I need to drive you to the hospital or call an ambulance."

"Don't want no ambulance." He looked bewildered and sounded like his throat was full of sand.

"So where's your car?"

"Somewhere around the block back there." He gestured with his left hand over his right shoulder, wincing as his right arm dropped into his lap. "I parked it a long time ago. Don't remember where."

She'd have to run up and down many streets, hunting his car. She couldn't leave him. He was probably in shock.

Maybe she could reach Tessa in anatomy lab. "I can't go after your car, Jimmy. What the hell happened?"

"Those Black guys," Jimmy said. "I told them, 'Hey man, I'm you're brother,' but they just kept kicking me. Jonas Bey kept yelling, 'You honky deserve to die, understand? Don't matter what you say, you gonna pay!'" Jonas Bey the Nationalist—Stephen's friend. Somewhere a siren rose from a growl to a high whine and held it. "Fuck Jonas!" Jimmy said. "I thought he..."

"He's messed up," Jane said. "He's *really* messed up," she added, as if repeating the phrase would somehow make things clear. The siren echoed and lowered into the distance. Jane tried to squelch the fire in her chest; her anger should not be directed at the Nationalists. They were the front line of the struggle; Jimmy hadn't known enough to give them space. And Jonas *was* messed up. She closed her eyes and swallowed. "I'll get you some water," she said. She needed some, too.

She drank down a mug of water from the tap in the bathroom and took four aspirin tablets out of the bottle above the sink. Then she refilled the mug for Jimmy. "Where did this happen?" Jane asked him, as she put the aspirins in his hand. "You didn't go to the Lakewood Tavern?"

"No, man!" Jimmy was crying—a good sign. "I was just walking along. I'd been to the African culture shop on Hough Avenue. I went to buy some of Ahmed's stuff—he's got those little carved giraffes, beads made of brass, shell, bone, very cool. Paintings," he added. He pronounced Evans' Arabic name "Ahk-med."

"And a lot of astrology books." Jane knew the shop, fragrant with Moroccan leather and sandalwood.

"Got a big sign: Republic of New Libya," Jimmy said. "I'm walking from there to my car, which is on 118th, now I remember. Goddamnit, those guys broke my arm! I heard it snap." He took two more aspirin and drank the rest of the water.

He was right; an ambulance would draw attention—violence in the Movement for Democratic Society! Sirens, a police report. Jane rolled a stack of *Guardians* into a splint; she'd learned how to do this in Campfire Girls. She also needed a sling. Someone's sweater hung over a chair; it had been there since the Vietnam slides. Jane folded the sweater around the paper, tied the arms around Jimmy's neck, and got him a damp paper towel for his face. He rotated and pulled up his legs, his bare golden knees sticking out of the torn jeans, the toes of his sneakers wrapped in duct tape, and lay back on the couch. Jane brushed the greasy wisps of hair away from his face. "Snuggle-dude," she thought. The bathroom had aspirin. What would it take to keep a clean washcloth in there, too? A revolution?

"Marvin will be here soon," she said. "We'll take you to the emergency room." Had Jimmy really been doing what he said he was doing? Would that question have occurred to her before her mother's phone call? Damn the boy, she thought. Damn all boys who can't quit fighting. She called Marvin and told him to hurry.

"My arm's killing me!" Jimmy's bellow rose out of the couch and echoed in the empty office. "Tell Marvin to bring some alcohol! I wanna pass out!"

"He wants to be anesthetized," Jane said to Marvin. "You got any vodka? That would do it. You know what? The office needs a refrigerator with food. And vodka. I could use a couple shots myself. We should..."

"Cool it, Jane," Marvin's voice was as mild as ever. "I've got a little bourbon left over from...a kind of party. Will that do?"

"It will," Jane said. Strange, how Marvin put it: *a kind of party.* He'd probably been entertaining a woman he didn't want anyone to know about. Except that he did, or he wouldn't have mentioned a party. And why bourbon? Marvin was so complex.

"Keep him conscious," Marvin said. "He might have a concussion."

She sat with Jimmy and let him sob on her shoulder. "I want to be their brother, man. I do. Why don't they get it?"

"Sh, sh, Jimmy. Of course you want that, and of course they don't believe it. Sh. Shhhhh." She half-held him, trying to keep clear of the sling. He blubbered with pain and shock. So sad, and so stupid, thinking he could say "brother" and make it happen, just like that. Outside the sky glowed with evening; it was only 6:00, but it felt much later.

Chapter 9

June 27, 1968
The Big Penny & The County Hospital

A Black man with blue eyes watched Ivy set his glass of ice water on the paper mat. She pulled out her order pad. "What would you like to eat?"

"Grilled cheese sandwich," he said. "Does that come with a pickle?"

"Sure. You like pickles?" Ivy was fascinated: along with blue eyes he had clear acorn-brown skin, and his lips were astonishing—"like a fresh-cut fig" from *Siddhartha*. She had wondered what a fresh-cut fig looked like: now she knew.

Working at The Big Penny, you could learn a lot. How to carry three dinners at once, for example. At the kitchen window she collected one platter in each hand and balanced the third in between, resting the plate on her baby finger to keep the cheeseburger-with-everything-plus-fries from touching the spaghetti, using the green-bean side, rather than the meatloaf side, of the Special to support the cheeseburger platter. The construction workers wore clean knit polo shirts and remembered her. "Here's our girl! Hi, Girl!" They worked down Euclid, where Claude Foster Hall was still being jacked off its foundation. The meat loaf guy winked and said, "Finally! I been looking forward to this all day."

The spaghetti man stubbed out his cigarette in the ashtray. "Don't mind him."

Their cheeseburger pal asked, "You got any hot red peppers, hon?" All three spoke with southern drawls.

"We have Tabasco sauce," Ivy said, and went to the kitchen thinking how marvelous feats of engineering and construction were wasted on the most boring building on campus, a dorm nobody liked to live in. But the university didn't care. "Growth," the Development Corporation president had said. The project was churning up wealth (Chuck explained) for workers from Georgia and executives from Cleveland. They would build a new building on the vacated space. Architects! More construction workers! Landscapers! Meanwhile the ghetto would not change. The war would continue.

Ivy found the Tabasco sauce and thought about the Black man's blue eyes, how he'd looked as though he carried an important message, a secret or a confession especially for her. She put three pickles on the plate next to his grilled cheese sandwich.

"Hold it!" Kreb, the manager, stepped away from the grill and put his arm across the doorway. "Aren't we being a little generous with the condiments here?" He speared a pickle with his knife and plopped it back in the jar.

"Keeping the customers happy." Ivy scooted under his arm. Kreb was not a complete jerk; he did have a teeny-weeny profit margin. But he also paid exactly one dollar an hour—in cash, to avoid taxes. Tips often came to $1.50 or $2.00 an hour.

"I almost got you three," she told the man, and his startling eyes glinted at her sideways as he smiled. He was about to speak. But she heard the cheeseburger-man: "Hey Girl, you got some of that hot stuff for me?" His table-mates laughed.

She twirled toward them and plunked the Tabasco next to the cheeseburger platter. "Anything else I can get for you gentlemen?"

"Yeah," said the man with spaghetti. Bald, with a very pink scalp. "How about some coffee and pie?" He wiggled his eyebrows as if he'd prefer his girl-waitress for dessert.

Annoying, to feel interchangeable with pie. Ivy forced herself to be cool and took their orders: apple, blueberry, banana cream. Across the diner a couple fitted themselves into the clean booth: Woman in a powder-blue skirt and jacket, a blonde bubble and little curls on her cheeks. Man in a military uniform. Ivy brought them water and menus thinking her shift was a kind of economic microcosm: the Development Corporation paid its workers for doing unnecessary construction while Kreb's little restaurant had to skin profits off a single pickle or a dollop of milk in order to nourish them. And now the military would give Kreb a few cents more.

A man with a torn T-shirt and the dirtiest, weariest face she'd ever seen clambered onto a stool at the counter and asked for a glass of ice water. Ivy gave him one and handed him a menu. Then she took the water pitcher to the Black man, wondering which economic niche was his. He wore a starched light-blue shirt; perhaps he worked for a church organization or for the mayor. Perhaps he knew Ken Shapiro, her boss. The march against poverty was basically over, yet Shapiro had told Ivy to put another ad for workers into the newspaper. "Why raise more funds *now*?" she'd asked. He didn't answer.

She refilled the Black man's water glass, thinking how to find out more about him. "Anything else?" She was always supposed to ask.

He raised his eyebrows and smiled with his ripe-fig mouth. "When do you get off?"

"Late," Ivy said. She had to close The Big Penny at midnight. She should scoot water over to the couple in the booth, but she lingered to wipe up the spilled water drops.

The blue-eyed Black man made a sound, a laugh or a throat-clearing. "I like watching your little ass twitch in that yellow skirt," he said. "So I thought it'd be nice to see it without the yellow skirt. What do you think?"

"Oh." Ivy was embarrassed. She'd imagined a conversation, asking about his life, listening to his voice, watching his lips move in his smooth brown face. Had she invited him to think about sex? She turned away clutching the dirty rag. "I'm sorry," she said, not looking at him. "My boyfriend will be expecting me." Jane would criticize her for using Chuck like that, especially because Chuck would be asleep. He'd spent eleven hours that day at the Savings & Loan. In the kitchen she washed her hands, rinsing away the idea of kissing a blue-eyed Black man. When she came out, he was gone.

The military guy and the blonde-bubble woman wanted sandwiches with coffee. The construction workers wanted more coffee, too. She cleared and wiped the now-empty table; she hadn't even known that she'd wanted to kiss him; meanwhile his mind had raced ahead. He'd eaten only one pickle, and he'd left only a quarter.

In the kitchen, Kreb yelled at her for putting too many potato chips in the baskets with the couple's sandwiches. She apologized and dumped half the potato chips back in the box. Three hours to go, and she was deflated with shame, ready to crawl into bed right now.

In the Cuyahoga County Hospital waiting room, Jane sat next to Marvin on the sofa, once blue vinyl, now a stormy gray. Jimmy had been swept away by the Emergency Room staff to have his arm examined, X-rayed, set, and casted. "I didn't think you were a bourbon drinker," Jane said.

Marvin had come to the office with a bottle half-full; Jimmy had gulped it down. Jane and Marvin had walked him to the car and driven across town with Jimmy slumped between them emitting bourbon-scented moans. Now Marvin sat hunched with his elbows on his knees, staring thoughtfully toward a spot on the linoleum floor. "Bourbon was half-priced," he said. "And every now and then you have to test a theory. So I did."

"And the results?"

"I'm not a bourbon drinker." He examined his hands as if they could tell him whether not liking bourbon was a serious failure.

Maybe he'd tried to have sex, and couldn't. Jane wouldn't ask—not in a public waiting room where two stout women scolded a young thin man about straightening up. "You got so much *potential*!" one said. Then she said it again. Across from them, a gray-haired man slept open-mouthed in an armchair. Jane and Marvin were the only white people in the room. "Who are you seeing these days?" she asked him.

"Seeing? You mean dating? Oh..." Marvin looked around; no one else was listening. "Oh, she's interesting, ex-Peace Corps, working on her master's in social work." A couple of seconds went by. "Eleanor."

"Ah. Is she in the Movement?" Maybe Jane had met Eleanor without getting her name. Maybe Eleanor would like to help with the MOP project. Neither Marvin nor Jane would get to the MOP meeting, now, unless...

"We haven't talked politics much," Marvin said. "We've been trying various drinks together, that's all. Lucky I had that half-bottle to spare, isn't it?" His face flushed, naked without glasses. He wasn't going to tell Jane any more secrets. She had an odd sensation—like the step you take in darkness when, expecting the staircase to end, it keeps going and you trip on empty air. "Where does Jimmy go from here?" Marvin asked. "Back to your Glenville apartment?"

"I guess so. He refused to let me contact his parents." Jane thought about the logistics of getting Jimmy up the stairs, drugged and casted. "I can curl up on the couch while he takes my bed." The lover she'd thought fondly about this afternoon had vanished inside the wounded boy with snot on his cheeks. And something else. She should be terribly concerned, full of tenderness. Instead she was annoyed. The waiting room smelled sour, and the lights were too bright; a rip in the gray-blue vinyl revealed dirty foam rubber inside. What was wrong with her? Next to her elbow, frayed copies of *Good Housekeeping, Reader's Digest*, and *The Watchtower* spilled over each other on the table. She felt a chill and thought of the gray street outside the phone booth. Then she remembered Jimmy was a suspect.

"We have an infiltrator," she told Marvin. "My mother got a letter from the FBI."

"With information about you that no one but an infiltrator would know?" Marvin took his glasses out of his shirt pocket and put them on. "Your mother's not the only one," he said. His pensive expression returned.

"Yours too?"

Marvin nodded. "And some others." He didn't say who.

"Tell me I don't have to suspect Jimmy Fulero," Jane said. "Jonas Bey and the other bozos who beat him up...They could be just pissed at a white kid who's invading their territory. But maybe they know something."

"Jonas Bey plays at being Nationalist, but I heard Harllel Jones doesn't like him. And if Harllel doesn't like someone..."

"I *hate* what happens to my brain when I stop trusting!" Jane wailed—too loudly. Marvin pressed down on the air with the flat of his hand to shush her. The gray-haired man woke and sat up straight in the armchair.

"Jimmy's an innocent," Marvin said firmly, as if saying made it so. "He knew nothing when he got here a couple weeks ago. His parents live in University Heights. He's been growing his hair for at least two years. Doesn't fit the profile of a federal spy."

"Some people's hair grows really fast." Jane thought of Jimmy tossing his mane out of the way so he could kiss her. After they'd made love he got a glass of water, dipped his finger and drew wet patterns on her breasts and belly, cool in the hot little bedroom. Not what she'd heard about FBI agents: neat, anxious, explosive people, dimwits who didn't know enough to get rid of their shiny black lace-up shoes.

"I'm getting to know the faces of the Subversive Squad," Marvin said. "There's one, now. Detective Sgt. Bill Janczi." A blue-suited man was talking to the receptionist at the desk in the hall. Jane strained, but she couldn't hear the conversation, and within a few seconds Janczi turned away.

"Someone here must have told the police Jimmy got beaten up," she said.

"What specifics did the letter report?" Marvin asked softly, one eye on the two women, who were reading, and the young man, who played with a yoyo. The wooden disk zinged out of his hand and snapped back up its string four times without a snag. "If even one thing happened before Jimmy got here..."

Jane thought back. "The letter mentioned that meeting at Cleveland State about the same time the office opened. Was Jimmy there?" She couldn't remember.

A nurse came in. "We're ready for you," she said to the two women. They rose to follow her; the youngster stuffed his yoyo back in the pocket of his jacket and put his hand on the shoulder of the woman who'd scolded him about his potential—his mother or aunt, Jane guessed. Then they left to see the sufferer behind curtains in the ward.

"He wasn't there," Marvin said. "We were sitting in a circle in a classroom."

"If it's not Jimmy, then..." Jane could picture the classroom, the people—Ivy and Chuck, Tessa, Marvin, Bert, a few more. Larger than the circle in Glenville, the night of the Columbia takeover, when Ivy's eyes had filled with tears as they sang "Eyes on the Prize." At the time Jane had felt critical of the singing which didn't work the way it had in Mississippi or at the Welfare Rights sit-in. Now, she realized, they hadn't sung like that since, hadn't linked arms—couldn't, any more. Mom's phone call marked the change—but it was bigger than the phone call. Jane watched Marvin return from the drinking fountain and settle into a grime-streaked chair. But if Jimmy wasn't a spy, if *any* of the others had slipped information to the spook who'd written Mom, any *one* of them..."That's almost worse," she said aloud.

"What? Oh, you mean Jimmy," Marvin said. "I know. I've been imagining the face of every Movement person I can think of, asking Have *you* lied to us? Have *you*?" He stared into the dim air of the waiting room. Then he sighed and shifted to face Jane. "For now, we can either talk about everybody we know as if they were betraying us, or drop the subject entirely."

"Drop it," Jane said. "I should call the MOP ladies. Got a dime?" Even before Marvin shook his head, Jane had removed one loafer and was prying the dime out of the leather slot.

"Oh, I'm *so* sorry," said Peggy the MOP hostess. The story of Jimmy Fulero's broken arm touched her. "You kids be careful," she said. "The County Hospital emergency room isn't the safest place."

Through a door came a yell—"I'm a-tell you people, *the police* did this!" Out burst the two women who'd been in the waiting room earlier, their faces stony with rage. The youngster came behind them, big-eyed, scared. Someone they loved had been beaten or perhaps shot by police, and no one here would listen. By the time she returned to Marvin, Jane had her head straight: the detective had come to suppress news of the brutality, not to investigate Jimmy's assault. Jimmy was not the informant, and she would not start a campaign of distrust. This was no time to be stopped by fear. Peggy had excellent intentions, but caution was counter-productive to the Revolution.

"What I admire about Bert is his *chutzpah*," Marvin said as Jane reclaimed her place on the couch. "The balloon drop was perfectly suited to Reserve Officers in Training—all so serious about marching in step, you see what I mean? Each squad's trying to out-drill the next, then Bert and Ivy unleash a cloud of gentle white balloons, each weighted with a little slip of paper..." he raised his hands and brought them floating down. "Oh, by the way, remember napalm? Remember what all this marching is for? A lovely move." Marvin had been going over events in his mind, as she had. The balloon drop had slid far into the past.

"I wish Bert weren't so morose," Jane said. "Three weeks, and..." She thought how Bert might have been influenced in jail—strong-armed or bribed or worse. No. She had dropped such thoughts.

"I think he must have been humiliated, somehow," Marvin pulled at his nose. "Takes a long time to get over humiliation, you know."

She didn't know, but evidently Marvin had thoughts similar to hers.

The emergency room doors boomed open to let in a pudgy middle-aged couple looking anxious. "We've come for Jamie Fulero," said the man to the information desk. He had an assertive voice with a hint of Chicago.

Jimmy's parents? Jane got up and stood in the waiting room doorway to speak to the woman, who clutched an olive-green leather purse to her middle. "We're friends of Jimmy's," she said. "We brought him..."

"He hasn't told us about you," the woman said, ignoring the hand Jane offered. She peered intently, and Jane suddenly felt grubby in her T-shirt and short denim skirt, legs bare, braid fraying over one shoulder. She hadn't combed her hair since morning, and it was past 8:00.

"Here he is," said the man. A nurse came pushing Jimmy in a wheelchair, his arm in a sling, his eyes unfocused. But he smiled.

"I'll go get the car." Marvin pulled the keys from his pocket.

"He's coming home with us," Jimmy's father said. "I'm Dave Fulero." He and Marvin shook hands. Jimmy's mother was quizzing the nurse, getting instructions.

"They're my friends," Jimmy said in a blurry, drugged voice. "I guess I'll see you soon," he called, as his parents wheeled him out the door.

Marvin turned to Jane, shrugging, palms held up. "Take me home," she said. "I want to tell you about my idea for the MOP ladies' action."

"You want to drive the Valiant to the Spock rally on Sunday?" Marvin asked, as they walked across the parking lot. "I won't need it. I'm going with, um...Eleanor."

Chapter 10

June 30, 1968
Public Square

Chuck stood alone in the afternoon heat, surrounded by a forest of posters on sticks. Another anti-war rally, this time for Dr. Benjamin Spock, and where was Ivy? She'd gone shopping with her aunt and promised to meet Chuck right here. Not her fault if she couldn't find him; the crowd filled a whole quadrant of the Square, its collective back to the Soldiers & Sailors Monument. Arthur, a local Mobe organizer, was introducing Dr. Spock. "We are your children!" Arthur cried into the microphone. Spock crossed the dais looking incredibly cool in his navy blue pinstripe suit, with a high stiff collar and a choking necktie, smiling with his even teeth: the living image of civilization. "War is not healthy for children and other living things," said the banner behind the podium. Pretty naïve, that statement. The Mobe wanted a broad-based anti-war movement, so their analysis stopped in platitudes you couldn't argue with. No awareness of the wider revolutionary surge.

Chuck stood on a bench to see better while Spock, in his Boston-Brahmin voice, said he was gratified to be here. He faced ten years in prison for conspiring with draft-resisters. Chuck thought anyone who sentenced Benjamin Spock to prison would be risking his career. But in 1968, he reminded himself, no telling how foolish men in power would be. "Illegal, immoral, and unwinnable!" Spock was saying. Bert Augustin appeared on one side of the platform with a long pole, a Viet Cong flag attached. Jimmy stood next to him, one arm casted and wrapped in a sling. They had brought the Revolution—the furthest wing of it, heedless of damage to children and other living things—to an *anti-war* rally?

Not a good idea. Chuck thought of an officer at Lake Erie Savings & Loan who liked to quote Curtis Le May: "Bomb them back to the Stone Age." Chuck could've told him that once atomic bombing started, they'd all be lucky to have a Stone Age to live in, but he'd kept his mouth shut so far, except to compliment tellers on their hairstyles and encourage customers' hunger for their own firms, their own houses, their own, their own...he spat, *phooey*, caught his chewing gum in his hand, stuck the wad in a trash can, wiped his hand on his jeans. Nice to be wearing jeans in Public Square, but after spending most of the week in Oxford wingtips, his feet hurt in sneakers. Loss of support. His arches were falling. Flat feet could get you a 4-F exemption, he'd heard.

Bring the troops home, the crowd was chanting; *Hell No We Won't Go!* Spock's fingers were raised in a V-sign, and suddenly Bert sprang to the platform, shouting *Ho Ho Ho Chi Minh!* waving the flag, red on top, blue on the bottom, yellow star in the middle. *NLF is gonna win!* Arthur and his Mobe committee (wearing *ties*, for Chrissake) rushed to center stage, and Arthur's voice came over the microphone. "Thank you so much for coming, Ben," he said. "Thank you for everything you've done for us since we were babies. Let's give Ben a cheer!"

No sign of Ivy amid the cheers. The Viet Cong flag waved over the crowd. A folk-singing couple took over the microphones with their guitars—"Blowin in the Wind" again. Tired of that song, Chuck jumped off the bench and stumbled on a pop can, almost falling. He picked it up and hurled it into a trash barrel. The Mobe's approach was not enough. Bert's was too much. You don't stop war by changing sides, Chuck realized. That much was clear now. Inside his head, Bert taunted: So how *do* you stop war, Motherfucker? What have you, Chuck Leggit, done lately? Chuck had been reading, that's what. Franz Fanon and Regis DeBray. Vonnegut. Ginsberg. Oh, he loved to read. "How many times can a man turn his head, pretending he just doesn't see?" the couple sang. He was disgusted with himself.

"Hello, brother, what is hap-pen-ing?" Enunciating with Spock's Boston-Brahmin accent, Sheldon emerged from among the posters. Chuck grinned, glad to see his almost-friend; they'd had a couple of long talks in the Movement office, just the two of them, while Ivy worked nights at The Big Penny. He'd caught himself telling Ivy about "my Black friend" and realized that he couldn't quite say just "my friend," but he wanted to.

Especially to Sheldon, who'd said he didn't know what it would mean not to be lonely. "Ralph Ellison's 'Invisible Man' could've been my twin," Sheldon said, "except then there'd be two of us." They'd talked a lot about books, and a little bit about women. Sheldon liked the way the Supremes looked, but he didn't like Motown. He preferred coffeehouse music—Baez and Judy Collins. "Not how they *look*; it's how they sound," he explained.

"So what do you think of this?" Chuck asked now, pointing with his chin to the stage where the singers were doing "Universal Soldier."

Sheldon shrugged. "With a little work on the melody and the lyrics, this could be a good song, you know what I'm saying? Wait, now it's getting interesting." A drummer had set up behind the guitarists, the beat was picking up, and the song turned into "I Ain't a Marchin' Anymore." "That's better," Sheldon said.

Nothing quite explained Sheldon's isolation. He managed to be in the Movement without attaching himself to anyone. No girlfriend he was willing to tell Chuck about. He'd gone through junior college, had a job as a keypunch operator, and lived with his mother, who worked at the Karamu theatre. His father was a musician in Europe. In the office when someone brought pretzels and beer for an impromptu party, Sheldon stayed apart. To be sure, he was usually the only Black man. "Why not get involved with your own people?" Chuck had asked once.

"Which people?" Sheldon had responded. "Why are they *mine?* I have no interest in wearing a dashiki, don't approve of the Afro Set."

"It's too damn hot," Sheldon said now. "Someone should put bottles of water in vending machines. We could buy two and pour them over our heads."

"I liked your idea of the bookstore with coffee and marijuana better," Chuck said. The unlikely-new-business game had begun when Chuck revealed his own half-assed fantasy that Sheldon would apply for a start-up loan so they could charge Lake Erie Savings & Loan with racism. Sheldon wouldn't set foot near Chuck's workplace, but every time they met he had a new crazy idea for making money. Selling bottled water! Might as well try to sell rocks as pets.

A jug band had joined the drummer and the singers, and all eight of them were belting "I-Feel-Like-I'm-Fixing-to-Die Rag." The crowd swayed, joining in the raucous, macabre chorus. Sheldon clapped softly, turning his slender, long-fingered hands from one side to the other. He was admirable; it took guts to live so independently. Chuck himself needed people. Unthinkable, for example, to lose Ivy.

A thought flew into his brain: Sheldon might be homosexual. The thought flew out again.

"I'm supposed to meet my girlfriend," Chuck said, stepping away. He caught a glimpse of a short person with long dark hair, near the stage, talking to Bert. The Viet Cong flag was cocked over Bert's shoulder. As Chuck drew closer, Bert leaned into Ivy, stroking her cheek with his thumb, drawing her face up to his. Their foreheads bumped as Chuck landed next to them. Bert dropped his hands and straightened up with a crooked smile.

"Where you been?" Chuck put his arm across Ivy's shoulders and pulled her to his side. Her body felt stiff, resisting his hug.

"Looking for you," she said. He held her tight.

"I was right there," Chuck said. He thumbed over his shoulder, but when he looked, Sheldon had vanished. The crowd was breaking up. "Let's go home," Chuck took Ivy's hand. "What was that about?"

"What was what about?" She was watching traffic. At the first gap between cars she leapt off the curb and pulled him with her.

"Is it against your principles to take a few steps to the corner and cross with the light?" he asked. She smirked at him from the curb. "You were flirting with Bert Augustin. What's *that* about?"

"We were just having fun," Ivy said. "Doesn't mean anything. Come on." She walked ahead among the Saturday pedestrians.

"It does mean something," Chuck said, catching up to her. "You were about to kiss him in public."

"You think I should kiss him in private? What are you being stuffy for?"

"You're supposed to kiss *me* in public," Chuck said. They were under the Halle's canopy, about to go into the Terminal Tower. A block away the preacher raised his red face to the sky, his voice sing-songing in the noisy air. Ivy pressed against Chuck as he kissed her; he felt her breasts, her thighs, the rich triangle between them. He drank her lips open and touched her tongue with his. She must have felt him hardening; she pushed away and took a breath.

"Okay," she said, breathing out, a little too slowly, the way he'd come to know. "I'm in love with you. And I'm due at The Big Penny in half an hour." They ran for the Rapid Transit at the bottom of the Terminal Tower.

"Kissing is harmless," Ivy said, settling into the Rapid Transit seat. "During the love-ins at Golden Gate Park, everyone was kissing everyone else. Girls kissed girls, guys kissed guys. I love kissing." She turned and kissed Chuck sweetly.

He felt a little sick, an effect of the "guys kissing guys" image that had flashed through his head. He shouldn't feel that way. If a man was queer—if Sheldon was, for example (for an

awful split-second, Chuck was aware of Sheldon's round lips)—
then the correct thing, the kind thing, was to wish him
acceptance and a lover.

He wished he could be as sure of things as Ivy was. She
wore a bright green dress splashed with white and orange
flowers. Some time in the spring all her skirts had become
shorter and brighter; this dress ended near the tops of her thighs.
He put his hand on her bare knee. She patted his hand, but she
didn't look at him. "Too hot?" he asked.

"Aunt Peg wants us to go to Kelley's Island with her,"
she said.

"It'd be nice." He'd heard of Kelley's Island, somewhere
in Lake Erie; people had a lot of fun there. "It'd be even nicer if
we could find a couple of days when neither of us is working.
I should quit. The Savings & Loan isn't the most ethical place
I've ever worked." And where would that be, he wondered.
Charley Leggit's Chryslers? The ice cream truck he'd driven
last summer? When was he going to make his contribution—
and how? "I hate that job. I can't afford to quit, that's all."

"You don't hate it," Ivy said.

"You've never even seen the Savings & Loan." Sometimes she could be so wrong about what she was sure of.

"You smile when you're getting dressed in the morning,"
she said. "I know you like the air conditioning. And your stories
about the other people are..." She hunted for the word in her
mind: "affectionate." They were riding through the bottom of
a man-made canyon lined with trash and bedraggled vines. Ivy
smiled. "It's okay," she said. "I understand it's a secret that you
like the job."

"No," Chuck insisted. "I really do hate it. Because..."
he blurted what he just now realized, "because it *pulls* at me. I
know how the tellers and the loan officers want me to behave,
so I do it. Without thinking. I've tried to stop, but I can't. I
want—no, I *need*—people to like me. I need to like them." He
hated the loan officers, junior and senior, their pompous
doughy necks stuffed into their buttoned-up collars. Yet he'd

skim *Reader's Digest* in the magazine racks at the Terminal Tower, memorizing one or two jokes they might laugh at. He was a pal to the head teller, a woman who should have his job. He complimented her clothes; she complimented his; that was their rapport. "It's a dilemma," he said.

Ivy sat back and leaned against him. "What you are is *ambivalent.* I love that word. Here's our stop." Two Black men (they looked like teenage boys, really) came aboard and stood together holding onto the overhead rail, though there were empty seats. They wore identical black leather jackets.

"I'll come to The Big Penny tonight," Chuck said, standing and reaching for Ivy's hand. "I'll have a vanilla milkshake."

"Okay." She held his hand while they made their way out of the car. Then she looked at him warily. "You don't *need* to come to The Penny, you know."

"I want to." Now that he'd revealed his messed-up feelings, he needed to be near Ivy.

"I thought you were going to the Movement office."

"First I'll go to the office, then I'll come to The Big Penny. What's wrong?"

"You're acting like you don't trust me."

They walked across the parking lot near the Case dorms, making their way downhill to Euclid Avenue. Ivy's voice echoed in Chuck's mind. Till now, he hadn't thought of not trusting her. He gripped her hand tighter as they approached the Monmouth.

"What's going on at The Big Penny that you don't want me to know about?" he asked, when they'd climbed the Monmouth stairs to the apartment. *Bert*, he thought.

"Come see for yourself," Ivy said, hopping from one foot to the other while he fiddled with the lock. The key never fit right; you had to jiggle it one way and the other, then jiggle the door before you could get the bolt to slide back. "I get the bathroom first," she said. He opened the door.

Chuck felt good about the newspapers and coffee cups on the table by the window, the tangle of sheets, books, and India-print on the bed. But some of the chaos—the sink full of food-crusted dishes; the dirty clothes strewn on the rug, half under the bed, near the bathroom door—was depressing. "We're supposed to live in squalor," Ivy had said. She never cleaned house. Chuck sat on the bed and kicked off his sneakers. He wanted her with him. So what if she flirted with men? She'd get tips that way. He could hear her in the bathroom, waiting for the water to get hot so she could clean up for work. He trusted her; of course he trusted her. He would ask her to marry him, but not yet.

She emerged from the bathroom dressed for work. He watched her yellow waitress skirt slide up her thighs as she bent to tie her sneakers. Then she was gone.

When Chuck got to the office fifteen minutes later, Bert was sitting at the new work-table, drawing on brown paper—a grocery bag that had been cut apart and spread out. His back jerked at the clap of the screen door.

"Sounded like a gunshot," Bert said. "What's goin' down?"

"Not enough," Chuck admitted. "Making plans?" He gestured to Bert's lines and scribbles.

"Oh, I'm just fooling around," Bert said, as if he hadn't been intent on the diagram, weren't fingering the ballpoint pen, eager to draw more. "This is a kind of map. You ever been to the steam tunnels under the Reserve campus?"

"No." Chuck had heard about the maintenance tunnels from Ivy, who thought it would be an adventure to go there. Chuck had no desire to go underground.

"There's an entrance by the nursing school," Bert said. "Another in the library basement. We walked around the stacks in the middle of the night, could've made off with a thousand books, if we'd had a way to carry them."

"Why would you want to steal a thousand books?" Who had Bert been with? When?

"I'm not planning to steal books, Leggit. The point is, you *could*. In fact, I think you could live down there, stay undiscovered for weeks, as long as you had food. Students looking for some free love have stashed mattresses in the corners here—and here." With his pen he touched little squares on his diagram. "The hard part is crossing Euclid Avenue; you have to climb down an iron ladder; the iron burns your hands. He dramatized with his hands and shoulders. "You can hear traffic way overhead."

"Free love," Chuck said. Better than having sex in cars and in obscure grassy corners. Oh, of course: Bert had gone there with Shelly. Now he was unreeling a detailed fantasy: check out the maintenance crews' schedules so "you" could hide from them, locate more exits.

"I figure there's an entrance under the architecture school, and maybe Severance Hall. Maybe the Art Museum!"

"The museum would have a ton of security," Chuck said. "Stolen art is much, much hotter than stolen books."

"Yeah, and Severance has all those elite instruments to protect," Bert conceded. He drummed the cement floor with the heels of his cowboy boots. "I'm just playing with the idea," he said. Bert would commit civil disobedience, but not burglary, Chuck knew—especially not major theft that involved dealers in stolen art.

"Hey Bert—let's go." Jane appeared from the shadowy back of the office. "Hello, Chuck!" Funny, how Jane's face turned pretty when she smiled. "You'll keep the place open for us, man the phones?"

"I guess so," Chuck said. That's what he'd promised to do, but he'd been hoping for company, too fed up with himself to spend another evening pretending to be an activist by reading books.

"We gotta go meet with Marvin about the fuck-head infiltrator," Bert said. "At least we know it's not you."

"Infiltrator?" Why would an infiltrator be needed? Chuck wondered. The Movement for a Democratic Society was transparently subversive. He thought of Ungvary's pale-blue unmarked car, parked in Public Square for this afternoon's demonstration, the dark suits inside watching something they couldn't understand. Maybe they'd hired someone to explain to them. He could explain. We don't like being used for others' purposes any more than you do—especially when the result is more money and power for a few men. Especially when we end up in the line of fire.

"My mother got a letter from the FBI." Jane was not smiling now. She looked sweaty and exasperated. "You're one of my subversive influences."

"I am?" Chuck suddenly felt much better. "Subversive influence?" Kind of like a promotion. "Well then, I'll give this place my best subversive supervision. Can you wait till I go across the street for a Dr Pepper?"

"Nope, we're off," Jane said, swinging her purse over her shoulder. It had once been the kind of high-class bag you'd buy from a Halle's showcase. Now the leather was worn, ink-stained purple on one corner, the long strap knotted together. Bonnie Leggit would've thrown that bag away.

"There's a case of Nehi orange pop in the basement," Bert said. He folded up his brown paper map and tucked it into his paperback book. Chuck tried, but he couldn't read the title.

Then Chuck was alone with his free orange pop. Now what? He picked up Bert's pen and found his own notebook —Was where he'd left it!—in the pile of papers on the literature table. He settled into the big stuffed chair near the window and leafed to the last thing he'd written, scrawled large to fill a whole page: "I claim to be a conscientious objector by reason of my religious training and belief and therefore request the local board to furnish me a Special Form for Conscientious Objector (SSS Form 150)." He'd copied the note from a CO handbook he'd found on Sunday, nearly a week ago.

He'd been walking alone on a shady street lined with big old dark-brick houses with complicated windows and heavy roofs. Two were fraternity houses; one was the Music School Settlement; another was the Society of Friends, which had its door wide open, and a sign: "Welcome. Meeting for Worship at 11:00." It was 11:05—yet the place was silent. Curious, Chuck had gone softly up the walk and looked in. In a large room open to the hallway, people sat on unfolded metal chairs. A man saw him and smiled, beckoning to an empty seat. Quaker meeting. Chuck had heard about them, seen pictures: the Quaker Oats man, women in caps and long skirts. But these people looked normal. He sat still and listened to the soft noises: breathing, a sigh here and there, rustles of position-changing, a tiny grunt as someone pulled out a Kleenex and wiped his nose. A man stood up and asked God for a way to live with fear so he could work in the most violent part of the city. Then he sat down. In the silence, everybody could think about what he'd said. They could think whatever they wanted, Chuck realized. He thought he might ask God for a way to live with his job till the end of the summer, but his thoughts kept wandering, and he kept looking around the room. He'd forgotten who he thought God was, if He existed at all. The silence went on for hours, days even. Chuck wondered why he couldn't just leave. Finally a gray-haired woman next to him turned and shook his hand. Meeting was over.

"You seem to have a question for me," she said. Her eyes were wide, curious. "Do you study here?" She had a slight European accent and large blue-enameled earrings, the kind his mother would call "Chi-chi."

"No," Chuck said, stumbling as he stood, unable to break from her open gaze. "I mean, not now. Can you tell me about being a pacifist?" He hadn't meant to ask; polite introductions should come first. But she responded as if she believed he was sincere.

"Are you thinking of conscientious objection?" she asked, and when Chuck nodded, she steered him into a room full of books on shelves. "Pacifism is a practice, no? It takes a long time. But we have a little book I can lend to you." She put into his hands the CO Handbook, plain, bound in gray paper. "Someone else will need it soon," she said. "My name is Mrs. Nelson."

He'd sat on the couch to read and found the statement that should have been in his letter two months ago. Rather than borrowing the handbook, he'd copied down the sentence in his notebook. Then he'd come to the office and left the notebook behind.

Evening light slanted into the office, and Chuck studied the statement again. *Religious training and belief?* He imagined being cross-examined (the book had said that could happen), having to explain how he'd come to the conviction that the war was...what had Spock said? "Immoral, illegal, unwinnable." Yes, and there's more, he thought again. He'd like to talk to Mrs. Nelson about pacifism being a practice.

Nah. He was out of luck. His religious training had come from Pastor Snowdon at his parents' Episcopal church (higher class than Baptist). Snowdon was a veteran of the European front who sang "Onward Christian Soldiers" with tears in his eyes. Father liked to sing "Praise the Lord and Pass the Ammunition" and would be enraged to think that Chuck's religious training would keep him from fighting for his country. But I *would* fight for my country, Chuck thought, if I could figure out how fighting would bring it back from...

He took a sip of orange pop and wrote "What *do* I believe?" at the top of a fresh page. He didn't know why, but he had to start with Ivy. "Dark hair spread across the pillow," he wrote, thinking of her naked, propped on one elbow reading in bed. Thinking of Ivy lifted his heart. At work, he'd watch the junior loan officer walk by and think, *If you saw Ivy, you'd envy me.* She was inviolable. He wrote "Ivy, inviolable" and thought maybe it should be "inviolate." There was a difference, but he wasn't sure what it was.

"I've no desire to possess you," he wrote. He would write her a letter to explain exactly how he felt. "I am yours as you are mine—perhaps more. We have formed an inviolable entity. A single *us*." No one had the right to violate their love. Bert Augustin's attentions were indeed meaningless. Augustin was busy fucking Shelly in the steam tunnels. Ungvary's plainclothesmen must have been thrilled when they saw Bert's NLF flag this afternoon.

"The Viet Cong are fighting for their country's independence," Chuck wrote. "So Americans are on the wrong side—which is why 'What We Can Do for Our Country' has become..." What had it become? Resist the draft and go to prison. Work for a group that demanded participatory democracy and get spied on by the FBI. Discover how the ruling class hoards wealth and power. "Work on overthrowing the System: that's what you do for your country. How?" Chuck wrote. *"By any means necessary,* said Malcolm X," he wrote, and then said the words softly, evenly, through clenched teeth, the way Bert said them.

Chuck had once asked Marvin what means were necessary. Marvin said he didn't know, but he'd just come upon an idea for designing really cheap houses. "Easy to build, with a mix of free and inexpensive materials. You'd put up your own house, and other folks would help you. Then you'd help them with their houses." Chuck was dubious. He'd told Marvin about the time he'd tried to build a house for his sister Bonnie's dog, sawing and hammering for a whole Saturday, bruising himself, wishing he were elsewhere. The result became a family joke.

Suppose Lake Erie Savings & Loan found out the FBI had called Chuck "a subversive influence." He put his fingers to his cheek and felt the cold bone inside. He went to the back door and looked up and down the alley, gravel-strewn and weedy. The air was cooler than it had been during the day, but it warmed his hands.

Chapter 11

July 8, 1968
Liberty Boulevard

Her back prickling against a rough-barked oak, Ivy sat next to Jane watching children play in Rockefeller Park. She wanted to talk about Ken Shapiro, whom she'd begun to distrust. And about the fight with Chuck over dishwashing. Chuck had said it was stupid for Ivy to cry. Then he ran the sink full of soapy water and sponged each dish, handing it to her to wipe and put away: two cups, two bowls, three plates. He hadn't rinsed. The towel was dirty. She couldn't tell him he was doing it wrong. Jane would understand. Jane had lived with a man for a couple of years. But Jane was absorbed in making faces at the baby perched on her lap chewing the end of her braid: Dora's baby. Two of the children on the jungle gym were Dora's as well, and while Dora was visiting her mother in the hospital, Jane was looking after the kids. To talk with Jane, Ivy had to drive them all to the playground in Chuck's Pontiac. He wouldn't find out till she picked him up after work, but he couldn't object: she'd filled up the car with gas. They'd been here for an hour, and so far there had been no chance to talk with Jane.

A boy on the topmost monkey-bar stepped on Kelvin's fingers. He squawked and fell. Jane leapt to her feet, and the baby jerked with a scream.

"I'll go," Ivy said, needing to move, thinking five-year-old Kelvin would be easier to comfort than a baby; she sprinted across the grass. But he was standing when she got there, brushing off the dirt and pebbles.

His sister Tina was yanking his arm, saying "C'mon, let's go," dragging him away from Ivy. They charged straight up the hill, bypassing the stone steps. Ivy followed, eyes to the ground to keep from stumbling over knobbed roots. When she got to the top they had disappeared. "Kelvin!" she called. "Tina! Hey! Where are you?" She stood in a rectangular garden with a slate path. At the end stood Goethe and Schiller, much larger than life. Schiller held a book; Goethe held out a laurel wreath as if he were about to crown someone who stood on the ground below—someone ten feet tall; the pedestal itself was huge, even the poets' shoe-toes were out of reach.

A scuffling noise: Tina and Kelvin squatted behind the statue. "We hiding from those giants," Tina said. "They gonna eat us up." Her eyes were big.

"They're not going to eat you," Ivy said. "They're nice giants. Look, they're smiling."

Tina clambered out to see for herself. "Giant brothers," she said, studying the beneficent faces. "They know they about to *eat*." Kelvin had started to creep forward, but Tina's "*eat*" sent him scuttling back. He crouched in the bushes, peering up toward Goethe's and Schiller's enormous marble calves.

Ivy laughed. "Let's get out of here," she said. Kelvin sidled away from the statues; if either poet had leapt to the ground and lunged for Kelvin, he would have missed. She began to decipher the German sentences on the pedestal, ornate letters painted gold. Then she felt the children's small brown hands, one in each of hers—gifts. So she went with them down the steps this time, away from the hungry giants.

They stopped in front of a marble stone. *Denkmal* would have been the German word for it: *Think-a-minute*. Someone had slathered the profile of another famous German with black paint and written "Black Power!" in clumsy letters all over the white marble. Ivy strained to read the original lettering as the children tugged at her hands. "That's Beethoven!" she told them. *Why him?* she wondered.

"Who?" Kelvin asked.

"He's a musician," Ivy said. "When he was little his daddy hit him on the ears, so he got deaf. But he wrote beautiful music anyway."

"Oh." Kelvin shrugged. "C'mon." They turned and ran again, down the hill to Jane.

"Someone painted 'Black Power' on the Beethoven memorial stone," Ivy said. Jane held the baby who was sucking on a bottle of water.

"I know," she said. "Happened over a year ago." She stroked the sole of one baby foot with her thumb.

"I like Beethoven," Ivy said. "It feels like a desecration."

"Sometimes we get jerked awake to our background conditioning," Jane said. "You really know better."

Stung, Ivy walked away. She did know better. Bert would have scorned her bourgeois blindness. He'd say, "You gotta ignore a lot of reality in order to like Beethoven these days." She thought again of Bert at the Spock rally, his hands on her bare shoulders, his face bending over hers, his long hair brushing her cheek—almost kissing, but then Chuck had shown up. She had said it was no big deal, convincing herself and Chuck. But that moment his lips and eyes and breath had filled her like a revelation, a glimpse of something she had to know in order to understand the world and herself.

She pushed the memory back into darkness and looked at reality: the park lay before her, peaceful, sunlit, filled with Black families. Children and adults, babies and old people walked along the sidewalks, sat on benches, sprawled on the thick grass and under the enormous shade trees. Children swarmed the jungle gym, the teeter-totter, the slide, and the swings. Several men fished from the stone wall that lined the creek. Beethoven did not belong here. If she let him go, she could rejoin them. She turned back to Jane and the children.

"Why don't you go play on the swings?" Jane was saying to Tina and Kelvin. "We'll stay here." They trotted off.

"Hi," Ivy said, and drew a breath. "I was thinking..."

"Leatha," Jane said, fondly. "My only chance to be with a baby. I feel so peaceful."

"Why say it's your only chance?" How could she introduce the fight with Chuck? The situation with Shapiro? Her feelings (still there, crouched, ready to spring out) about Bert? The way she had tried to tell Kelvin about Beethoven? *Icky*: that's what Ivy felt, and besides, she wished she were Black. "You'll have your own kids, right?"

"No," Jane said. "I won't bring children into this world."

"But if this makes you happy..." Ivy studied the baby, who was sitting up now, gripping Jane's fingers, putting them in her mouth, jouncing restlessly. Across the lawn, Kelvin was trying to pump, but the big heavy swing wouldn't move.

"But I don't have to be with them all the time," Jane said. She drew a snaky line in the dirt with a twig, then threw the twig to keep it away from the baby, who whimpered. "If I were their mother, with never enough money, never enough time even to *think*, I'd go crazy." Leatha was fussing and squirming, trying to get out of Jane's arms into the dirt.

Ivy found Chuck's car keys in her purse and held them out, jingling. Leatha grabbed eagerly and put the biggest key in her mouth. There was a quiet moment.

"Yesterday, Ken Shapiro..." Ivy began.

Jane wasn't listening. Her gaze was locked onto kids who were circling Kelvin, hollering insults, threatening to knock him off his seat. The keys fell from the baby's fist to the ground. She began to cry. "Leatha wants to walk," Jane said. "She's almost ready to do it on her own, so she needs practice." Ivy took Leatha's small hand and helped her stand. The baby crowed. "Ah!"

"Ah!" Ivy answered. Sunlight poured over the playground; the afternoon was getting hot. A teenage girl gave Kelvin's swing a push and he soared, grinning.

"Yesterday I went for groceries," Jane said. "Peggy drove me out to Shaker Heights for fresh fruit and low prices. I got dizzy looking at all the melons, peaches, nectarines. Then suddenly the injustice got to me: I wanted to smash peaches into the super-clean floor, toss bananas into the fluorescent lights, heave a cantaloupe through the plate-glass window. I get so mad sometimes."

"I know," Ivy said. But when she'd gone to Heinen's with Aunt Peg, she felt only the pleasure of buying good fruit and fresh-baked bread.

"Peggy bought a bag full of peaches and nectarines, made me promise to get it to a mother with children," Jane said. "So I took it to Dora. She hates handouts; I got her to accept it as a favor to me."

"Wait a minute, who's Peggy?" Ivy asked. The baby took another laborious step, clutching Ivy's fingers, and then another.

"One of the MOP ladies, Mothers Opposed to Poverty," Jane said. "Her last name starts with a B. I can't remember it. Spanish, I think."

Suspicion confirmed. "Barcelona. She's my aunt," Ivy said. "But she's not a mother." Then suddenly Aunt Peg's lost child came to life, a cousin Ivy would never know. Where did the child live? Not a child: she—or he—would be grown now. Full of sorrow for missed chances, she stroked Leatha's little hands with her thumbs and watched the next lurching step.

"No kidding," Jane said. "Oh shit, there he goes," She leapt and ran to the swing; Kelvin sprawled in the dirt, yelling at another boy who was trying to break Kelvin's hold on the chain. Even after the other boy thrust himself onto the seat and pushed off, Kelvin held tight and got dragged, the chain wrapped around his arm, until he dropped with a yell, "Muh-fuck!" Tina came running and got to her brother just ahead of Jane.

Leatha settled into Ivy's lap and leaned against her chest, sucking two fingers. Ivy felt her warm damp weight and shifted to make her lap wider, her back more supportive. Near the swings, Jane was kneeling, eye-level with Kelvin, listening to him and to Tina, calming them both. How *could* Jane deliberately close off the possibility of children, at age 25? Ivy watched them come across the lawn, arms around each other. One of Kelvin's elbows wept blood.

They tended his wounds with Kleenex, which Tina moistened and pressed into soggy balls at the drinking fountain. "Perfect," Jane said, dabbing the blood off.

Kelvin winced, cried "Ow Ow Ow!" and Jane laid dry Kleenex over the scrape on his elbow. Then she brought out the snack: a box of animal crackers for each child. Kelvin took out a cookie. "This here's a lion. *Rahr!*" He lunged at Tina.

"That's some puny lion," Tina said. "I got a elephant, *stomps* on your lion!" Her hand holding the elephant cookie knocked Kelvin's lion to the ground; he began to cry. Tina gave him another, from her box. "Animal crackers is fun," she said, settling next to Ivy. "I like M&Ms better, though." She popped another animal into her mouth. "Can I comb your hair?"

"What?"

The child reached to touch Ivy's ponytail—not quite pulling, just feeling the hair with her fingers. "Let me comb your hair. Please!"

Ivy reared away. She hated anyone to fuss with her hair, had refused to let her mother comb it, had loathed her few trips to the beauty parlor. "I don't have a comb," she said.

"Jane always lets me comb her hair," Tina said. "She has a comb. Jane!" Jane was naming cookie-animals with Kelvin, her braid hanging down her back. "Don't I always comb your hair real nice?"

"Yep, you do." Jane smiled. "But not now. I promised your brother I'd..."

"Ivy don't have a comb," Tina said. "I want to do hers."

"Oh. Well, mine's in my purse," Jane said. She rocked back onto her heels and got up, scooping the baby out of Ivy's lap and reaching for Kelvin's hand. They headed toward the drinking fountain.

Ivy felt trapped. Tina found a 10-cent comb in Jane's purse and reached for Ivy's ponytail. "Yours is straighter than Jane's," Tina said.

"Hers is longer, though," Ivy said, jerking her head away. "*You* have pretty hair," she said to Tina. "Nice and thick." She touched one of Tina's five springy braids: one above each ear, two at the back, one atop her head.

"My hair's nappy," Tina said. "I want it long and smooth." Her gentle fingers, her sweet triangular face—wide-apart eyes, sharp little chin—made foolishness of Ivy's fear.

Bert had told her how the community day-care children liked to play with his hair. She pictured Bert sitting still with the fingers of three- and four-year-olds in his long gold-tinged hair and knew what he would say: *Let go of your bourgeois conditioning.* "Here," Ivy said, ripping the rubber band from her ponytail. "Don't yank, okay?"

"Okay," Tina said, and Ivy felt the teeth of the little comb pull at her scalp. The little girl tried to be careful, stroking the hair back, making a part. She didn't yank at the snags. Ivy forced herself to sit still. Bert was in her mind again. Her lips swelled with wishing she could kiss him.

"Time to go?" Jane stood, the baby asleep on her shoulder, Kelvin jumping at her side.

"It's not done yet," Tina said.

Ivy couldn't move; Tina held a clump of her hair firmly in her fist.

"We got to pick up your mother, then take you all home," Jane said.

"I got to be downtown by 5:30." Ivy tried to be gentle as she pried the comb from Tina's hand.

"What you doing downtown?" Tina asked. "Take me with you!"

Ivy recoiled from the idea. "Meeting my boyfriend." *Next time*, she promised herself.

"Boyfriend! Woo-woo!" Both children hooted, almost in unison.

"You in *love*?" Tina asked as they walked back to the Pontiac.

"I guess so," Ivy said.

"What's his name?"

"Chuck."

The car was sweltering after an hour in the sun. Ivy was awkward with the stick shift on the steering column; she started too quickly, stalled, and had to start again. Tina and Kelvin rollicked in the back seat, telling stories about Ivy and her boyfriend. "Oh, *Chuck*. Oh, Mr. Woodchuck, oh, Ivy and her Mr. Woodchuck are in *love*. He says, I love yoooo, Miss Ivy." Jane pointed out interesting cars for Kelvin, tried to get Tina to read signs, but they kept returning to the story of Ivy and a fat, hairy woodchuck. How had they known just what would sting her the worst? Ivy tried to ignore them as she drove into downtown traffic. Baby Leatha began to cry.

While Jane ran into the hospital to find Dora, Ivy sat behind the wheel as Tina and Kelvin climbed into the front seat and pestered her with questions. When you gonna take us to the zoo? How about Disneyland? O*kay!* We going to Disneyland! Why not? Ivy tried to explain that Disneyland was 3,000—no, 4,000 miles from here. Did they know what a thousand miles was? How about one mile? They didn't care; they laughed at her discomfort. "You know what? Ivy gots witch hair," Kelvin told Tina.

"She look like Morticia in the Addams family," Tina said. "You *are* Morticia, that's who you are. You playing around with Ghoulardi, cheating on Mr. Woodchuck."

Ivy glared at them. "Stop it, you guys! Right now!"

They laughed louder. "Woo, she getting mad," Kelvin said.

"We blowed her cover," Tina said. "She don't want to be caught cheating on her boyfriend." They began to sing the Addams Family tune.

Ivy turned up the Pontiac's radio, loud, to a station playing jitterbug music. "Hello, Mary Lou." An awful song— but she refused to change the station. They tried to attack the radio. Ivy grabbed a wrist of each child; they squirmed and protested. "You *mean*, Morticia!" Kelvin reached the dial and the radio squawked up and down.

"Tell me what station you want," Ivy said. A concession too late. They didn't want music, they wanted her angry, and they had what they wanted: she was ready to hit them. She had imagined herself leading children from the inner city through Disneyland—where she'd never been, but longed to go. Not if they hurt her like this. "Cheating on" stung painfully.

Jane appeared in the parking lot with baby Leatha on her hip and next to her a tall woman wearing a blue sheath dress. Dora. "There's Mama!" Kelvin cried. He and Tina slithered over into the back seat.

Dora climbed in between them. She had Tina's large eyes and pointed chin; her figure was long-limbed and thick in the middle, her hair pulled to the back of her head.

Jane settled into the passenger seat with the baby snuggled on her shoulder.

On either side of their mother, the children were quieter than they'd been all afternoon. "You had fun in the park," Dora said. It was an order, not a question.

"Yes, Mama." Instantly obedient children.

"That's good," said Dora. "Now let's go home. Your grandmommy's doing better; you're going to visit her tomorrow."

"Mommy, Tina made a joke on Ivy," Kelvin said. "Called her Morticia."

"That's not nice, Tina," said Dora.

"Kelvin did too," Tina protested. "We was playing."

"Yeah, I know. You say you're sorry?" They sat quiet.

Ivy should say, *Never mind, it was just a game.* But she did mind. "Why are you mumbling like that?" Dora's voice rose in pitch. "Let me hear it: we're sorry, Ivy."

"Sorry, Miss Ivy." Kelvin's voice.

"We're sorry," Tina said.

"Now you thank Ivy for driving you all to the park."

"Thank you, Ivy," Tina said. And Kelvin said, "Thank you very *much*!"

Jane glanced at Ivy and smiled. "Morticia," she said. "Those kids."

"They turned on me," Ivy told Jane, after they'd delivered Dora and the children to their house. "It's like they ganged up on me, all of a sudden."

"Why take it personally?"

"I don't know," Ivy said, miserable. She felt ugly and racist. And selfish, deprived of Jane's attention to her personal worries and failings.

"They like you," Jane said, getting out of the car at the Movement office. "We'll do it again soon."

"Okay," Ivy said, and smiled (she realized, driving downtown through hot wind) only because she needed Jane's approval. If Jane knew how she felt—if Ivy had told Jane everything that was bothering her—Jane would not approve. But maybe, next time...oh, she roiled with possibility, with not-knowing, with longing for Jane's calm sureness.

The clock at the corner of Ninth and Euclid said 5:40. Against the Public Library, a white marble statue of a lady seemed to be languidly pulling at her bodice; it had slipped off her shoulders and was about to slide off her breasts. Next door was a very Caucasian young man made of bronze with huge muscular legs and arms, wearing nothing but a cave-man skin and a crew cut. His eyes were wide, as if he were startled to find himself in downtown Cleveland without enough clothes. Both were outsized, like Schiller and Goethe, but the German poets had been fully dressed in eighteenth-century suits with knee-breeches.

Cleveland had a population of giants who watched from their pedestals as the 20th Century walked by. All the giants were white people. Suddenly the languid marble lady and the surprised bronze man seemed sinister in their foolish half-nakedness—dangerous to anyone not descended from white Europeans.

But it had been a good afternoon, after all. Hadn't it? Jane had said "They like you." Ivy still felt polluted in a way she couldn't begin to clean up.

What could she tell Chuck? He appeared now on the library steps, his jacket and tie over one arm, walking aimlessly, then grinning when he spotted her in the car. He came around to the driver's window and reached for the keys. "I'll drive."

Not much, Ivy answered her own question, crossing to the other side of the car. Better keep quiet.

Chapter 12

July 23, 1968
The Crystal Grille & Glenville

"You're invading the Selective Service Center at 6:30 in the morning just to *see records*?" Bert challenged Chuck across the table. "Jesus, take the fucking gloves off. When you're at the intake valve on the death machine, you don't just stand around politely. Pour blood on those files. Burn them!"

Jane saw Ivy's fingers tight-laced in Chuck's; Ivy pressed her lips closed and her cheeks grew red.

Six of them filled the large booth and two chairs at the Crystal, a cheap comfortable place with vinyl seats ripped near the corners and mended with tape. Over Marvin's shoulder Jane could see the counter where a lemon meringue pie, one wedge removed, glistened sweetly yellow and white, so magnificent she wished she hadn't squandered her dollar on the chicken dinner she was about to eat.

"Strategy, man, strategy!" Chuck was saying. "We got some law students planning with us; they're not radical enough yet, but they will be soon enough."

Stavros arrived with two stacks of sliced white bread on little plates. He wore a cook's apron with the strings wound around his lean waist and tied in front, a rhinestone American Flag pinned at one hip. "See here?" he said. "I brought you extra. I treat you people good. Here's butter, too." He grinned, showing his gray teeth.

"Stavros serves the people!" Tessa raised her water glass in salute.

"You need more water," Stavros said, and went away. On the jukebox Johnny Mathis began "Unchained Melody."

"Come with me and Marvin after dinner," Tessa said to Jane. "We're going to see *Rosemary's Baby.*"

"I promised Tina and Kelvin I'd read them a story tonight," Jane said. The children's grandmother was home from the hospital now, but not back at work. Dora needed help.

"What we're spending to destroy Vietnam," Marvin said to Tessa, "would buy every Vietnamese family a two-bedroom brick house, a new Chevy, and a color TV."

"Make real estate, not war?" Chuck shifted his attention to Marvin and Tessa's corner of the table. He pulled his mustache.

Ivy had freed her hand and was frowning. "I'm not making the Revolution so everyone on the planet can live in little square houses," she said. "That's not what they want."

"Don't make assumptions about what people want," Chuck said, as Stavros set a plate in front of Jane. A quarter of a roast chicken steamed between green beans and mashed potatoes. The fragrance alone was nourishing. Chuck was right. How could anyone presume to know what another person wanted?

And yet when she thought about it, Jane did know. Dora wanted that brick house, the lawn, the car, and the keys to both; she wanted to pay the bills with money of her own. If she couldn't have those things, she'd sacrifice herself till her children would.

Chuck was stroking Ivy's hair, pulling a strand off her cheek, tucking it behind her ear. Did Ivy want him to do that? Jane couldn't tell. Obviously Ivy had outgrown her parents' house and lawn. She said she loved Chuck's one-room apartment, but Jane could see stronger fondness for the traditional idea of beauty found in museums and well-groomed parks.

A few weeks ago Ivy had put the Emperor Concerto record in Jane's lap, saying, as if it were an intimate secret, "Oh

Jane, *this* contains ecstasy—you know, that place where extreme pleasure and extreme pain meet each other?"

"You mean orgasm," Jane had said. Curious, she'd started the record late that night and lain on the couch listening to the slow chords. She couldn't imagine Ivy making love to herself with this music, though it was fun, in a way, to try. She thought she had succeeded in turning herself on when Tessa burst into the room, talking rapid-fire, and Jane pulled her hands quickly out from under her nightgown. Tessa didn't notice. "Oh, Beethoven's Emperor," she'd said, and disappeared into the kitchen. The piano began to crash and gallop up a musical hill. But Jane's hands stayed quiet, and soon she fell asleep.

Tessa wanted to fix things. At the moment she had the showerhead in her purse; she wanted to find a part so she could repair it and they could take showers again. Tessa was a good roommate. (The green beans were bland and rubbery. Tessa saw Jane looking at the salt shaker, picked it up, and handed over the salt.) She'd been thrilled when she learned to sew people up after surgery, eager to report. "The body's torn open, literally reduced to blood and guts." She pantomimed the violent tearing. "You take away the diseased part—and finally, carefully, you stitch it together. And it works. Within an hour the eyes are open, the mouth is smiling." Tessa's approach was the same to poverty, to the war in Vietnam, to the government. Identify the problem—a worn gasket, a gallstone or a tumor, advanced Capitalism—and fix it: buy a new gasket for the showerhead, stitch up the abdomen, make a revolution. Add salt.

At least Tessa would never be without something to fix. Jane wished she could be as single-minded. Instead her focus kept shifting. She wanted to join Dora's family. No, she wanted to be left alone to plan the Revolution until she'd figured out all the details. No, she wanted to educate the Heights mothers. She took another bite of chicken and chewed, feeling nourished but not satisfied. She wanted pie, after all.

Bert had given up the draft board argument and was lambasting patriotism and objecting to all nationalism. He wanted all borders erased, all walls leveled. "Love of one's country is a dead idea!" he insisted.

Chuck disagreed: "Think about Zapata. Fanon. Bernadette Devlin." Chuck loved the small movements for independence, the secret meetings in basements, the collections of outdated rifles, the songs to get your blood up till you ran in the streets screaming "Freedom!" He practically yelled that word—unusual for Chuck. Marvin and Tessa's conversation halted. Stavros stopped clearing a table and turned to look.

"You're such a fucking romantic," Bert said, and Jane couldn't tell whether that was disgust in his voice, or admiration.

"What about the Black Nationalists?" Ivy asked. She was leaning against Chuck's arm, a girlfriend who wanted her hair stroked.

"They're not really making *nations*," Chuck said fondly. "They're resisting colonization." Yes, Jane thought, Chuck wants romance. Not the Battle-of-Algiers kind, the Ivy's-champion kind.

Bert added, "The Republic of New Libya isn't a *place*, it's a group of people, here and in Detroit." Stavros collected plates, stacking them on one hand. "Hey, Stavros," Bert said. "You're an American, right?"

"You betcha," Stavros said. "I am citizen five years now. I tell you, this is God's country!"

"It is that," Bert said, grinning. Wolf-grin, Jane thought.

"You want dessert, yes?" Stavros asked. Jane ordered her pie. She could afford it: tomorrow she'd eat oatmeal for free. The others ordered coffee.

Marvin touched Jane's hand. "You've been awfully quiet. What are you thinking?"

"About us," she said. "What we *want*, most of all."

"That's easy." Marvin nodded. He adjusted his glasses to watch with hungry eyes as Ivy sipped from Chuck's water glass. "Community," he said.

"Isn't community what we have?" Jane asked. She thought of the dinner on the night of the Columbia takeover, how the phone call had pulled them all together.

"Only part way," Marvin said. "For one thing, we're all white." And for another, Jane thought, you need a girlfriend. She hadn't met Eleanor at the Spock rally, where they'd split into factions: Arthur ("We are your children!") Cohen and the Mobe on one side, Bert and his NLF flag on the other.

"What's with Jimmy?" Tessa asked. "He seems to have disappeared."

"He's still living with his parents, I guess," Jane said. Weeks had passed since he'd stumbled into the office cradling his arm, and he hadn't called, hadn't appeared. It occurred to her that she didn't miss him. The intoxicating sexual steam between them had vanished. "Bert will know," she told Tessa. But Bert heard them and shrugged: he didn't know, after all.

The lemon meringue pie slice, so tempting when it was part of the whole, slumped alone on its small white plate, wilted at the edges. Jane cut off the point and put it in her mouth— sweet-tangy lemon, sweet-foamy meringue. The Campfire Girls had a legend: if you ate the point of your pie first, you'd never get married.

Campfire Girls' camp-outs were fun, but they weren't Jane's idea of community—which came, she realized, from long-ago picnics where the adults roasted brats and metts over coals while Jane's mother played guitar and sang "Joe Hill." Jane was allowed to stay up late, curled in her father's lap watching the fire. The feeling was even stronger in Mississippi. No conflicts over purpose, no question of trust. "We shall over-come," they sang. Overcome *what*? She ate another bite of pie. They didn't know then how long and confusing the struggle would be, how much had to change.

"Nonviolence was dead long before King was killed," Bert was lecturing Chuck on yet another subject. "Gandhi's tactics worked against the British; they could be shamed. Americans have no shame at all. We're the most violent nation in the history of the world. *If you don't fight, we will crush you—* that's the national stance."

"Who's *we*? Who's *you*?" Chuck demanded. "I can see why the Blacks need to carry guns to protect themselves, but you and I would be stupid to walk around armed."

"All your nationalist heroes started small like that. Castro and Che..."

"This is the U.S., 1968," Chuck said. "C'mon, what are you proposing?"

"Bring the war home," Bert said.

It was Bert's favorite slogan since the East Lansing conference. Jane watched him chopping the air with his mangled hand to emphasize what he was saying. He burned inside, more consistently revolutionary than any of them, the Movement's self-appointed Everyman. The price of a can of baked beans rose, and Bert rose up against the Campbell corporation. Napalmed children ran screaming down a road in Vietnam, and Bert longed to catch them in his arms, douse the fires and carry them to Washington to show McNamara what he'd done. Che Guevara's body was laid out like the corpse of a lion in a ruling-class safari picture, and Bert kept chanting the hero's words. Closer to home, Ahmed Evans, quietly developing his little African curio business and organizing "New Libya," was harassed by his landlord and the police—and Bert felt personally thwarted, held down while the handcuffs clicked shut behind his back. He'd come to the Crystal this evening jubilant, drumming his boot heels along the Euclid Avenue sidewalk, singing Dylan, busy being born.

Chuck was floundering, trying to find a way to love Che and argue for nonviolence too. He was unusually red in the face, and Bert was half out of his seat, leaning over the table, poking at the contradictions in a mean way. Bert's hostility had deepened; it was more than saying "fuck" all the time, more than the humiliation of three weeks in the County Jail.

"Violence is not the same thing as revolution," Chuck said.

"It's necessary though." Bert interrupted before Chuck could go on. His hair fell over his eyes, lurking dark among the strands. His hands gripped the table's chrome edge. *"By any means necessary.* That's where we're headed."

"Let's go," Jane said to anyone who would listen. "I can't be late for Dora's kids." She pushed her chair back and stood up.

"I'll go with you." Ivy rose. She woulf stop being with Chuck for a little bit. Jane smiled approval. They stood in line at the cash register together, and then they left, while the others finished paying inside. It was still light, but the air had cooled.

"I'll go back home," Chuck said, approaching behind them, calm now. "By 6:30 we gotta be at the draft board. Not militant enough for Augustin, but we'll do our best. See you soon, Babe." He kissed Ivy and turned away.

Bert slammed the red door of the Valiant on Marvin and Tessa, off to the movie. Then he ran to stop Chuck. "Hey Leggit! Let's go to my place and get drunk." His ferocity gone, suddenly he wanted company. "You girls join us when you've got Dora's kids to sleep."

Chuck looked at Ivy, who nodded; then he shrugged and reversed course.

The sky had turned gray with creeping darkness. The air was thick with moisture and car exhaust. Jane felt queasy: she shouldn't have eaten the pie.

Tina's and Kelvin's beds were mattresses in a curtained alcove off the kitchen. Ivy was reading aloud on the floor between them when a *crack* sounded from outside the open window. A gunshot? Probably some fool at the Lakeview Tavern, Jane thought. "The moon will shine on th crumbs we dropped on the path," Ivy read, as though she had not noticed. Another shot. Dora shouted in the living room.

"She callin out the window to somebody," Tina said. "Go on, Ivy."

"But the birds had eaten all the crumbs, and Hansel and Gretel were quite lost."

Heavy footsteps on the porch, sound of bolts, more footsteps. A voice exclaimed, "Crazy out there!" White male.

Dora stuck her head through the curtain. "Y'all stay in bed, hear?" She looked sternly at Tina, then at Kelvin. Then she disappeared. Water gushed in the kitchen sink. A subdued exclamation—"Ouch!"—from the man.

"Mama!" Kelvin yelped.

Dora re-appeared. "I'm-a help this man who got hurt," she said. "Be cool, now, son. You got Ivy and Jane to look after."

"I want some water," Kelvin said. "Please, Ma'am, may I have some water?"

Ivy closed the book and put it on the floor. A cupboard door banged in the kitchen. Dora's voice: "You go ahead and sit on this towel."

What white man, Jane wondered, shot but still on his feet, needed shelter? Not a policeman. She remembered that half an hour ago she and Ivy had passed two police cars near the Lakeview Tavern. Early for the police to park there, she'd thought. Sitting on the floor with her arm around Kelvin, Ivy breathed rapidly, the little hollow at the base of her throat moving in and out. If Chuck had figured out that Bert wasn't attacking him personally, then they'd have gone to the liquor store together. They might now be walking down 125th toward Lakeview, on the way to Bert and Marvin's apartment.

Two more shots. Dora appeared with Kelvin's cup of water. "You want one too, I suppose," she said to Tina.

"No thank you," Tina said. "Who that man?"

"Tow-truck operator," Dora said. "Come to move that Cadillac on Beulah. Some fool shot him—not too bad, he's walking and talking. I gave him the use of the phone." Her nervousness showed only in the way her head was cocked, listening as the man slammed the phone and cursed, and in the way she held a dishcloth, rubbing it between her fingers as if it were a remnant of something precious. The phone clicked and rasped as the man dialed again.

Jane heard soft mews. "Is that Leatha waking up?"

"Yeah," Dora looked back over her shoulder. She backed out of the alcove.

Suddenly the air went wild with sirens. Tina leapt out of bed, but Kelvin was ahead of her, pawing his way through the curtain. Jane caught up with them in the arch between living room and kitchen. Ivy stood looking at a blood-soaked cloth in the sink.

"He a policeman," whispered Tina.

True enough, the man's uniform was policeman-blue. "Uh-unh, look," Jane showed Tina the tow-truck company patches on his shoulder. He was young, his hair yellow-blond under his cap, his pale eyes red-rimmed.

"It was an ambush," he said. "Somebody punctured the tires on that Cadillac, waited till we came to tow it, then started shooting." His breath came in gasps, and he clutched a wad of bloody rags between elbow and rib cage. More sirens wailed. "All the lines at police headquarters are busy. I'll have to go out there for help." He pointed to the front door and then coughed. The coughing hurt: his face crumpled, and he leaned against the wall. Then he pulled himself up straight. It was an act of extreme manhood, a fierce denial of the dark stains on his jacket, blackish streaks on his pants' legs. "What are *you* doing here?" he demanded of Jane. "Boy are you ever in the wrong place."

Lights, spinning on the top of a police cruiser, sent flashes of red through the cracks around the living room window shade.

"Thank the lady of the house for me," the tow-truck man said. He clenched his lips and his nostrils flared, pulling air in, letting it out. He turned the door handle but couldn't undo the bolt without raising the arm that pressed the rags to the wound in his side; Jane undid the bolt, touching his hand— colder and whiter than hers.

"I will," she said and watched him stumble across the porch and down the steps. The police car spun its lights on the other side of the street; they'd take him to an emergency room. Dora had let him into the house where her children were trying to sleep, given him water and let him phone while bleeding onto the rug. Jane closed the door hard, made sure it was locked and bolted. Whoever shot him had probably mistaken him for police. That Cadillac had been sitting on Beulah for weeks.

Ivy stood by the window, holding Tina's hand, lifting the shade so they could both see out. "Chuck?" She spoke softly. "We should leave," she said.

If only we could find Bert and Chuck, Jane thought. They'd all drink rum & Coke in Bert's little white-radical digs. On the old sofa, with the coffee table made of cement blocks and a scrounged cellar door, they could wait out whatever this was. A bar fight would be over by now.

Gunshots rattled, too many, too close together to count—as though someone were shooting a machine gun in back of the house. The air smelled of gunpowder.

No. Jane wouldn't leave two terrified children with their mother's arms full of their baby sister. Dora had come in from the bedroom, Leatha crying on her shoulder, Kelvin crowding her legs. Jane held out her arms and took the weeping baby as Dora picked Kelvin up and held him. "Get *away* from that window, Miss Tina!"

Ivy let the shade fall back over the window, then turned with a guilty look. Tina slumped onto the floor. "Didn't see nothin," she said.

"Thank goodness," Dora said. "Now you both goin to bed."

"Uh-*unh*!" Kelvin shook his head vehemently. "No Mama, I'm-a stay here with *you*." He buried his face in his mother's neck. Dora petted his back, her face creased with distress. Tina crept across the floor on hands and knees, settling cross-legged next to her mother, holding one of Dora's ankles.

"Does Bert know where Dora lives?" Ivy asked Jane. "Maybe he'll come for us."

Jane shook her head. "And the phone's unlisted. We'll call him." She swayed side to side, rocking the baby while Dora rocked her little boy. Ivy slumped onto the couch and pulled one of the throw pillows into her lap. Dora had sewn the pillows by hand out of bright scrap material and stuffed them with old stockings. Tina settled next to Ivy, two fingers in her mouth. After a minute she picked up the other throw pillow and held it tight. They stayed like that, holding and being held, while shooting continued outdoors. Cars squealed, driving too fast down the narrow streets.

Leatha finally relaxed into sleep. Jane could tuck her into Dora's bed, then phone Bert. But he might not be there yet. And Marvin was still at the movie with Tessa.

Dora put Kelvin down; he leaned against her as she held out her arms and Jane delivered Leatha. "Come on now, we all gonna sleep in my bed." Tina slid off the couch. "God help us, it'll be over soon." Dora took all three children down the hall and into her bedroom. Ivy went to the window and lifted the shade again to look out.

The phone rang. "I'll answer!" Jane picked up the receiver. It was Dora's mother.

"One of the Donaldson boys got shot," Mrs. Williams said. "He may be killed."

"You shouldn't be alone," Jane said. "I could come be with you." Dora's mother lived two houses down from Jane's and Tessa's building.

"You can't go running around these streets," Mrs. Williams said. "The air is dangerous. I'm not even going near the windows."

"I shouldn't stay here, either," Jane said. If she mentioned Ivy or the tow-truck operator there would be a barrage of questions.

"Maybe not, but now you're there, you stay put. Get Dora on the phone."

Dora was already coming. "What if the tow-truck operator told the police he saw two white girls?" Jane whispered. "I'm worried you'd get in trouble."

"Can't think about *what-if* stuff," Dora said. "Hello, Mama?" Jane heard a choke in her voice. She joined Ivy at the window. Three police cars were parked near the corner, still and dark except for their reflecting stripes. Was that a person underneath? A dark shape seemed to move, a liquid flicker in the deep twilight.

"I've got to make sure Chuck's all right," Ivy said.

"Call him. Maybe he's home."

"He's with Bert. I know it. I'm going out there."

"The air is dangerous," Jane repeated.

"Okay," Ivy said. Her voice was level, uncompromising. "You don't have to come with me." She unbolted the door, pulled it part-way open, and slipped out.

"Wait," Jane said. She held the door so Ivy wouldn't close it behind her. "You can't go alone!" Jane called. She looked back at Dora, still on the phone, and waved. Dora frowned and shook her head. Jane waved again and went through the door; behind her, she felt the lock click into place.

Ivy had already run to the corner. From the porch, Jane could see her crossing Beulah Street—the wrong direction, away from Bert's apartment. She scrambled down the porch steps and ran through the smoking darkness to catch up. Across Beulah, Ivy stopped, and then Jane saw. A young black man lay on his back on the sidewalk. The blood spreading underneath him shone glossy under the streetlight. Two bandoliers criss-crossed on his chest, glittering with bullets. His elbows were scraped and bent, his arms in the air. He was wearing sandals—and one of his feet moved.

"We gotta help him." Ivy rushed forward. *Crack.* The streetlamp shattered. Jane's brain pulsed emergency, a red silent scream.

"Young ladies, get away from there." The deep voice came from darkness on the porch nearby. "They's a hundred men runnin around this block," he said. "In the bushes, between the houses. They shoot at whatever moves."

"Why'd you shoot out the streetlight?" Ivy asked. Jane felt her companion's hand grasp hers. She reminded herself to breathe. In. Out.

"That wasn't me. I called for an ambulance." The man's voice rumbled cool as old earth. Impossible to see his face; he stayed in shadow. "Tried to go out there but a bullet stopped me, same sharpshooter stopped you."

"We're looking for two white guys," Ivy said, climbing the porch steps, clutching the railing with one hand, pulling Jane along with the other. The man on the porch didn't respond. Flashing police car lights made the street glow red, then vanish, then re-appear. On the porch Jane felt a little safer; she squinted into the darkness. Somewhere in that narrow driveway or this clump of bushes or behind a car over there, a sniper lurked. More than one: the sniper had used a rifle. Someone else had fired an automatic. Jane heard a groan and saw the injured man drop one arm. She lunged toward the steps.

"You can't help that boy," the voice on the porch came deep and clear. Jane froze.

"So where's the ambulance?" Ivy asked, indignant.

"Soon as it's safe, they'll come. A hour? A day?"

"But he'll ..."

"He already dead, poor boy. This here's a war zone. I know, I been there. Women in war zones—you don't belong, you hear me?" In sunlight, Jane had thought she did belong. If she could see this porch-sitter, she'd recognize him. He probably recognized her, and he wanted her gone. "Let's get going," she said to Ivy. "That way." She pointed.

"Keep safe; go through this house and out the back door," the man said. "Don't turn on any lights, you hear? Go to the kitchen, then out."

She could hear him following as they crept down the dark hallway. He might be carrying a gun, but he wouldn't shoot if they kept going. The kitchen smelled of old bacon grease. Then came a closed-in porch crammed with auto parts. Then wobbly steps; Jane clutched the rail and felt a splinter jab into the palm of her hand.

More gunshots. A flurry of gunshots. "People on the roof!" Ivy whispered, pointing to shadows on a flat-roofed garage. She pulled Jane close, and Jane felt her sturdiness; Ivy's arms and legs were stronger than Jane's. Her breath rasped. They pressed against the aluminum siding of the next house; a woman's voice keened inside.

"We have to go that way," Jane said, pointing across the yard. She held Ivy's hand as they stepped forward. Ivy tripped over a tricycle and they stopped. Listened. Then moved again. Jane felt a blow to her chest—the cross-bar of a rusty swing set. They turned to enter the driveway between houses when two men emerged—police in white helmets. Jane dropped to the ground behind the privet hedge and felt Ivy squatting next to her. "Let's ask them to escort us," Ivy whispered.

Jane's visceral revulsion to the Cleveland police told her this firefight was somehow their fault. But Ivy had a point: a police escort might be their only way across Lakeview. She looked at the two white-helmeted men. They'd be suspicious at first, but then they'd get all protective. Then they might kill someone. She shook her head, *No.*

A shot came from the garage roof, and a policeman dropped. The other fired toward the sniper, *bang bang bang,* then dropped to his knees to check out his partner.

Jane felt Ivy's hand on her knee as they watched through leaves: one man in uniform put his injured partner's arm around his own neck, struggled to help him stand, held him close around the waist. They disappeared together down the driveway.

"Let's go." Ivy pulled Jane's hand. The splinter dug in. They peered around the house. Lakeview was crammed with police cars. "My god," Ivy said. Two policemen crouched behind one of the cars aiming guns toward the street.

"Bert's apartment is right there." Jane pointed across the street and two doors down. They should have gone around by Oakland Avenue; now there was no other way. "We'll crawl behind the hedge." She dropped and felt broken cement bite into her knees and hands, reality's sharp edges.

They were caught between Black men and policemen, aliens trapped in a no-woman's land. Ivy stoppered her mouth with a knuckle, as if to keep from talking or crying. Jane wanted to scream. The bushes scratched and clawed at her hair. The ground under her knees was littered with cigarette butts and broken glass. The air stank horribly of gunsmoke and burning rubber. Dim shapes moved in the darkness. Sudden bursts of light illuminated only smoke.

Ivy stood up. A few yards away something sparked and cracked. She dropped again. "I just got shot," she said. Weird wonder in her voice. "Look at my shoulder."

The bullet had torn into Ivy's T-shirt; blood was seeping, but not (thank goodness) spurting. Jane folded the T-shirt sleeve and pressed the wound. "Put your hand here," she said. "Keep it there." She'd been preparing to spend the rest of the night here behind the privet hedge, if necessary; now they couldn't do that.

Ivy kept her arm across her chest, her hand clamped to her shoulder. She was biting her lower lip and her forehead was sweaty. Her voice squeaked. "Where the hell is Chuck?"

The blood wasn't spurting, but she was in danger of shock. "He's with Bert," Jane said, forcing her voice low and even. "Can you walk?" What would they do if Ivy couldn't walk?

Ivy coughed and took a deep breath. "I can walk fine," she hissed.

"We'll go to my place, then." They doubled over, Ivy clutching her shoulder, and crept back into the yard with the swing set. No sign of movement on the garage roof. Jane straightened in the darkness, trying to unclench her body. Her palm throbbed around the splinter.

Ivy moaned in a high wee voice, *"Hnnnn. Hnnnn."*

Another driveway led to 123rd Street, where police cars sat silent and dark along the curbs. No one moved on porches or behind upstairs windows. They rounded the porch-man's house. At the corner of Beulah, the man with the bandoliers lay twisted, absolutely still. "He's dead," Ivy said, in a half-strangled, unbelieving voice.

"Yes." Jane felt lemon meringue putrid in her belly. "We should keep going." They passed Dora's, dark and silent as the other houses. On Oakland Avenue the smoky, crowded darkness popped with gunshots. A canister hissed. Steam? Tear gas: that's why her eyes hurt. The streetlights blurred overhead. Jane stubbed her toe hard on a piece of broken slate and her sandal broke. She bent to take it off. When she stood up, she saw Ivy running clumsily, one hand still clutching her shoulder, staggering toward two men on the sidewalk. Their hands shone pale under a streetlamp. White men. Bert's and Chuck's faces came into focus.

Ivy collided with Chuck; the two became one shadow under the street lamp. Bert's face was streaked with dirt and tears. "You got gassed," Jane said.

"Yup. Down on Auburndale. Police car burst into flame two yards away from us. We couldn't get near my place." Bert pressed the words out, his voice thick with significance. "It's begun," he said. "Here. Cleveland. If I weren't so white, I'd go down to Superior. There's gonna be action there."

Chuck's arms were wrapped around Ivy's waist; he was holding her up. "She needs to lie down," he said. "Get a car, we gotta go to the hospital." His voice rose.

Jane felt a kind of inner earthquake—first nausea, then anger. Then came a wave of tears—not for the beginning of *it*, nor because she'd brought Ivy here and now had to somehow get her to an emergency room. In her mind the dead man stared at her with a pleading, puzzled expression. A teenager who bled to death on the sidewalk. She felt Bert's hand on her back. "You okay?" he asked.

"We didn't help that kid," Jane wept. "We should have gone to Dora's again, should've stayed on the phone till we got an ambulance." Crying embarrassed her. She let her hair cover her face and turned away.

"Let's go inside, put Ivy to bed." Bert's hand parted the curtain of hair and turned palm up. "Your key," he said. "It's not gonna be safe to drive anything for awhile." The key was in Jane's purse, which had been over her shoulder the whole time. She brought it out and threw her hair back. All their faces were wet, the air still thick with tear gas.

PART THREE

The old books tell us what wisdom is:
Avoid the strife of the world, live out your little time
Fearing no one,
Using no violence,
Returning good for evil—
....
I can do none of this:
Indeed I live in the dark ages!
From "To Posterity" by Bertolt Brecht

"Hot Town, Summer in the City" played on car radios, transistors, stereos, and jukeboxes, filling Cleveland with gleeful menace from the Lake to the Heights, from Rocky River to Parma.

The Movement discovered Brecht's "To Posterity"— copied it out by hand, typed it on onionskin paper, ran it through ditto machines, mailed it to friends, taped it to bathroom walls, kept it folded and wadded in pockets. In the midst of an argument, someone could demand: "What times are these, when to speak of trees is almost a crime?" The poem told us: this is how we must live now.

On Wednesday morning, July 24th, the newspapers reported seven deaths in a two-block area of Glenville and four more a few blocks away. Three of the dead (and seven wounded men) were police officers. Three of the dead were members of the Republic of New Libya, headed by Ahmed Evans, who was under arrest. One death was labeled "civilian"—a man on his way home.

Wednesday afternoon Mayor Carl Stokes set up a barrier around Glenville, keeping out all white non-residents, including police. Black Nationalist leaders and Black policemen patrolled the streets together, talking to residents, calming them down. Within days the Ohio National Guard drove north in armored cars to patrol the perimeter that kept Blacks in and whites out. At Dora's urging, Jane and Tessa moved out of Glenville; Bert and Marvin followed.

In *Point of View*, Roldo Bartimole quoted Eldridge Cleaver and Frantz Fanon; what Republic of New Libya members had done, he wrote, "must be viewed as a deliberate, revolutionary, and political act. It may be the first such act in the ghetto rebellions plaguing this nation." By the end of the summer Evans would be charged with seven murders; the following spring he would be found guilty by an all-white jury and sentenced to death. He would die of cancer, still in prison, in 1978.

In Chicago the Mobe continued to request permits to demonstrate peacefully at the Democratic Convention, and Chicago's Mayor Daley continued to refuse. He'd given orders in April after King's assassination: *Shoot to kill arsonists. Shoot to maim looters.* Over the phone, in meetings, and in coffee shops, the Movement argued. Should we march peacefully with the Mobe? Join the Yippies' Festival of Life? Perform creative, symbolic acts of vandalism? Bert Augustin drew a street map of Chicago on brown paper, filling in the details by phoning SDS organizers who lived there. "Shoot to maim," he muttered. "How do you shoot to maim?" When Jimmy and Greg invited him out for beer, he snarled at them for lack of revolutionary consciousness. Then he pulled "To Posterity" out of his back pocket and hammered it to the basement door.

Chapter 13

August 17, 1968
University Circle

Chuck crossed the vacant lot behind The Monmouth, next to the used-car place. Saturday morning, alone again. He liked to walk with the streets empty, the light pale, the air still cool. His sneakers crunched cinders; an oily breeze lifted his hair. He'd wakened in Ivy's arms, her leg over his hip, tongue-kissing, tangling and untangling, rising to climax, then more kissing—oh, delicious; while darkness faded they came three times—and now she was doing the breakfast shift at The Big Penny. Chuck felt good in his body, loose-limbed and thriving. He had no particular destination, no particular time he had to be anywhere.

So he walked onto 115th Street and kept going, past crowded-together houses losing their paint, with a window boarded up here and there, past a corner shop still closed, with "Air conditioning!" painted on the wall. He crossed Wade Park and saw an olive-drab truck: National Guard. Crossed Ashbury: another truck. Two soldiers leaned against it, smoking. Lakeview was one block from here. He'd returned to the Glenville neighborhood for the first time since the fire-fight.

They had all stayed away. Bert and Marvin moved to a place in East Cleveland. Jane and Tessa had an apartment on Coventry Road. For the extra monthly payments they relied on parents. Chuck had given up any wish to do that; in six weeks or so he'd be done with Lake Erie Savings & Loan. He stopped walking. Sunlight filtered through the maple leaves.

He'd been filling his notebook with information about the Glenville firefight. Roldo had loaned him a copy of the police report which counted three dead and eleven wounded as "suspects," another dead man and three more injuries as "civilians."

"So now the Republic of New Libya officially has a military?" Chuck wrote. The tow-truck operator's bullet wound was in the police report; Ivy's bullet-torn shoulder was not. She'd told the emergency room doctor she'd been practicing with a borrowed rifle. That made sense to the doctor: a lot of Clevelanders were learning to shoot guns. Ivy's shoulder wound had closed within a week, and the dark red scar itched and burned. "With rage," she liked to whisper, "in solidarity with the oppressed peoples of the world."

After the guns had stopped, about 11:00 that night, Ahmed had walked out of an attic and surrendered to the police. He'd been there for three hours and hadn't fired a shot because his carbine had jammed. No spent shells were found in the attic. Sheldon had talked to the attic's owner, who confided that Ahmed was "kinda sorry he hadn't killed those policemen. In the neighborhood we been watching them all afternoon, sitting in the patrol cars parked on Lakeview, drinking beer and hard stuff, too." Chuck wrote the whole thing down.

His collection of facts was lining up against police. Evans was the only one who'd been charged with any deaths, yet his jammed carbine had been found in the bushes where he'd tossed it before he went to the attic. Roving white men had killed two Black men waiting for a bus on St. Clair, but no one had been charged with those deaths. During the Mayor's cordon, the police radio had picked up comments like "Fuck that nigger mayor!" from white policemen in their cars. Chuck just kept writing, though he didn't know what he'd do with the information. It didn't seem like it belonged to him.

Now, rather than turning away from the intersection where a man had been killed in Chuck's presence, he forced himself to keep walking. Three weeks—no, he forced himself to be accurate: it had been three and a half weeks ago. He'd encouraged Thomas to open his car door to a wounded policeman.

He and Bert had come from the State liquor store down Auburndale, oblivious to the sirens until they saw the intersection aswarm with running figures. A couple of rifles popped. Then came the rattle of a semi-automatic. A police cruiser exploded into flame, and Bert swore—"Holy shit!"—while Chuck clutched the rattling paper bag carrying bottles of Coke and cheap rum.

Ivy and Jane were somewhere in the foul-smelling dusk. Thinking to use the phone in the Lakeview Tavern across the street, Chuck paused on the curb, but Bert took his arm. "The pigs are carrying fucking automatics." Chuck followed Bert's gaze and saw the machine guns. The policemen wore large white helmets. "We got to figure out what's going down." Bert backed up a walk and sat on some porch steps.

Chuck sat next to him. "Do you know the people who live here?"

Bert shook his head *no* and then pointed. "Look there." A man lay half-under a cruiser: dark pants, white helmet—a policeman taking cover. "Open that rum." He slid the paper bag off the bottle and twisted the cap.

"No thanks," Chuck said. He wanted his wits about him. Flames and smoke swirled in the red cruiser-lights. "If we made it around the corner, could we get to your building?"

"Yep," Bert said. He swigged the rum. "And what that means is, my building is probably surrounded by people and pigs with guns. And what *that* means is," another swig, "the Revolution's begun." He jiggled his knees, incapable of stillness.

A young Black man came around the corner of the house.

"Hey, Thomas," Bert called softly. "What's happening?"

"Just trying to get home." Thomas obviously knew Bert, but the look was wary. When Bert shifted on the stoop, an invitation to sit, Thomas took a step backward. "My car's over there." He pointed with his chin toward a Ford Fairlane across the street. "Looks like hell, doesn't it?" The car was barely visible in the flickering darkness.

"Want a sip?" Bert passed the bottle to Thomas, who took a careful swallow and coughed.

"Not very good rum," Thomas said. He passed the bottle back. "Thanks."

Shouts erupted. Thuds. More gunfire. A figure flitted around the corner of the house—a youngster with bandoliers crossed on his chest, clutching a rifle—and darted into the garage next door.

"Where you going?" A policeman had come out of hiding and stood on the walk in front of them. "You boys won't have any fun here tonight," the cop said. "Tavern's closed."

Bert stood up and tossed his hair back over his shoulders; he was leaner and a head taller than the white-helmeted cop. "Actually, I live on Lakeview, two blocks from here," he said. "These are my friends." He waved toward Thomas and Chuck.

The cop looked at the three of them, assessing. "We could use your help," he said. "My partner's down. We need to get him some medical care. Where's your car?"

"I'm on foot," Bert said.

"Thomas has a car across the street," Chuck said.

"I'm going home. Wife and kids." Thomas shrugged and adjusted the half-rolled sleeves of his shirt. His hair was clipped close to his head, Chuck noticed: no Afro. He shrugged again and looked at Chuck. Chuck gave a nod. "If you keep me covered while I help your pal—" Thomas told the policeman.

"Let's go," the cop said. He put his hand on Thomas's shoulder, and the young man shrugged it off. They crossed the street and got into the Fairlane.

"Bad move," Bert said. "You just handed a brother over to the enemy."

"He needed to get to his car, get home," Chuck gritted his teeth. "And there's an injured human being. A life could be saved."

"No, a *pig*'s been injured," Bert insisted. "Not a life worth saving."

"That thought was not worthy of the Revolution," Chuck had written days later. Now, looking at the porch where they'd sat drinking rum, he felt a wave of wretchedness.

The Fairlane had nosed away from the curb and made its way toward the corner, then rolled into the intersection, stopping by the fallen man. The passenger door opened, then shut again as rifles cracked. There was an eruption of automatic fire. Flames appeared—gasoline leak?—on the pavement. The front of Thomas's car smoked.

"Let's split," Bert said, already running. Chuck caught up with him on 124th Street. They should've gone this way to begin with. Every shadow looked like Ivy charging into a street without looking; he would run till he found her. And then, thank God, he recognized her fast stumpy walk, her swinging hair. She came close and he saw blood streaking the hand she had clamped to her shoulder.

The bullet had ripped through the flesh and gone out the top of her shoulder. She was numb and weepy, rigid in his arms. Inside the apartment Jane cleaned and bandaged the wound, and Chuck held Ivy next to him on the couch till the middle of the night, after two houses had burned to the ground and Evans had been arrested. Then he got his car and took her to the emergency room where a doctor gave her five stitches and a knock-out pill. Chuck had left her asleep and gone to work.

At the Savings & Loan, every Black person in Cleveland had become a sniper or a looter or both; Junior referred to Stokes as "head coon." Chuck kept his mouth shut and tried to keep his eyes open. Days later he remembered the Draft Board Invasion. A few young men had been permitted to see their own records, as prescribed by law. That was all.

Not until last week did Chuck learn how Thomas had died—not in the spray of bullets or his own burning car; rather, he'd been shot in the head at close range with an automatic.

Not until yesterday had Chuck learned there was a law against police carrying automatic weapons.

Guilt stuck like a fishhook in his throat, Chuck walked away from the boarded-up Lakeview Tavern, the blood-stained asphalt, the charred ruins of two houses. He kept seeing the policeman, his face flicking, like one of those striated plastic pictures, from partner-rescuer to killer. He couldn't remember the cop's face, but the voice had been mild. He'd nodded *yes* to Thomas and then felt the *clang* of his own certainty against Bert's.

He'd disliked Bert's calling policemen *pigs*, but in that moment, when one of them fired into Thomas's temple, Bert had been proven right. "That's his car," Chuck had said to the policeman/cop/pig. Thomas had shrugged and smiled.

Now Chuck was walking along Magnolia Drive, the land of aging mansions where there was no police stake-out, no surveillance, no young men wearing bullets across their chests, no one getting killed by police illegally firing automatic weapons. Not yet.

Mrs. Nelson was weeding the flowers in front of the Quaker meeting house. Chuck hoped she wouldn't notice him. He didn't want to be asked why he had not come again to the Sunday silent meeting or what he'd done about Form 150. But just as he crossed the front walk, she sat back on her heels and waved at him. "So. Have you applied to be a conscientious objector?" She wore a straw hat with a brim, like a farmer; her face was open and friendly without demanding anything. He'd forgotten that he liked her.

Chuck stopped walking. "It's on my desk," he said, "asking if I believe in a Supreme Being." He'd been stumped on the first question. "The form's got only two boxes, *yes* and *no*."

"Ah." Mrs. Nelson pulled out a weed and laid it on the pile beside her. "You can't choose *no* if you want to be a conscientious objector," she said. "You must choose between *yes* and the blank space." Her hands in oversized gloves stirred up the soil, then patted it tenderly. "Please will you reach me the watering can?"

He found it and gave it to her. "How do I choose the blank space?"

"Write something like 'see attached.'" She tilted the can, dribbling water around the base of a rose bush. "Then you write exactly what you believe, in detail—two or three pages should be enough." Mrs. Nelson spoke with crisp European syllables, pronouncing the *t* in *exactly* and *detail*. She had come from Germany.

"But I'm not sure exactly what I believe," Chuck said. The existence of God was the least of his doubts. The sight of the National Guardsmen, just a few minutes ago, had made his hands itch for a rifle—just to carry, not to shoot. Unless he needed to.

"Of course, you are full of doubt," Mrs. Nelson said, as if she'd read his mind. "You are a thoughtful young man." She began to dig a hole in the soft soil of the flower bed. Under her rough apron she wore wide-legged jeans, Swedish clogs, and a light blue sweater over a blouse with a white collar closed at the throat with a silver pin. Her earrings were also silver.

"I have to send the application by the end of the week," Chuck said. It didn't seem like enough time to figure out exactly what he thought, much less to write a long explanation.

"But you have thirty days, haven't you?" She pushed herself up to her knees and then stood.

"Thirty days from when the re-classification letter was *mailed*. July 22nd."

"You received Form 150 three weeks ago and you let those *yes* and *no* boxes stop you?" Her voice was even. "Are you sure you *want* CO status?"

"Yes of course," Chuck said, too quickly. "It's just complicated."

"Complicated," she said, stretching, then dropping her arms. "Come with me while I clean up." Chuck followed her to the back yard.

"I'm thinking 1-O, community service," he said, while she laid the uprooted weeds on a pile of compost. The alternative was 1-O-A, noncombatant military service. He'd prefer a job as a hospital orderly or teacher in an inner city school. "The idea of service fits participatory democracy." *Participatory democracy* stood in his mind next to a man in overalls, holding a cap in his gnarled hard-working hands, speaking out at a meeting. A picture by Norman Rockwell. "Everybody has a voice, and everybody takes a turn cleaning streets or volunteering for the fire department."

"That idea fits into several major religions, you know," Mrs. Nelson said. "Now we go to the kitchen where I wash my hands." They went through the back door to the mudroom, where she slipped off her clogs. Chuck kicked off his sneakers. His feet were bare. Mrs. Nelson wore white socks. "What you are talking about is a society without heirarchy—and without war."

"No war, ever?" he asked.

"No executions, either," she said. "No guns."

A song danced in his head: *I dreamed the world had all agreed to put an end to war.* Ivy had sung that song on the way back from the Pentagon. Then Chuck had returned to school and learned about the Treaty of Versailles. The League of Nations had agreed to put an end to war and failed spectacularly. "Hitler had to be stopped," he said.

"Ah yes, Hitler had to be stopped," she nodded. "I escaped before he was stopped—and we did it without guns. The Friends helped me."

"Is that why you became a Quaker?"

"I suppose so. But we believe Hitler could have been stopped without war."

"How can you possibly believe that?"

She bent over the sink and turned on the water, washed her hands carefully with soap, rinsed them and turned off the water. Drying her hands on a very white towel, she turned to him. "What stopped Napoleon?"

Chuck shrugged. "The Russian winter?"

"Exactly," she said. "There is always another alternative to war."

"What would that have been, in Europe, twenty-five years ago?" he asked.

"I don't know," Mrs. Nelson said. "But thirty-five years ago the war could have been prevented." She sighed. "It's my faith, you see?"

"I'm not sure I have that kind of faith." Who could prevent the Cleveland police from shooting Black revolutionaries? What if the next uprising took place in the land of mansions? Bert would gladly wear bandoliers across his chest. And would Chuck attempt to help a wounded enemy? Or would he hide in an attic? Sometimes there were only two choices: shoot, or stand aside while an innocent man gets shot. If you're not prepared to shoot, you are part of the killing anyway.

"So you must learn what kind of faith you do have." Mrs. Nelson finished drying her hands and hung the towel on a hook next to the door. "I go now."

Chuck shook her clean, strong hand. "I'll get to work on that essay." Or maybe I won't, he thought, on the sidewalk again, walking past college fraternities closed for the summer. There were other ways to refuse induction. Some men enlisted and organized GIs. The Movement was growing inside the military. In Chuck's mind the essay changed from an attachment to Form 150 into a broadside, printed and handed out in front of the induction center. The title might be "Who is my Enemy?" The answer was something about recognizing one's humanity and keeping it alive, about how guilt was part of the process. *We are all complicit*, he thought. Mrs. Nelson drove by in her Volkswagen bus, waving and smiling. Even she was complicit, no matter how much faith she had, no matter how white her socks.

Near Guilford House, Chuck thought of Ivy, now flouncing around The Big Penny in her yellow dress, being adorable. Flirting was good for tips, she'd said. He thought, but I'm the one who made love to Ivy Barcelona this morning. He pictured how the tip of her tongue touched her upper lip while she wrote an order for biscuits and gravy, the neck of her dress open to that area right between her breasts. He pictured her on Bert's lap in the office, laughing, shaking her long hair over her face. Having fun, she'd said later. She refused to see men's lust. She was inviolate.

He crossed the church parking lot to Euclid Avenue, walking near the Church of the Covenant's great doors under its round stained-glass window. He and Ivy could get married here. They'd make invitations on the mimeograph machine in the church basement. Across the top, a slogan from Che Guevara: *At the risk of seeming ridiculous, let me say that a true revolutionary is guided by feelings of love.*

As if Che could bless their wedding? Slogans were false comfort. Chuck walked west and stopped. The landscape had been strangely disrupted. A beige brick tower protruded into Euclid Avenue, filling one lane behind a massive tractor. Claude Foster Hall was moving—yes it was, a few feet at a time. The monstrosity was flanked by workmen in hard hats who stopped traffic and guided the tractor. Ivy must have fed these men breakfast. Chuck came closer and heard them calling to each other in short barks, moving the thing that had never been meant to move. And now it was impossible to stop, inexorable as a glacier.

"Chuck! Hey, Chuck—over here!" Tessa stood on the Severance Hall staircase, waving, standing next to (he squinted to be sure) a bucket. "I'm cleaning the steps in exchange for a pass to the symphony," she explained, when he'd climbed up to her. She lifted her big push-broom and he grabbed the handle; she let him pull her near. "They're doing Mahler and Dvorak next Thursday," she said. "I'm a sucker for those guys."

The bucket was full of water; the broom was wet, and the steps above Tessa were wet. She'd scrubbed from the top down to where they stood. Her arms and legs were streaked with gray, her hair tangled; a strand hung over her forehead between her close-set eyes, making her look cross-eyed. Chuck took the lock between his thumb and fingers and tucked it behind her ear. Something about playing with the broom gave him permission to do that. Tessa smiled. Then she raised her arms over her head and stretched, turning her interlaced fingers inside out. The stretch raised the hem of her damp cotton shift to her crotch. "I like mindless work," she said. "Especially when it means wet stone in the middle of Saturday in August. And I get to go to the symphony." She wrinkled her forehead. "I guess I'm elitist about music. You coming to the meeting this afternoon?"

"The meeting?" Chuck had forgotten.

"We're planning for Chicago."

"Of course." The convention wouldn't start for another ten days. He hadn't even figured out how to take off work. "What kind of plans?"

She looked exasperated, and guilt pricked his throat. "Affinity groups. Specific actions. Transportation: who's driving, who's paying for gas. Someone needs to be in charge of food. We all need Vaseline and helmets."

"Helmets? Vaseline?"

"Police are going to use billy clubs. Maybe worse. And the Vaseline protects you from tear gas and pepper spray."

"Oh." Chicago, not Magnolia Drive. He'd been letting Ivy do the planning. She talked about going to Chicago as a kind of vacation: they'd travel together in the Pontiac, stop for hamburgers and soft ice cream cones along the way, stay in a motel on the way back. She'd bought him a used sleeping bag at army surplus, for three nights in the church basement. "This will be so *fun*," she'd said. "I can't *wait*."

They hadn't talked about what they'd actually do there, besides join the demonstrations. Chuck thought he should have a new notebook. He'd go one way, Ivy would go another; then they'd come together and tell what they'd seen, like Hemingway and Martha Gellhorn in the Spanish Civil War. He didn't want to wear a helmet or smear himself with Vaseline.

"What kind of actions?" he asked Tessa. She exuded superiority even holding a wet broom. Her bare feet were dirty too. And she turned him on, which made her even more provoking; he didn't want to get hard. The meeting would probably hash over the same stuff they'd been discussing for weeks, but if he didn't go he might miss an important decision. And sometimes, he thought, he was needed to help keep the Movement sane.

"So we'll see you around two?" Tessa was smiling with one side of her mouth, as though she could see that Chuck was aroused. Her nipples showed under the damp cloth of her dress.

He meant to just touch her shoulder and say 'bye for now, but when he felt her hands on his waist, he reached across her shoulders, pulled her to him, and kissed her mouth. *Kissing is nice.* He heard Ivy's voice in his head as if to give him permission. But he felt Tessa's cold breasts through his shirt. She was taking little sips of his mouth, her tongue flicking the delicate insides of his lips, and then his hands moved to her buttocks, pulling her close. He heard the broom clatter on the stone steps.

"You're a sweet man, Chuck Leggit," Tessa said, letting go, stepping back, smiling on one side of her mouth.

"You are...something else," he said. He tried to smile, but his mouth twitched several ways at once. He ran one hand through his hair, pulled his mustache. "I need to go now. See you this afternoon. Ivy and I will be there."

He walked down the steps and sprinted across Euclid to avoid the passage of Claude Foster Hall; then he looked back. Tessa was pushing her broom along the step. Her head bobbed with the strokes; the long handle thrust into the air behind her.

Chapter 14

August 19, 1968
Shapiro's Office & The Big Penny

"I'm curious." Ivy set Mr. Shapiro's coffee on his desk, her own coffee on the other desk. Bringing both coffees was part of her job; "You fly, I'll buy," he said every morning. Her shoulder was practically healed; the stitches were out, and there was no pain when she carried a large cup of coffee in her right hand. But she wasn't about to go sleeveless in front of Shapiro. He'd ask about the scar, and she couldn't tell him how she got it.

"You're always curious," Shapiro said. Then he winked. She distrusted his winks. Her father winked too, but only when he meant *This is a joke; get it?* Shapiro winked to signal a kind of friendliness, but Ivy had learned that his winks masked hostility. He meant, *Do what I say, and quit asking questions.*

He knew she did not like what she was supposed to do for the next several hours: phone for donations. Shapiro wouldn't explain where the money was actually going. Keep the job, Chuck advised; $3.25 an hour is better than $1.00 waitress-pay, and *fund-raiser* will look better on your resumé than *waitress*. "What if it's a scam?" she'd asked.

"If you find that out, you quit." Then Chuck told her about quitting his camera-selling job. "I needed money more than I needed to expose that camera outfit. Besides, the business was small potatoes, one guy up against a hard edge. He'd invested in a lousy product, and if he didn't sell it, he had nothing."

"How do you know all that?" Ivy asked.

"Just logic," Chuck had said. In other words, he was guessing.

If Shapiro was using donations for something other than the Poor People's Campaign, he needed to be exposed. She sat on her desk, swinging her legs and sipping her coffee. It was an old wooden desk; no donations had been spent on the office. "It's just that I've had questions from people on the phone; they want to know where their money is going."

"Tell them Ralph Abernathy," Shapiro said. "They'll recognize King's right-hand man. He's been in all the papers wearing those denim overalls, driving those mules all the way to Washington."

"But Resurrection City's been torn down and the marchers have all returned from Washington," she said. "The leadership's dissolving in squabbles over money."

"Smarty-pants," Shapiro stirred more sugar into his coffee. "Listen, the money's going to help poor people. Tell them about poor people. You've got statistics." He winked. "You're a talented young lady. You could have worked anywhere—but you care, so you chose this job. Now do it."

"If they paid attention, they'd learn that the PPC national coordinator recently lost three million dollars."

"I was just about to say—" Shapiro aimed his dark eyes over the rim of the Styrofoam cup. Eyes the color of beef gravy, the skin around them gray. "The money's in the bank. When it reaches $5,000 I send it to Abernathy, Martin Luther King's second-in-command. And he'll be happy to accept it."

"We haven't raised $5,000 yet?"

"We never will, if you don't stop asking questions and get on the phone, Ivy. Line up some bigger checks." Shapiro winked again as Ivy picked up her coffee and turned toward the phone desk in the corner.

Six hang-ups and ten no-homes. The next person answered and gave her scripture—"The poor you will always have with you"—in a reassuring voice, as though "the poor" had to be kept that way to fulfill some kind of duty to God.

Then came a ten dollar donation. She delivered profuse thanks and went back to dialing. How much of that particular donation was needed for the phone bill, the rent, her hourly wage, Shapiro's income? No wonder he'd been unable to amass even $5,000. No one was home, no one was home.

Then a vehement, ragged voice: "You want me to give my hard-earned money to those Blacks so they can buy guns and kill policemen? Shame on you! Shame!" Ivy wanted to scream facts—most of the poor in Cleveland are white; most Blacks would never kill a policeman—but the woman had hung up. Just as well.

Once upon a time, Ivy had believed in the land of liberty and justice, committed to equality or at least fairness. But when she looked, she'd seen that equality and fairness had always been limited to white male property-owners. Glenville had exposed the brittle hypocrisy. Ivy's bullet-wound was proof: she had been a witness to the police carrying automatic weapons. She'd seen houses in flame and burning to the ground because no fire trucks would come. She'd seen a young man die on the sidewalk.

The amazing thing was that the asthma, even that night in the Crystal constricting her lungs, had vanished with the gunshot. Adrenaline rush, of course, but it was still gone. She felt better than she had in months, energetic and clear-headed.

She kept calling, doggedly, counting telephone rings, delivering lines, politely taking *no* for an answer. She no longer cared what Shapiro was up to. She was ashamed of this job, even right now, dialing another Pepper Pike phone number, counting the rings, two, three, four. Yet she liked how it felt to be in an office downtown, dressed in a shirtwaist, stockings, and new bone-colored slingback pumps. She liked having money to buy shoes, and she liked having a title: office manager, fund raiser for Dr. King's campaign, for the Poor who would always be with us because what would we do without them? We'd have to beg for ourselves. Plead for mercy.

"Hello?" A woman's voice answered on the sixth ring. Quavery. An old lady had taken a long time to come to the phone.

"Oh! I've got the wrong number," Ivy said. "I'm so sorry."

"Never mind, dear," the voice said.

Ivy hung up. She *was* sorry. Her ear and her palm were hot from clutching the phone. "I'm going to get lunch," she told Shapiro, handing him the name and the address where he could pick up the ten dollar check she'd raised with two hours' work.

She should have given him a bogus address, she realized, waiting in the coffee shop for her Coke and BLT, his coffee with cream and pastrami on rye. She should have called the ten-dollar donor back and said, *Don't do this, okay?*

When she returned to the office, he was looking out of the window. There was something odd about him, even from the back. "The money's gone," he said. He stood completely still: that's what was strange.

"You sent it to Abernathy?"

He turned, but he didn't look at her. "Stolen," he said. "One of those college boys that worked for us last week. The head teller described him."

"The guy who raised $77 in one day," Ivy said.

"Yeah." Shapiro rubbed the back of his neck, where the short hairs were gray. "Took a check out of the drawer and withdrew it. We'd raised $4,328." All that hard work down the drain. His face and shoulders drooped.

"What are you going to do now?" Ivy asked. She looked around the room: bare grimy walls, scarred and mismatched desks, rickety chairs. For the Movement, this office would be just fine, but for a middle-aged man who spent his days begging donations for a cause he wasn't involved in, this was a shabby life.

"Raise more," he pulled away from the window and faced her. "Call *The P.D.* and *The Press*, will you? I'm putting another ad in the Help Wanted section. Call it 'Charity, Unlimited,' this time. Nice name, don't you think?" His wink looked like a twitch or a spasm.

"Right now?" It was just barely possible that Mr. Shapiro was still on the legal side of honesty. Ivy thought of that $77 kid—working door-to-door on commission, way ahead of what any other door-to-door worker had been able to do, unable to match his own surprising record, and gone within five days. She would not call the papers.

"Yes, right now!" Shapiro said. "How do you think we're...?" He leaned forward, hands on his desk, his face pink and his eyes wide, looking at her now, almost pleading. It occurred to Ivy that whatever he was up to, he desperately needed money. Her face must have shown her thoughts, because he didn't finish his sentence. "Never mind," Shapiro said. "I shouldn't have asked. I was wishing I didn't have to let you go. I can't afford to pay you."

"Oh," she said. "I'm fired?" Her curiosity had settled the matter.

"You'll turn out fine. You're a smart cookie. I'll write you a reference, any time."

"Thanks," Ivy said. "I may need one." They shook hands before she left; his hand was wet, his face greasy with sweat and weariness.

She got off the bus near the Art Museum lagoon, thinking maybe the thief was Shapiro's partner. Maybe those two men would divide the money and start "Charity, Unlimited."

*Fund*amental change, she muttered, balancing along the low white marble wall edging the sidewalk. Funda*mental* change. Not funds, minds. She imagined a society where everyone had shelter and enough to eat. No one should have to beg. King and Abernathy hadn't intended their campaign to be about pleas for money, but that's all white liberals knew. Give money.

I'll give you revolution, Ivy promised. Three meals a day for everyone. And a telephone. Free medical care. No war sucking up young people's lives, no crime. Tonight she'd ask Kreb for more hours at The Big Penny, let him yell at her for being generous with pickles, cream, or Tabasco sauce. He couldn't stop her from caring about people. The People.

"Refill?" The man held up his coffee cup as Ivy came by. He'd occupied the corner booth for an hour, drinking coffee and water, reading Sunday's *Plain Dealer* someone had left behind yesterday.

"You need a sandwich with that," Ivy said. "The grill's turned off, but I can make you a chicken salad sandwich." Kreb would have ordered the guy to buy some food or quit taking space meant for paying customers. But it was 8:00; Kreb had left for the night. There were only two other booths occupied and a stout woman eating apple pie at the counter. Ivy needed tips, and the customers needed to know she didn't tolerate free-loaders.

"No thanks," the man said. "I'm not hungry, just need some more coffee. And I sure do like to watch you do your job." He was over thirty, with short hair and a blue polo shirt and glasses with plastic frames—middle class, not broke.

"You should see me make a chicken salad sandwich," Ivy said.

He sighed. "There's other things I'd rather watch. I'll bet you're a good dancer. Where do people dance on a Monday night in Cleveland?"

"I don't know." She avoided his eyes. Why bring up dancing if you're too cheap to order a sandwich? Ivy did not want a friendly chat with this man—not because Chuck hated her flirting and said it was dangerous, but because the man seemed faintly repulsive to her. Maybe she just wasn't in the mood.

Some conversations were useful. At The Big Penny Ivy learned things she'd never know otherwise. The Claude Foster Hall movers, for example, had a lot to say about cement blocks. Who would've thought there was so much to know about cement blocks? They introduced Ivy to Loretta Lynn and poor Patsy Cline. They let her try a bit of chewing tobacco, laughed when she chomped vigorously as though it were gum, kept laughing when she ran to the kitchen to flush out her mouth with water.

"They're not really interested in *you*," Chuck had said. "They're competing with each other, showing off."

Sometimes Chuck was wrong. One of the construction workers had asked about her art history major, then got her talking about the Dutch Masters and how they were different from Velasquez and El Greco. How Rubens was almost Spanish.

"You stand there running your mouth about great painters, and he's looking at your breasts," Chuck had said, "wondering when he'll get to fuck you."

Ivy had been too upset to ask Chuck if *he* liked to think about fucking waitresses. Just as well that he was now at the Movement office a mile away. When he was at home she felt as if he were spying on her from his third-floor window. She refilled the man's coffee cup, set it down, and felt the heat of his shoulder near her breast. "Okay, let's see you make a chicken sandwich," he said, smiling. Leering.

"On toast?"

"Mm hmm." He licked his upper lip. His tongue was disgusting. She never set out to be seductive; it just happened. She did not want to know the man's name—did not want his *desire*, which she could feel across the diner as she returned the coffee pot to its hotplate and bent over to get the bread from under the counter. He'd look better if the back of his neck weren't naked, if his ears didn't stick out, if he weren't wearing those glasses with pinkish frames, if his skin weren't so white and moist.

That scene with Shapiro still soured her. Had *he* been focusing on her boobs the whole time? Chuck had hinted as much. Did all men fantasize about sex with women, all the time? She felt the chill of the fridge on her face as she took out the white plastic tub of chicken salad. Why had she invited Mr.

Pink Glasses to watch her spread this pale, bland mess onto his toast? Why had she deliberately smiled and reached for Shapiro's hand when he'd fired her? Did *she* want to attract all the men? It would be dishonest to pretend she didn't have a quick throb of delight when the construction worker had asked to go with her to the Art Museum. She had noticed how his nose wrinkled when he smiled, how his forearms were tan and strong. Shame, Ivy.

"We could dance in my living room," said Pink Glasses, as she set down his sandwich. "Right after you get off work."

"Sorry, I've got a date," Ivy said.

"I mean it," he insisted. "When do you get off?"

"Too late for you." She turned away, roiling inside. How had she let this man think she might accept his invitation? She should have said, *My boyfriend, whom I live with and sleep with every night, expects me home.* But the truth was, she didn't want Chuck's expectations to bind her life. If he expected sex tonight, he'd get it, whether she felt like it or not. That's how things had been going.

The couple in the booth near the door had left, and now the fat woman had finished her every-night pie and was rolling off the stool by the counter, as if she were drunk on spices and sugar, apples and lard. Ivy cleared dishes and wiped the tables, feeling the moist pale eyes of the chicken-salad man on her back, wishing he would leave or someone else would arrive. Now, while she wiped down the counter. Now, while she replenished the salt and pepper shakers. Now, while she reached to the top shelf for the box of little sugar packets...

At last the door opened. Ivy flooded with warm relief: she knew these people—Bert Augustin and Shelly Kaplan, who said, "Oh good, there's Ivy." Shelly's smile took up half her face. Her collarbones stood sharp above the gathers of her gauzy blouse, her knobby knees white below her cut-off jeans.

Shelly settled into the booth across from Bert, who said, "All day long I been thinking about a grilled cheese sandwich," and slumped when Ivy told him the grill was off. "There's nothing to eat in this whole fucking city." His golden-brown hair fell over his face as he sank onto his elbows and opened a paperback book, as if to say Forget You.

"I can make a sandwich," Ivy said. "Chicken salad? Egg salad? Ham and Swiss? Bert shook his head no, no sandwich, nothing at all, and glared at his book.

Shelly ordered a Coke. "Hey Ivy, I been wanting to ask you," she said, ignoring Bert. "There's a place on Hessler Road opening up this fall. We could rent it if there were three of us— me, you, one other. What do you think?"

Hessler Road! A living room and a kitchen. No housemother. They could have meetings. Chuck could spend the night. "Does it have three bedrooms?"

Shelly nodded. She was an art major, had been in Sherman Lee's Asian art class. They'd been together at SDS meetings and anti-war marches, but they'd never talked politics. Nor had they talked about Bert; as Ivy poured Coke over ice and waited for the foam to settle, she wondered how long Bert and Shelly had dated. If they shared the place on Hessler Road, would Bert sleep over? She pictured Bert and Shelly with Chuck pouring wine, the four of them gathered in comfortable chairs, talking into the night. She loaded her arms and slalomed across the diner carrying Coke, straw, napkins, and ice water. Bert was talking now as Shelly listened, her eyes big under her cloud of hair.

"I could ask Gail Richards if she wanted to go in with us." Ivy placed drinks and did a wrist-flourish with each napkin. "She was on my hall in Guilford."

"I know Gail," Shelly said, nodding approval. "You talk to her, and when she says yes I'll call the landlord. Better ...What?" She asked Bert, who apparently disapproved of his ice water.

"Coffee," he said. "You got coffee at least?" He reminded Ivy of a hawk—head up, alert, with far-seeing dark eyes, looking at Ivy as if he didn't really mean coffee-at-least. Could she fall for *this* man? He was in her mind too often. In real life, as now, she could be cool around him. She turned her back with a swish and went for coffee.

Behind her came Shelly's voice: "No, Augustin, turning on the grill after 9:00 is *not* a revolutionary act."

Oh. He'd thought she could just fire up the grill and fix his sandwich. On Hessler Road, Ivy thought, we could fix grilled cheese at all hours. She admired Bert, that was all. He knew a lot of history: Russia, Cuba, China. He was in contact with SDS all over the country. He understood Marcuse and Debray.

"You wouldn't know a revolutionary act if it wore a sign around its neck, saying *This Way to the Ruling Class Yacht*," Bert said to Shelly. "And handed you a drill to bore through the hull."

"You're underestimating me again," Shelly's voice rose. Ivy got out sugar packets and poured cream in a little pitcher, moving slowly, pouring herself coffee, taking a sip, eavesdropping: they'd come from another meeting about Chicago, nothing was settled, and Bert was pissed off.

"No one *gets* it!" Bert slammed the table on *gets*. "If a little sorry-ass group like Ahmed's cultural nationalists could bring out the pigs and unmask all the bigoted reactionaries in Cleveland, then think what thousands of principled, educated revolutionaries can do if we get our act together in Chicago. If nothing else..."

"Why are you telling me this?" Shelly blew two lungs' worth of cigarette smoke at him. "You think can sell it to *me* when you couldn't convince Marvin or Jane?" She looked up as Ivy put down Bert's coffee. "Say, how's the Penny's pie?" Her face was flushed.

"Blueberry's good. So's apple." Ivy shielded her chest— her breasts, her heart—with the order pad.

"Listen up," Bert opened his book and read aloud. "'Wherever death may surprise us, let it be welcome, provided that this, our battle cry, may have reached some receptive ear and another hand may be extended to wield our weapons.' That's the attitude for Chicago." He saw Ivy cock her head toward the book. "*The Diary of Che Guevara.*" He stuck his thumb between the pages to mark his place and showed her the cover. "Just published by *Ramparts.*"

Che was an asthmatic. Ivy knew that government troops located him by finding the store where he'd bought his inhaler refills. Then they shot him down with automatic rifles. Maybe he'd written about asthma in his diary. She half-reached for the book.

"I'd like a slice of blueberry pie, please," Shelly said, pulling the elastic neck of her blouse back up over the edge of her shoulder.

"Apple pie," Bert said. "Why not?"

Ivy sliced pie and slid it onto dessert plates, thinking about Che. The Bolivian jungle was suddenly close: a small band of comrades moving through the trees, hands extended to push branches out of the path, clearing the way. Soldiers, hiding in the leafy shadows, raise their guns. Battle cry. Welcome death. *That* much commitment was required. The pie knife was huge and pointed, a weapon if she needed one. She looked toward the booth where the chicken salad sandwich man had flirted with her—menaced her, really. With his naked ears and his shaved neck, he looked like a soldier or a cop.

She came out with the pie slices and saw the man's booth was empty; on the table sat a glass, a coffee cup, and a balled-up napkin on the empty plate. He hadn't even asked for his check. Ivy tripped—not much, just enough to tip the blueberry pie off its plate. Purple goop on the floor, her legs, her dress. Missed the apron entirely. Dammit. Shelly and Bert laughed as Ivy delivered the apple pie and went to get another slice of blueberry.

Then she went to the rest room to clean up. Her skirt was soaking wet and still purple-stained when Shelly burst in. "I'm sorry. We weren't laughing at you," she said.

"Yeah, you were laughing *with* me," Ivy said. "It's okay. This has been a hard day." She took a breath, planning to tell all of it—the loss of her job with Shapiro, the leering cheapskate in the polo shirt, and Chuck's...no, nothing about Chuck.

But Shelly spoke first. "The thing is, I'm really worried about Robbie."

"Robbie?"

"Bert. Sorry. His real name is Robert. We went to high school together. I forget that he changed his name. Shit, Ivy, he was such a good-hearted kid in high school."

"Isn't he still?" Ivy asked. She was bent like a half-folded jacknife, wiping down her stockings, the wet nylon skirt clammy against her arms. "I think he was galvanized by Glenville. He doesn't mean we should all carry rifles in Chicago; he means..."

"I was with him all day," Shelly said. "I know what he means. He's pissed because Marvin got critical, and Marvin was right; if it weren't for Rob...Bert, we could've come to agreement. He knows what I think; that's why he read Che Guevara out loud."

"What else happened at the meeting?" Ivy looked in the mirror. Her hair was wild, her dress soaked with water and splotched with blueberry stains. What a mess.

"Oh, Tessa Buchanan gave us a protective armor-list: helmets, goggles, baggies with damp washcloths for the tear gas. We talked options—guerilla theatre with the Yippies, Zengakuren with the Mobe, radicalize the McCarthy kids, put up daily bulletins on walls all over the city. I'm not going."

"Why not?" Ivy looked in the mirror at Shelly's teary eyes. Chuck would write the bulletins, Ivy thought. She and Jane planned to visit the Ohio delegates—listen to them, try to radicalize them.

"Because," Shelly said, her teeth clenched. "I'm going to spend two weeks with my family—Mom, Dad, Aunts, Uncles, Cousins, Grandma—who I haven't seen since the last night of Hanukah, and I miss them. We've got a beach house on Long Island. I am going to take a fucking *vacation*."

"I guess you told Bert."

"Yeah. What else should I do? Lie?"

"That's why he's in a funk." Ivy could see Bert's point of view: he must have been furious—his girlfriend, of all people, returning to the bourgeoisie.

"He was gloomy long before I told him I wasn't going." Shelly lit a cigarette. "I'm not really *his*, you know what I mean? We're not exclusive or anything, just old friends. Although," she inhaled smoke and blew it out, "Just before I came in here, I thought he was gonna hit me."

"Just now? Did you just tell him about Long Island?"

"I didn't make up my mind for sure, till then." Shelly shrugged. "He was showing me the sap he'd made."

"The what?"

"A weapon. A piece of hose with a metal fishing-sinker on one end; that's what he tried to hit me with, and it would have hurt like hell. I had to get out of his way." Shelly dragged on her cigarette—in, out. "I just want to leave. I don't want to even talk to him. Will you go first? Then I can sidle out behind you. Here, he probably won't pay." Shelly handed Ivy two dollars.

Stuffing the bills in her apron pocket, Ivy calculated the price in her head—Coke, coffee, and two pie slices; she'd lose fifty cents, if she couldn't get it from Bert.

He hunched over *The Diary of Che Guevara*, not even looking up as Shelly slipped out the door. Ivy got a rag from behind the counter to wipe down the table where the chicken salad man had sat leering—and hadn't paid a cent. "Jerk," she muttered.

"Hey, Ivy, saw your man at the meeting." Bert spread-eagled his book and beckoned.

"Yeah. So?"

"Talk to me, okay?"

"Okay." Ivy sat down across from him. "You got another disagreement with Chuck?"

"Nah." Bert combed back his hair with his fingers. "Unless he's got one with me. He and Marvin were still at it when we left, round and round, trying to avoid what's coming.

It's gonna come." He leaned into the middle of the table, hands clasped, staring at the dark gray Formica. "Che had *heart*, you know what I mean?" Bert patted himself on the chest. "You do know. You got shot in Glenville. We can't join the Black vanguard. But we can support them and commit to the struggle. We're the hope of the world. If we fail...oh fuck, we *can't* fail."

"Hard rain's gonna fall," Ivy said. She couldn't think of anything else to say.

"Yeah. Also: there's just more *people* in our generation than in theirs. And we'll live longer. We're the first generation living with nuclear warheads. We all watched the same TV shows. We're going to take over, and they know it. The Chicago pigs are preparing to slam us. It shows their weakness, but we got to be ready." He was dead serious now. "It's heavy, man, and I guess I shouldn't expect too much of people. But shit: Long Island beach house!" He had noticed Shelly leave, after all. He noticed everything. He just couldn't understand why others hadn't kept up with him. Ivy hadn't kept up with him. Suddenly she wished she could.

She understood there had to be a revolution. But carrying a weapon to Chicago, even a homemade sap, seemed crazy. "People have different skills," she said, carefully. She didn't mean to touch Bert, but her knuckle brushed his mangled finger, and he grasped her hand. "Different ways to contribute," she went on, thinking of Chuck's writing, and his leaning toward pacifism. Bert was no pacifist—but Chuck might be. And Ivy might be, too. She wasn't sure.

"If everybody goes in his own private direction we get nowhere. We need discipline." Bert sat straight, looming over her. "We don't have the luxury of each-his-own, do-your-own thing—not when we go for a comfortable drink among friends and get shot at by cops. Not when we get infiltrated and betrayed to the FBI. Discipline," he said again. "We're soldiers for the cause."

"If we turn into soldiers, doesn't that defeat what we're working for?" Ivy thought of the "Spy vs. Spy" cartoon in *Mad*

Magazine: the black spy looked exactly like the white spy, and every month they found new ways to kill each other (death signified by little crosses in the pointy faces where their eyes had been). Neither one was the good guy. Or the bad guy.

But Bert had mentioned the infiltrator. The betrayer. They had a spy in their midst who couldn't be a good guy.

"Sometimes you have to accept being a soldier." Bert tapped the back of her hand three times. "We're *right*. That's the difference. We *know* imperialism is bad—in Algiers, in Guatemala, in Cuba and China and Vietnam. We're young, that's all. And we're in the belly of the beast."

She should read Che's diary. "I've got to close this place," she said. "And you owe me fifty cents. Shelly paid the rest. I wouldn't ask, but it's been a pretty bad day."

He didn't ask what had happened, just dug two quarters out of his pocket, pressed them into her hand, and hugged her. He held her close for a full minute, one hand stroking her back.

Ivy hung up the "Closed" sign and swept the floor. In the soft strokes of the broom, the gathering of crumbs, cigarette ashes, and torn napkins, she thought how Chuck would tell her what really happened at the meeting. Shelly was surprised by Bert's militancy, no doubt; she hadn't been in Glenville. All of a sudden Ivy wanted Chuck—wanted to have sex with him, starting with her tongue in the hollow at his throat. She and Chuck would plan their days in Chicago together.

She washed the dishes quickly, quickly, and ran out the door of the Big Penny, across to The Monmouth, up the first flight, the second, the third, worked the key in the lock. "I'm back," she called.

Chuck stood in the middle of the room in his work suit. He must have gone straight from the Savings & Loan to the Movement office and then the meeting. If he'd been home for longer than two minutes his shoes would be off. "Long meeting," he said. "You got stains on your uniform."

"Blueberry. I hope it'll wash out." Ivy began loosening his tie. "Bert and Shelly came to The Big Penny arguing about Chicago."

"We all were arguing," Chuck said. "And..."

Ivy felt his hand on the back of her head. "And?"

"I'm not going," Chuck said.

She stepped away from him. "What the hell happened?"

"Someone needs to man the office. Our people will be all over Chicago, getting arrested, getting hurt. The jail allows one phone call: so call the office. Or if you get lost, you call the office. Here, we keep track of where everybody is. It's a communication center." He yanked at his tie as he talked, took off his jacket, hung it over a chair, and rolled up his sleeves, not looking at Ivy. She stopped herself from crying and turned off the red flood of anger so she could think.

Chuck and Marvin would have been working this out while Ivy was spilling blueberry pie and talking to Shelly. Chuck would offer to sacrifice for the good of the Movement; he wanted to be the good guy, not a coward. Watching him step out of his banker's wingtips, she thought he could easily be both. And in the process he'd agreed to abandon her—after all that concern about her *flirting*. Why?

"Look," he said, putting his arms around her, still not looking at her. "We'll have fun, you and me in the office, sleeping bags on the floor, reading, writing, taking turns on the phone."

Oh. He'd volunteered her, too. "Couldn't anyone else do it? Anyone?"

"Had to be someone who couldn't be suspected of informing," Chuck said.

She wasn't satisfied. For the past two months she'd aimed herself like an arrow toward Chicago. "I'm cleaning up," she said, taking her nightgown with her into the bathroom. There she peeled off her stained dress and stockings, scrubbed herself with a washcloth, and stopped thinking. She let herself cry, briefly, and washed her face.

When she came out, Chuck was in bed with *Ten Days that Shook the World* and she'd made up her mind. "I'll miss you, Babe," she said, "when I'm in Chicago."

Chapter 15

August 23-24, 1968
Minneapolis, Chicago

Jane stood on her parents' porch watching a Packard the color of a lima bean crawl by; the driver must havebeen looking at house numbers. Were the police watching her even here? It was not yet time for the Minneapolis SDS people to pick her up on their way to Chicago. The FBI? She felt trapped and furious. The Packard stopped at the corner, then went on. Maybe the driver was just a normal person. At any rate, she'd given him nothing to watch. She might not even go to Chicago.

Daddy's second heart attack had come on Tuesday, and Chuck had driven Jane to the airport. They didn't talk; she'd been choked silent with terror (Daddy in Intensive Care) and guilt (her promise to phone, broken and broken again). Chuck was kind—the most selfless guy in the Cleveland Movement. Jane was glad he'd volunteered to stay in the office; they'd need him. He didn't ask questions, just turned on the car radio, so they heard when the Russian tanks rolled into Prague, crushing *that* revolution.

And today, Friday, the National Guard tanks were on their way to Chicago. Maybe some were finally leaving Glenville. "Those guardsmen must be angry," Mom said. "They've given up summer vacations." She'd come to the porch with a broom and was sweeping in short, quick jerks. One side was clean when she stopped. "You haven't finished packing," she said.

"I'll stay here," Jane said. "The counter-convention will go on in Chicago whether I'm there or not." How small and fragile her parents' lives had become. Daddy was in bed, keeping still to avoid upsetting his weak heart. Mom had taken leave without pay to look after him, so now she worried about money on top of everything else. Because she couldn't share the bed with Daddy while he was so weak, she'd been spending nights in Jane's old room, sleeping only fitfully, exhausted all the time. "And this is what they call a successful heart operation," she'd laughed.

For three days Jane had been running errands in their Ford, putting away all the half-finished sewing and throwing out the wrapping paper and old magazines so her mother could be comfortable in the little room. She'd cooked Daddy's low-fat, no-salt foods. She couldn't leave now. They needed her. For the past five years she'd been a terrible daughter, abandoning them as they scuttled in ever-narrowing circles between their jobs and the couch in front of the television. They'd talked of traveling through Canada when they retired, then through Europe. They'd planned to buy a boat for pleasure trips on the river. Now they would go nowhere. She should stay at least till Daddy was well enough to be alone while Mom went to work. Across the street the sun was setting between two houses, a flaming inverted bowl sinking into the trees.

Mom swept the porch dirt onto a dustpan. "Dad wants to see you before you leave," she said. "Take him some Jell-O. Go. He's hungry."

From the bedroom doorway he looked terribly small and pale. He smiled at Jane weakly and raised his hand when she approached—a warding-off gesture.

The bedroom was stuffy, with a sick smell she couldn't peg to anything. Her father was slumped to one side. "Let's prop you up a little better," Jane said, reaching behind him to straighten the pillows. He took the bowl of Jell-O and held it in both hands.

"Czechago, Czechago, your kind of a town," he sang feebly. A little joke.

"I've decided not to go," she said. "You and Mom need me here."

Dad spooned Jell-O slowly to avoid spilling. He swallowed and said, "Wrong decision."

She thought she'd misheard until she looked at his eyes—intelligent, piercing. "But Dad, it's important to me..." She was going to say, "to make sure you and Mom are all right."

He cut her off. "It's more important that you go," he said. "Give those Democrats hell in my name. Show the world they can't keep on the way they've been doing."

"Oh." Jane felt like crying. "I'll worry about you."

"Likewise," said her father.

"You represent me too," Mom was standing in the doorway. "I'll get you some cash—with some change so you can phone us."

"I'll get stronger, Jane," he said. "Next time you see me, I'll be bounding around."

"Don't kiss him," Mom said. "We've got to be really careful about germs."

It was time to pack; the sun had set and the trip would take most of the night. The local SDS people had said they didn't want to wait around.

In Chicago on Saturday Jane found Tessa in the women's demonstration and forgot all her doubts about coming. The sidewalk in front of the Conrad Hilton was filled with women—all women, *only* women, marching in a circle. A few men on the sidelines watched with dour, puzzled faces. Jane raised her *Women Strike for Peace* sign high and straightened her shoulders under her backpack.

What do we want? When do we want it? Next to Jane, Tessa shouted *Peace! Now!* The old question-and-answer cry rang hollow, divorced from its words. Jane began to substitute "Liberation!" for *Peace!* Tessa added "Justice!"

At the last meeting in Cleveland they'd agreed, finally, on nothing but to keep close and go with the flow. They would be an affinity group—Jane, Tessa, Marvin, Bert, and Jimmy; Ivy would come later. Bert chose a large maple tree in Lincoln Park where they could post messages to each other. They stowed thumb tacks, paper, and pencils in their backpacks. "Revolution!" Tessa yelled, as she passed the Conrad Hilton door. Chicago police in sky-blue helmets and matching short-sleeved shirts watched with hands behind their backs. A police van stood at the corner, its windows reinforced with wire—waiting to be filled with protestors under arrest. The police had already killed a teenaged boy, an Indian, two days ago.

Jane remembered her first picket line: She'd had to reach up to hold onto her mother's hand outside a department store. Strikes seemed to be always in cold weather, and they were always called "strikes" rather than "demonstrations." They dressed in hats and sober coats—dark blue, brown, or gray, collars buttoned, with scarves and gloves. Mom smiled as she marched, sometimes talking with the other men and women, sometimes laughing. Daddy walked silently with his shoulders hunched, his sign over one shoulder, his jaw set. When people scuttled across the line, trying not to meet anyone's eyes, he shouted "Scab!" Those people were hurting the strike. "A scab puts his own greed ahead of the people's welfare," Daddy said. "It's worse than stealing."

In front of the Conrad Hilton, the air was cool under the awning and hot in the sunshine. The loop of marchers moved from shade to sun and back to shade. Most of the women wore dresses and sandals—moderate, conciliatory outfits. Jane and Tessa wore jeans. Jane was happy: here was the Feminist Movement. Tessa was bored with circling. "I'm jumping out of my skin," she whispered. "Sorry Jane, I'm going back to Lincoln Park where there's action. Music, too." She bolted from the line, leaping across the path of two women, blew a kiss to Jane, and loped up Michigan Avenue. Policemen turned their heads to watch her go, their helmets a row of enormous swiveling robins' eggs.

Inside the lobby, delegates and politicians glanced at the protesting women and turned away when they saw they were being looked at. Two bellhops stared; one smiled and made the V-sign with his hand. Jane laughed and waved. The inside of the hotel looked like an aquarium, with dressed-up people moving silent as tropical fish, glassed-away from the gritty world. "Those policemen look as if they're hiding erections or trying to keep from peeing," said a voice behind Jane. Sure enough, the cops stood with their legs spread, holding nightsticks across their crotches.

Jane turned to look at the speaker, a round-faced woman with freckles.

"Nothing threatens men like organized women." She took two trotting steps to walk next to Jane. "They can't charge a peaceful picket line in front of the Conrad Hilton: the most important Democrats are staying here. McCarthy headquarters are here." Jane glanced through the glass: A red dress and two black suits stood stiffly: slim, hard bodies, bland faces. They looked like mannequins.

"I'm Patricia," the woman said. She was older than Jane, past thirty, dressed in a polka-dot shift. Her low, conversational voice made her words shocking. "Men are chiefly concerned about the size of their dicks, whether they're in bed with us or in political meetings. The Vietnam war makes sense only as an effort to keep America's big dick from going soft. But we know American men are getting the pants beat off them by a bunch of barefoot soldiers in pajamas—men and women both. Where you from?"

"Cleveland. Movement for a Democratic Society. You?"

"Boston Female Liberation. I came here with Women Strike for Peace."

Behind them two girls started singing "The Battle Hymn of the Republic," a tired old patriotic war-song. But at the second line Jane realized they had changed it—"She is trampling out the vintage where the grapes of wrath are stored"—and joined in. There's action here, Jane thought; patient, determined, female; Tessa had missed the point. "Her truth is marching on."

At the message tree, a policeman in jodhpurs and riding boots was talking to a man in a white shirt. Jane crouched behind a bush and peered through the foliage. The white-shirted guy was Marvin with a haircut, bullet-headed and beaky. "At least they won't be able to put the LSD in the water supply," the cop was saying. His shirt and his helmet were horribly blue. His club dangled from his hand. "We got a permanent guard on the reservoirs. You can't be too careful. Those people may seem innocent, all peace-and-lovey-dovey." He jerked his chin toward the Yippie festival on the lawn. A crowd swirled among the tents and tables. "Okay, I'll grant your point: some of them mean well. But why do they have to get so hairy and refuse to bathe? When you get down-wind, whew!" He fanned away imaginary odor with his hand.

"You'd think they'd just settle for a few stink bombs, wouldn't you?" Marvin said placidly. How long had he been playing with this cop? Had he cut his hair just so Chicago police would talk to him?

"Oh, they can't get enough of stink, they wallow in it," the cop said. "All that marijuana messes with their smell systems." He delivered this bullshit with astonishing authority.

Tessa appeared, wearing a football helmet and carrying a loaf of bread under her arm. She dropped next to Jane. "There ought to be festivals like this in every city, all the time," she said. "Free books. Free food. Thousands of people." She broke off a hunk of bread and handed it to Jane. "Free rock concert soon. The Motor City Five."

Jane bit off a mouthful and chewed, wondering how many thousand people milled around the tables filled with food, pamphlets, jewelry made of beads and leather, more stuff she couldn't imagine. The bread was dark and crumbly, with whole grains of wheat and sunflower seeds. "I don't know if I could stand being this groovy all the time," she said.

"You'll feel better when you've had a drink." Tessa pulled a bottle of apple juice out of her backpack and set it on the grass next to Jane's knee. The policeman was still talking, and Marvin was nodding soberly. He flapped his hand toward Jane, a hi-there-but-stay-away movement. Jane ducked behind the bush again.

"The bad smell is just a way to annoy us, a sign of their *sociopathology.*" The policeman rolled out the word with knowing assurance. "We're really looking for the masterminds. We know they're here."

"You mean...?"

The policeman leaned in close and muttered something.

"Communists!" Marvin said loudly. "You don't say! Well, they certainly have changed. The last Communist Party members I met would never have come up with something called the Festival of Life."

The cop glanced down the hill at the tent-village. A crowd of hundreds seemed to have congealed around something. "Hey, hey—what'd I tell you," the cop nudged Marvin. "Trouble. You better go on home." He trotted toward a cluster of blue helmets at the edge of the field.

Tessa stood up, pulling Jane with her. Through the trees, Jane saw a flatbed truck surrounded by police and a swarm of park people. There was a flurry—police were attacking with clubs, pushing park people to the ground. "The truck was supposed to be a stage for the rock concert." Tessa swigged apple juice and passed the bottle back to Jane. "There's Bert with Jimmy Fulero." Long hair streaming from under their helmets, the two men loped toward the flatbed, urging others to join them, yelling "Come on! Come on!" and beckoning.

"Aren't you going down there?" Jane asked Tessa.

Tessa shook her head. "I'm going that way." She pointed to the edge of the tent city. "Medical Committee for Human Rights tent; we'll be needed for First Aid."

"Who knows what violence folks might commit with a flatbed truck?" Marvin joined them. He nibbled bread and squinted into the distance where police were dragging three people by their arms. The flatbed truck was leaving.

Jane felt her head fizz inside. "Did you put vodka in the apple juice?"

"Took you a while, huh?" Tessa smiled.

Jane was too dizzy to run down the slope and swell the ranks of the crowd. She decided to wait until her head had cleared and lay down next to Marvin. "What did you do with your hair?" she asked.

"I figured I should stay cool," Marvin said. "Long hair gets hot." He put one arm around Jane and pulled her closer, so her head was on his shoulder. The concert had started after all. The opening chords swelled and burst like glowing soap bubbles in the greasy air.

"It's good to be here with you," Jane said. "And Tessa."

"Actually," Marvin said into her ear, "I cut my hair for my mother. She lives in Evanston. I paid her a visit yesterday." Jane had not known that about Marvin's mother. Drowsily, she wondered what else she didn't know about him. He turned and nuzzled Jane's hair with his long nose. Then he kissed her on the cheek, reached with his hand to turn her face so he could kiss her lips.

"Don't," Jane said. "I'm so fond of you, I don't want to be kissed." She wasn't sure why kissing Marvin felt so wrong. "What kind of political confrontation is it when cops fight kids over an impromptu band stage?"

"The police are pretty easy to provoke," Marvin said. "You heard that goon in the shiny boots. I let him talk just to get the full extent of his craziness—which I'm sure has been passed along as official information." Jane thought again of that young man dying on the sidewalk, at the corner of Beulah and 123rd—his eyes, trying to look at her, trying to focus, his lips moving to say something. Dora had told her he was seventeen. Dora also knew what had happened at the bus stop on St. Clair; several white men had pulled over, jumped out of their car, beaten the two Black men to the ground, and shot one in the head. No one had been arrested for that murder. Jane's loathing for anonymous white men festered in her stomach.

"I'm fond of you too," Marvin said. He passed the apple juice bottle.

"Thanks," said Jane. "No, no more." She hadn't meant to get drunk. *I'm sorry, Daddy,* she said to her father, who sat among pillows in her mind. *Czechago, Czechago.*

Tessa reappeared. "Something's going down—holy shit, let's go." She pulled Jane to her feet. Marvin stood and grabbed her other hand. Jane wasn't ready, but she ran anyway, down the slope, among people who stood watching and murmuring, then among people who were running too, until it was no longer possible to run amid the bodies. Her head reeled.

Bert and Jimmy were overturning picnic tables to make a barricade. "We're claiming the park," Bert yelled. Suddenly Jane was shoved from behind; weighted by her backpack, she landed on hands and knees. Marvin pulled her up. Police billy clubs waved above the crowd.Cries, shouts, thuds. Jane clutched Marvin's and Tessa's hands. They had to run to stay upright. A blow landed on Marvin's head, cracking like a rifle shot.

Tessa swooped down to kneel beside him. "He's out cold," she said. "Keep people away, would you? Give the man some room!"

Two police yanked Tessa's arms and pulled her away so they could kick Marvin, who was not out cold; he held his hands to his face, knees to his chest. Kick kick to the head and back, kick kick to butt and groin. Marvin groaned and lay still. The police vanished in the crowd, and Tessa crawled to Marvin's side.

Jane put out her arms and called, "Stay back!" making a great fan of her body, trying to be as big as three people. A little space formed around Marvin and Tessa on the ground. Outside that space, the clubbing continued.

"Motherfuck!" Jimmy yelled, to no one Jane could see. He held up a forked stick with a piece of rubber tubing and put a marble in the slingshot.

Jane lurched forward. "What the hell are you doing?"

"Protecting us," Jimmy said. He let fly. The marble *thunked* against a blue helmet, and the cop whirled around. Three helmets popped up next to his.

"Now you've done it, you little shit," Jane muttered. She put her arms out, to give Marvin space. He was trying to rise. Jimmy loaded another marble. The helmets surged closer, clubs bobbing over the crowd.

"He's getting up now," Tessa shouted at Jane. "Help me lift him."

Marvin looked sheepish on all fours; Jane put her shoulder under his arm as he stood up slowly, Tessa on the other side. "I think I should..." Either he didn't finish, or Jane couldn't hear him because a club thwacked her shoulder, above her backpack.

The next blow hit Jimmy, who staggered. "Ow!" He threw the marble.

"Cut it out!" Jane yelled.

"Didn't mean to throw that one." Jimmy rubbed his neck. "Fuck those motherfuckers!"

"I'm getting Marvin to his friends' place in Old Town," Tessa said, close to Jane's ear. "It's only a few blocks from here. He's probably got a concussion."

There was a surge from behind Jane; the crowd was moving into the street. Cars screeched and honked. Jane dodged the traffic and wriggled between two parked cars; then she felt sidewalk beneath her shoes. The crowd had thinned, and she was running through a neighborhood with front stoops. "The pigs are on a fucking rampage," Bert said, appearing next to her. Jane tripped over a child's tricycle and fell flat. She sat up and took off her backpack. It was an old Campfire Girls pack she'd used on camp hiking trips. The strings on top were frayed and knotted; she fumbled to open them.

"Hand that over, girlie." A policeman reached for her pack.

Jane clutched it. "I'm getting a handkerchief," she said. Her fingers touched the plastic bag with her wet washcloth.

"I don't care what you're doing," the cop said. Another cop stood close behind her; Jane felt a tug on her hair. She was yanked to her feet.

The pain was like nails and needles driving into her head, knives stabbing the nape of her neck. A hand twisted her braid, pulled her up to a face with flat blue eyes, a purplish nose, bad teeth, a double chin. "You fucking whore dyke." The face spewed the words. He had a thick red tongue. He literally spat in her eyes and let her drop. Off-balance, she landed on her tailbone; her hands and elbows slammed to the pavement behind her.

*Get back up now, quick...*her mother's voice in her head. No one could spit in her face and expect her to crumple into a weeping heap. Kicks thumped her back, her butt, her thighs, as she struggled to stand and was thrown down again. Pebbles dug into her hands. "Pig" was too good a word for such thugs. Even "goon" was too mild. The kicking stopped. Jane lay sprawled, prone, aching. The noxious spit burned her face. The words "whore dyke" boomed in the cavern of her skull. But her hair was still on her head. She stood, claiming one square of sidewalk on a street in Old Town. Four of them in blue shirts and helmets were assaulting people who ran, crouched, or scrambled behind trees. In the street Jimmy was fighting back, kicking, spitting, screaming "Cocksucker!"

"This guy bit my hand!" a cop yelled. "I need a rabies shot. We're taking him in." Jimmy struggled as two cops carried him off. Jane glimpsed his face, lips parted, teeth bared. He held up a solidarity-fist; one of the cops grabbed it and wrenched it behind his back. He screamed—it was the broken arm, not long out of its cast. They lugged him to the paddy wagon at the corner. "Long live the Revolution!" he screeched as they threw him in.

Jane picked up her pack: the cops had taken her Swiss army knife and her "Join Us!" leaflets. Her washcloth was still there; so were her pencil and paper. Her money, of course, was in her pockets. Bert came out from behind a tree. "Little Jimmy's got guts," he said. "They've got him on assaulting an officer and resisting arrest, at least."

"How are you?" Jane asked.

"Not bad. Got a few billy club licks," Bert said. He took off his helmet, shook out his hair, and massaged the back of his neck with one hand. "This jean-jacket's protective." He held out his arms and rotated them experimentally. Two blue pigs were coming back from the paddy wagon, looking for their next victim. "Let's get out of here," Bert said. "It's too soon to get arrested. The convention hasn't even started."

"Let's find a phone booth," Jane said. She wanted to talk to her mother.

"Right," Bert said. "We should tell Chuck about Jimmy."

Jane was tingling all over as she ran, the soreness of her limbs and head and back waking up her body. She had been spat on. She had felt what it was like to be scalped. But she knew where she was: crossing Clark Street. She was coming to her senses, and she was not tired at all.

"They're terrified," Bert said. "They think we're monster zombie hippie vermin, gonna destroy the world."

"Whore dyke, the guy called me."

"Whoa—what an honor! Welcome to the ranks of the reviled!" Bert said. They could walk now; no one was chasing them, no fellow protestors pushing past. "And we thought we were just disorganized politico schmucks," he said. "We aren't even doing a tenth of what we said we'd do." He stopped at the corner, looked both ways, and charged across, pulling Jane with him. "And now they think we're taking over. In their minds, we're winning!"

"How do you know?"

"Anybody who's threatened by Jimmy and his marbles has got to be seeing bogeymen," Bert said. "Here's a phone."

Bert seemed too cocky, Jane thought. While he called Chuck, she wiped her face with her damp washcloth and looked at a police car parked nearby, its occupant a shadow backlit by streetlights. She missed her Swiss Army Knife. She'd always carried it, to open letters, cut cord, slice apples; but it was sharp enough to make a hole in a tire. Terrible image: Marvin huddled on the ground. *Kick kick.* Windows glowed with lamplight in the apartment building nearby. "We could go inside, pound on all the doors, yelling *Wake up!*" she said. "Tell everyone what Chicago's finest do in the dark streets."

"Some of them are gonna say *Hurrah for Chicago's finest.*" Bert's eyes narrowed. "We're the enemy now."

"We're not who they think we are," Jane said.

"I think maybe I am," Bert said, scratching his chin, which bristled unevenly.

Jane thought of Dora leaning out the front window in Glenville, calling to the wounded white tow-truck operator, giving him a glass of water, letting him use her phone, not mentioning him the next day as she soaked the blood-stained rug with cold water, scrubbed it with soap, and soaked it again. Jane had thought she was a humanitarian like Dora. But tonight she wanted to slash tires and rouse sleepers, drag them into the streets.

"Let me call my folks," she said to Bert. "I'll be quick."

He leaned against a wall smoking while Jane told her mother she was fine. "Glad to hear it," Mom said. "We didn't watch the news tonight." Her voice had the sharp-edged chirpiness she used when she was scared. If they didn't watch the news, they were busy with some immediate crisis: pain or worse. But Daddy was okay, on his feet a couple times a day. "Call earlier next time, okay?"

Her mother was covering up, and Jane could do nothing. She hung up, then burst open the phone booth doors and said "Let's go" before Bert could ask questions. Mom had been right to shut her out; Jane was where she belonged now, whore-dyke of the streets, the law-and-order man's worst nightmare.

Chapter 16

August 25-26, 1968
The Movement Office & Chicago

The screen door banged as Ivy stepped into the office. Chuck hung up the phone. "I had to close The Penny, lots of dishes and mopping," she said, putting her arms around his waist. It was well past the midnight closing time. She'd also taken a bath and washed her hair; he felt the damp strands, her clean, naked arms and legs. "It's nice and cool in here," she said.

Chuck decided not to tell Ivy he'd been trying to call her. The thing was Chicago, where twenty Cleveland Movement people were running around the streets. "I've been on the phone all evening," he said. "The police attacked in Lincoln Park. Jimmy's been arrested and Marvin has a concussion."

"Oh God, already?" Ivy's turquoise eyes flicked wide; she covered her mouth with one hand and spoke through her fingers. "Why?"

"Something about a rock concert—Bert was squeaking he was so excited. I guess the police went crazy with their billy clubs." So don't go to Chicago, Chuck wanted to add. The calls from Chicago had left him feeling useful and eager for company. Ivy had sunk into the lumpy couch. "You're staying tonight," he said, settling next to her.

"Okay," she said. "I'm too tired to walk to the Monmouth again." Her face was full of shadows. "The demonstrators were on the evening news. Kreb says 'Those kids are raising all kinds of Hell.' I didn't tell him I was about to join them."

"You've got a ride?" Chuck kissed her cheek; he just needed to touch her. If she didn't have a ride, maybe she'd stay.

She shook herself free of his hands. "I'm riding with Pastor Joe Griever. He leaves in the afternoon." She'd wait tables for the Sunday brunch crowd; then she'd meet Pastor Joe in the Church of the Covenant parking lot. "I should be packing now." She inched away from him on the couch. He looked close to see if her lips were tight-pressed with anger. A few days ago, when he'd suggested she stay in the office with him, she'd flared up: "Why? So I can make you sandwiches and fuck you at night?" That had started another brief, hot quarrel.

Now her lips were slack and soft. "I can't even think," Ivy said. "I need to lie down. Where's my sleeping bag?"

He got the bags out from under the table, and Ivy sprawled on top of hers without undressing while he called Jimmy's parents. "Yeah, Jamie already called us," his father said, refusing to use Jimmy's chosen name. He hung up without even saying good night.

Chuck straightened his sleeping bag so an inch of cement floor was between him and Ivy. Then he lay down. Oily night wind came through the screen door. It was hooked shut, easy to break open, but he didn't expect to sleep. On the other side of the cold strip of cement, Ivy's breathing slowed and softened.

Four more phone calls came before morning: two arrests, a broken leg, a woman looking for her man, who called looking for her. Chuck gave him her number and lay down again. Then he reached for Ivy, kissing the nape of her neck, rousing her so, loppy and half-asleep, she let him make love to her. He loved her intensely, loved that she was brave and even that she was going to Chicago on her own.

She had to leave in the dawn. "Call me," he said. Helpless, sleepy, he accepted her kiss, dry on his lips, and watched her go out the door, sleeping bag under one arm. When the door slapped shut he was rolling up his own narrow bag, unable to look as she walked away; she'd have to hurry to get into her waitress outfit.

Then he was disgusted with how hard it was, her leaving. She'd be back in a few days, for Chrissake. She would dress up to visit Ohio delegates and McCarthy campaigners in hotel lobbies. She had no plans to block streets with Bert, write on walls with Tessa, or scatter marbles under police-horse hooves— Jimmy's awful idea.

She might get arrested anyway. One call came from a guy who'd been standing on a porch in Old Town, talking with the people who owned the house, when police pulled him down the steps, threw him to the ground, and took him to jail.

Chuck put a pot of water on the hot plate for instant coffee and shaving. He wished he could get someone to cover for him. He'd like to go to The Big Penny for pancakes, see Ivy once more before she left. But it was too early to phone anyone. He was stuck in the office.

He looked at himself in the dirty bathroom mirror, watching the razor scrape over his cheek and jaw. *Coward*, he thought. He was safe while his girlfriend was going to be with Bert: tall, handsome, hair-in-the-wind, so fearless he was scary. The delegates would be committed to their candidates; they wouldn't get talked into supporting the Revolution. So Ivy and Bert would run through the streets from one demo to the next.

Don't think that stuff, Chuck told himself. He poured boiling water over the Nescafé and walked outside to look at the empty street. Staying here would be a lot easier if he had a television. Maybe Sheldon had one—or Greg Lambert. They'd both offered to help when they weren't at work. Later he could phone them. Now, if he wasn't a coward, he could write the essay for SSS Form 150. Chuck took out his notebook and opened to a clean page. "Dear Uncle Sam," he wrote.

"Since you asked, here's what I believe about the Supreme Being—as of Sunday, August 25th, 1968, the first month into the 22nd year of my life. (Beliefs must change, of course, as the world changes.)" He crossed out the sentence in parentheses. "God probably exists, but if so, He is by definition vast, all-powerful, and unknowable, not white not black not yellow. He is not an American. He does not take sides." He crossed out "probably" and "if so," to sound certain.

Where was God this morning? Not in his parents' Baptist church, where true burning reverence was reserved for the passing of the money-dish on Sundays, the net profits on the rest of the week. "The word of God," they taught him, and then they acted as if the Word did not say what it said: "Thou shalt not kill."

He could never un-know the Vietnamese woman killed by American soldiers in her own village, the picture showing her earlobe with its silver ball intact, her brains glopped onto the grass of her conical hat. Or Thomas, trying to be helpful on his way home to his family, his brains blown out by one of Cleveland's finest. And what the fuck did that cop believe?

"You ask about my religious teachers. First: my grandfather, Baptist church deacon and loyal Republican. How did he teach me religion? He took me hunting."

At nine Chuck had killed a squirrel. He remembered how it dropped from the branch to the forest floor and lay there limp and whole, except for blood leaking out its nose. "Rudolph the red-nosed squirrel," he'd crowed.

"Show respect," Granddad said. "That animal gave its life for you." He showed Chuck how to skin it and take out the guts. They made squirrel stew. It tasted fine. "The squirrel is inside you now," Granddad said. "It's a part of you." Since then, when church people mentioned taking communion he'd thought of the squirrel inside of him. Body and blood.

Maybe God was with Joe Griever, now about to start the Sunday sermon, soon to drive Ivy to Chicago. Chuck began to write about Joe, who opposed the war in Vietnam and said the atomic bomb made war obsolete. He let the Movement meet in his church basement and use the mimeograph machine. Was God there, in the mimeograph machine?

"Griever's acts speak louder than his words," Chuck wrote. "If a man joins the military, he must kill other men in order to stay alive. He's trapped, in other words, and so is the other man, who would not be his enemy if they met on the street." Chuck had not killed Thomas. He'd had no way of knowing such a thing was possible. Yet he'd found himself praying for mercy often in the past month. To whom did he pray? He wasn't sure.

"Third," he wrote, "is Mrs. Nelson, of the Religious Society of Friends, a total pacifist who says that all wars are avoidable, illegal (according to U.N. charter), and 'not healthy for children and other living things.' She should know, having escaped Hitler's Germany."

Even if she was right about Hitler, which Chuck doubted, she hadn't mentioned the Japanese imperialists. And what about the revolutionaries? Weren't the NLF justified in the killing they had to do? Fanon, Guevara, and Bert Augustin would say so.

"I will not be sucked into your war," he wrote. If another war had begun—in Glenville, in downtown Chicago—he would not claim it yet.

Friday at 5:00 he'd cleaned off his desk at Lake Erie Savings & Loan, put the stapler, staple-remover, and pencils into the lap drawer, dumped his scratch papers full of arithmetic and tic-tac-toe into the wastebasket. On his way out he'd stopped at the head teller's booth to tell her he'd be gone for a few days. She'd raised her plucked and penciled eyebrows and said, "Okeydoke, I'll tell the boss." Then Chuck pushed the heavy door open and stepped into the street, where he removed his tie. Since then he'd worn his work shirt, jeans, and sneakers. The bosses had not approved his leave-without-pay, even though he'd requested it in writing. They'd expect him tomorrow morning. He could still show up—No, out of the question.

He called Greg Lambert at nine; if Greg wasn't already up he should be. The phone rang four times: still asleep. Eight rings. At demonstrations, Greg exuded the joy of battle, shouting as though he wanted to be attacked. Chuck wondered if he'd taken the live grenade from his desk. Just as well Greg had a job this summer at Republic Steel; he'd get into big trouble in Chicago. Twelve rings.

Chuck hung up and called Sheldon, who answered right away. "You want me to bring my TV? *Give* you my TV for the whole week? Oh, man." Sheldon was no altruist.

"Just four days. You'll be at work most of the time. If you want to watch something, come to the office."

"You must think I got nothing better to do," Sheldon grumbled. He was busy—"Church! Yeah, I go to church!"— but he said he'd come later.

The phone rang: Tessa. Marvin's concussion was real, but not terrible; he'd be back on the streets in two days. Meanwhile, she'd be in the medical tent if anyone called looking for her. "How's it going for you, Chuck?" They hadn't spoken since last week on the Severance Hall steps; Chuck felt his heart beat in time with her breath on the phone. He wanted to keep talking. He wanted to hang up. "Twenty-five thousand police," she said. "They're smashing journalists' cameras. People are getting radicalized right and left. Got to hang up; out of money."

"Okay," he said. "Bye." She'd already hung up.

The phone rang again: Jimmy's mother wanted to give him the jail address. She was friendlier than her husband. "I'm watching the news," she said. "In a strange way, I'm really proud of Jamie."

"Me too," Chuck said. He turned to a clean page in his notebook. "If I were with Tessa Buchanan right now, I'd..." He thought of billy clubs cracking on shoulders and skulls. What would he have done if he'd been with Marvin? What if he were with Ivy as she was attacked with a club? He looked at the ballpoint pen between his fingers; he could use it to stab a man in the eye. He jabbed the pen into the air, imagined the eye smeared with blood and ink, the howl of pain, the handcuffs round his wrists, his own brief satisfaction as he was locked into a paddy wagon.

He remembered Ivy's hand clutching her shoulder, blood dripping over her fingers. In Glenville, he had longed for a gun. "If I'd been Thomas's brother," he wrote, "I'd go after the cop who shot him, knock him to the ground and beat his face to a pulp. The urge to avenge is so basic that no one can wipe it out completely. Mrs. Nelson's peace is a garden, nothing more violent than light rain—extremely naive." Chuck remembered her in the silent meeting, how she sat with her eyes closed, smiling slightly. He realized she didn't *want* to know what beasts people were, didn't *have* to know, wearing her jewelry and silk blouse with blue jeans.

Ivy woke with Pastor Joe's wife looking at her over the seat-back; the car had stopped at the church. It was Monday morning. "Here's your hotel," Mrs. Griever smiled. They'd left Cleveland late; Ivy felt bad for not seeing Chuck once more— but she hadn't wanted to risk fighting with no time to make up. She knew he was doing a good thing, but she couldn't help being pissed at him for staying behind—for not being *here*, on the sidewalk, as the Grievers drove away to visit their college-professor friends in Hyde Park. The morning was cool and bright; the church door was open.

The linoleum floor of the basement was littered with sleepers, humped in bags and blankets; the air was warm with their breaths, sour with body-smells. If Chuck had come, he and Ivy would be waking up together, making detailed plans; he'd tell her to be careful. She found the lavatory and washed her face with cold water. She looked in the mirror at her pink cheeks, and then felt a crazy surge of joy: she was free, flying solo, making her own decisions. She folded her wet washcloth, slid it into the Baggie and twisted the top shut. Then she put on her visit-the-delegates dress. Among the sleepers, she'd find someone she knew. She tiptoed in white-stockinged feet among the breathing mounds. Near the wall she saw a familiar long braid. She tugged it, and Jane turned over with a squawk. "Ow, watch it!"

"Good to see you, too," Ivy said.

"What time is it?" Jane asked. "Got my hair pulled yesterday. It's sore, that's all." She winced as she hitched herself onto her elbows.

"Ouch! I'm sorry," Ivy said, and she was. "It's 9:00." Light spilled from windows near the ceiling. "I'm going to visit the Ohio delegation. Do I look like a McCarthy kid?" She twirled on one heel.

"You look like you're about to rush Phi Kappa Zeta."

"You're coming too, aren't you? The delegates are in the Holiday Inn. I've no idea how to get there."

"I can find it." Jane sat up and yawned. "It'll have a coffee shop. Let's go." She slithered out of the bag. She was wearing a T-shirt and filthy jeans, her face streaked with grime. Hair had escaped her braid, straggling over her neck and cheeks. Carrying her knapsack, she picked her way barefoot across the floor to the lavatory.

Ivy strapped on her patent leather Mary Janes and followed with her toiletry kit. She put on eye makeup and tied a red ribbon behind her bangs and over the tips of her ears: the Alice-in-Wonderland look.

Jane came out of a stall. "You need a McCarthy button."

"Got one." Ivy fished the button out of her purse and pinned it over her left breast while Jane soaked and rinsed her washcloth, stripped to the waist and began to wash, shivering. Apparently the church didn't want to waste money on hot water. Jane's arms and ribs were blotched red and purple. She was gaunt. "What will you wear?" Ivy asked.

"I didn't bring a skirt," Jane said. "Don't McCarthy kids wear jeans?"

"The boys do," Ivy said.

"Oh." Jane dug out a pink T-shirt and pulled it over her head. "I brought this," she said. "It's long enough to be a dress." On the front, someone had drawn flowers with red magic marker. She dropped her jeans. "Will it pass?" On her thin body, the shirt hung loose and wrinkled to the middle of her thighs.

"You look hippie-ish," Ivy said. "Not exactly 'clean for Gene.' But maybe if you brush your hair..."

"Rat's nest, isn't it?" Jane picked up the end of her braid and broke the rubber band as she pulled it off. "You don't have a brush, do you?"

"Of course, I do."

Ivy watched Jane gingerly unweave what was left of the braid, then pull the brush slowly across her scalp, wincing. She brushed one strand, then the next, then the next. "My ribs hurt," Jane said. "Is this only Monday? I feel like I've been running for weeks."

Two other women had stumbled into the john and shut themselves in stalls. They'd need sinks and mirror space in a minute; Ivy went into the big room, where people were moving, sitting up, hoisting themselves to their feet.

Jane came next to her, still brushing. "A braid makes people want to pull it, you know that?" she said. "I feel like I'm twenty years older than I was on Saturday."

Ivy loaded her shoulder bag and began to repack her suitcase. Jane handed Ivy the brush full of hairs. Her eyes were teary. "That hurt." Loose, her hair fell sleek and wavy past her waist.

"Where's Tessa? And Bert?" Ivy looked around the big room.

"Tessa's at the medical tent. Last I saw Bert he was in a strategy session. It was one or two in the morning. There." Jane pointed to a quilted hump in the corner. "That's him, I think." She got a fresh rubber band and re-braided her hair. "I'm all right now." She breathed—in, out—and blew her nose. "Do I still look too freaky for the Holiday Inn? I know; I'll wear this." She picked up Ivy's London Fog, pulled it on and buttoned it.

"I was going to carry it," said Ivy, "but you need it more."

By the time they were walking briskly through the gray stone canyons of downtown Chicago, Jane was limber and confident again. "I'm glad Chuck wanted to stay in the office," she said. "It's a good idea."

Chuck *wanted* to stay? Didn't want to be in Chicago? *Why?* For a scary minute Ivy felt adrift—cut loose without a map. She had to remind herself that she knew what Chuck wanted: to stay away from Bert, for one thing. And to be able to go to the bank if they called him; he liked his job.

"Here we are." Jane climbed three stone steps and pushed through a brass revolving door. Inside the hotel three men in uniform carried luggage for three people in suits, two men and one woman in stiff lacquered hair. They had brought trunks as well as suitcases. "Files," Jane indicated the trunks. "They're setting up the offices. There's the coffee shop." She pointed at the sign. She went ahead as Ivy stopped to check herself in the long mirror in front of the elevators. The pattern of her dress, red with black and white lightning streaks, hid its wrinkles. Her hair was smooth and flipped just a little at the ends; she tucked a couple of wisps under the red ribbon and put on lipstick. She was watching herself smear her lips together when the elevator opened and a man stepped out. He was rotund, white-haired and blue-suited; his nametag said *Columbus, Ohio.* He also wore a Humphrey button. Ivy started for the coffee shop, but he blocked her way, smiling as though she were his long-lost niece.

"Honey," he said. "I'm sorry to tell you: your man is just not going to win." He shook his head sorrowfully: too bad.

Her man? Oh, McCarthy. She was wearing his button. This was what delegates did: argue about the candidates. "Easy for you to say," she smiled. She would banter a little and then find the McCarthy delegates for the real discussion. "My candidate's against the Vietnam War," she reminded the white-haired man. "Your candidate isn't. Why should I want him to win?" She started to walk away.

"I know just how you feel." The delegate stopped her with his hand on her arm. "You're young and idealistic. But you need to understand." He tilted till his face came within an inch of hers, though they stood two paces apart. "Politics is like a baseball game." His voice was hushed as though he were imparting a profound secret. "You should root for the winning team."

"What do you mean?" He seemed to think she was a dumb chick dazzled by thick carpets and gleaming brass. Baseball game! "Humphrey will win anyway so I should work for him?"

The man nodded as if he were proud of being shallow. Suddenly she was angry. Didn't he *know*? She wanted to shove pictures and facts in his face. "I'm not playing a sport," she said. "Children are being killed, whole neighborhoods are on fire—not only in Vietnam, but in Cleveland..." The words poured out in a rush, exactly what she meant, for once: everything made worse by that awful war, no end in sight but nuclear holocaust. "All because of *your team*," she said, "and you talk about baseball games!"

The delegate looked at the floor as if the wrongs of the world were accumulating around his feet. But when he looked up, his face was serious and calm. *I've lived a long time*, his expression said, *and you are very young*. "Honey," he said, "you don't know how important a baseball game is."

"I can't think of anything less important than a baseball game," Ivy said. Rage made it hard to be civil. "Unless it's..." She tried to imagine something less relevant than baseball and couldn't. "Hubert Humphrey as president," she said.

"You got spunk, honey," the delegate said. "But you're way outta your league. I don't believe for a minute you know what it means to change the world. You're not *really* committed. You're not poor." He held out his arm in a look-at-you gesture. "Poor people are thin. You're fat!"

No one had ever said that before. Muttering, "Baseball game!" Ivy found the ladies' room; she was so angry, so angry.

Jane stood at one of the sinks. "I saw you talking to that guy," she said, "So I came in here to scrub with hot water and soap. I feel better."

Ivy looked at herself in the mirror. Did the dress make her look pudgy? "I should change out of these clothes. I hate playing McCarthy girl."

"That was fast," Jane said. "What happened?"

"He said that politics is a baseball game," Ivy said. "And baseball games are more important than people's lives."

"I see." Jane raised a lipstick: "Cherries in the Snow," she read the label. Then she filled the mirror with thick red letters: "Power to the People! Dare to struggle, dare to win!"

Now they had to leave quickly. "Let's take the bus," Ivy said. As they rode through the Loop she scuffed her shiny black shoes and tried to make herself small in the seat. *Fat.* Her jeans *had* felt a little tight, lately. She'd been eating more because she could breathe more easily. And she'd cut down on cigarettes. Obviously that man expected activists to starve. What did he know? More than she did, about how the ruling class made money on war. He knew, and he did not care.

Chapter 17

August 27, 1968
The Movement Office & Chicago

The shadows were slanting across Euclid Avenue when Tessa called the office. "Great speeches in Grant Park," she told Chuck. "Can't talk long, just have to exchange messages."

"Everyone okay?" Chuck asked. She would be wary of a phone tap.

"I think so," Tessa said. "Ivy's in Grant Park with Jane; she says Hi. Marvin too. Do you know where we can find Jimmy?"

Chuck told her the jail address. "It's good to hear your voice," he said.

"Good to hear yours," Tessa said. "Got to go. See you soon." She hung up. Chuck thought he should have asked about Ivy and realized that Tessa would have said, "Just fine," unless she'd had bad news. He couldn't have asked whether she was obeying stoplights or whether she was flirting with anyone. Dumb questions, Tessa would've thought.

With the convention in session, Chuck kept the television on all the time. Knowing his comrades could not see inside the Stockyards, he was useful just watching and taking notes. When he didn't want to watch, the voices kept him company. When he couldn't stand what they were saying (this morning the Democrats voted down the peace plank—idiots!) he turned off the sound and focused on faces—excited, astonished, aghast, and grief-stricken by turns.

It was 5:30. Chuck was enjoying his time here. The quietness, the shabbiness, the insufficient lighting all added to its comforts. But now he needed a walk and a Dr Pepper. He could use a meal at the Crystal. He phoned Greg Lambert; no answer. Lambert had dropped by yesterday, offering to sub. "I'm raking in the moolah," he'd said. "Let me know if you need anything—anything at all." Now he couldn't be reached. Count on Greg to be unreliable.

Chuck wasn't envious of Greg's job—heavy lifting within ten feet of white-hot molten steel. But he loathed the prospect of returning to Lake Erie Savings & Loan even for three more weeks of being cool. Junior had said they might keep him working, even after school had started: Chuck had done that well at hiding his thoughts. If he were someone else he'd be proud.

He turned on the television without sound. CBS cameras panned a band shell with a stage and musicians, then crossed the audience; the mass of young people resembled an audience at any folk concert. Suddenly police were charging through the seats, clubs rising and falling in unison. The kids scrambled to get out of the way. Then the camera zoomed in on Ivy. She stood all alone between two rows and watched the cops come—her eyes and mouth three holes through which her spirit poured out; as the camera veered away, her face became a gaping mask. Chuck felt as if she could see him, was accusing him. His mind scrambled for a way to get to her: gas up the Pontiac, force Greg and Sheldon to take turns manning the office...

A reporter's face appeared, nose bloody, glasses shattered. Chuck turned on the sound and heard the reporter's hot, urgent staccato. The police had attacked newsmen. The police had closed access to the bridges. The police were wading into this crowd, now. With the sound on, there was no mistaking the clubs; Chuck heard their sickening *thok, thok.*

Ivy! The camera moved too fast for him to see faces. The drive would take seven hours. He had the church phone number; they'd give him directions, and...

The phone rang. It was his grandfather. "Heard you took a leave of absence from work," Granddad said. "Something wrong with your body? No? Something wrong with your head?"

"I'm fine," Chuck said. He turned off the sound and moved close to the TV. "Everything all right with you?" Stumbling people were being attacked by police; no sight of Ivy. She could be right there, off-screen.

"Well, I thought everything was just swell," Granddad said, "till I phoned my friend George at the bank. Who do you think you are, some salaried executive? You were on your way, but now you've quit in the middle of things, and you've made me look like a fool. I don't need that, Chucky. George did me a favor, hiring you."

"Wait. Stop. I wrote a letter, explaining that I wanted four days' leave *without pay*. They never got back to me, so I figured..." On the TV screen, two cops ran after a protestor and knocked him to the ground. A newscaster's face appeared, the mouth moving silently.

"They never gave you permission, then, am I right?"

"Right. But listen: It wasn't like they needed me. I was correcting arithmetic and running errands, for Chrissake; I guess I should have called, I guess..." Chuck heard his own babbling begin to whine. He stopped. National Guardsmen marched across the screen, their bayonets fixed. "Listen, Granddad, I'm busy. Let me call you back."

"I'll call *you*, Chucky. In half an hour."

The TV was full of running screaming people being beaten by police in shiny pale helmets. One protestor, moving a sawhorse, looked like Greg Lambert. No. Greg wouldn't leave the mill or the moolah. Another commercial came on. Then the news was over until 11:00. Chuck closed his eyes and saw Ivy running from the clubs. People would be calling him soon; he had to stay.

The next call, however, was Granddad sounding friendly, as if there were nothing wrong. "How's that girlfriend of yours— what's her name?"

"Ivy Barcelona. She's fine." Chuck crossed his fingers. *Please, let her be fine, please please.*

"You know, I'm afraid that girl's turned your head. That's why you forgot yourself." Granddad had a message after all. "She's got you thinking you're some kind of peace-and-love missionary. Your mother says she's one of those New Left people, involved in plotting that trouble in Chicago." Suddenly he shouted. "Do you know what kind of shit you're in?"

Chuck held the receiver away from his ear. "The truth is, Granddad, I got her involved. And of course there's no law against protesting in Chicago, but I'd be in deeper shit if I were actually there." He wasn't quite lying. "Where does Mom get her information?"

"A little bird told her," Granddad said. "Or women's intuition. I don't care. I want to know why you left the job." So Mom hadn't mentioned the FBI letter.

"I didn't," Chuck began. But he knew why Granddad had called. If Chuck showed up at the office Friday, he would not be allowed in. To save face, Granddad had told George about Chuck's subversive girlfriend. "Is Mom really upset?" he asked.

"Yes, she's upset. Who wouldn't be? Are you gonna marry that girl?"

"Yes," Chuck said. "I am. Tell Mom."

"Oh dear. Are you sure? Have you popped the question?"

"No. I'm waiting till..."

"Good. You could get yourself in a mess with a woman like that."

"Granddad, Ivy's a terrific person. She's... If you met her, you'd see how sweet she is, how good-hearted, how..."

"Yeah, yeah, I know. She's beautiful and intelligent, too. Son, the first woman is always that way. Always." The old man sighed. "Your mother will probably feel better if I tell her you're determined to marry this girl. Meanwhile, get yourself straightened around. You hear me?" Another sigh. "Goodbye now."

The phone rang almost immediately with an arrested woman making her one call. Chuck took the name and number and called the woman's husband. Then came another: a man in the hospital with a broken collarbone. He couldn't drive, but if someone would wire money he could take the bus home. Chuck made connections and watched the light fade on Euclid Avenue until he could no longer see the derelict gas station across the street.

After a while Sheldon came, and together they watched the 11:00 news, looking carefully for faces they knew during the replay of the police riot (the newscaster called it that, now) at Michigan and Balbo. "Look—is that Greg?" Chuck pointed.

"Nah," said Sheldon. "That guy looks thoughtful."

They saw Ribicoff shout "Gestapo tactics in the streets of Chicago!" in the Amphitheatre, and they saw Daley's wide mouth yelling, too far from the microphones to be audible.

"Did you hear?" Sheldon said, when it was over. "Ahmed Evans' gun money came from Cleveland:Now!"

"What! All of it?"

"He didn't need *all*. Guns aren't that expensive."

"I'm surprised you know that," said Chuck.

"I am too," Sheldon said. "I surprise myself all the time with what I know."

On her fifth day in Chicago, Jane had lost track of everyone. She'd left Ivy at the band shell and gone to soak their washcloths in a drinking fountain; more cops had arrived, which meant more tear gas. While she was trying to find a fountain that worked, the police charged, and Ivy was swallowed up in the crowd.

Jane walked among shoulders and frightened voices, sorry she hadn't gotten Ivy's washcloth to her; the air was thick with fumes. Her bruises made her aware of all the little movements involved in walking, the bunch and release of thigh muscles, the side-to-side rocking of hip bones, the rasp of lungs.

Jackson Street Bridge was crammed with chanting Mobe kids, police herding them from the sides, calling "Keep moving!" and nudging people with their nightsticks. Jane's voice had died within her. She needed to call her parents. She needed to pee. Ah—there, at the end of the bridge, was a café with a restroom.

She stared at her face in the mirror: bumpy nose and bony cheekbones, her lips invisible, thin, the same color as the rest of her face. The eyes were narrow, dark, angry. Street fighter's eyes. She washed her hands and wet her face, and went back out. On her way through the coffee shop she scooped a handful of sugar cubes into a napkin and stole a knife. She'd become an outlaw, vandalizing mirrors with lipstick, stealing sugar and flatware. She sucked on a sugar cube and looked for a phone.

Daley had ripped the compassionate mask off the Democratic Party and set the cops on them all. In the press of people on Michigan Avenue she saw Bert, blood on his face, being dragged toward a paddy wagon, waving his fist, yelling, "Long live the Revolution!"

Jane thought of her mother saying "Represent me." *How?* She skirted the melee, avoiding nightsticks, dodging legs and arms that flailed the air, and got caught in a press of people so tight she felt herself lifted off the ground and carried by elbows crunching her sore ribs. She couldn't breathe. They were protesters, her people, and still they pressed against her as if they didn't know she was there. She heard the crack of club on bone, again, again, again. "A whole window just fell in!" somebody yelled in her ear. "Cops are pushing people through the broken glass!"

Then she was free, running down Michigan Avenue toward a phone booth on the corner. Clutching the quarters in her pocket, she pushed the door and had one foot inside when she felt a hand on her shoulder.

"Go somewhere else to make your call," a helmeted cop snorted, gripping both her arms; he was wearing tight black leather gloves.

"I've got to call my folks," Jane said, as he pulled her out. She kicked the air.

He wrenched her backpack off her sore shoulder. "Gotta check for weapons," he said, untying the top of the pack. Out came the pink T-shirt.

Fury boiled through Jane's legs and arms; before she could think she had twisted around to kick the piggy rump, the porky thighs, pummel the fleshy back with her fists. And then she was lifted and thrown into a paddy wagon, slammed among protestors sitting thigh to thigh. Across from Jane was a boy who looked like he'd come through a windstorm that had blown away all his landmarks. "You look bewildered," she said. Her voice rasped from tear gas.

"I'm stoned," he rasped back. "And I really, *really* wish I wasn't. It's too weird."

Jane was not stoned. "This situation is not weird," she told him. "In fact, it's becoming normal." Being thrown into a police wagon was just the next thing after being clubbed, manhandled, and nearly scalped. For others it had been normal for years—generations. And except for that one poor guy, no one had been shot. Yet.

It was normal (she reminded herself at the station) to be fingerprinted, to be pulled along by the upper arm, bruised on top of bruises, to be silenced. It was her due: no matter how she equivocated, she was on the same side as the NLF, the Cuban revolution, and the Communist Chinese. She'd phone Chuck as soon as she could. He'd know where the others were and tell them. She'd call her mother some day when she had a chance.

Women were crammed into one room. "We'll be out by morning," someone was saying. "They've arrested hundreds of people in just a few days. Can't afford to take each one of us through the arraignment, the hearing, whatever happens after that."

A deep chuckle. "I don't know. I wish I could sit down." Jane recognized the voice—and when she looked, she recognized her acquaintance from the Women Strike for Peace march.

"Hey!" she called, waving, grinning through a forest of women's heads and shoulders. The freckled woman waved back. Jane looked down to avoid stepping on toes as she squeezed between bodies toward her friend. What a collection of women's shoes—hiking boots, sandals, bright leather pumps. Jane stepped over a saddle shoe and smiled at the woman who wore it. The night ahead would be long and uncomfortable, but Jane felt a strange euphoria.

The woman from Boston, Patricia, patted her on the arm. "You know," she said. "This is just the beginning of a huge change. History will prove us right."

They had nothing to do but talk. Patricia had left her husband finally a few months ago. "When Kennedy was assassinated," she said, "I was standing in the kitchen beating eggs, waiting for my husband to come home from work. I barely had a thought for Kennedy because I was concentrating so hard on being Paul's wife. Can you imagine?"

Jane couldn't.

"I can't either," Patricia said. "What a tight little mind I had."

Ivy's lungs had begun to solidify. Tear gas, she thought. She stopped running; then she stopped walking. She had to work on breathing out. Then she had to bend over to get enough air, hands on her thighs to give the lungs more room. Time to use the inhaler. Shit. Goddamn it. The demon always returned at the wrong time.

The inhaler was buried in the depths of her shoulder bag; she rummaged, then leaned against a wall to use it—right here in the milling and shouting. She coughed and inhaled again. It was almost empty, the medicine stale and weak.

She'd been moving since the moment at the band shell when the police arrived swinging their clubs like Fess Parker playing Davy Crockett at the Alamo, clubbing anyone who didn't scurry out of the way—an attack on the audience, whose only assertive act had been to chant *AAOOUUMM* along with Allen Ginsberg, so hoarse from days of tear gas and *oming* he could hardly do it alone. *AAOOUUMM*. Then a band came on, and an idiot kid shinnied up the flagpole, people around him yelling *Half-mast! Don't take it down!* and the police waded in. Watching them club their way toward her: that was the moment when Ivy knew Bert was right about the war coming home. George Wallace was right, too, she realized: *Not a dime's worth of difference between Republicans and Democrats*. They were all thugs. They would destroy democracy—destroy their own children—rather than give up their fucking baseball game.

Then she saw the mules. Real live mules pulled a wagon—three wagons, with Ralph Abernathy driving the first, dressed in overalls and a straw hat. The Poor People's Campaign had come to Chicago, to Michigan Avenue, surrounded by police on motorcycles, trailed by chanters and singers. *Ain't gonna let nobody turn me round, turn me round*...Suddenly the wagons stopped and were engulfed by the crowd. Ivy felt a little shaky, but she could breathe well enough to walk away. Behind her came thuds and yells. People next to her began to run, so she trotted along with them, her shoulder bag banging against her side. Too soon to run fast; too soon to use the inhaler if her lungs seized up. Get away from the tear gas, she told herself, and stumbled against a manhole cover. She put her arms out to break the fall and felt someone grab her hand.

"Come on," said a male voice. "Just a little further." There were two of them, each holding one of her hands; they pulled her with them for another block, and then another. Then they were walking on an empty side street, three kids in a skyscraper canyon. They introduced themselves: Ed was short and stocky; Mike was tall and thin. "Were you at Michigan and Balbo?" Ed asked. Ivy shrugged; she wasn't sure.

"I was at the band shell," she said. "Then I crossed a bridge. Saw the mule train."

"They were stopped at Michigan and Balbo," Mike said. "Those cops went crazy, pushed a bunch of bystanders through a plate glass window. They're like Nazis on Kristallnacht."

"Let's go to Grant Park," Ed said. "We'll be okay there." They rounded a corner and walked through an alley. Ivy could walk now: no teargas here. But a barrier made of sawhorses forced them to walk single file—Mike, Ivy, then Ed.

They were passing a phalanx of National Guard standing motionless, bayonets fixed. Mike stopped, so Ivy stopped. Bayonet points glittered an inch from her face. Behind her, Ed reached for her hand. The nearest guard was less than a foot away; she heard him sniffle. He would not catch her eye. His lips shut over his teeth.

In front of her Mike suddenly screamed "*Fuckers!*" dropped to a squat, and scrabbled on the sidewalk with his fingers. Ivy could feel the guardsman next to her lean forward, and she stepped back. Mike hurled a pebble; it hit a wall and dropped harmlessly. He bent again, spluttering, and found an empty cigarette pack which he threw onto a guardsman's helmet. The guardsman stood still, but under the rim of his helmet, Ivy saw him glare. "Assholes!" Mike hissed, and threw a chip of cement.

It hit a helmet, and the guardsman turned his head and shook his bayonet. "Don't make me use this, you idiots," he said softly. Ivy met his eyes and thought she saw his upper lip twitch.

Mike acted as if he didn't hear, but Ed apparently had. "Hey Buddy, hey," he took his friend's arm. "Cool it, Mike. Cool it now." He tugged at the arm as Mike muttered and fumed.

"Police state. Fucking police state. Not going to just *take* it. There's gotta be some loose bricks."

"Unh-unh, no man," Ed was holding tight to Mike's belt. Ivy took Mike's hand; as he struggled to break loose, she put her other arm around his waist. They got him across the street to the park. In the darkness between trees he relaxed.

"Something cracked inside," he said. His cheeks were wet with rageful tears. "For two days I've been thinking how it was for my grandparents in Warsaw. *Police state.* Those bayonets—I couldn't stand it another second."

In Grant Park's leafy darkness, a world away from bayonets, people sat in clusters on the grass. Ivy held Ed's and Mike's hands, stepping over blue-jeaned legs, brushing strange backs with her own. Colors had been erased by darkness.

"Dellinger's talking," said Ed. The president of the Mobe held the bullhorn, a wide man in a suit. Ivy dropped to the ground—dirt and grass: *earth*—between Ed and Mike. Across the street stood a tall grid of glowing squares: the windows of the Conrad Hilton. Close at hand were rustles and murmurs. Dellinger read messages from famous people. "We're with you," he read. "You're doing what we should have done long ago." Below the noise of traffic came a roar with no source that Ivy could identify.

Someone put a paper bag into her hands. "Have some and pass it," a voice said. Fritos. Another bag came by with Oreos. Then came a jug of KoolAid. Then came a jug of wine. More KoolAid. Food was circulating throughout the park; everyone helped themselves, no one worried about germs. Ivy was more thirsty than hungry. When she found a ham sandwich in her lap she passed it to Mike, who ate half and passed the rest to Ed, who stood leaning against a tree to see the speakers.

Standing next to him, Ivy looked around the crowd: surely Jane was nearby—or Bert. She needed to find someone from Cleveland. She squinted to see better; no good. She wished Chuck were here with his arm around her. Fear had opened her lungs in the bayonet line; now they were beginning to tighten again. Back at the church, her suitcase had aminophyllin and an inhaler refill. What if she couldn't find her way back? She had three dollars in her pocket—enough for a taxi? She didn't know. "This is legally our turf; the police won't attack here," Rennie Davis said into the bullhorn. "See those cameras? The whole world is watching."

Then Marvin, his head bandaged, one eye blue-black, reached for the bullhorn and Davis gave it to him. "The whole world may not be *listening*, yet," Marvin said. "We need to reach out to our brothers and sisters in the jails and the emergency rooms, in the McCarthy campaign headquarters, the newsrooms, and in Lincoln Park. We are The People. The world sees; now it needs to understand and feel included—even policemen." The bullhorn made his voice boom like a prophet's, reciting Debs: "*As long as there is a lower class, we are in it. As long as there is a criminal element, we are of it. As long as there is a soul in prison, we are not free.*" A few people chanted the words with him; then came the other chant, louder: *The whole world is watching! The whole world is watching!*

Ivy felt an arm across her shoulders—oh, it was Ed's. His other arm came round her. "We've won this time," he said, and kissed her. She felt as though she were kissing an anonymous person, as though the people in Grant Park had melded into one vast person; she was kissing that collective person. They kissed again, one with the crowd.

"Look," Mike said. Ivy pulled out of Ed's arms: a dark man had the bullhorn, his eyes hidden under a black hat with a wide brim, a Black man so tall he could sit on a camp stool and still be seen by the crowd. "Brothers and sisters," he was saying, "the Blackstone Rangers are among you." The mysterious street gang had resisted white domination, resisted the Daley machine, and would show them all how to take the streets. The crowd erupted in cheers.

Nearby crouched a girl Ivy's own age, a Black girl in a leather jacket, her clear-eyed face shining briefly in the roving glance of a flashlight. "Vote for George Wallace," she said. "So we can have a revolution." She clasped her hands under her knees and rocked with excitement.

The thought had occurred to Ivy, but she'd never heard anyone say it: Let the government get so bad, citizens must revolt. The idea was manipulative, terrible. But it made sense. Ed was reaching to kiss her again. She felt his hands travel up and down her back, fingering her shoulder blades, her waist, rounding her buttocks, pulling her close. His kiss was soft and smoky and warm. His hand covered her breast and his fingers moved, feeling.

She stopped him. "I want to listen," she said. Someone was holding a transistor radio to the bullhorn, broadcasting a voice, the words coated with radio-fuzz, barely intelligible. *Delegates are with us*—the whisper traveled from one cluster of park people to the next. *Senators and congressmen are with us. In that hotel across the street.*

A shadow took the bullhorn away from the radio and spoke into it. "See all those lights in the Conrad Hilton?" He turned the bullhorn toward the grid full of yellow squares and yelled: "If you're with us, blink your lights!" The chant echoed out of the crowd. "Blink your lights if you're with us! Blink your lights!"

Up and down the face of the Conrad Hilton Hotel, lights winked off and then on again, off and on.

"Power to the People," sang the Black girl, rising onto her boots. "Power to the People." The crowd took up the song. She raised both fists, singing.

PART FOUR

There was little I could do. But without me
The rulers would have been more secure.
This was my hope.
So the time passed away
Which on earth was given me.

from "To Posterity" by Bertolt Brecht

After Chicago the amazed media turned its attention to the Movement, twirling its lenses and clicking its shutters from different angles. *Who are those kids? What the hell happened? Who's at fault?* In back-to-school issues of fashion magazines, models wore army jackets, helmets and combat boots. *Fortune* reported that Che Guevara was more popular with ambitious young men than Johnson, Nixon, Humphrey, or Wallace. *Reader's Digest* warned the country against "Engineers of Campus Chaos," and quoted J. Edgar Hoover: "...to put it bluntly, they are a new type of subversive, and their danger is great."

To be sure, some of us dreamed of menacing the System, but we were disorganized and divided, not threatening. The government's Walker Report called it a "police riot"; didn't that vindicate us?

The "new type of subversive" had become popular. That fall's SDS pamphlet said, "There ain't no place to be today but in the Movement" and "if you're tired of the Vietnamese eating napalm for breakfast, if you're tired of the Blacks eating tear gas for dinner, and if YOU'RE tired of eating plastic for lunch, then give it a name: Call it SDS, and join us." Membership swelled by thousands.

To be so publicly loved and hated is to possess a weird form of power. We were offered microphones and podiums, but most of us could not explain the events we called "Chicago." If, for a little while, we knew that the Revolution had begun, an hour later that certainty would be undermined.

Norman Mailer wrote an adventure story in which an author roams downtown Chicago during the convention. The demonstrators become his "troops." After his arrest (for blocking a Jeep with a barbed-wire fence mounted on the front grill) the author goes to Hugh Hefner's Playboy mansion for more drinks. Hefner's been clonked on the head with a nightstick himself. "Dear Miss," Mailer says to one of his troops, "we will be fighting for forty years."

The Walker investigators counted 12,000 Chicago police; 5,000 army soldiers, 6,000 National Guardsmen, and 668 arrests. They couldn't count the protesters. Many came from the Chicago area; after demonstrating for a while, they'd go home. The next day, they'd go to work. No one counted the hundreds of infiltrators placed by the FBI. Most of the wounded stayed away from the local hospitals, who nonetheless reported more than 100 protestors. Movement medical centers treated 625. Twenty reporters were hospitalized Sunday night alone. That was the big mistake of Chicago's finest: attacking messengers who made the attacks into history.

There is still no agreement about what exactly took place. We were there, that's all. We still discover each other. *Were you at Michigan and Balbo?* we ask. *Remember that guy who climbed the flagpole near the bandshell? I heard he was an infiltrator. Do you know?*

Meanwhile (between August 20 and September 2) Soviet troops killed 72 protesters in Czechoslovakia and wounded 702. In Mexico City, students organized all summer, anticipating the Olympics. Those who tried to put up posters or write graffiti were shot. In the week of the Democratic Convention, 308 Americans were killed in Vietnam. 1,134 were wounded. The enemy dead were estimated at 4,755.

Chapter 18

September 7, 1968
Atlantic City

Jane stood on the Boardwalk facing the ocean. Waves unfurled onto the beach and were dragged back, then swelled— great salty breaths made visible. In the distance, ocean met sky at a thin white line that barely separated two pale blues. Salt wind blew Jane's hair away from her face and made her squint; she removed her coat—not hers, Ivy's—and felt her arms and legs and torso begin to unknot in the wind.

She had arrived by train at dawn and slept on the beach, wrapped in the London Fog, among grassy sand hills that turned hard under her body. Now the sun was somewhere in the haze at its zenith, and she wanted to be alone in sea and sky so the noise in her head could fade.

She kicked off her sandals, trotted to the shoreline, and let the cold water wash over her feet. Sand slipped away under her soles. Five days past Labor Day, no one sprawled on beach towels. Only a couple of young men with pale naked torsos swam and bounded in the waves. Two teenage girls in bikinis stepped past Jane on stalky legs, their shoulders rigid. One wrapped her arms around her body, clutching her rib cage; the other looked over her shoulder, and Jane met her furtive, troubled eyes. These girls had tan, slender, smooth bodies, new breasts and hips, graceful ankles and high-arched feet. But they held themselves tightly, as if they would fly apart if they didn't. Jane thought of a doll she'd had, its legs and arms and head fastened inside the torso with rubber bands that snapped; in an instant the doll went from being a small replica of a girl to six plastic pieces, grotesque in their bare round pinkness. She recognized the painful inner knot without which a girl might come to pieces.

"Right there," said the girl looking over her shoulder, pointing to the Convention Center. "Miss America will be in there tonight. I wish I could go."

"You gonna watch on TV?" the other asked, still clutching herself. Jane felt chilly as the wind blew through her T-shirt and jeans, cold water splashing her ankles. She stepped away from the water, sand grating between her toes.

"Of course," said the other girl. "My dad wouldn't miss it, and besides..." The rest of the conversation was lost as they walked away. Jane watched their backs grow smaller in the distance. She was alone. She'd come here for the No More Miss America demonstration, but she didn't have to participate. She didn't know the organizers. No one expected anything from her. What a strange feeling.

She and Tessa had set out together, but they got only as far as Long Island, staying overnight with the Buchanans, when Javier the med student showed up. Jane had been introduced to him in Cleveland, a swarthy handsome fellow in a lab coat, and glimpsed him in their apartment, once on her way to the bathroom, once as he was heading out the door. Now, it seemed, Javier's political consciousness had been raised—and he wanted Tessa to go with him to Mexico, right away. *Vámanos, Chica!*

"I need to further my Third World education," Tessa explained. "Mexico has peasants as well as workers, and the organizers are very politically advanced. Besides," she added, "Miss America *is* pretty trivial."

"That's exactly the point," Jane had insisted. "Trivial gets the attention, and real women get ignored." But she knew Tessa could not choose women's liberation over a chance to visit Mexican Marxists, especially with a handsome Mexican lover.

Jane sat on the sand among sea-grasses, glad to be far from Cleveland.

More precisely, far from Bert. He had met her on the steps of the Cook County building when she was released from jail, hours after his own release. He put his arm around her—a nice gesture, but he wouldn't let go, and as they settled in the blue van he started to feel her up. "Oh man, Jane, I've got to get laid," he whispered. "You do too, I know you do, it'll jolt you out of your pissy mood. Let's fuck right here. Now."

Jane pushed him away. "We both need a shower," she said. "Phew! Be decent." Bert's overtures were usually half-joking, easy to resist; now for the first time he persisted.

"I don't care how funky you smell; funk is a turn-on." He poked one grubby hand under her waistband, fumbling the buttons on her jeans. She'd had to practically knee him in the groin.

He finally admitted he was high on speed; then all the way back to Cleveland he talked about battles with police, spouting his analysis of the Revolution's new phase. "Two, three, many Chicagos!" he proclaimed. "We won an important victory."

"If that was victory," Jane said, "I don't know how many we can stand." She sat next to Tessa, who drove; neither woman had combed her hair—much less washed or eaten—for days. Marvin slept among the sleeping bags on the floor at the back, and Bert wouldn't quit talking. And she couldn't get rid of her anger, even when Tessa scolded her for overreacting.

When Jane asked about Jimmy—had he returned to Cleveland? How was he?—Bert didn't know. They'd held demonstrators for 48 hours and released them on their own recognizance—no names. Jane's mother had returned to work; that's how much better Daddy was. "There's support for what you did in Chicago," Mom said. "Read *The New Republic*. I'm feeling hopeful, in spite of Humphrey." Jane couldn't feel hopeful. She was too sore and tired. For two days she'd stayed in the apartment, taking hot showers and sleeping, barely noticing Tessa or Javier. Then she and Tessa took the bus to New York.

Sitting in her grassy hollow, Jane cleaned sand from between her toes and felt free. She rolled up the London Fog and tucked it under her head to lie on. She was damned fond of this coat. She'd worn it while running through tear gas. She'd worn it when the police pulled her out of the phone booth, and in the jail, that thick-doored room packed with women. All night long they'd taken turns sitting on the cement floor with their legs layered over and under, backs against others' backs, sometimes putting sleepy heads on others' shoulders. Jane talked mostly with Patricia, who'd come to the Movement through feminism, whereas Jane had come to feminism through the Movement. Periodically a deputy would pound the door and tell them to shut up. The noise was significant: a group from New York kept up chants and songs that grew increasingly bawdy. A few women quarreled. One who looked Chinese retreated into a private hell, eyes squeezed shut, arms wrapped around her knees, keening in a high, thin monotone till her voice gave out. No one could calm her down or talk her into opening her eyes and joining them. "Power to the women, fuck the pigs!" sang the New Yorkers. One of them yelled "Fucking pig!" just as a female deputy opened the door, and for that she was refused her chance for the toilet. She screamed in frustration and had to pee on the floor, apologizing as she soaked the shoes of others around her.

They were escorted to the toilet one at a time by deputies who insulted them as they walked down the hall. Jane's deputy, older and not as beefy as the blue helmets on the street (more like an old mongrel dog than a pig), kept his hand on Jane's shoulder and told her to take off her coat. "Take your hand away," she said, "and I might." When he dropped his hand to his belt, close to the gun and the nightstick, she said, "I think I'll just leave the coat on."

"Hey, Marilyn," he called. "Need you to come search. Got this bitch here who refuses to take her raincoat off."

"Do it yourself," came the female voice from another room. "Have fun."

The deputy did not have fun. He searched Jane as though he were rifling a chest of drawers, reaching into her coat pockets, then the pockets of her jeans, stuffing the contents into a paper sack. He felt under her shirt, inside her bra, his face impassive; then he made her bend over and poked his fingers into her anus and her vagina. "Now I got to warsh my hands," he said, making a disgusted face. "You can use the toilet." The toilet was filthy with shit and vomit. While Jane peed, the deputy stood at the sink lathering his hands. He dried his fingers carefully and put on gloves. Jane asked to wash her hands and face, and he refused. "I know you don't believe in warshing; you're just being difficult," he said, steering Jane by the shoulders out of the bathroom and back to the holding cell.

Never before, not even in Mississippi, had a jailer probed Jane's softest places, pressed her bruises as though she were fruit he was testing for ripeness, left her shaken and trembling. She stepped high over women's laps, careful not to bump or knock—others were bruised, too—until she got to Patricia, who said, "Another male chauvinist pig did his dirty work, huh?" Then Jane crumpled, hands covering her face.

"Listen to me," Patricia said. "Don't you be ashamed. Men have been setting up women to feel filthy for ages, and we're not filthy. You know that."

Jane had thought she knew that. She'd learned to talk about body parts calmly; she was no longer repelled by menstrual blood, phlegm, urine, or shit. But in the conversation with Patricia and five others, Jane saw she'd felt ashamed for years, since her breasts first started to bud. She'd blamed sore breasts for hurting her, rather than blaming the sixth-grade boys who poked her to see if she'd cry out like a doll with an internal squawk box.

Even now, after the hot soapy showers, after laundering all her clothes (but not Ivy's coat; she'd pay a dry cleaner, eventually; then she'd give it back), Jane still felt filthy—and sore in some deep place impossible to reach. No wonder Bert's pawing had been so hard to take.

The two pale boys ran from the sea to the beach, and she hid behind a thick clump of grass. "Hope we get to see one of those babes," called one boy.

"Ah, they got 'em locked up," the other said. "Gotta keep 'em virgins till tonight's over."

"You really believe all those Miss America girls are virgins?" They were walking together now, past Jane. She clutched the coat, redolent of smoke, urine, tear gas, sweat, and fear. She inhaled it deeply; the smell was awful, but it told her where she'd been and who she was. It eased the shame.

On the Boardwalk, women were gathering in pairs, in threes, in clusters; their hair blew in the wind. They talked excitedly with one another. Some carried signs which they laid in a heap on the boards. "This is the first thing I've ever organized without any men involved," said one woman to another. Jane half-recognized her—from New York SDS, maybe.

The first time. Jane thought of the all-women Welfare Rights movement to which Dora's boyfriend Stephen had objected. She thought of Mothers Opposed to Poverty, a group with no men—but they kept arranging meetings around their husbands' schedules. Even Jane asked Marvin for advice. The Women Strike for Peace March in front of the Conrad Hilton had been her first all-women demonstration. She wondered now if men had helped organize it.

"It was a little scary," the woman was saying. "I came up against getting the permit, thought, *Gotta ask my old man how to handle this.* Then I realized: *no, not his action.* And I did it myself, my way."

Frieda, that was this woman's name. She wrote for *New Left Notes.* "This is a great day," she said to Jane. The haze was clearing, the line was forming, and women were having fun. Jane picked up a sign that said "Welcome to the Miss America Cattle Auction" and joined the pickets in a great circle.

"Here comes the sheep!" Voices rose, excited about the sheep, led by two ropes attached to its collar. The women coaxed it along, alternately tugging on the ropes and patting its haunches. It wore a thick coat of wool and a bewildered look. "Our new Miss America!" Frieda hollered. If the Yippies could nominate a pig for president, then the feminists could nominate a sheep for Miss America. Jane put on her coat, settled her backpack on both shoulders, and joined the line. "We're going till midnight," said a voice behind her. A flyer came into her hands.

"It should be a groovy day on the Boardwalk in the sun with our sisters," the flyer said. "In case of arrests, however, we plan to reject all male authority and demand to be busted by policewomen only. (In Atlantic City, women cops are not permitted to make arrests—dig that!)" Male reporters would be refused interviews. Jane read the ten points of protest as she walked, sun on her cheeks. The language was fresh and witty, not strident. If Chicago was a new phase in the Revolution, then Atlantic City, ten days after Grant Park, was an even newer phase.

It would have done Ivy good to be here. The girl played up to men; she was charming, naïve, and cute without even meaning to be. In some moments (watching Ivy swish through the hotel lobby, for example, pursing her lips as she looked in the mirror by the elevators) Jane envied her ease with femininity. But at the rate Ivy was going, she'd be married to Chuck and mothering three babies within the next five years. Jane had known Civil Rights workers who got buried alive in housekeeping and baby care. She didn't want to split Ivy apart from Chuck; they were sweet together, and Chuck was a good guy. But Ivy needed to be herself first, Jane thought.

The sheep had been duly crowned and paraded, and a life-sized paper puppet with women chained to her ("women enslaved by beauty standards") was being auctioned when Jane heard her name called. The voice came from somewhere high up, behind and above her. "Over here! Look up!"

The bridge spanned the road next to the Convention Center; a red-haired woman waved her arms. Patricia. Jane danced in the picket line, waving her poster, and Patricia called, "Stay there! We're coming down."

She emerged onto the Boardwalk with her friends and caught Jane in a full-body hug. She felt Patricia's soft ampleness, hands stroking her back; women didn't hug like this in Cleveland. Her parents didn't hug like this. She heard Patricia's deep sigh and felt herself relax, fully welcomed, and safe. *Safe.*

"Meet my pals." Patricia introduced the Boston group: five women. They were not dressed like the women striking for peace, or like the Heights MOP. No makeup, for one thing. One wore a Movement button that said "The Bread Is Rising." Another had almost boy-short hair. A stocky woman with large breasts wore a man's seersucker vest. The fifth wore a long dress made of India-print. They seemed delighted with each other.

"I thought of asking you that night we were in jail together," Patricia said, "if you're a lesbian, too. You look a little shocked. Guess not."

"I'm not shocked," Jane said, and immediately felt a little less shocked. "I can't see what difference it makes." Was she flushing because she had lied? No, she was embarrassed that she'd felt such happiness at seeing Patricia and a little frightened that she'd loved the embrace. "We're all fed up with the Miss America meat-market," she added. The five lesbians smiled.

"Let's go." The woman with the seersucker vest tapped Patricia on the arm. "They're opening the Convention Center."

"You need tickets, don't you?" Jane said. She wanted to stay with them in solidarity. She also wanted to be free of them.

"We have three." Patricia pulled the tickets out of her shirt-front pocket. "Want to come?"

Jane shook her head. "I don't want to take up anyone else's space. And I'd rather be outside." She wasn't afraid of them as much as she was averse to the contest. She remembered bits she'd seen on TV last year at Bert and Marvin's apartment.

All the contestants looked alike. Their comments were superficial, their talents amateurish. During a baton-twirling act she'd talked with Marvin about travelling to meet the North Vietnamese. Bert had stayed rapt.

Patricia and her friends had the Women's Liberation banner to show when they got the chance. They hoped for audience reaction, a contestant who'd take the Feminists' side. "In any case, we get to be a bit disruptive," the friend said. "And we might be on TV."

After they left, Jane wandered into the crowd of women on the Boardwalk. The march had ended; the afternoon light slanted onto glittering waves. It would be fall soon. Ivy was moving back to campus. She couldn't live openly with Chuck and stay enrolled in college; she was too honest to live with Chuck and keep it secret. She'd applied for permission to live in an apartment. Maybe there would be an extra room, Jane thought. She didn't want to share space with Javier. A group of demonstrators sang, "Ain't she sweet, making profit off her meat."

"*You're* the cow!" someone yelled: a woman's voice, harsh, flavored with New Jersey. She had long blonde hair— brassy and too straight: dyed and ironed. Jane had forgotten that her sign said "Miss America Cattle Auction." Oh. She was the cow.

"Moo!" She grinned and came closer.

The woman wore a short skirt made of white plastic, with a wide belt that made her hips look large. Next to her, a man with an earnest face under the pomaded curl on his forehead asked, "Which one of those girls is your husband, or do youse all sleep around?"

There it was again: *whore-dyke.* Loathing him, Jane inhaled, exhaled, and felt a fist inside her chest gather her together. "Moouhooh," she said, making the sound rise and bawl like a real cow's lowing. "I don't belong to anyone. I come and go as I please. I'm into freedom."

"Right on, sister!" One of the women on the Boardwalk beamed at Jane.

"Oh, you'd love to be Miss America, if you could," the man said.

"You're just jealous!" shouted the girl.

The sister and three other demonstrators had stopped to watch Jane handle this couple. Others were being heckled farther along the Boardwalk. Jane heard calls: "Get on your broom and fly out of here!" "Go back to Russia!"

"You couldn't be Miss America if you were the last woman on earth," said the blonde. "You're too ugly."

"I wouldn't wear high heels with a bathing suit," Jane said. "I don't know any self-respecting person who would. Actually," she said straight to the blonde, "I think you're more beautiful than any of the Miss America contestants."

There was a hush.

"Hey, she's hot for you," the man said to the blonde. "Stay away from my girlfriend, bitch."

"Who does he think you are?" Jane asked the girl. "Does he think you'd be taken in by anyone who gives you a compliment? You're strong."

"How do you know?" the girl asked. Suddenly, a real question.

"Your voice," Jane said. "You've got a good strong way of saying what you think. Do you sing?"

The man snickered.

"Shut up!" His girlfriend nudged him. "Yeah, I sing, pretty good too."

"For a church choir," the man said, his upper lip curled.

"What's wrong with a church choir?" Jane demanded of him. "Doesn't a church need good strong singers? Does a woman have to win a contest to be good at what she does?" I'm good at this, she thought, and wondered if "this"—the connection she'd established with the blonde in the white-plastic skirt—had a name.

"Let's get out of here." The man took his girlfriend by the arm. "This bitch is messing with you." He said "with you" as *witchah*. He pulled the blonde; she hung back.

"Tell me true," she said. "If you *could* be Miss America, or even Miss New Jersey or Miss Hoboken—if you had a real chance, you'd take it, wouldn't you?" Jane shook her head firmly. "Why *not?*"

Jane had ten answers, wittily summarized on the paper in her pocket, but none of them fit this moment. Between the hanks of artificially lightened and pressed hair, under the plucked eyebrows, this girl needed a specific, personal, direct answer. For the moment, at least, she trusted Jane to be honest. "Because it's a lie," Jane said. Which lie? She asked herself. Purity? Success? Picture Miss America sitting on a shit-stained toilet, watched by the deputy who'd probed her ass with his fingers. "You wear the crown and carry the roses for one day, one minute, and then what? For the next year, people tell you where to go and what to say, you smile and wave at strangers, but what about your own thoughts, your own aspirations?"

"What about them?" The blonde pulled against her boyfriend, who still gripped her arm. "You go on. I'll come in a minute," she told him.

"Uh-unh, you're coming with me," he said. "Now."

"I wanna talk to this person, she's interesting." Blonde hair flapped as she turned toward her scowling boyfriend. "Now get off my case!" Her voice rang.

He pulled harder. "You do what I say."

"Ouch!" she yelled. "You're giving me bruises!"

"Do you?" Jane leaned forward, her voice low. "Do you always do what he says?"

He heard anyway. "She sure as hell does! She's a good girl. We're getting married in two months."

"Really?" The blonde looked up in surprise. He let go and put his arm around her shoulders. "You're really gonna marry me?" Her voice rose to a squeak.

"You bet I am," he said. He kissed the top of her head, right on the dark roots at her part, and looked defiantly at Jane. "No one'll marry *you*, ever," he said. "You're gonna be one sorry old maid. Let's go, Milly."

Now he used her name. He'd marry her, and then he'd probably order her around. But Milly's eyes had connected with Jane's. For a minute she'd understood. Would she keep singing in the choir? Would the church tell her she had to obey her husband? Pondering Milly's life, Jane thought, He's exactly right. I am a woman who'll never get married. If I feel like a sorry old maid part of the time, so be it. The decision was made. It had been made a long time ago.

"Right on, Sister," said a woman standing nearby. "That was impressive."

Four women rolled a huge barrel to the center of the circle and tied a sign around it with string: *Freedom Trash Can.* Women held aloft high heels, long chiffon scarves, bras, girdles, and fishnet stockings—emblems of male control over women's bodies—to become trash. Jane walked away from the Boardwalk.

She'd known. Whenever she ate the point of a wedge of pie, she'd known she would not marry—yet at the same time she'd assumed she would. After Norman had left, she'd let Jimmy into her bed; she'd even let him grope her possessively in public. She'd taken shelter under Marvin's arm. She'd resented Javier partly because she envied Tessa.

Early in the visit with her parents, Jane had asked her mother: "If you wanted to go to Italy that much, why didn't you just go on your own?"

Mom had given the response Jane had heard before: "When you get married, you'll know." Jane had thought of saying, *But I'll never get married.* But she didn't know then. Now it was settled as finally as the posts holding up the Boardwalk.

She never wanted to be tethered like Ivy and Chuck. It seemed impossible to know each of them separately. Ivy was always mentioning Chuck, and he was completely hung up on the idea of "his" girl. Jane had thought, if Ivy weren't around, it would be pleasant to sleep with Chuck. But like every man she'd been close to, he'd probably want to "score." She never again wanted to add to a man's score.

On this part of the beach, demonstrators blended with ordinary beachgoers, buying drinks at the refreshment stand, watching the waves lick the shore. Their bodies threw long shadows in the late-summer twilight; the edges of buildings and boards were sharp, the cracks between very dark. The women's restroom—a latrine really, with a cold shower and changing areas—was set between two former concession stands, now boarded up. Jane relieved herself in the cool briny stall, its smells cleansed by sea air, rinsed her feet in the shower and sluiced her face with water from cupped hands.

She stretched her arms overhead, then swung down and touched her toes, and felt her body fill with well-being. Gone, finally, was the burning rage that had propelled her through the Chicago streets. Fear was lifting and floating away like mist. Maybe it was the ocean that calmed and strengthened her inside.

She thought of climbing the dune behind the restroom for a better view, and entered the dark space between two buildings. Two women stood there, kissing each other. They held each other close, cupped each other's cheeks with their hands, and moved their heads and mouths, nibbling, sipping, drinking each other in. Jane could not stop herself from staring.

They were beautiful, these women—fleshy; one was even stout. They made little soft sounds that reminded Jane of eating strawberries. She thought she'd never seen such loveliness before in her life.

One of the women glanced up and saw her. "Sh," she said, and pushed the other away gently. Patricia and her lover.

"Don't stop!" Jane whispered. She realized she was intruding—"I'm sorry"—and spun around and ran, her ragged braid flopping against her shoulder, loose hair blowing across her eyes and into her mouth. *Lesbians*, they had said. *No difference*, she'd replied. She hadn't expected beauty. She trotted toward the Convention Center, back to the Boardwalk, where women were filling the Freedom Trash Can with symbols of their oppression. A gray-haired woman walked past with a book, *Tropic of Cancer*, and heaved it into the can. Then she raised her arms in a giant V for victory, her face shiny with tears.

Three women in pastel dresses with tight waists and poufy skirts were performing a guerrilla theater stunt—painting red circles on each others' cheeks, spraying each other with a perfume atomizer made of a two-quart jar and a balloon. One shouted "Down with body odor!" in a shrill voice and sprayed another who coughed elaborately, then raised a pair of enormous scissors and began to cut away the yellow skirt of the woman with the paint brush. "Skirts are short this year!" They went into a frenzy of cutting, spraying, and painting.

Jane watched the scissors. They looked like hedge clippers. Bits of cloth fell into a pile, and the woman in yellow scooped them up to toss into the trash can, leaving the scissors on the ground—an invitation. Jane picked them up. "Do you mind?" she asked the woman whose dress was now in tatters around her knees. The actress gave a wide red-mouthed smile and stuck out one hip. "Cut right here," she said, lifting a train of yellow netting and chiffon that fell over her rear end to the ground. Jane clipped once, twice, and again to part the last threads. "Piece of tail!" the actress yelled, holding it aloft and dumping it into the trash can. Everyone cheered. The actress did a little jig in her high-top sneakers.

"My turn," Jane said, handing over the clippers. "Time to get rid of the braid." She lifted it off the back of her neck. Five years she'd been trailing this rope of hair, growing relentlessly heavier and longer. It stuck in her coat and got tangled in her backpack straps. The blue pig in Chicago had not been the first to pull it, just the most vicious. Washing, combing, letting it dry, braiding took hours—for what? "Cut it off!" She stretched the braid and held it still, a snake with its neck on the guillotine.

The clippers came together with a metallic shearing finality; Jane felt the braid writhe between the blades. Then it was in her hand, held high, and women around her cheered. "Freedom!" she cried, and threw. The braid sailed into the can, a furry arrow with a rubber band at the end.

"Freedom!" they yelled. Someone threw in a bottle of dishwashing soap; someone else threw in hairspray. The three actresses began a can-can, kicking their bare legs high. Another can-can line formed. All over the Boardwalk women danced as the sun set behind the Convention Center. Jane joined a *Hora* circle. Her head felt light, her neck felt cool and free; the short ends of hair blew around her face.

Chapter 19

September 14, 1968
Hessler Road

Ivy stepped between two fluted pillars into the past. Heights women strolled among divans and clusters of prim chairs. Leather bound books stood in matched sets behind glass doors in cupboards ornamented with wood carvings. Above the marble mantelpiece hung a portrait of a lady in dark blue velvet, her white hair piled high, pearls in a long rope around her neck and dangling from her earlobes. She glared as if she recognized that Ivy did not belong. Aunt Peg, fingering price tags on the china dishes on a table, had called this a house sale. Then she brought Ivy to a mansion. Someone had died, maybe the pearl-hung lady over the mantlepiece, and the descendants wanted to empty the place. The prices were low: a stuffed ottoman for $3.00; a pair of silver-plated candlesticks for $5.00. Why were only Heights people here? Dora would like the candlesticks. Ivy put them back on the table. All she wanted was a dresser for her bedroom on Hessler Road, in the duplex she shared with Gail and Shelly—a place full of life.

Unlike this place: an ancient canopy bed reigned over the bedroom. A white china basin and pitcher, $2.50 each, sat on the marble top of an old-fashioned commode. In a cabinet underneath Ivy found a chamber pot shaped like a giant teacup with a lid and roses painted on its side. Gleaming clean.

A Dylan song played in her head: *You must leave now, take what you need, you think will last.* Good, here was the dresser: $12.00, a huge mirror included. The top drawer stuck—no, it opened to a firm tug, and inside were scarves, each straight-pinned with a tag. 10¢ per scarf, 25¢ for a purple shawl with fringe that slid over Ivy's fingers. *But whatever you wish to keep, you better grab it fast.* Ivy forced the drawer closed. Other drawers held tablecloths, tea towels, and napkins. Too big for Aunt Peg's Corvair, the chest without the mirror might fit into the trunk of Chuck's Pontiac. Ivy leaned against the fuzzy wallpaper and closed one eye to see the mounts and screws on the back. Yes, the mirror would come off, so the pieces could be transported separately. On the floor stood a pair of knee-high sheepskin boots. "Airman's boots WWI," said the tag. $2.00. Ivy removed one sneaker and slid her foot into a boot. With thick socks, it would fit. She stepped into the other boot, tugged, and felt the leather tear. She pulled it off her foot. The sheepskin was rotting. Mum would say she must offer to pay. *Look out, the saints are coming through*...She stood the boots neatly against the wall and fled the room. Time to find Aunt Peg, close the deal, get out of here. How come "It's All Over Now, Baby Blue" was stuck in her head? Nothing was all over, except this world of mansions and marble-topped commodes.

At the top of the polished oak stairs Aunt Peg was inspecting a bedspread, dark red brocade. "Hold up that end, Ivy. I want to make sure it has no holes. It's such a steal."

"Everything's a steal," Ivy said. She folded the corners together. "I found my dresser, $12.00. Who should I pay?"

"Just a minute." Peg adjusted her half-glasses and peered at the bedspread. Her permanent had grown out; she'd put her hair in a French twist and wore gold hoop earrings. Still tan from summer weekends on the Lake Erie shore, her body seemed to have grown softer and more elastic. "Only a couple of snags on this side," Peg said. "It'll suit your purposes."

"I don't have any purposes." This spread was much too large for Ivy's bed—an old rollaway cot. "Come on. Somebody might buy that dresser before we get to it."

"Cover that horrible plaid couch in the front room," Peg said, her arm curled protectively around the red brocade. "Nothing like a used bedspread to improve old furniture. Have you checked out the kitchen? I bet you could find..."

"Aunt Peg, I don't have time to roam around buying stuff I don't need." Ivy was secretary of the SDS chapter; interested students were trying to call her at home. She'd been talking to them all week, handing out her phone number.

"Heard you were in Chicago," one freshman said to her. "I wanted to go, but I couldn't."

"My older brother climbed the General Logan statue," said another. "I'm ready to join."

SDS had invitations to speak to a class, a church youth group, a high school Junior Council on World Affairs. Ivy didn't know what to say to these people; she needed discussion. But instead of planning the Revolution, here she was in the heart of Old Establishment Cleveland on a Saturday afternoon, among women who murmured reverently as they fingered linens and lace and glassware. Gold bracelets clinked against antique china teacups. None of the ruling-class spoils in this room could relieve anyone's pain.

Last weekend in Bloomington, Ivy's lungs had seized up; she'd brought neither inhaler refills nor aminophyllin, so she'd had to ask her father to write a prescription. "*Now* you tell me," he'd said. "Minutes away from dinner. Which your mother's been working on all afternoon."

"Just write it," Ivy said, clutching the back of a chair. "I'll go to the pharmacy. Back in minutes." Pent-up air threatened to burst her lungs.

Her father relaxed against the couch cushions, his tie loose, a glass of Dewar's in his hand. "You can't drive like that," he said. "How about I pour you a little Scotch?"

The drink made Ivy cough, and the muscles in her back crimped painfully. Tears spilled over her lower eyelids; more coughing. Pee ran down her leg.

Her father gazed at the painted landscape above the fireplace. "I thought you knew better than to let your medicine run out," he said. "But hell, I was sure you knew better than to run through tear gas." His voice stayed even, clinical.

"I was fine," Ivy said, forcing air out. "in Chicago."

"Sure you were," her father said. "So were all those unhinged self-styled revolutionaries. All you did was make matters worse for the Democrats." He leaned forward, elbows on his knees, pink in the face. "You do understand, don't you, that Nixon's election is now a sure thing?"

Was he so angry that he welcomed her suffering? If only she could breathe, she'd tell him what was going down. Che had known how it felt to be strangling from deep within the chest.

"America thrives on the two-party system," her father went on, explaining how each party cast a net with nodes to which its members attached themselves. You connect to the net, then you get your people elected, your legislation passed.

You'd be on the winning team, Ivy thought. She realized suddenly she could die while her father lectured on the merits of the two-party system.

Her mother came in to announce dinner. "Do you have any of that Scotch for me? Oh, I'll just have white wine. Ivy, will you light the candles?"

Ivy straightened and pulled herself up to standing. All right, she would die lighting candles. She got as far as the dining room doorway.

"Goodness, you're in rather bad shape," Mum said.

"She let her meds run out," Dad said from behind Ivy. He put his hand on her back. The warmth of his palm eased the soreness, but it lay heavy against her struggling ribs. "She wants a prescription."

"Well, John, you'd better write it," Hetty said. "Ivy, this is extremely annoying. Home for only two days, and you've managed to ruin our one nice dinner. Beef tenderloin."

Extremely annoying doesn't begin to describe the situation, Ivy thought. She couldn't speak. Her mother had made a centerpiece of daisies and purple asters. The china plates, the glasses, and the silverware all gleamed balefully. The little tubes in her lungs, the bronchioles and alvioli, would not *would not* let air out. "Couldn't help it." Her voice emerged in a whisper, her eyes leaked shame, and her legs were damp with pee.

"Let's not forgo the dinner, Hetty," Dad said. "If she sits quietly the asthma will ease up. Give her some tea; tannin is a natural antihistamine."

"Can't sit," Ivy insisted. Dad was an obstetrician, not a lung specialist, but how could he not *know*? Maybe if she passed out, he'd get it. She shut her eyes, willing herself to pass out.

Her mother bent to look at Ivy's hands clutching the chair. Then she looked at Ivy's mouth. "I'm afraid we'll have to do something, John," she said. "Your daughter's lips and fingernails are blue."

"Ahhhh." Her father groaned with disgust. "The hospital pharmacy is the only one open at this hour." He avoided Ivy's eyes as he put on his jacket and got a prescription pad out of the breast pocket. "What do you take?"

She whispered precise amounts and correct spellings. Her mother gave her a cup of tea and went upstairs without a word. Alone next to the gleaming, flowery table, Ivy breathed in tea-steam and stopped thinking.

The medicine, when it finally got to her, made it possible to go to bed. She slept fitfully, waking every two hours, waiting a third hour so she could use the inhaler, sleeping another two hours. She vomited her first three aminophyllin tablets; the second three stayed down. The next day she called Chuck, who drove to rescue her. He didn't understand what had happened, and she only said, "Take me home. I'll never do that again."

"Do what? Visit your folks?"

"Maybe," Ivy said. "I think I might be allergic to them."

So a week later here she was with Aunt Peg, who did not mention a conversation with John and Hetty. They found the man to pay: Kevin Waterson, a grandson of the lady in blue velvet who stared over the mantelpiece with such hostility. As Ivy and Peg emptied the dresser drawers, Waterson complained about how troublesome the sale was, how he needed to get back to the bond market, how boring the bond market was. His voice grated against Ivy's spine.

"Do you know the Watts, near Chestnut Hills?" Peg asked.

"My parents did," Waterson said. He and Peg dropped names—Watt, Halle, Crile—ruling class people, as if the names were passwords to an inner circle of power and money. Ivy piled scarves and tablecloths on the bed. Once they had been expensive; now they were bland and boring. The china basin and pitcher appealed to her as relics of a time without plumbing: no ugly pipes, no taps clogged with rust, as in The Monmouth. But she knew how servants would have heated water on a stove that burned coal or wood, then poured it scalding into the pitcher. Someone had the job of emptying the wash-water; someone dumped shit and cleaned the china pot. So there: flush toilets promoted equality, and Ivy would never buy the china.

"My niece was in Chicago," she heard Peg say. "Ask her."

Kevin Waterson was regarding Ivy as though she'd grown older or something. "I admire people with the courage of their convictions," he said. "But throwing bags of excrement and dressing outrageously and smoking LSD just hurt the cause."

Ivy wondered what he thought the cause was. "LSD isn't smoked," she said, keeping her voice patient. "And nobody threw any bags of excrement."

"The newspapers said they did. The police reported it."

"We ran around the city for days. Can you imagine carrying a bag of excrement with you all that time so you could throw it at some cop?" If she'd been a servant carrying the grandmother's shit in the chamber pot, she would have longed to throw it.

Mr. Waterson's nose wrinkled. "Are you telling me the police lied?"

"Why did they say they were under attack when they were the ones with guns, clubs, and tear gas?" Her voice rose. "Why did they charge into the seats at the Grant Park bandshell clubbing people who were just standing there chanting OM?"

"I'm sure they had their reasons."

"Mystery to me," Ivy said. "We were outnumbered five to one."

"You certainly made an impression," Aunt Peg said, as they settled into the Corvair. Kevin Waterson had accepted $1.50 for the bedspread and nothing for the shawl. Ivy didn't mention the torn airman's boots.

"That shawl is absolutely royal purple," Aunt Peg said, as Ivy led her into the apartment on Hessler. "It would be perfect draped over a baby grand piano. Didn't your dorm have a grand piano?"

"It did," Ivy said, wishing she'd refused the shawl, "and a nosy housemother and a stairwell that made all phone calls public. I like inviting you for coffee without having to ask permission first." She put a saucepan full of water on the stove.

"You *do* need a kettle," Aunt Peg said. "I'll cover the couch, okay?"

Ivy liked the apartment's worn couch and the two stained stuffed chairs. They were comfortable; she could put her feet up or drink coffee without worrying about the fabric. She liked Shelly and Gail. When she'd announced she was moving to Hessler Road, Chuck had said, "It's stupid you couldn't just keep living with me." But in truth, Ivy was relieved to be out of the grimy efficiency at The Monmouth. Here she could be her own person.

Right after Chicago, she'd been glad to be wrapped in Chuck's long arms, her head against his blue shirt, clean and safe. He'd given her a kaleidescope. Lovely, to spin the tube and watch patterns form, then dissolve. Each design was a mandala, Chuck told her, whole, perfect, and transient, never to be replicated. She spun the tube, delighted as the patterns formed and dissolved. She tried to show Chuck several particularly good ones, but he couldn't hold the kaleidescope still enough; by the time he looked, the pattern had changed again. "I've been thinking," he said. "It's time to change your name to Ivy Leggit."

Oh no! Too soon! She clung with her arms around his waist, heard the rasp of his hand stroking her hair. The obvious response was to kiss him and say Yes. *Yes!* But she couldn't. "That's too big to think about right now," she mumbled, her mouth close to his ear. "Anyway, I've got to graduate before I can get married. So do you."

"No," Chuck said. "I'm not going back to school." He'd paid his father and gotten two part-time jobs, one at the university bookstore, the other at Underground Books. He could earn enough for rent and food, but not tuition. "I can make my own way," he said. "The Cleveland Movement needs an underground newspaper."

"Chuck's starting an underground newspaper," Ivy said to her aunt. Peg sat on the couch draped with the dark red bedspread, stirring milk and sugar into her coffee. "He'll want to do an article on Mothers Opposed to Poverty."

Peg brightened. "He should," she said. "Welfare Food Allowance Month is under way. We couldn't get Shirley Stokes to sign up; her husband's been so embattled since Glenville. But we did get Mrs. Louis Stokes, the state representative's wife."

Shelly burst into the room, carrying a bag of apples. "I've been in the country!" she said. "I didn't know Ohio could be so pretty." She was flushed and breathing hard; her hair rippled around her face and down her back. "We picked apples. I ate so many! We could just pick 'em off the ground, take a bite off the good side and throw the rest away. I'm drunk on apples, I have cider-breath." She blew into Ivy's face. "Great couch cover!"

"Who's with you?" Ivy saw at first a young boy looking around the living room. Shelly's brother? Then the figure turned, showing a girl's face under the bill of a Greek Fisherman's cap.

"This is Angela," Shelly said. "She's a freshman..."

"Fresh*woman*," Angela corrected.

"Anyway, she's in the Movement."

The phone rang: Jimmy Fulero. After Chicago, he had transferred from Kalamazoo to Case Western so he could stay in Cleveland and organize. "You know, Ivy, I don't think Bert should come to the first SDS meeting," he said.

"We can't tell him not to," Ivy said.

"Why not?" Jimmy's two nights and two days in the Cook County jail had made him years older and more imperious. Full of himself, Chuck had said.

"That's what participatory democracy means: we don't exclude people. What's wrong with Bert?"

Jimmy sighed. "If you don't know, I can't..." Then silence. Then: "Okay. He's pushing too hard for direct action. You and I know we have to do a lot of educating first, especially with all these new students."

"And we both know that action is the way people get radicalized. Listen, Jimmy, I can't talk right now. Can you call back later?" Ivy thought frantically; *this* was why she needed to talk to people—but not just Jimmy. Maybe Jane or Marvin could help make sense of how to get Jimmy and Bert working together. The Movement needed both action and education.

"You call me," Jimmy said. "Don't wait too long. Is Gail there?"

Gail picked up the phone upstairs, and Ivy hung up, more bothered than she could say. "There's a little disagreement," she told Aunt Peg.

"Men are like roosters," Shelly said. She put a dozen apples in a wooden bowl on the coffee table. "Look at all the reds and greens."

"Admirable apples," Aunt Peg said, stressing the *A*s. Then she looked at her watch. "Oh my dear, I've enjoyed this. And I must go. I have to meet, um"—she bit her lip. "Someone," she finished.

Maybe Peg was just sensitive enough to get out of the way. Maybe she wanted Ivy to ask about her boyfriend. But if Ivy did ask, suddenly there'd be a man to meet, or to avoid meeting, another person to feel guilty about not being nice to.

She thanked her aunt and felt a bit sad, watching Peg go out the door alone.

"I hope you're staying at Chuck's tonight," Shelly said. "A guy I know from Nyack's coming through on his way west; could he use your bed?" A guy Shelly didn't want to sleep with? She'd come back from Long Island in love with nature, makeupless, determined (she said) to play the field. She had not mentioned Bert. Hard to remember that the two of them had ever been close enough to quarrel in The Big Penny.

"As long as your friend doesn't get stuff on the sheets," Ivy said. "That's my only set."

Gail came down the stairs. "Jimmy and I are going to *Planet of the Apes.*" She took an apple and bit into it. "Yum," she said. "Hi, Angela."

Jimmy and Gail? But Gail had said yesterday she was loyal to Joe. Ivy tried to picture the SDS meeting with Jimmy and Bert in the same room. Maybe if Chuck came to take notes for the underground paper, they'd talk reasonably.

Maybe if she and Chuck could talk just about how to balance action and education, they could figure it out. Chuck liked to think about abstractions like action vs. education.

"Thanks for your room," Shelly said. "Actually, my Nyack friend is on his way to Canada. He'll never come back. *Never.* The word gets me right here." She pressed her sternum.

Ivy was about to say, But you could visit *him*, when the phone rang again. Bert. "Ivy, we gotta talk," he said. "I'm coming over." Oh shit. Jimmy was on his way too.

Then she had a good idea. "Can you bring the blue van?" she asked. "I've got to pick up a dresser."

Half an hour later she met Bert at the curb and said "Fairmount Boulevard."

"La dee dah," Bert said. "A Heights dresser." He drove uphill talking in fragments. "Action's all there is. You get what I'm saying? Little Italy's quiet today. Ever been to that restaurant? Mafia. We live in a police state, now. That much is clear to everyone. In Chicago I was Toto, biting the leg of the little man behind the curtain."

"The wizard was fake, but he had a lot of backup," Ivy said. What had been so urgent? "There's the house. No! Here." She leaned into him to point out the looping drive in front of the Waterson mansion.

"Jesus, this is a fucking palace," Bert said. He checked himself in the rearview mirror, parting his summer-gilt hair with his fingers. "I feel like I'm casing out a joint."

But he got on well enough with Mr. Waterson, who now seemed to approve of the counterculture; Ivy couldn't tell why. The two men loaded the dresser together, and Waterson gave them two old blankets to use as padding. "Peace!" He held up his fingers in a V for peace as they drove away.

"Jimmy's gone over to the national Mobe," Bert said, when Ivy finally asked what *exactly* he'd phoned to talk about. "He's heading the college Committee to End the War with a whole different line than SDS. He shouldn't be at the meeting." Now neither guy wanted the other to be there.

"The Mobe is part of the Movement," Ivy insisted. "And we're an open group. Are you going to fight him if he comes?" They were parking on Hessler Road now; the duplex was quiet. Ivy unlocked the front door and called inside; no one was home.

"I'm not starting any fights," Bert said. "But listen, he's joined the Young Socialist Alliance, and they take orders from the central committee of the Socialist Workers Party; it's the opposite of participatory democracy. They will have told him to skew the agenda to avoid revolutionary action. Have you got that corner?" They were carrying the mirror in its frame upstairs. They went back down for the dresser drawers.

"I won't let him fuck up the revolutionary agenda," Ivy said. "I *won't*. Dig?" They lugged the dresser drawers, two at a time, then the dresser itself, up to Ivy's room. The labor made her breath short, as it seemed to calm Bert down.

He screwed the mirror onto the back. "Hold right here, will you?" he said. To hold the connecting boards steady so he could put in extra screws, she had to lean close over his shoulder and twist so he had enough light. The afternoon had turned gray and rainy, the light dimmed further by dust on Ivy's one small window.

"All my stuff is still in suitcases," Ivy said. "I really needed this. Thanks much."

"There," he said, and stood next to her. Close to her. He seemed huge in the small room, with fragrant bits of sawdust on his shirt. His large hands moved down her back to her hips. She felt her breath rise to the top of her chest, felt her breasts lighten as though they were hollow. Then they were kissing, deep rich tongue-kisses. His breath came warm on her cheek and she breathed high and light. "I've wanted to do this for so long," Bert said. He opened her shirt, pulled her bra to one side and kissed her breast.

Ivy felt something like an electric shock and squirmed away.

"You're thinking about your boyfriend," he murmured, inhaling deeply and exhaling, a huge breath. "Just as well," he said. "I could really get a case of you, and I don't want to."

"A case of me?"

"I could fall in love," he said.

"Oh God, don't do that," Ivy said. "How about tea or coffee?"

They kissed again while they waited for the water to boil—his hands on her shoulders, hers on his belt, sweet lip-kissing this time. Over coffee he told her how great Bob Dylan was. "You can't stay," Ivy said. "Shelly could show up any minute, and Gail's out with Jimmy; I guess they'll..."

"Hey let's be *inclusive!*" he said. "No, never mind, you're right."

He left quickly, and the rain thundered on the tin roof over Ivy's little bedroom. She inhaled her medicine and turned on the shower. When Chuck called, she was clean and quietly putting things into drawers. A narrow escape: she'd been about to get a case of Bert Augustin.

They went to Cusumano's for pizza, and she told Chuck about the hostility between Bert and Jimmy. "I don't know how he found out Jimmy's 'gone over to the Mobe,' do you?" Ivy asked. He shook his head, so she went on. "Bert says it's too late for education; the police state is here."

"Even more reason to put radical education first," Chuck said. "Action's exciting, but without analysis, it's just...thrills. Or mindless rage."

Ivy remembered Mike's eruption in front of the glittering bayonets. Lucky for him that he hadn't found a brick or one of those phantom bags of excrement.

The waiter brought two glasses of Chianti, and Chuck kissed her hand. "I love you," he said, raising his glass. "Let's set a wedding date. Right after your graduation."

Ivy said her first thought. "But I haven't gone around the world."

Chuck sat back, surprised. "What does that have to do with marriage?" he asked. "What kind of around-the-world do you have in mind?"

"Traveling the whole planet." She had a vision of herself coming down a gangplank onto a wharf filled with strange colors and scents. "You know: Florence, Cairo, Athens." She didn't know, really; she might as well have said Prague, Havana, Peking. She just didn't want to be married. Not yet. "I want to visit my brother Glen in India," she said. That was true.

Glen had sent her a letter last week. The village needed clean drinking water, but he hadn't yet figured out how to get that. He'd begun to learn how to handle cow dung with his hands, to keep fires going and to build walls. "I feel like a rather inept hired hand, most of the time," he wrote. Ivy told Chuck about Glen's letter.

"Visiting your brother doesn't mean you can't marry me," Chuck said. "We can go together." Then he frowned.

"Look, I'm going to Cincinnati again tomorrow," he said. "I'd like to tell my mother we're engaged, and we've set a date."

"Tell her we're thinking seriously about it," Ivy said.

"Working out the details of the engagement?"

"You can say 'almost engaged,'" Ivy conceded.

He wouldn't be at the SDS meeting, then. She'd have to control the agenda without him. She'd never be able to keep both Jimmy and Bert quiet. "Give each man time to strut his stuff," Chuck said, "and let folks make up their own minds." That was all the advice he had.

It was a decent plan, Ivy thought, though it didn't address what to do if one man tried to kick the other out of the meeting.

But Chuck was asking her what kind of wedding she wanted, and she didn't know. They talked about some weddings they'd attended: the best part, Ivy thought, was the dancing. Chuck agreed—but then he asked her to go with him to the Church of the Covenant. "Just to look," he said. She couldn't say no.

Everything weighed on her like a low cloud, and as they got to The Monmouth and Chuck started unbuttoning her shirt, she couldn't get Bert's kisses out of her head. She felt guilty going to bed with Chuck, whom she loved, while thinking about Bert, who was (she had to admit) more exciting. Chuck moved over her, and she thought of Ed in Chicago—that feeling of kissing everyone at once. She loved it, and she wondered what was wrong with her. They both came together, fast and hard, and Chuck was exultant. "Oh darling!" he whispered. Then again, "My darling." She stroked his familiar back, fingered the vertebrae close to the skin, and kissed his hands that she knew could never, never hurt anyone, and imagined Bert's mangled finger in her mouth. She would probably marry Chuck, finally; the important thing was to keep the Movement going, to make a good Revolution. If only she knew how to get through the next week. And would she ever see her parents again? While her lover slept, Ivy lay in the dark weeping. She could not have told anyone what she was crying about.

Chapter 20

October 5, 1968
Underground Books & Public Hall

Chuck checked the sky: no buzzards. Of course not. Why would buzzards circle over Euclid Avenue? It was 10 a.m., time to work at Underground Books. The buzzards had been in his dream: that's why he felt them overhead. He unlocked the door to the cellar and entered the warren of books and papers, glad for sunshine only because it meant fewer customers.

Radical poet d.a.levy had left his new paper—*Buddhist Third-Class Junk Mail Oracle*—in a stack on the counter, next to his old paper, *The Swamp Erie Pipe Dream*. Chuck moved *Swamp Erie* to the bench by the door under the "Free" sign. Someone had yellow-chalked "God is Dog spelled backwards" on the blackboard. Like Ferlinghetti's "Dog," Chuck thought, to whom everything was equal—"puddles and babies/ cats and cigars/ poolrooms and policemen...Congressman Doyle is just another/ fire hydrant/to him." He climbed onto the stool behind the counter and spread out his notebook.

"Dear Uncle Sam, I've given up school in exchange for sanity," he'd written. He'd typed the letter and enclosed a cartoon picturing the draft board as a pair of American eagles looking rapaciously at a hapless kid, drawn to look like both student and baby goat. "Your loving victim..."

The response had come yesterday: 1-A. "Registrant available for military service."

He'd thought of calling Mrs. Nelson, but he knew what she'd say: *Why were you so foolish as to send that letter?*

He'd sent it because he was alone in the Movement office when everyone else was in Chicago, and because he'd thought he might die if he didn't do something. Because he'd drunk a full tumbler of Scotch, and because he'd tried so many times to write the essay about how his religious beliefs kept him out of the military and failed. "*Never* is it too late to send in Form 150," Mrs. Nelson had said. "It gets more difficult, that is all. You must explain why your mind has changed."

Why did his mind keep changing? It flipped like a coin or a card. He turned the page and wrote "VIOLENCE: an eight-letter word—twice as bad as any four-letter word."

He liked Mrs. Nelson, liked being around her as she calmly kept on gardening, liked her white socks. "Peace is like housework," she had said. "It feels always like drudgery, has to be done over and over. You miss it only when you haven't done it." She seemed to "do" peace by tending flowers and listening to Chuck, hearing what he meant though he hadn't yet said it. But she also believed Hitler had "that of God" in him and World War II could have been avoided. *Do* peace by putting up with Hitler? A delusion.

Chuck's father had *done* war. In the Battle of the Bulge, Charley Leggit had acquired a piece of shrapnel that traveled around in his body. Once he'd let Chuck feel the hard lump below his collarbone. When it reached his rib cage under his arm, it hurt. Father never said exactly what he'd been doing when he was shot. "I was a corporal, serving my country," he'd say. "Lucky to get out alive."

Charley Leggit and Mrs. Nelson: both lucky to get out alive.

Chuck thought how, in Cincinnati this last time, his father had sharpened the big carving knife to attack the slow-baked chicken. Only the skin needed slicing; a dig with the knife point popped out the leg; a single sweep over the breast, and the white meat fell on to the plate. But Father flourished the big knife as though the chicken were putting up a resistance. Somewhat like Mrs. Nelson, Charley Leggit loved his enemies: he couldn't live without them.

They'd all reconciled; Chuck shook hands with his father, and his mother kissed him on the cheek, tears in her eyes. He'd said, "Looks like Ivy and I are tying the knot," which wasn't a lie, and Bonnie thumped him on the back. When Granddad burst in the front door, hungry for dinner and calling "Where's your girl, Chucky, I want to see her!" Chuck would have given up his wages and mooched for a year if only he could have Ivy in the chair next to him.

"When I was 17," he wrote under VIOLENCE, "I killed a deer. I watched the light die in its eyes and knew I could never kill again. I want to help others, to nourish the bit of God everyone carries inside, like blowing on a coal to keep the fire warm."

Liar, he thought, and crossed it out. Then he wrote, "When I was 21, I caused a man to die; he was, like me, an accidental bystander in a battle between police and militant Nationalists. I am now terrified of holding a weapon in my hand, even a slingshot, even a rock."

"I kill in dreams, firing guns at menacing dogs or people whose faces are hidden. Last night I stabbed a man. I felt the cloth of his shirt, the solid softness of his stomach underneath. I pushed the knife in and heard a scream, high above; the man was very tall. I pulled the knife out and stabbed again. Blood poured over my hands, and I saw buzzards circling overhead. The buzzards kept coming back." Funny how the dream returned as he wrote. And scary. Chuck turned the page.

If there was a glowing spark of God in everyone, there were also hot coals and live grenades. The man in the dream wasn't Bert. But now Chuck was thinking how Bert had stormed out of an SDS meeting—mad that people were listening to Jimmy—and Ivy had been hurt. She and Bert needed to have a long talk after that. Then another long talk, a few days later.

Yesterday Greg Lambert phoned to say, "Hey Leggit, guess what I saw—Ivy and Bert Augustin in each other's arms. You better watch her. Who knows what would've happened if they hadn't seen me?"

"Don't talk filth," Chuck had said quietly, and hung up.

"We hugged," Ivy said, last night. "What is the big deal? You're not jealous of Bert Augustin, are you?"

"No," Chuck said. "I just want to punch his lights out." Ivy frowned, and he said, "Not really," which was true: he couldn't imagine attacking Bert with his fists. But then he'd had the stabbing dream.

Greg was envious, Chuck decided. Ivy said "I love you" at least once a day, and he felt the cord that bound them together as if it were a tendon or a muscle. She liked the silver hoops he'd brought her from Cincinnati. Every time he saw her she was wearing them.

This afternoon he'd meet her at the protest march downtown. The Cleveland Fraternal Order of Police had more Wallace supporters than any local group except the Hungarian Freedom Fighters, and they would all come prepared to club for law 'n order. If Chuck's grandfather were here, he'd be on their side.

"Now see here, Chucky, you're falling into that leftist habit," Granddad had said, when they were alone on the front porch, Mom and Bonnie in the kitchen, Father walking the dog. "Hoodlums burn and loot their own neighborhoods, a few hot-heads kill policemen, and the lefties say *Spend more money!* That makes no sense atall. Rhodes says: law and order first. And I say he's right. So does Nixon."

"I don't trust Nixon," Chuck said.

"Neither do I. No one should trust any politician."

Granddad had forgiven Chuck for leaving the Savings & Loan. "No man should work where he doesn't belong," Granddad said over the glider's squeak as he moved back and forth. "You just need to study human nature, Chucky."

"Human nature," Chuck said, "will blow us off the planet."

Granddad chuckled. "It might do that."

"Don't you care?" Chuck asked.

"I care about you and your sister Bonnie, and your hardworking parents, and a few other people. I care that you have the freedom to be idealistic and wrongheaded for a while, and I want you to have a good life, but God only knows how long it'll be. I've lived 78 years, and I still have my wits about me. I can't control what the Communists might do, now that they have the Bomb. And that's as far as it goes. Leave the rest to the good Lord." He leaned forward, elbows on his knees, looking out at the yard. "Bats." He pointed. Dark shapes flitted among the trees. "If we all get blown up, you know, our worries are over."

Remembering that night with Granddad in the dusty morning air of Underground Books, Chuck thought of the World War III joke, with endless silence for a punch line.

The door opened, Sheldon came in, and Chuck closed his notebook. "Hi." Sheldon picked up the top copy of the *Buddhist Third Class Junk Mail Oracle*. "d.a. levy's new rag, far out." He turned a page and read out loud, pausing at the line breaks: "'A wordless knowing/Grasps my wandering/Through another/Day of rain.' Beautiful, isn't it?"

"Gentler than usual," Chuck said. "Where are the obscenities he's famous for?" He'd heard the poet read at the Well Coffeehouse and remembered his own thought—*he makes even the pain and filth of Cleveland marvelous*—better than the words themselves.

"What's obscene is how he's been hounded by the authorities," Sheldon said. "d.a. knows dirt is holy. Think about it: Fucking. Shitting. Those are God-given acts. Want me to read more?" He leafed through the *Oracle* and found a page. "Look here."

Chuck looked at the stanza next to Sheldon's thumb: "WE CANNOT TOUCH EACH OTHER

except/perhaps thru our minds
THIS IS THE REVOLUTION
and they have outlawed communication."
Here was a man who faced prison for writing poetry, and Chuck
couldn't even write honestly to his draft board. He'd enclosed
a stupid cartoon instead.

Sheldon sat on the bench to load his pipe. "He's
something else, levy. Refuses to compromise."

"Easier said than done—*refuse to compromise*," Chuck
said. But Mrs. Nelson did. So did his father. They had refusal in
common. Maybe when the induction notice came, Chuck
would refuse too. Maybe levy was truer to the Revolution than
anyone in the Movement—and his oppression by the police
proved that.

"I'll buy this," Sheldon picked up the *Oracle*, "with good
money earned by compromising." He produced a Kennedy
half-dollar and spun it on the counter. "Will I see you later,
when we welcome Mr. Wallace?"

"Right on." Chuck nodded. "Ivy says a George Wallace
presidency would be so repressive, it would bring on the
Revolution."

"I wouldn't count on that," Sheldon said. "People can
get used to anything. You finished writing that Glenville
article?"

"Almost," Chuck lied. Scribbles in his notebook hardly
counted as "almost."

"I think I can interview Evans," Sheldon said. "My
mother knows his lawyer."

"No shit! That's fantastic! When?"

Sheldon didn't know, exactly, so Chuck could confess
that he didn't know, either, when he'd finish the article.
Friendship. They talked a little longer, and then Sheldon left.
The air in Underground Books stank of cherry blend tobacco.

Chuck paged through his notes, flipping past Glenville,
then Chicago, then the Milwaukee 14, to a new blank sheet.
"Nobody's talking about the violence that starts way before a

cop gets killed," he wrote. "Poverty. Harassment by police. Fear. Silence heavy with words unborn." Yes, and now what? He tried to be honest, but under every thought, inside every word, crouched its opposite. And d.a.levy knew that. "Wordless knowing." Behind Chuck on the wall, God was dog spelled backwards.

He looked at *The Plain Dealer* again; the police wanted better cars. Today they'd show up in full riot gear. Wallace was their "law 'n order" man. Carl Stokes had refused to welcome him to Cleveland, and he was coming anyway, almost here. What would Chuck *do* if the police attacked? He felt buzzards circling high above the city.

Two hours later Tessa waited for him at the corner of East Sixth and St. Clair, in loose army pants and combat boots. Above her belt: breasts round as water balloons, shiny lips and rippling hair. Chuck turned away to watch the crowd gathering at the other end of Sixth Street. "Where's Ivy?" he asked.

Tessa shrugged and walked ahead of him past the Hungarian Freedom Fighters' bus with its window sign: *Wallace for President!* They stopped at the next corner and Tessa put her hand on his arm. "Police shot hundreds of students at *Tlatelolco*," she said. "Yesterday. They were holding a peaceful rally. Javier phoned his mother; she couldn't talk for crying."

"What's *Tlat*...what you said?" Chuck asked. He looked anxiously for Ivy.

"Mexico City," Tessa said. "There they are." Movement organizations clustered on the lawn under banners: *Youth Against War and Fascism. Cleveland Area Peace Action Council. Mothers Against War.* Young Republicans in blue suits carried signs for Nixon and freedom of speech; they didn't like Wallace, either. "Stop Wallace!" Tessa yelled as if she were screaming about the massacre in Mexico City. A guy with a crew cut led the Cleveland Mobe, waving *Stop the War!* and *Stop Wallace!* signs. Good God, that was Jimmy Fulero with hair like a frat boy's. "There's Ivy." Tessa pointed.

Ivy stood between Bert and Shelly under a banner: *Bombs Away with Curtis LeMay!* Next to them Marvin carried a sign quoting Mayor Daley: *The Police Are Here to Preserve Disorder!* Much better than the Mobe signs. Ivy had been gaining weight—the Pill, she said: her jeans were tight at the hips and crotch, and her shirt strained against its buttons, revealing skin between her breasts. She had not set her hair, and her bangs hung into her eyes. Chuck had a thought—*this is not the girl to take home*—and erased it immediately. He trotted toward her, nearly colliding with old Ted Dostal, the Socialist, striding in his orthopedic shoes. "Scabs!" Dostal shouted, pointing at the *Vote Wallace* group across the street. "Scabs!" Behind him two men carried flags—one starred and striped, the other hammered and sickled. Six high school students (*Shaw High Shows Up for Peace*) passed, their cheeks soft and pink.

Ivy up close was beautiful, as always, her blue eyes shining, her upper lip pert and moist. Chuck reached round her back and tugged a hank of hair. "Glad to see you too," he said, and kissed her.

"The FBI was looking for me in Bloomington," Ivy said. "They woke up my parents in the middle of the night."

When, exactly? What did they want? How did the Barcelonas react? He wanted to ask, but the lines had formed, and he was marching now between Ivy and Tessa. Up ahead he glimpsed Mrs. Nelson in the *Women Strike for Peace* contingent. She wore a neat black armband on her beige sweater-sleeve.

"What the hell are you talking about?" Ivy asked. She'd taken up casual swearing since Chicago.

Chuck hadn't known he was saying it aloud: "Tlate*lol*co. *T*late*lol*co. Tlate*lol*co. I'm just trying to say it right."

"How do you know for sure what's right without asking a Mexican?"

"I can tell by the sound." Chuck wished that were true. He moved close to Tessa and spoke in her ear. "Where's Javier?" Her breast almost brushed his arm.

"In psychiatry rotation, I guess," Tessa said. "I don't really know."

Police in dark-blue uniforms lined both sides of the entrance to Public Hall, their faces stern and beefy. Preservers of disorder.

The march quickened; feet sounded in unison now, and conversations broke into sporadic comments. "Jane looks more cheerful with short hair," Ivy said. He hadn't even recognized Jane; her hair curled and waved like Bob Dylan's.

"Why would a haircut make anyone look cheerful?" he asked.

Tessa was telling Ivy about Mexican students. "They know about Paris, Prague, Columbia, *and* Chicago. We're abysmally ignorant in comparison."

Chuck counted two hundred anti-Wallace people spread along the mall. "Hey Chuck," Tessa called. "There's an SDS caucus in Boulder next week. You're not in school anymore; come with Bert and me!"

"Maybe," Chuck shrugged. "I could write about it for *Underground News*." A trip to Colorado with Tessa and Bert? Uncomfortable.

"Are we making the Revolution now?" Sheldon's deep voice.

"Shh. Listen," Ivy said. Drums, a tight bongo rhythm.

"It's all theater," Sheldon said. Fist raised, he boomed, "Power to the People Right On!"

They stopped marching and hushed as a double line of Black men marched past. Their black berets had the red, gold and green African National Congress insignia, and a man at the head of the line carried an ANC flag. Six drummers beat time with their hands, perfectly synchronized, and the crowd parted for them. They stopped at the entrance. The Black men stamped *bam-bam* into place a few feet from the police.

"Afro Set," Sheldon whispered in Chuck's ear: Harllel Jones's group. Clusters of messy-haired white people stood bewildered or mesmerized. "That's Harllel." Sheldon nodded

279 — Susan Streeter Carpenter

toward the trim handsome man at the end of the line. Every policeman lifted his nightstick and held it poised, one hand clutching the handle, the other holding the tip.

Drums beat again, fast and hollow. Ivy clutched Chuck's arm, and he saw Mrs. Nelson, on the other side of the crowd, her mouth open to gasp or scream.

Harllel Jones strode to the nearest policeman and spoke quietly. The door was opened, drums went silent, and Afro Set filed in. The white contingents followed.

Chuck and Ivy were directed to the balcony with the rest of the group. Cheers filled the ground floor. "Oh my God, he's so small," Ivy said. Wallace marched to his bulletproof lectern as a trio of bubble-haired girls performed a Country & Western song. More applause.

"That's where we dropped balloons," Ivy pointed. "There were four bands marching at once down there." She showed Chuck the ocean of people that filled the main floor.

Wallace looked up and shook his finger. "Turn those TV cameras to the balcony. Show the people of America what kind of folks they are," he said.

Cameras were already on the Nationalists—how could they not be? Stone-faced Black Power asserted itself calmly, relentlessly, chanting to the TV cameras, now with a side-step— "Power to the People!"—like the Miracles and the Panthers combined.

There was a flurry higher in the balcony behind them. A scream. Two policemen popped up at the end of the row and ran out.

"Calm down, let the police handle it," Wallace spoke again. "You know, if one of those demonstrators ever laid in front of my automobile, that would be the last automobile he'd ever lay down in front of." The audience cheered on the ground floor.

"Shelly had her Curtis LeMay sign torn up by a couple of Wallace fans," said Jane from behind Chuck. "The police took her outside."

"She wasn't doing anything illegal," Ivy said.

"She was creating a disturbance," Jane said. "Good for her."

The little candidate was promising to fill Washington with rednecks and peckerwoods (cheers from the ground floor) and to make life miserable for shiftless people with no jobs (more cheers).

"Ah, life without a job is so *easy*," Jane said, almost loud enough to be heckling.

In front of them, Afro Set started a new chant—*You don't have a job! You don't have a job!*—pointing toward Wallace on *you*, clapping after *job*. The claps resounded like gunshots.

Outside the auditorium, the crowd fanned across the mall, and police moved in with nightsticks raised. The Afro Set had resumed drumming as they marched quickly toward Superior. Not one man got out of line.

Out of the corner of his eye, Chuck saw Greg Lambert pick up something and lift his arm like a baseball pitcher. "Stop that, you idiot!" he yelled. He flew into Greg, landing with his shoulder against one large arm; the hand held half a brick. Two policemen came rushing. "Drop that!" Chuck yelled. Greg dropped it. The police hesitated. Then came a cry from another direction. "Motherfuckers!" And the two police moved away.

"I get so mad," Greg said, rubbing the upper arm Chuck had hit with as much of his weight as he could hurl. "Those pigs are such..."

"I know, man. Hope I didn't hurt you," Chuck lied.

"Nah," Greg said. "I'm fine." For a change he didn't seem to want to stay near Chuck; he hurried back into the crowd. The police were clubbing and making arrests. Old Ted Dostal went down. Bert Augustin went down.

"Time to go," Jane said. "Come on." She led the way to Public Square.

Minutes later they climbed onto the Rapid Transit and found seats. With the tracks clicking under them, Chuck remembered how quickly the police had turned away, how

Greg had suddenly vanished—and it occurred to him that Greg could be one of those provocateurs hired by the FBI to make trouble, giving the cops an excuse to club. "Nah," he muttered. Too far-fetched.

"Are you going to write this up for *Underground News?*" Jane asked. She sat across from him and Ivy.

"I should," Chuck said, "but I'm still working on Glenville. And the Milwaukee 14. You write this one."

"I'm writing about Women's Liberation," Jane said. "We should get Tessa to write about the student massacre in Mexico. She's quit school till after the Revolution."

"But the Revolution needs doctors," Ivy said. "She was so close."

"Not that close," Jane said. "Hey Ivy, why not write about SDS on campus?"

"I'm taking a pretty heavy load this term," Ivy said doubtfully.

"What about Shelly?" Chuck said. "She got elected chapter president; you could work together."

"She'd say *sure I'll do it*, then she wouldn't," Ivy said. "Where did Shelly go? They didn't arrest her, did they?" If they had, there was no way of knowing. The Rapid Transit rumbled through a gorge littered with dead wood and garbage. "Maybe she'll be home when I get there." Ivy slumped and bit her lower lip. "That first meeting, with Jimmy and Bert coming off different walls, left everybody confused. We elected Shelly— that was the only decision. And the second meeting had only twelve people. If I wrote about it, there'd be one paragraph. Not even that much."

"They're both so extreme and so *sure*," Chuck said.

"They're crazed," Jane said, shaking her head. "We all are, though. Jimmy came out of jail in Chicago and nobody was there to meet him. None of us waited. He took the bus back to Cleveland all alone."

"Was that why he was mad at Bert?" Chuck asked.

"Of course not," Ivy said. "They differ on some basic principles. You saw the signs today. Jimmy's with the Mobe. But we need to work together, don't we?"

"Bert had the blue van in Chicago," Jane said. "He could have waited for Jimmy."

"Why didn't he?" Chuck asked. Jane shrugged and turned her head to the window. The real question, Chuck thought, was why Ivy had gone to the office for all those long talks with Bert. Why had she given him sexy hugs? He'd ask her later, when it wouldn't make a scene.

A good reason to go to Boulder with Bert and Tessa: keep Bert away from Ivy. He could figure out what was happening with the SDS nationals, and if they were making Bert crazy. Something was wrong when the Movement couldn't finish a meeting without a leading radical activist walking out. "You haven't failed," Chuck hugged her with one arm. "You've done fine. Don't get discouraged."

He rubbed his cheeks: time to shave. He would take Ivy home and help her find Shelly, if Shelly wasn't already there. Then he'd clean up, buy a rose, and present it to her. He'd buy two roses, if they weren't expensive, one for each girl. Ivy would love that.

Chapter 21

October 10, 1968
Coventry Road

A harmonica sliced the air like a siren, yanking Jane out of bed. "There must be some way *out* of here!" Dylan again. Even in the bathroom, with the water on full, she heard the saw-edged voice. "Too much con*fu*sion, I can't get no relief."

"It wouldn't be so bad if you'd play the whole album," she told Tessa, who stood at the stove stirring oatmeal. The metal spoon scraped the aluminum pot and grated against Jane's spine alongside the electric guitar.

"Bert will be here soon, and I haven't packed." Tessa banged the cupboard door and plopped two bowls on the counter. She ducked into her bedroom, which opened onto the kitchen, picked up the record-player needle and moved it back to "All Along the Watchtower." The harmonica wailed like a hyper-amplified mosquito.

Since Chicago they'd shared this place, the back half of what once had been a good-sized apartment on Coventry. Jane wanted to talk, as they used to, make sense of what was going down. But Tessa seemed to be in constant motion, internal engine revved. She talked to herself in Spanish—"practicing for Cuba"—and quoted Chairman Mao. She'd played "All Along the Watchtower" for three days straight.

"I need that song," Tessa said. "It's stone *revolution*: businessmen and ploughmen keep right on digging our earth and drinking our wine. So they don't recognize worth, don't hear the wildcat yowling in the darkness, don't know the riders are approaching." She set a bowl of oatmeal in front of Jane. "Us: we're those riders, Jane. Why don't we have any milk or sugar?"

"We didn't buy any." Jane was not going to apologize for the lack of groceries. "Besides, I like it plain." She should point out the song was a conversation between a joker and a thief.

"You do not like it plain," Tessa said. "I know you." She spooned oatmeal into her mouth, said "Blecch!" and shielded herself with the newspaper. Cold came through the cracks around the window. Wind ripped oak leaves off the branches, and empty twigs bumped against the glass.

"Try some salt," Jane said. She sprinkled salt on her oatmeal and willed herself to like it. Maybe Tessa was right on, and Jane was too irritable and irrational to see that. She'd stayed up most of the night trying to write her article for *Underground News*, but it had turned into a sort of play, *Female in America*.

"Look at this." Tessa slapped the paper onto the table. "Student *unrest*," she said. "Never expect *The Plain Dealer* to get a story straight, but even so."

Jane studied the picture: Jimmy Fulero, his pea-jacket collar turned up against the wind, talked into a microphone. He looked older with his hair short, and boring. Ivy stood beside him in knee-high boots. They were protesting Dow recruiters at Case. The article quoted the students' message—"Dow makes napalm, bring the troops home"—but the story belonged to the recruiter, who explained that his company was Dow *Corning*, not Dow *Chemical*: "Our company makes cookware; we have nothing to do with war or weapons." He did not say *napalm*. "These kids should have checked their facts."

"Even so—what?" Jane asked Tessa.

"Let us not talk *falsely* now," Dylan yelped. "The hour is getting late."

"*Of course* Dow wants to separate burning flesh from those white dishes with blue flower designs," Tessa said, "but Dow is Dow, napalm or dishes, a juicy hunk of the military industrial complex. What the hell were Ivy and Jimmy thinking?" She slammed her fist on the table. Bowls and cups jumped. "They should stop the recruitment, rather than walking round and round with signs. Jimmy's Committee Against the War just says 'American Troops Out Now!' over and over—and Ivy and Shelly are going along."

"Have you talked with Ivy?" Jane asked. "Or Shelly?"

"And if the university won't stop recruiters, shut it down," Tessa went on. "*You* meet with Ivy and her pals about Women's Lib all the time; can't you even discuss how capitalism works?" She half-rose, accusing Jane. Her close-set eyes said *fury.*

Jane swallowed the bitter-salt taste in her mouth. "I'll see Ivy later this afternoon," she said, standing, reaching for the papers she'd left on the table. "We're doing a counter-homecoming action." *Action.* Rather than talk, they'd *do* surprising, revolutionary things, galvanize onlookers into thinking.

"I read your play this morning," Tessa said.

"Well?" Jane wondered if Tessa minded that Jane had borrowed her stories—the broken high heels, the male chauvinist professor, the Movement guys who expected her to make coffee and take notes but not actually strategize.

"The problem is," Tessa said, "it's all about middle class white people. Yeah, okay, some are Movement people, and in *that* scene you've trivialized the Movement."

"I think you've missed the point," Jane said, as Tessa dumped her oatmeal bowl in the sink on her way to the front room—still Jane's bedroom until the bed was folded into a couch. "You didn't ask to read it," Jane said, following her. Maybe it was a stupid play, a self-indulgent exercise written when she should have been doing real work.

"It's not terrible," Tessa said. She stood by the window, looking out at the parking lot. "Women's Lib training can get middle class co-eds in touch with the system's oppression. Maybe you need to write personal shit for therapeutic reasons.

But the hour *is* getting late." She stood with her arms crossed. "Don't be upset; if I was being counter-revolutionary, I'd expect you to confront me." She picked up the end of Jane's bed to collapse it. "I can't get this to close." She heaved against the metal frame, but sheets and blankets made the mattress too bulky. "You should go to the Boulder Caucus convention with me and Bert and Chuck, that's all."

"Leave the bed open," Jane said. "Feminism is not counter-revolutionary."

"If Chairman Mao were here now, he'd say that play is artistic, and *all art* is counter-revolutionary," Tessa said. "Bert thinks we should fill the marble foyer of Severance Hall with garbage, and he's right." Tessa had scrubbed that foyer on her knees so she could listen to the symphony; she knew she was shocking Jane. "Yeah, I winced," she said. "But that's the leftover bourgeois in me; the point is, I didn't take Bert's criticism personally. You shouldn't take mine that way."

"Politics *are* personal," Jane said, "and I've got commitments. See you when you get back from Boulder." She didn't want to argue, especially if Bert was about to arrive and likely to join the fray. She pulled on her jacket, hoisted her backpack, and ran down the stairs. Slamming the door, she saw Bert in the blue van, looking over his shoulder as he backed it into a parking place. She took off running.

Tessa's criticism hurt. *Only middle class white people. Trivialized the Movement.*

Jane ran along Coventry Road; open-air exercise would clear her head, maybe straighten out her analysis. *Good politics, the correct line.* Tessa used those phrases as if there were only one way to think responsibly. Had she always been like this?

Jane slowed at the window of a new shop full of clothes from San Francisco: loose pants made of dark purple velvet and bright green satin. A silvery dress. Inside, one wall was paneled with old wooden boards; leather bags with fringe hung from hooks. The counter was strewn with colored glass beads, scented candles, and hand carved pipes for smoking marijuana.

A longhaired kid sprawled in a red beanbag chair. "Need help?" he asked.

Jane shook her head. "Just looking," she said.

He shrugged and returned to *The Two Towers*. In the case lay earrings made of curly silver. A day-glo poster on the wall said, "Do your own thing." Another said, "Feed your head." The smells of sandalwood and patchouli said, *Down with the ruling class and New York fashion.* If this store could survive in Cleveland, the Revolution was unstoppable, much bigger than Tessa's narrow correct line.

Some of the earrings were pretty. If Jane had any money...but no, she'd spent most of this week's $5.00 bill on typewriter ribbon and onion-skin paper. Now she was down to 75 cents—a street-woman, traveling on foot. The backpack pulled at her shoulders as she walked past Irv's delicatessen, the shoe repair shop, the hardware store, the gas station, registering each smell—cured meats, shoe polish, metal, ancient grease. She swung onto Mayfield and down the hill, cemetery on one side, apartment buildings on the other. On down through Little Italy, where snipers had lurked during the Hough riots. Chuck said they'd returned last summer after Glenville.

She stopped to wait for a light and saw a woman glaring at her. And here it came, again: the face of the boy dying on the corner of Beulah and 123rd. He looked at her and Ivy—dim white-girl figures across the street from where he lay, unable to move except for the jerk of one sandaled foot. His eyes weren't pleading, but puzzled: *What are you doing here?* Then they lost expression: *Oh, never mind; goodbye.* His face had become Jane's emblem for all the dying kids, Black and Vietnamese. She crossed to the corner grocery, its walls painted red, green, and white, the colors of Italian pride. Glenville was only a 15 minute run from here, and yesterday she'd missed the birthday party of a living Black kid. Kelvin had turned six.

Inside the Italian grocery, a dim place with crowded shelves, a chubby woman stood behind the counter; she wore cherry earrings and lipstick to match. Jane picked out a Snickers bar. "This is for a Black kid in Glenville," she said to the cashier, stressing *Black* just a little. "It's his birthday."

"So?" the woman said, handing Jane the change. "Hope he likes it."

"Me too," Jane said, pocketing coins and slipping the candy into her pack.

The saleswoman pressed her lips together; then she leaned forward. "You know what," she said. "My kid's father's in Da Nang. Been there six months. Six more to go."

"How old's your kid?" Jane asked.

"Four," the woman said. "Too young to remember who his father is."

"I'm so sorry," Jane said. There were sad and important things they hadn't told each other. None of those things, so far as Jane knew, had yet been put into words, though she'd tried last night, writing *Female in America*. But she'd left out this particular anger, about mothers and small boys and men at war. Soldiers dying.

Glenville was quiet again, with newly-boarded windows and two empty holes on 124th where the houses had burned. "Your hair's *cute*," Dora said, pulling Jane in the door. "Sit down awhile."

In the living room, still ballooned and streamered from yesterday's party, Leatha high-stepped for her grandma in a white dress and a white hair ribbon. Kelvin sat cross-legged on the floor, running little cars into a box he'd made into a garage under the coffee table, his lips *brrrring* engine noises. He looked up when Jane settled on the couch. "Oh, Jane's here! Hi, Jane!" She presented the Snickers, and with his Grandma's prompting Kelvin said, "Thank you very *much!*"

Dora picked up the candy before he could tear the wrapper. "This is for after supper," she said, and put it on top of the refrigerator.

"Dag!" said Kelvin. So Jane knew he liked his gift.

Tina came from watching TV in the bedroom. "Oh mercy, Jane, you cut your hair." She fingered Jane's curls. "Still soft, though."

"Been wanting short hair for years," Jane said. "How are you, Ms. Williams?" she asked Dora's mother. "Since when has Tina been saying *mercy*?" she whispered.

"Maybe she got it from me," Ms. Williams shrugged. "Kelvin says it too."

"Want some ice water?" Dora put two glasses on the coffee table. She was beaming in a pink dress with a bow under her bust.

"You're happy today," Jane said.

"I got me a job," Dora said. "Because you helped me get my GED. And the Welfare Rights got me experience." She would start next week as community outreach worker for the new Neighborhood Family Health Care Center.

"I'm proud of you," Jane said. "It's a good job. Stokes' people did something right." If they'd let Dora organize as she knew how to do, then maybe one small bit of the Revolution could be accomplished quietly, without street fights. The ice water tasted of their old friendship.

"Soon as I can, I'm gonna move out this neighborhood," Dora said. "Get us a house over by Kinsman Road. Mama'll quit her job and live with us. The baby will have her all day long. Work a couple years, then I'm-a go to *college*." Her ambition uncorked, buoyant as the balloons that Tina and Kelvin were batting back and forth, Dora sauntered to the counter and cut Jane a slice of leftover chocolate cake. "Saved it for you," she said. "Mama made it."

Jane didn't deserve cake, but she cut off the point and put it in her mouth, analyzing: Dora's mother cleaned for wealthy white people like the Buchanans, Tessa's parents. Meanwhile, the Buchanans sent money to their daughter so she could pay rent while making the Revolution, after which everyone would have a guaranteed income and clean his or her own house. Or maybe, after the Revolution, housecleaners would be paid as well as, say, plumbers.

Dora, however, would not wait till after the Revolution to live well. She wasn't waiting for men to come to their senses and grant women equal rights, either. Tessa might say she was co-opted by the System, but Tessa was living off Marjorie and Tom Buchanan. *Surfacing of contradictions*, Jane thought.

What about the Revards, her own family? As long as Jane could remember, a cleaning lady had come once a month for tough jobs like scrubbing floors and windows. A Black lady in the city had ironed Daddy's shirts. And even now, Jane could fall back into that household as if it were a soft mattress under a tightrope. But if Dora's job got wiped out, or if something happened to Mama (Jane thought of Ms. Williams' surgery and her own father's fragile heart) any little crisis would send them spiraling into poverty—*splat*. The Revards' mattress was cushy in comparison. The chocolate cake was moist and sweet, and Jane couldn't take a second bite.

Fix it, Tessa would say. *Overthrow the Capitalist-imperialists.*

Jane put her cake on the table. "How does it feel to be six?" she asked Kelvin.

"Fine," he shrugged. "I almost got a bike, but Mama say wait another year."

"Hard to wait, but it'll be worth it, 'cause you'll be bigger," Jane said. "Show me the new car." She turned over the little vehicle in her hands, let Kelvin point out the moveable steering wheel, the door that opened, the wheels that spun, until it was time to go. She and Ivy had to pick up the counter-homecoming queen.

Gathering clouds darkened the sky over Hessler Road. Ivy answered the door looking flushed and upset. "Oh God, Jane, I forgot. I just woke up. Stuck a paper under the professor's door at three in the morning and crawled into bed." Jane shrugged (what else could she do?) and followed Ivy into the kitchen. It was 5:00 in the afternoon. Ivy cut up an apple to share.

"Let's go get our girl," Jane said, chewing an apple slice. "Where is she?"

"At the Art Institute," Ivy said. "with a friend of Shelly's." She pulled on a jacket, and Jane thought sadly of the London Fog, which lay at the bottom of her closet.

"I don't have a car, since I don't live with Chuck anymore," Ivy said.

"But Chuck's on the way to Boulder in the blue van with Tessa and Bert. Didn't he leave you the key?" Jane had been on foot for hours, from Coventry to 124th and back to Hessler. The car would have been welcome.

"I didn't ask for it," Ivy said. She walked faster. Rain had begun.

"I hope it's not heavy," Jane said. They had several blocks to carry their homecoming candidate, a plastic mannequin. *It's supposed to be fun*, she told herself. Ivy's group had reserved a hall and publicized the dance, with a band and refreshments. "Who are the other contestants?" she asked.

"I'm Suzy Creamcheese," Ivy said. "Shelly's the Glamour Puss. Lots of eye makeup."

"Suzy Creamcheese, huh?"

"Jimmy's idea. He's a Frank Zappa fan. I get to wear my patent leather Mary Janes and set my hair in ringlets."

"How is Jimmy?" Jane asked. She thought of the young stranger in the newspaper.

"He's okay," Ivy said. "Too serious, most of the time. A bit paranoid. I was glad he got the band; it'll be fun. I don't think he'd be involved if Bert were here." She climbed the steps of the Art Institute and led the way down the hall to the studios. Jane admired how Ivy, working so well with Jimmy, managed to get along with Bert too.

They carried the naked-plastic-woman pieces into the rain, the arms and legs reaching over Ivy's shoulder, the chin digging into Jane's collarbone. "Let's stop for coffee," Jane said, when they got to the Student Union. The mannequin was amputated and bald, but recognizably a woman. She'd sit between them, "the perfect female": silent, slender, dismembered.

"We need to keep her a secret," Ivy said, looking to Jane as if she wanted approval. "And I don't want to talk to people right now."

"Not even to me?"

"Oh Jane, oh...I didn't mean you."

If Ivy wanted to hide the mannequin, okay. "So where do we deliver, um, what are we going to name this person?"

"I hadn't thought of that." They trudged abreast up the stairs, plastic body parts clicking against each other. "Rosie the Reserve Raider?"

"The Raiders will have their own queen," Jane said. "How about Boob Girlie?"

"Dolly Sweetheart," Ivy said.

"Madonna Hooker," said Jane.

They decided to have a vote—*Name the Queen!*—with little slips of paper in a fishbowl on the literature table. After shutting their candidate in a closet near the ballroom, they got coffee.

Jane put two sugar cubes in her coffee and stirred.

"Here's what I've been thinking," Ivy's blue eyes were liquifying, her lips wobbled, but her voice was steady. "I need to break up with Chuck."

"What?" Jane said. "Why?" Ivy was holding back tears. "This isn't anything to do with Jimmy?" Ivy shook her head *no no no*. "Or Bert? Or Chuck's going to Boulder?"

"I need freedom," Ivy said. The tears spilled onto her cheeks.

Jane handed her a napkin. "Chuck certainly loves you."

"I love him," Ivy's voice tightened into wet tiny screams. "But I don't know what that means. Chuck seems to think love means getting married. Having sex and then getting married."

"Sex has almost nothing to do with love," Jane said. She thought of Jimmy and realized she wouldn't have sex with him now, even if she had the chance—which she wouldn't.

"Sex without love," Ivy said, "would be kind of like eating, wouldn't it?"

"I guess so," Jane said. "You'd get bored and want variety." Norman had been pastrami-on-rye after years of peanut butter and jelly. Jimmy Fulero was chocolate creams—too much for a steady diet. Suddenly she thought of strawberries: Patricia and her lover in the shadows near the beach. A letter had come from Patricia a week ago with news of an International Women's Conference to be held at Thanksgiving. Jane wanted to go. She needed to sign up. Now. "I've been working on a play," she told Ivy. "*Female in America.* Want to read it?"

"Oh God, I'd love to," Ivy said. "When?"

"I've got it with me." Jane hauled the manuscript out of her backpack. "I wrote it last night while you were writing your paper." Ivy wouldn't be as critical as Tessa. "I think it needs a second act, maybe about welfare mothers."

"Looks cool," Ivy said, turning pages, stopping to read, turning again. Jane sipped coffee and closed her eyes. She liked Ivy very much. "Where'd you get this letter from the girl who loves books and doesn't want to be kissed? Sounds like what I would've said at thirteen."

"*American Girl*, I think," Jane said. She had written the letter herself, at fifteen, the only one in her class not excited about boys, in agony over the possibility that she was backward or had a disease. She had not kissed anyone till she was in college. But the Jimmy affair had proved she was not a lesbian.

"Yeah," Ivy murmured, chuckling as she turned a page.

"Which scene?" Jane asked.

"The meeting where a woman says something smart and the men ignore her. Except..."

"What?"

"It's more complicated than this, you know? All the little things that go on underneath, between men and women, women and women, and men and men. Maybe they're not little; they're important. But we never talk about them, there's no time, no room…oh, never mind, I don't know how to say what I mean."

"If I tried to include all the things underneath, I wouldn't have a scene," Jane said. "I'd have a book. Except I don't know how to write that kind of book." Ivy had tears in her eyes again. "What's wrong?"

"Everything. I'm not much good, am I? Want some more coffee?" Ivy closed the manuscript and passed it across the table. "Thinking of Chuck, that's all."

"Talk honestly with him," Jane said. "Maybe you can work things out." Chuck was the kind of guy who could handle honesty—unlike, for example, Norman. She felt an urge to protect Chuck, keep him from being dumped into the cold.

"Yeah, maybe," Ivy said. Then, a few seconds later," Bert showed me the steam tunnels."

"His kind of thing," Jane said. So that's how Ivy was getting along with Bert. Her sex appeal, of course. Tessa had mentioned Bert's interest in the underground hallways—not tunnels, really, just routes to the steam pipes that heated the campus buildings, access for the maintenance staff. "Was it fun?"

"There's this ladder that goes straight down under Euclid Avenue," Ivy said. "You're descending into a pit, it's pitch dark, and you can't see the bottom. The metal rungs are so hot your hands are burning, but you can't let go."

"So you kept going," Jane said. Why was Ivy telling her this?

"It was incredible, standing deep under Euclid Avenue, hearing the traffic overhead. There's a mattress down there," Ivy said.

This was why, Jane thought. "Bert wanted to try it out with you."

"He would've, but by then, I wanted out of the tunnels."

Bert hadn't forced himself on Ivy; good. Maybe he and Tessa would start having sex again, in Boulder. Tessa was the one Bert really loved. But they were both so dogged right now.

"We kissed," Ivy added. "He's pretty sexy. I'm really glad Chuck went off with him and Tessa."

"He can be aggressive," Jane said. "He tried to screw me. We'd both just come out of jail. Sex to him has nothing to do with love, but it's more than food. It's..."

"Actually," Ivy said, "he started talking about symbolic bombings. Direct revolutionary action against the National Security Complex. I understand—I mean he's right, but..."

"His strategy's flawed," Jane said. "The National Caucus should straighten him out. It's full of sharp politicos."

"I hope so," Ivy said. "I'm not ready for war; I want to graduate first. And I may still be a pacifist. Do you think I'm being bourgeois and counter-revolutionary?"

"I'd be upset if I thought any of us was really ready for war," Jane said. "But I also think we're into something bigger than we can imagine."

She left Ivy at Hessler Road and walked in rainy darkness to the East Cleveland apartment Bert and Marvin were subletting from Norman, who was rising in *The Columbus Post Dispatch*. It had been a nice apartment, but Jane was glad to be out of it.

"Actually, Bert doesn't live here anymore." Marvin dumped a can of mushrooms into the spaghetti sauce and stirred.

"What? When did he leave? Why? Where did he go?"

"Several nights ago." Marvin leaned against the stove with one hip. "I kind of threw him out. I'd had enough of his obsession with armed struggle."

"Tessa's talking about 'the enemy' all the time," Jane said. "Listen to her talk, and the rationale for armed struggle follows logically. Except...I can't shake the feeling they're both too frantic. I told Ivy the SDS workers in Boulder would straighten them out."

Marvin looked at the floor. "If he were just reading DeBray like everybody else, I wouldn't worry. But Bert was making Molotov cocktails—here, in the kitchen." He stirred the sauce carefully. "So you think I was over-hasty?"

"Tessa has been pissy for weeks," Jane said. "She plays the same Dylan song over and over. Where's Bert been staying, since he left here?"

"I thought he was staying with you." Jane shook her head. Marvin looked at her and shrugged. "Somebody else's couch, then," he said. He didn't seem to care.

Reassuring Ivy had been easy when Jane didn't know about the Molotov cocktails. She couldn't kick Tessa out; the rent was paid by Tessa's family. If Tessa brought in explosives, Jane would have to leave.

"Bert's awful hungry for militant action." Marvin took a box of Choo Choo Wheels out of the cupboard. Jane laughed. "You got something against my favorite meal?" he asked.

Why couldn't they all work it out together? They were smart, committed, and they'd been friends for years. She should confront Marvin: *Listen, we need to remember how to argue constructively with each other. Tessa attacked me. She probably thinks I attacked her. You obviously attacked Bert.* "Tessa was upset about the Dow recruitment protests at Case," Jane said, as Marvin poured Choo Choo Wheels into boiling water. "Not militant enough. Dominated by the Mobe's Committee to End the War."

"Which is dominated by the Young Socialist Alliance," Marvin said.

"So I've heard." If Jimmy had joined the YSA he was getting Trotskyist analysis from the central office of the Socialist Workers' Party. Not just the analysis, but language and strategy. Jimmy would have to toe the line. Tessa and Bert, in contrast, were completely original thinkers. "I wrote a play Tessa doesn't like," Jane admitted. "Maybe I'm just annoyed because of that— and I'm sick of 'All Along the Watchtower.'"

"Bert's been playing that one, too." Marvin said. "Here's what I think. Tessa quit school because she was convinced the Revolution would happen without her if she didn't. Right?"

"Or it would fail, or it would bypass Cleveland. She said she couldn't make the Revolution as a med student," Jane said. "Not if she wanted to be a good doctor." Tessa did nothing half-assed; in med school she'd prepare frantically for exams and got ecstatic whenever she received a little praise from a professor.

"I think lashing out at you is a reaction to her own self-criticism," Marvin said. "She has to make the revolution now, every minute: otherwise why throw over her career like that?"

He dished up a bowl full of Choo Choo Wheels, added a glop of sauce, and put it in front of Jane. It occurred to her that he and Bert might be having some weird rivalry. She thought of Marvin's kiss in Lincoln Park and Bert's advances in the blue van. She didn't want sex with either man—but she did want the friendship that now seemed to be disintegrating. She wanted to work with both of them, if she could. They'd all gone to Chicago together, and they'd never put messages on their tree. They'd returned with no common strategy. The spaghetti sauce was watery, the Choo Choo wheels under-cooked.

"We disagree on strategy," Marvin said, munching, his voice muffled.

"It's not that simple, is it?" Jane speared a mushroom with her fork.

"What's interesting," Marvin said, "is how *angry* I've been since Chicago."

"The concussion," Jane said. "Those police were stupid thugs."

"I'm angry at the good-hearted liberals," Marvin said. "Even the ones who give us money. What's happened, in Glenville and Chicago and since then, is new and strange, and can't be pinned on anyone—not on Evans, not on any of those eight men they're charging with conspiracy in Chicago, not even on the police."

"Not on an infiltrator? Not on the Subversive Squad?"

"Okay, that explains the paranoia. But what can we do that we haven't already done?"

"You said we should do something constructive with our rage. And it's not paranoia."

"I did?" Marvin was pacing now. "I was right."

"So do you have ideas?" She would invite him to the counter-homecoming, for a start. Being with Marvin was comforting. He always had hope.

"There's a United Way luncheon," he said. "Do-good liberals will be there in force, all dressed up, patting each other on the back for their charitable work."

"So we should invade it?" Jane grinned. She wondered whether Eleanor was involved.

Marvin grinned back. "They need to be confronted by people who question what they're doing, all dressed up and comfortable."

Another action. Not quite what she'd come looking for, but it might help them—Jane and Tessa, Marvin and Bert, and Chuck and Ivy, too—figure out how to work together from here.

Chapter 22

October 11, 1968
Hessler Road

"This is my senior prom dress." Shelly held it by its puffed sleeves. "Awful, isn't it? Perfect for Suzy Creamcheese." The dress was baby girl pink, high-waisted, with smocking under the breasts and a white collar.

"You'd have no choice but to be demure in this dress," Ivy said, trying to imagine a quiet, well-behaved Shelly, her hair ironed straight. It was easier than thinking about the bubbly act she'd have to put on as Suzy.

"Last Saturday the demure-girl act kept me out of jail." Shelly put the dress into Ivy's hands. "Try it on." Then she attached a fall of red hair to her own, pinning it at the temples and the top of her head. "Needs a black hair band," she said.

"You need to flatten your own hair; it's poufing at the nape," Ivy said. "Zip me up in back." The pink dress was tight across her breasts and around her arms; the skirt rippled just above her knees. She'd have to keep her arms down all evening. "I should wear a pink ribbon."

"Cut off the sash," Shelly said. She was wearing her new black leather skirt. It looked extraordinarily sexy with Shelly's naked breasts, her nipples scarcely darker than the pink dress. "Where's your scissors?"

"You could wear suspenders and say it's a Rudy Gernreich outfit," Ivy said.

Shelly looked at herself in the mirror, arranged a hank of synthetic red hair over one breast, then flipped the hair back over her shoulders and displayed her naked chest, back arched, hands on hips. "I could make a shirt out of Saran wrap," she said. "Scissors in your desk?"

"Don't cut off the sash," Ivy said. "Suzy Creamcheese needs bows. I've got a white ribbon somewhere."

"Suzy Creamcheese will be *adorable*," Shelly said. "When's Chuck coming back?"

"Tuesday or Wednesday," Ivy said, poking through her top drawer. The white ribbon emerged. "I'm not looking forward to it," she added.

"You're not?" Shelly dropped the leather skirt and picked up her jeans.

"I've decided to break up with him." Ivy glanced at Shelly's surprised face. "It's time to be someone other than Chuck's girlfriend."

"You mean you want to play the field for awhile," Shelly said. "Every woman should do that. Kind of like trying on different shoes before you choose."

"Maybe," Ivy said. In the last month Shelly had spent every Saturday night out with a man—she wouldn't say who. The first time she appeared on a Sunday afternoon, eye makeup smudged onto her cheeks, her bushy hair snarled, eager for coffee and the newspaper, Ivy had asked where she'd been. Shelly leveled a close-lipped, world-weary gaze and left the room. So Ivy didn't ask again. But she doubted that even Shelly believed that sleeping around was like trying on shoes.

"Men do it; why not us?" Shelly had said at a Women's Liberation meeting. Yes. Why not? Thrilling, clandestine kisses with Bert were near the surface of Ivy's mind these days. Alone in her rollaway bed she'd been imagining sex with him: a smooth, satisfying impalement that slaked a kind of hunger aching just above her groin.

Sex with Chuck was too often a way to settle him down so she could sleep. She loved to snuggle next to him, she loved sex, too, sometimes; she felt...tethered, that was the trouble. When she thought of a future in which she was happy, she pictured herself alone, exploring cities, meeting people, uncommitted to anyone. When she'd told him she wanted to go around the world, she was telling a truth she hadn't known till then. She didn't want to sleep around (not much, anyway). But she'd discovered it was possible to love one man and long for another; the two feelings were quite separate. No, she should not continue to be Chuck's girlfriend.

She'd half-wanted to tell Jane what had happened when she and Bert came out of the steam tunnels; she would not tell Shelly.

They'd found a new exit through a door in the Mather gym basement and climbed the stairs holding hands. "I don't want to let go of you," Bert had said. So they walked to the Art Museum grounds above the lagoon, his arm over her shoulders, hers around his waist. The fall afternoon was warm and colorful; Ivy was skipping a lecture on ancient Greek literature.

Bert stopped under the statue of Tadeusz Kosciuszko, Polish hero of the American Revolution. "He's got cool boots," Bert said. Kosciuszko's boots reached his knees and folded at his ankles, tough stompers. His left hand was on his scabbard, his right held the sword as if he were leading a charge. Beneath the bronze statue, the marble pedestal was engraved with a story:

"'I come to fight as a volunteer for American Independence,' said Kosciuszco.

'What can you do?' asked Washington.

'Try me,' was the reply."

"I like this guy," Bert grinned.

The statue was stiff and a bit crude, the man's body submerged within the boots, cape, and his odd Polish hat. "You have to wonder about the Polish hero-worshipers who commissioned it," Ivy said. "Did they love the man or his clothes?" Bert thought that was a pointless question. They strolled over to the fountain, where naked nymphs and gods capered passionately in the spray, and back up the steps to The Thinker.

"Rodin meant this figure to be Dante, perched over the gates to heaven and hell," Ivy said. The statue loomed over them. Bert threw back his head to look carefully.

"You know what?" he said. "The Thinker doesn't have a cock."

"Are you sure?"

"Yeah, he's a fucking eunuch." Bert pointed, but the statue was too high above them, its body too thoroughly hunched over the knees, to be sure. Ivy didn't care; all afternoon she'd been aware of Bert's body, not hidden but enhanced by his work shirt and jeans. She felt her nipples reach for him like tongue-tips, her lips swell with blood.

They came together on the grass behind the marble wall, breathing hard, fumbling with buttons and zippers till they were skin-to-skin. Thrilling and uncomfortable to lie under Bert on the grass; Ivy felt a stone pressing into her back and squirmed. But her belly and thighs were silken and her whole body charged, trembling, eager. When they finished, they had to dress quickly so no one would see them. The ground was muddy where they'd lain.

Bert said he would never claim her. "I know you're attached to Chuck Leggit," he'd said.

"Bourgeois couplings are outdated," she'd responded. She knew Bert thought that.

He wanted her to quit working with Jimmy. "He's supposed to recruit members for the Party, not make the Revolution."

"There's more than one way to make the Revolution," Ivy said. "And we're a democratic society, so..." The thing was, she and Jimmy together had built a bigger protest against Dow than either could have individually. Bert was pushy in meetings, interrupting, urging students to use more inflammatory language. A few students admired him; more were turned off. Now Bert and Chuck were in Boulder together. What would they say to each other about Ivy?

Oh, Chuck. He'd said "I don't own you; it's a figure of speech," but marriage seemed inevitable as a tunnel ahead on the Pennsylvania Turnpike: she could argue against outdated bourgeois relationships forever, and they'd still have to go through the tunnel. She'd come out Ivy Leggit, someone she didn't know and probably wouldn't like. *How to break free?*

In the wastebasket, earlier this afternoon, she'd found a torn piece of a letter from Gail to Joe. "I love you, darling; I just need to be free for now," it said. "When you get back from 'Nam, maybe..." She hoped Gail had sent a more definite rejection. Joe was the soldier who cut off Vietnamese ears; Gail could never get back together with him now. She'd been spending whole weekends with Jimmy and joined his Mobe Committee to End the War in Viet Nam. Gail thought Jimmy was adorable.

If Chuck came back from Boulder hating Ivy, so be it, Ivy decided, peeling off the pink chiffon. Right now, she didn't want to sleep with anyone. She stood before the mirror, plump in her underwear, wishing she could fit into Shelly's black leather skirt. "Maybe I should write Chuck a letter," she said to Shelly. "Say something like *I just need to be free for now. Maybe we'll get back together, when...*"

"Cop-out," Shelly said. "The way to break up is to do it. The future will take care of itself. Have a good time tonight."

"So how do you feel about Bert Augustin these days?" Ivy said. Shelly turned around in the doorway with an exasperated sigh.

Then she laughed. "Got a cigarette and match?" Ivy retrieved the pack from her desk drawer. She'd promised Aunt Peg to quit smoking, and so far today she had. "You know? I was almost hung up on Bert," Shelly said. "He's got *charisma.*" She blew a cloud of smoke. "When he was in jail, last June, I went to see him, all teary, *Oh honey, what can I do?* God, I made a fool of myself. He was a fucking iceberg after he got out. Said things to drive away any sane girl."

"But you were still with him that night in The Big Penny, before Chicago."

"Oh, I can't help *liking* him. I stopped expecting anything, that's all. He doesn't love anyone. And since I went to Long Island when I should've gone to Chicago, he won't even talk to me. I'm president of the SDS chapter, but he talks to you. And I don't care. That's kind of a good feeling." Shelly stubbed out her cigarette on the edge of Ivy's metal wastebasket and let the butt fall. "Don't think about Robbie, I mean Bert, okay? Don't think about Chuck, either, till you have to."

"It's hard." What Ivy had seen in The Big Penny restroom didn't quite match Shelly's account of her feelings. "Chuck wants to be engaged, and I keep putting him off." She'd smoked half a cigarette without meaning to; now she stubbed it out.

"Like it's hard for Gail to cut the cord with Joe," Shelly said.

"Cutting Joe's cord must feel like letting him fall over a cliff," Ivy said. The cord connecting her to Chuck was muscular and ropey, pulsing with blood. The tethers to her parents were thinner and longer, strong as steel, and what about her brothers? The line to Glen would be solid; the line to Randy—the business man, the bully of her childhood—might as well be spiderweb. All the cords wriggled through her mind, wrapped around her chest, hobbled her legs; she was all tangled up.

"I don't want to be tied to anyone," Shelly said. "Not even my family. You want to use the shower first or shall I?"

"I'll go. I need to make ringlets." Ivy was running out of time.

When she came out of the shower the phone was ringing; Jimmy didn't like the SDS pamphlet. "Napalm for breakfast, tear gas for lunch," he said. "I wouldn't mind so much if it endorsed an anti-war candidate." Jimmy was pushing for Fred Halstead, from the Socialist Workers' Party. "The Trots," Bert called them.

"The SDS pamphlet goes on the lit table tonight," Ivy said. "Along with your Halstead sheets, the Women's Liberation statement, and *Underground News*."

"Bert's rhetoric is unacceptable."

"It's not Bert's rhetoric. That leaflet was written by SDS folks in Chicago."

"And Bert objects to *my* connection with a national organization," Jimmy sneered. "So why should I share a table with SDS lit?"

"I'm SDS," Ivy said. "So are Marvin and Jane. And we don't have a problem with your bringing copies of *The Militant* tonight. Listen, I gotta go."

"I'm not only bringing *The Militant*. I'm bringing anti-war flyers, too."

"And Fred Halstead for President," Ivy said.

"Not till people are ready," Jimmy said. "First they oppose the war; then we show them how the war is because of capitalism: Halstead's analysis. From there they join the party. *That's* how we make revolution."

"Halstead's is *not* the only revolutionary party." Ivy stood shivering, naked except for her bathrobe, her hair drying unset and straggly. "We don't have time for this discussion." Even last week she'd really liked Jimmy.

"Okay," Jimmy said. "I'll put the fucking pamphlet on one corner of the table, because this is supposedly an inter-organizational event—though it's really a Women's Lib event. I feel very coerced."

"If it's a Women's Lib event," Ivy demanded, "then why is Marvin Kaminsky the MC?"

"If you don't know, I won't bother you with some basic truths about parties on Friday nights," Jimmy said. "Listen Ivy, you're a smart person. We really should talk."

"We do talk," Ivy said. She needed to keep communicating with Jimmy and his committee, somehow. But it was getting harder. "I've got to go," she insisted.

Neither she nor Shelly looked as good as Ivy had imagined they would. Shelly wore a white sweater, not even transluscent, and her false eyelashes looked more sloppy than glamorous. Ivy's ringlets emerged from the rags in droopy spirals; she settled for two pigtails with white bows. She'd wanted big-bauble earrings like the girl in *The Graduate* wore, but all she had were her small pearl studs.

They had fun on the stage with Marvin, who gravely asked each of them her personal feelings about football and its importance to higher education. Shelly as the Glamour Puss answered, "It's a highly educational experience to watch guys crash into each other and get injured; it makes me understand men and patriotism and, you know, *life*."

Ivy gave her Suzy Creamcheese speech: "Those men are such gorgeous *hunks*. They're so tough! I just get all gooey inside thinking about them." She stood pigeon-toed, clutched Marvin's arm, and squealed.

The mannequin smiled, and Marvin said, "See that! She's beaming with joy! She knows when to keep quiet!" He put the crown on her and gave a sarcastic speech (more or less what Jane had written for him) about how Polly Plastics was the ideal woman.

Jimmy brought the band, and the event became a party, the counter-homecoming Queen irrelevant on the stage. Someone had brought jugs full of vodka-spiked orange juice. A guy from Ivy's biology class whispered, "You're so yummy tonight I can hardly stand it." She decided to avoid him.

Between numbers, she wandered to the lit table and found the SDS pamphlets buried by copies of *The Militant*. She pulled them out so they could be seen, even though no one would look at lit tonight. It had been silly to argue with Jimmy. They'd given up the *Name the Queen* jar when Marvin suggested "Polly Plastics."

Gail sat with her feet on the table, reading *Man's Fate*.

"Not good for your eyes," Ivy said. "Can I at least get you something to drink? Orange juice?"

"Coke," Gail said. "I've got a history paper to write this weekend. That's why I'm reading this." She wore slacks and a polo shirt. The shadows around her eyes were dark purple. Ivy couldn't help jiggling to the music; Gail was almost as still as the mannequin.

Eaten up by her dilemma, Ivy thought: Joe vs. Jimmy. Support the troops vs. end the war. She considered telling Gail she'd read the torn piece of letter as she got two Cokes from the refreshment table. When she returned, Gail said, "I almost forgot. You got a telegram delivered to Hessler Road, after you left. Here."

Chuck had sent it this morning from St. Louis: "Thinking how sincerely I do love you."

Ivy felt a painful visceral tug. *Shit!* Tears came into her eyes. She couldn't wipe them away without smearing Suzy Creamcheese's mascara, and she had no Kleenex.

"That's really sweet of him," Gail said, reading the telegram.

"Yes, it is," Ivy said. Like sweet potato pie. Like a parent who kept you on a leash for your own good. Jane danced by with Marvin, both wildly waving their legs and arms to the band's version of The Beatles' "Revolution."

"Shall I get another chair?" she asked. Gail might say how she was trying to break up with Joe, and Ivy might tell her about breaking up with Chuck; she might be able to learn more about Jimmy and the Socialist Workers Party.

"I've really got to finish this book," Gail said. She picked it up and turned a page.

Jane appeared behind Ivy. "Here," she said. "I've been meaning to..." She held out the London Fog. "*Thank you* for this coat," Jane said. "I couldn't afford to have it cleaned, but I washed it twice."

"It's fine," Ivy said, putting it on. It was wrinkled, but it hadn't shrunk. It fit over the pink dress. The band was playing "Theme from a Summer Place" and people were slow-dancing, shadowy snuggled couples scattered on the dance floor. She wished she were among them—not with Bert, with Chuck. No, not with Chuck either. "Thanks for taking care of the coat," she said to Jane. "Now my coat *and* my ID have done acts of historical significance."

"You have, too," Jane said. They were going down the stairs together, walking into the darkness.

Jane was a good friend. The night was cold; streetlights barely penetrated the mist, and Ivy felt the pink dress tighten around her chest and arms, felt a slow wheeze under the chiffon.

In the old white Valiant with one red door, Jane drove Ivy home to Hessler Road.

Showered clean, comfortable in her sweatshirt and jeans, she made some Constant Comment and added honey. She was breathing easier when Gail and Jimmy came in.

"Hi there," Jimmy did a little semaphore-wave. "You were pretty creamy tonight."

"I'm so glad to be out of that costume," Ivy said. "*This* is me."

"An old Reserve sweatshirt?" Jimmy wore a red sweater over a blue-collared shirt; his cheeks were flushed, his eyes unfocused. Drunk on vodka and orange juice.

"I'll be out of your way in a minute," Ivy said. "I'm about to cave with exhaustion." But after she was in bed she lay awake for a long time listening to the sounds downstairs: murmuring, couch springs groaning, then finally the front door closing. Gail came upstairs. Ivy heard her in the bathroom, thought of getting up, and didn't. The bedroom door closed; Gail's bed creaked. The house was quiet. What was this ache of regret? Unbidden, Ivy's mind swung toward the feel of Bert's hand creeping beneath her shirt. She felt her body soften, replaying the wild mix of sensations on the Art Museum lawn: the chill of grass on buttocks, the skin-on-skin friction, Bert's slippery mouth. If Chuck thrust his tongue into her that suddenly, would she want to stay with him? Chuck was tentative with his tongue.

He'd found a Western Union office, gone there, and composed his telegram. *How sincerely I do love you.* The words snarled around themselves. What a waste of money, to say what she already knew. Like the flowers he'd brought her after the Wallace demonstration, this telegram was romantic as hell, but it had a tether. Tears trickled over her ears and into her hair.

She was awakened by Gail pounding on her door. "Ivy! Get up! Chuck's here!"

"He can't be," Ivy said, still sleepy, a high note in back of her right ear whining *please, no, I'm not ready.* "I'll be down in a few minutes, after I've used the bathroom." Rising, she saw a streak of red on the sheet.

She washed herself and rinsed the blood out of her underpants, feeling relief, as always, that she was not pregnant. She fastened a Kotex pad onto the belt, put it on, and scrubbed the pink stain with soap, rinsing, scrubbing, rinsing again. Odd, how she'd dreamed that Chuck was here. The Boulder Caucus convention had barely begun.

Naked in the hallway except for the Kotex, she heard his voice, Gail's answering. He *was* here. She'd have to tell him now; that was the deal she'd made with herself. *Oh no. No.* Maybe if she explained how she loved him but needed to be free? He'd accept her feelings, and they'd keep going toward the tunnel. Maybe if they split up now they could come together again, some day, when she'd been around the world?

She ran cold water over her hands and wiped her eyes and cheeks with her fingers. If she took time to hunt for a towel, she'd lose her nerve. She clambered into her jeans and sweatshirt.

Here he was, in the big living room chair, handsome in the workshirt that made his eyes look extra blue. "Hi, sleepy girl." His mustache spread across his smile.

"Why aren't you in Boulder?" she asked.

"The blue van got a terminal case of transmissionitis." Chuck rose and came toward where she stood, halfway up the stairs. "We had to abandon it in St. Louis. Bert and Tessa flew on to Boulder. I took the bus home."

"How did Bert and Tessa get the money?" she asked. "And not you?"

"SDS money I guess." Chuck shrugged. "Bert and Tessa get paid by the central office." He reached for her hand, and she came down the stairs, wondering how come she hadn't known that SDS paid its organizers, and then they were hugging; she was loving Chuck and feeling guilty. "Let's go get some coffee, and a paper," he said. "Go comb your hair." He reached one finger to push the long bangs out of her eyes and looked at her, searching.

She shook her head. She wanted nothing so much as a chance to wake up slowly with a cup of coffee, to read the funnies across the drugstore table from dear old Chuck Leggit. But she met his eyes and knew: He'd sent the telegram because Bert had told him what she'd done. He planned to get her abject, weeping apology and then forgive her.

The knowledge felt like hardboiled egg in her throat. Her eyes were burning dry; she could not let him touch her again. "No," she said. "I've decided. I can't promise to marry you. And I can't go on being your girlfriend. It's over."

"No it's not," he said. "You can't just *end* what we have."

"I have to." Ivy closed her eyes so she could think. "You want to get married and I don't. I know that now."

"Oh," Chuck said, still close. "Are you sure?"

"Yes." She was sure only that she had to answer *yes*.

"What happened?" He grabbed her by the shoulders and shook—three hard shakes. "Tell me. Now. Now!" Ivy's head wobbled, and she brought her hands up to protect her neck, forcing him to break his hold. "Tell me," he said again.

"I need to be on my own," Ivy insisted slowly. Bert had said he would not claim her. She would not claim him. "Figure out who I am without being someone's girlfriend."

"You want to fuck around," Chuck said. "With Augustin."

"Bert has been with you, not me," Ivy said.

"Yeah, I drove the van while he and Tessa fucked in the back. But you've been *meeting with him* for months." His voice rose thick with disgust. "What I'm saying, Ivy, is I understand how overwhelmed you've been, with Jimmy pulling one way and Bert pulling the other. Out of your depth. What I'm saying is, come to me." He held out his arms. "We'll work it out together, whatever it is."

Out of her depth. He couldn't imagine her needing to work things out on her own. If she gave in, Chuck would claim her, with all her private thoughts and feelings, forever. The tunnel loomed dark, and she swerved away. "No," she said, stepping backward. "It's over. I'm sure."

There was more to say—I'll always love you? I'm grateful for the time we had? I'll be your friend forever? Even if those things were true, it was too late. He'd already turned away. Turned his back on her, opened the door, walked out. His steps rang on the porch, thudded on the steps, then he was gone. She wanted to lunge after him—*No, wait, I didn't mean it.*

She did mean it. She reminded herself of that constricting tangle, that tight cord; she wanted her connections with people from now on to be gossamer. She felt herself bleed, felt her Kotex soggy with blood between her legs. She sank onto the stairs.

When Shelly came home, red hair spilling from the paper bag that held her costume, Ivy was still sitting on the bottom stair. Hours might have gone by; she didn't know. "I broke up with Chuck," she said.

"Wow," Shelly said. "You've got guts. You guys were welded at the hip—oh, honey, here, here." She let Ivy cry in her arms, cry and cry, and Shelly's arms were not comforting. Nothing could be comforting ever again. Ivy hated her own skin, her own voice.

She felt like retching as she washed the blood out of her underwear and her jeans. Bless Shelly for making a whole pot of coffee. Ivy brought her cup to the living room couch and opened her medieval art book to statues of saints and kings. It was soothing to think how, for hundreds of years, all of Europe had held still on stone pillars and altars and tomb-lids, unchangeable, indestructible.

Chapter 23

October 12, 14, 1968
Liberty Boulevard & The Movement Office

Lake Erie slapped against rocks under Chuck's feet, its water greenish-brown, translucent and impenetrable as wax. The rocks heaved and scraped, a jumble of dark basalt, mottled granite, and broken cement. Spray bit into his sneakers; he shivered in the afternoon cold. He'd forgotten his jacket. Could he have left it at Ivy's house? If so, was it lost to him forever?

He'd walked the whole length of Liberty Boulevard to the Lake Shore, noticing only his feet, astonished that they kept appearing below his knees, one before the other, slapping the pavement. He looked at his right hand: it was clutched around a water-smoothed stone. He threw it *plop* into the lake and watched the ripples try to make circles, as they would in a pond, but they failed: the lake water cut the stone's ripples into snaky lines, and the water sloshed into nauseous billows without forming waves. He wished he hadn't thrown the stone. His hand missed it.

If he'd known the van was about to throw a rod, he wouldn't have sent Ivy the telegram. He'd been fantasizing her creamcheese outfit, knowing she'd borrowed a dress from Shelly, who wore diaphanous, low-necked dresses. He'd thought how bony Shelly was; underneath her clothing you'd find a creature scrawny as a wet cat. But Ivy in a dress of Shelly's, breasts tight against the cloth, fabric brushing all her soft curves—Ivy moved into his mind just as the Western Union office appeared across the street from the gas station where he and Bert waited for Tessa to finish in the bathroom. Chuck had rushed to send the first ten words he could think of. When he came out they were annoyed, eager to move. "What was the urgent message about?" Tessa had asked.

"Telegram to Ivy." Chuck sat next to Bert while Tessa settled in the back, arranging her sleeping bag so she could nap while Bert drove.

"Ivy's a wild and free babe," Bert said. Chuck had felt the back of his neck bristle; he hated the way Bert tried to show off his manhood with bullshit about any woman, much less Ivy. Then Bert went on. "She loves French-kissing, can't get enough of it." Chuck watched him maneuver the van into the left lane and gun the engine. "Don't ask me how I know," Bert said. Chuck told him to quit fucking around and turned on the radio. A few miles down the road, the transmission failed.

He shouldn't have surprised her. He'd taken the time to bathe and put on clean clothes; he could have called her. But he was full of his plan to take Ivy to breakfast, rushing stupidly from his apartment to hers. She came down the stairs all blowzy in jeans and a sweatshirt, barefoot, no bra, her ears sticking out between droopy spirals of hair—and for a second she'd come into his arms, her cheeks soft and pink with sleep. For that instant before she startled and pushed him away, he was able to deny that he knew the break-up was coming.

He'd known when he sent the telegram. He'd known before Bert had made his innuendos, but he hadn't figured it out till he saw Ivy's eyes grow dark and guilty when he asked her, "What happened?" And when he realized he was shaking her, he'd known. He'd blown it.

He wanted another stone. His butt ached from sitting on an edge of broken cement. He clambered down and slid into pieces of slate sharp as hatchets, and the cold wind blew through his shirt as he bent close to the water. His jeans were soaked to the knees before he found a good round stone and took his bearings. Lake Erie spread metallic-gray to the northern horizon. Beyond was Canada. East was Bratenahl, as snobbish and closed as its ancestor town in Connecticut. West stood the

Terminal Tower amid the lesser buildings of downtown Cleveland. Once, in another life, he'd worked there in a bank. He'd worn a suit and tie and held Ivy, his darling, in bed, her arms clinging to him, her sweet hair against his mouth as he kissed her. "I hate when you leave," she'd say, even though they'd be parting for only a few hours.

One more embrace, please, God! Then he could be strong.

He threw the stone. Cold forced him to move, pulled him off the rocks and across the Lake Shore traffic, running, his sneakers chafing his feet, the wet hems of his jeans rubbing his ankles raw as he ran up Liberty Boulevard. He ran past the bushes where a girl's body had been found the other day. She'd been raped and "disfigured," according to the newspaper—cut with a knife, probably, her face, her breasts, or her vagina. Predators lurked among the trees here, thinking a student-type would carry a wallet, thinking vengeance on the white oppressors.

He had no wallet, just $3.00 in his back pocket, meant to pay for coffee and sticky buns for himself and Ivy this morning. What if he'd held on when she first came to him rather than letting her pull away? What if he'd said, "Don't be silly, we need to talk over coffee," rather than losing control of himself? He could have begged for time.

No, walking away was the only thing to do. She'd as much as said it all before: she wanted to go around the world, to flirt and kiss at random. She wanted to be a girl who'd been around. What was the probability of a man in her bed this morning, a man still there when she stood on the staircase telling Chuck it was over? He'd give it fifty per cent.

Near a playground he got a cramp that felt like a knife in his ribs and stopped running. He wasn't going back to Ivy's. He'd ask someone else. He'd find Shelly in the Student Union; she seemed to do most of her studying there. *Hi Shelly, you didn't happen to notice a tan jacket with a plaid lining? By the way, what's Ivy doing? Has she said anything to you about...*

He didn't like the hang-dog tone of that speech. Today was Saturday: Shelly wouldn't be in the Union. He didn't give a fuck about his jacket. He didn't give a fuck about anything except that he could not let Ivy know how bad he was hurting. He didn't want to face the dirty laundry in his apartment. But he had a bottle of Scotch there. How much was left?

The words reeled through his brain—*I've decided. I need to be on my own. It's over, I'm sure.* He could not stand it, wanted to sob, thought he must go to Hessler Road, smash the glass on the front door, sneak in and climb to her bed. He no longer wanted to possess her, he'd decided before the telegram. She was a liberated woman. If she needed to sleep around a little, he'd force himself to live with it.

Bert and Tessa slept around, yet they'd stayed lovers, clutching each other in the back of the van as Chuck drove, kissing each others' hands in the Indiana diner where they worked on their manifesto. "Let Us Not Talk Falsely Now," they called it, and "The Hour's Getting Late." They boosted each other's rhetoric, talking "isolated acts of disruption," and "exploding the symbols of authority and power." They seemed to think a lot of noise and rubble would cause people to see the need for revolution. Chuck said as much, and Tessa suggested he work on sharpening his analysis. She gathered a pile of things he should read, but he pointed out that he could not read while driving. Bert's voice had grated like a saw blade and Chuck had wished he were home with Ivy.

He needed someone to grab onto (didn't everyone?) like you'd hold onto a horse's mane as it galloped, or like you'd hold onto the mast during a storm, in a ship headed toward a far edge where no one had ever gone. His mistake was not facing what he knew: Ivy was no tame pony, no mast to which you could lash yourself, not at all. Not wild and free, either. She was being tossed around by the storm even more than Chuck was. When he thought of them as two people wind-blown and reeling crazily into unknown territory, he could forgive her for fucking Bert.

Not yet, though. He climbed the Monmouth stairs, let himself in, and found his jacket on the back of a chair. The bottle of Scotch was one-third full. He poured it all in a glass and got out his notebook, writing all the darkest, most brutal words he knew, describing the most disgusting things he'd ever seen, from a headless dead bird in the back yard (he was six) to Greg Lambert's bare ass (one evening last week), fat, pimply, farting. "Greg's a child," Chuck wrote in his notebook, "self-centered, with a short fuse: that kind of child. And Augustin's the same, only worse, because he's smart. A thorough jerk."

The Scotch gone, the light waning, he was unfortunately still conscious. He took off his jeans, crawled into his dirty sheets and made himself sleep. In the morning he woke clutching a T-shirt: Ivy had worn it and left it in his bed, the last time she was here. The last time. It still smelled of her.

Monday evening he was typing the master sheet for *Underground News*, page four—again, the third time, when Bert somehow materialized in the office. "What are you doing here?" Chuck asked, without looking up. He'd been working like a robot. It was marvelous how his eyes dried up and his gut stopped churning as soon as he was at the typewriter, breathing mimeograph ink, thinking only about word counts, correct punctuation, and layouts.

"So much for the Boulder con," Bert said. He leaned against the wall and lit a cigarette. "They don't get it."

"Who doesn't get what?" Chuck mumbled, then saw another stupid mistake. *Ahcmed*, he'd typed. Disgusted, he pulled his hands off the keys. "Okay, tell me." He had to report what had happened at the convention.

"The only proposal that passed was a student strike on election day." Bert flicked cigarette ash to the floor and stomped as though it were a cockroach. "No class today, no ruling class tomorrow."

"Cool slogan: it would just fit into this space." Chuck held up the master of the first page carefully, by its edges, thinking he could draw the letters by hand, seeing how the words would space themselves.

"Fuck that shit!" Bert struck the page with the side of his hand, ripping it. "*Fuck* those hippie pacifists, those damn *consolidators*. Fuck especially the PLP and their Maoist class analysis..."

Chuck picked up the ruined page. It would take two hours to type again. He watched Bert walk to the front window and look out. For a long second he considered strangulation; his belt would do the job. Then Bert turned around and strode past him. "Pacifism is a ruling-class tactic to disarm the masses," he said, his boot heels thumping in time with his words. "And we *know*—we *know* that every *god*damn uni*ver*sity in this *coun*try is a *tool* for the *nat*ional se*cur*ity *com*plex..." He's crazy, Chuck thought, wondering if he could justify a blow on Bert's head—knock him out for awhile. Bert turned and paced, then turned again, raving about the hundreds of arrested students in Detroit, Illinois, and Oakland. Mass expulsions. "The university functions only to support the Establishment's aims; therefore it has no right to exist!"

Chuck picked up the cigarette butt and tossed it on top of the ruined mimeo master. If Bert didn't leave quick, Chuck would have to manhandle him out the door. The thump and scrape of those boots on the cement floor, the ranting voice and long limbs flailing against nothing but air, even the hanks of butter-brickle hair spreading grease around the jean jacket shoulders, stirred up a storm in the room that made logical thought impossible. This was the man Ivy thought was so *fun*, the man she had *so much to learn* from. Those thoughts led down a poisonous path. "Hey!" Chuck shouted, and jumped into Bert's path. Bert stopped in mid-stride. "I got a paper to get out. Go write all that down, if you want a report at all." He could edit Bert's words on paper; he'd be doing his job. "I gotta finish this issue." Chuck's hands were forming claws. "I thought I had the front page done, at least. Get the hell out."

"Hey! Be cool, be cool." Bert put his hands up as if Chuck had aimed a gun at his chest. A gun would be too easy. Chuck would prefer a knife. "No need to shout. I didn't mean to tear your fucking mimeo sheet, okay?"

It wasn't okay. Nothing was okay. Chuck's wound gaped, raw and crippling.

"We were at Glenville together," Bert said. "You know what I'm talking about." He backed to the couch and sat down. "I been stewing and stewing. Haven't slept. Don't remember how to sleep."

"I can tell," Chuck said. "Go write. That's what I do." Glenville was on the page in his typewriter: an intersection filled with flames.

"Writing takes so *fucking long*." Bert lit another cigarette. "We got no time—no time!" He fell onto his back against the cushions. "Forty-one burnings or bombings since September," Bert said. "The Movement did that. We're a bigger threat to the Establishment every day. There's a classified military research building in Ann Arbor..."

He really wants to blow something up, Chuck realized.

"All symbolic, no one hurt: we mess with their fucking property, and the university comes out of the woodwork to openly defend its right to inflict violence against living breathing people...And the public *sees*. Whenever people are threatened by us, we're getting somewhere." Bert's rationale made a kind of sense. "The Hough riots led to Cleveland: Now!—all those millions for the inner city, pacify the natives. The seeds of revolution have started to sprout..." His voice dropped to a mumble. Chuck stopped listening, turned to the typewriter, and tried to figure out where he'd left off. Hard to focus on the line of words.

Suddenly Bert hauled himself out of the couch and came around to look at Chuck over the typewriter. His face was puffy; his eyes slitted. "You're right, I've been rambling," he said. "You know that girl Angela? I thought she might be here."

Angela. Chuck had met her. She was SDS at Case Western, had a fierce way of looking out from under the bill of her Greek fisherman's cap and a loud voice. "*Down* with the damned rulers! Pitch Edgar Hoover out on his ass!" Bert's interest in Angela made Chuck feel a little safer.

"Do you know which dorm she lives in?" All freshmen lived in dorms. "Does she know you're looking for her?"

Bert shrugged. "I told her I had a bottle of bourbon stashed in here, and she said she might come to meet me. I want to show her the steam tunnels."

"You've got a bottle of bourbon? Where?" Suddenly Chuck felt more friendly. Amazing, how that worked. He thought of pouring bourbon down his throat, like hot healing syrup.

"In the basement, if someone hasn't liberated it." Bert went to check, and Chuck turned back to *Underground News*, page four. He looked at the next spelling error—*violance*—and decided to let it stand. He could re-type the first page, print all four pages, and Issue II would be ready to distribute tonight. Then he'd get back to the hard work on the typewriter: Glenville.

"If you're about to meet a girl, you really should go home and clean up," Chuck said, as Bert came up the stairs with the bourbon.

Bert shook his head. "No facilities," he said. "She'll have to take me as I am." He swigged from the bottle. "You don't have anything to eat, do you?"

"But you were living with Marvin," Chuck said. He was hungry too, and the fridge was stocked with bread, bologna, and mustard. He accepted a teacup full of bourbon and sipped. Could he let Bert stay here without killing him, after all?

Bert was talking again, his long arms on his knees, cup of bourbon cradled between his palms. "Someone asked me why a Marine would cut off a Vietnamese ear, and I think I know, now. You come out of the jungle, your camouflage pants stink of shit, you haven't slept in weeks, your ears are ringing.

And there's your enemy, dead. He's had power over you for months, he's made your life hell, killed your friends, and this time you did something real. You *acted*. Now, you gonna walk away without a token? No! You take a piece of his power." Bert stared at his imaginary dead enemy. "I wish to God I could've been with Che in Bolivia," Bert said. "I was at the Pentagon instead; how far is Washington from La Paz?"

"You are a crazy fucker," Chuck said. "You know that?" But he could see the dead enemy, could imagine slicing off an ear. Suddenly he got up. "I'm making sandwiches," he said. There was a bologna-slicing knife in the desk. He felt supremely Christian, making a sandwich to feed his enemy, and supremely hypocritical, hoping Bert would be threatened enough by a kitchen knife to leave.

He kept the knife in his hand as he brought the plate over with two bologna sandwiches. Bert was staring morosely at the bulletin board over the desk. Bobby Seale's photo stared at them from among a scattering of little messages and a raised-fist print. "Eat," said Chuck. "Then get out of here. I need to work." He wondered where Bert would go. Then he didn't care.

"You know, Leggit, you're not a bad guy," Bert said, helping himself to the top sandwich. "The paper's a good idea; it'll grow. And you quit school; I respect that."

"You seen Marvin since you got back?" Chuck asked. He wished Marvin were here to talk to, wondered why Bert was no longer living with him.

"Kaminsky is not interested in action," Bert said, chewing. Then he swallowed, and his voice rose. "*Organize*, he says. We've got to build our jungle base. That's bullshit!" He threw the cup against the bulletin board; it bounced off, leaving droplets on Bobby Seale's chin, and shattered on the cement floor. "Organizing just means going slow. We could organize for the rest of our lives and get nowhere."

Still overreacting, Bert had answered the question Chuck hadn't asked. He collected the pieces of cup, dumped them in the wastebasket, and poured himself a little more bourbon. Alcohol softened the air. "You better go." He put his hand on Bert's shoulder to guide him out. Bert jerked away. "Put that knife down," he said.

Chuck realized he'd held the blade an inch from Bert's chest. He dropped his hand, still holding the knife. They stood next to each other facing the office door. Bert stank of sweat and road dirt. He'd left Chuck at a bus station in St. Louis three days ago and probably had not slept since. Chuck had not slept much, either. "Go get some sleep," he said. "Tessa will let you crash on the couch."

"You know what?" Bert turned, with a red-faced truth-imparting stare. "Marvin Kaminsky is a fucking father figure."

"I would've thought that was obvious," Chuck said.

"You don't get it: he's *my* father figure." Suddenly Bert's face was tragic, all its muscles drooping, and fear in his eyes.

Chuck wondered if Bert had seen his real father lately. He knew Augustin Senior had bought his son a lawyer, but hadn't visited him in jail or welcomed him home on release. Marvin was fatherly, all right: past thirty, friendly, full of experience cooked down to wisdom. That's why Chuck had wished him here. Everyone in the Cleveland Movement sought Marvin's advice about things.

Chuck thought of his own father, whom he no longer feared or hated, now that he'd paid the tuition back. He just couldn't stand to be around Charley Leggit for long. There were good memories he didn't know what to do with; they made him sad. "We all have to outgrow our fathers," he told Bert.

"Easier said than done," Bert said. He picked up the bourbon bottle, took a long swig, and threw himself back on the couch. Chuck watched his eyes close.

"I'm going to finish the paper," Chuck said. Bert didn't respond. All right, let him sleep. He hadn't come to the office to see Angela, after all; she was an excuse. He didn't have anywhere else to sleep.

Chuck set to work again on the first page, bourbon and sadness coursing through his veins. The work of re-typing required just enough close attention to keep other thoughts at bay. Getting the words spelled right was the most important thing in the world—spelling, and hitting the space bar in time to keep the margins straight. Each *ding* brought him closer to the steady thumping productivity of the final print.

He had been typing for an hour, slowly and perfectly, finishing the Dow-demo story and beginning Jane's MOP report, when the door slammed open and Greg Lambert staggered in with a television so big he couldn't hold its bottom edges and still see over the top. "Do we still have the antenna you and Sheldon rigged up?" Greg's voice woke Bert, who looked around as if he'd forgotten where he was. Then he closed his eyes again.

"Right there," Chuck pointed to the corner where Sheldon's TV had been, and Greg set down his load with a groan of relief.

"Hiya, Augustin," Greg said to Bert. "How was the meeting in Boulder?"

"Shitty," Bert said, raising himself up with a groan. He swung his feet to the floor. "SDS got too big, all of a sudden. What's the TV for?"

"I found it," Greg said, "and I already have one, so I thought it'd be useful here. For watching the news and all that. I'm glad to see you, Bert, because..."

"Let's turn it on." Bert suddenly moved into action, swooping to the corner to plug in the television and hook up the wire ends of the antenna. "C'mon baby." He turned the knobs and patted the sides.

"I got that stuff you wanted," Greg said to Bert. "From the steel mill?"

Bert stiffened. "No shit? Where is it?"

"In my garage," Greg said.

Greg meant his mother's garage unless the steel mill had paid him unbelievably well this summer. And what "stuff" would Bert want badly enough to be excited, buttoning his jean jacket, screwing the top on the bourbon bottle? "I'll just take a piss," Bert said, "and then we'll go to your garage." He disappeared into the john and pieces clanged together in Chuck's mind: The live grenade on Greg's desk. Bert's talk of "exploding the symbols of authority and power." Would a steel mill use dynamite?

Bert had slung his pack over his shoulder when the television came on with a blare of suspense music. He spun around. "Hold it, we're not going anywhere."

Tony Curtis ran across the screen, handcuffed to Sidney Poitier. Railroad cars in the background. "You know this movie?" Greg said to Chuck.

"*The Defiant Ones.*" Chuck had seen it years ago. It was coupled in his mind with the line *Black and white together*. "Curtis and Poitier are escaped convicts," he said.

Bert returned to the couch. "We missed most of it, but my favorite scene's coming. Look." They watched the two men stumble into a grove of trees near a river. Leaves buffeted their faces. The law officials came over the ridge with baying dogs. The convicts' choices had narrowed to two: Keep running, or stop and get caught.

Life is rock-bottom basic for men in chains, about to be caught. Same with being a soldier, Chuck realized. Nobody expects you to sharpen your analysis, to keep re-examining and adjusting your mind with every new event or theory. You kill or are killed, live or die.

Tony Curtis was killed. He lay dead in the ditch next to Sidney Poitier, who watched the dogs pull the sheriff nearer, his choices narrowed to one. Greg sat cross-legged on the floor, shoulders slumped and head thrown back, rapt as a kid watching *The Fugitive*. Bert softly pummeled one palm with the other fist. "This is it...the best moment of all the moments in all the movies I've ever seen."

Poitier looked up, a smile on his handsome Black face, and made the one choice. He crooned off-key: "Bowling green, sewing machine, bowling green..." Bert on the sofa leaned forward, mouthing the words with Poitier as the camera moved in; Chuck saw his face, spellbound, singing with Poitier: "Sewing machine!"

For awhile after Bert and Greg left, Chuck worried. What would he do if Bert and Greg brought explosives back to the office? He couldn't call the police. He finished the front page and returned to the fourth, and as the night deepened he realized they weren't coming back. He'd been wrong to think that Greg could smuggle explosives out of the steel mill. Maybe "explosives" was entirely the wrong conclusion. Could have just as easily been information; maybe Bert wanted to research a connection between Republic Steel and the military. Maybe he was after free beer.

Chuck finished typing, tenderly wrapped his mimeo masters in a folder, and made his way to the Church of the Covenant basement, where he fired up the machine and printed 200 copies of *Underground News*, Issue II. A good night's work. He returned to The Monmouth at dawn, his head swimming with mimeograph ink fumes and exhaustion, ready to sleep for days.

PART FIVE

For we knew only too well:
Even the hatred of squalor
Makes the brow grow stern.
Even anger against injustice
Makes the voice grow harsh. Alas, we
Who wished to lay the foundation of kindness
Could not ourselves be kind.

from "To Posterity" by Bertolt Brecht

"What will you do after the Revolution?" we asked each other, leaping past the cataclysm into the future, a green-pastures-still-waters place where we'd dance, make love, have babies, and learn to play guitar really well. We'd sentence the corporate rulers and the masters of war to Disneyland where they'd spend the rest of their lives waiting in line, riding little trains through decorated tunnels, and drinking chocolate milk. They'd never again be able to harm anyone.

For guidance we borrowed words from people who had actually made revolutions in Russia, China, Cuba, and Algiers. We fought over theory and practice, strategy and policy. The arguments helped to make the Revolution logical, but only up to a point: History told us our circumstances were unprecedented.

What we had intended, along with Civil Rights, was to stop the war in Southeast Asia and the march toward nuclear holocaust. In the process we discovered the System—a vast metal-minded matrix of technology, bureaucracy, and money. And the System discovered us. It seemed that law enforcers, bureaucracies, and government officials were threatened before we'd planned any real damage. Decades later, when some of us requested our FBI files, we discovered with a kind of appalled fascination the extent of COINTELPRO's messing with our lives—spying, wiretapping, sending letters to our families. They also disrupted, provoked, and spread false stories.

A myth has spread that we left the Movement because we gave up our unrealistic "ideals." Or that we'd never had them: the whole effort was fueled by personal ambitions rather than our fondess for humanity or for the planet. These are the kinds of stories people tell to ease their own guilt and sadness. This is what actually happened: we grew older. We came to know the strength and pervasiveness of the System.

Some of us recognized our lost image of Revolution in the final explosive scene of *Raiders of the Lost Ark*—as if the movie had read our dreams.

If we felt, by leaving the Movement, we had missed a train we should have been on...

If we felt regret when we found Bernardine Dohrn's letter from the underground in a Berkeley Bookstore: "We are outlaws, we are free!"...

If so, we could only cast about for new paths forward. There are many. Resistence against the System is now vast and diffuse. We are still here.

Chapter 24

November 4, 1968
Hessler Road

Ivy looked at the Camel cigarette between her first two fingers and willed the hand to quit shaking. Camels were uncompromising: no filters, no gold paper, no menthol. No calories: she could not allow herself to be fat. She tapped the ashes into the little brass ashtray next to her knee. Her mouth tasted foul, and there were sore spots on her tongue.

Cigarette butts piled up like little turds; ashes flaked onto the rug and her clothes. Her jeans had a gray smear where she'd wiped her hand. Her father had said, "You're not risking emphysema—you *will get it*. Slow, early death by strangulation from the inside." She would quit right after midterms.

Now smoking was necessary so she could concentrate on medieval art and then on Helena Curtis's biology text splayed beside her on the bed. If nothing else tonight she had to learn the Krebs cycle. When she finished both exams tomorrow, she had to write a paper on *Antigone*.

On the cover of her medieval art book was a painting of God removing the rib from Adam's side. God had dark hair, a gold halo like a plate on the back of his head, and an expression of wide-eyed tender concern. Adam slept, his hand covering half his face, as if he had a headache. He had pubic hair, but no penis. The rib that God held out looked like a penis. God seemed to be saying, *Here, try this. You'll feel better.* The painting made her sad.

Gail pounded on the door to her room: "Phone for you!"

"I'm hiding," Ivy said. She'd put the Movement on hold for the week.

"You'd better take this one. It's the FBI." Gail had been sleeping: there was a crease on her cheek and her hair stuck up in back. She disappeared into the bathroom, and Ivy picked up the receiver. From Gail's double bed she could see out the big window to Hessler Road. The sycamore branches waved and creaked, pale in the blue evening light. "Am I charged with anything?" she asked. Tessa had said she didn't have to tell the FBI anything if no one had pressed charges.

"No," said a man's voice. "But we know you were at the meeting on June 11th."

"Okay," Ivy said. "It's been nice talking with you."

"At 13805 Euclid Avenue," he went on, "you were planning to disrupt the Chicago Convention."

"Goodness, June was a long time ago. I don't remember." But she did remember: a group in the office basement had argued about what the Bobby Kennedy assassination meant for the Movement. Chuck had been eager to go to Chicago. Greg Lambert kept pounding his knee and grunting "Up against the wall, Motherfucker!" till Jane told him to quit. Glenville hadn't happened yet. They'd been different people than they were now.

"While you were in Chicago," the man persisted. "Did you see Robert Augustin? Was he carrying a smoke bomb?"

"I don't have anything to tell you," Ivy said. She thought of the thrilling conspiratorial darkness in Grant Park, with the whole world watching.

"We know you're a person who believes in honesty and openness," the FBI man said.

"That doesn't mean telling everything I know to strangers. I'm going to hang up now." She dropped the receiver into its cradle and moved from Gail's bed to the window. Below on the street, two men stood talking under the sycamores. The streetlight came on above them. One was a stranger. The other she could see only from the back—a bulky, round-shouldered man with a blond butch cut. He reminded her of Greg Lambert.

"Sorry to wake you up," she said to Gail, who'd come into the room and was putting on her jeans.

"I wanted to get up," Gail said. "What time is it, anyway?"

"Five o'clock, I think," Ivy said. She hoped Gail had heard her refusals. But she was oddly pleased, clumping downstairs, that the FBI had called. She was *wanted*; she had made an impact. The clock in the kitchen said 5:20. "Want some tea?" she called up the stairs to Gail. Tea had no calories.

"Make a whole pot. I want some too." Shelly stood over the sink in a cloud of steam, dumping a pot of macaroni into the colander. "This is for a tuna casserole to last the rest of the week." She'd lined up ingredients: cans of tuna, a little box of frozen peas, cream of mushroom soup.

"Thanks." A thought flew like a moth into Ivy's mind: one person in that June 11th meeting had told the FBI that she was honest and open. Who? They had been a small group—six or seven people. She couldn't remember now. "Medieval art exam tomorrow morning," she told Shelly. She turned for the stairs and heard the kettle slowly gathering itself to boil. In a minute it would scream.

Someone pounded on the front door. Ivy peered out the front window and saw the stranger on the sidewalk. He looked familiar, not a complete stranger. She opened the door, and Jimmy walked in. "Barcelona!" He held out his hand. The kettle set up a yell.

"Sorry, the kettle's making a non-negotiable demand," Ivy said. "Gail's coming." She backed away as Jimmy peeled off his peacoat.

In the kitchen, Shelly was packing the tuna fish and peas and soup into a casserole dish. "I'll crumble Saltines on top," she said. "I'd rather not talk with Jimmy."

"Me either; I'll just carry in some tea," Ivy said.

She found Gail sitting on the couch next to Jimmy. "You voting tomorrow?" Jimmy asked.

"I'm not 21 yet," Ivy said. For election day, Shelly had distributed flyers saying "No class today; no ruling class tomorrow." Gail had made hand-written signs in dripping red letters: "Support the Troops—Bring Them Home." Nobody would go to class. Ivy poured the tea into cups and chose one to carry upstairs. Then she stopped. "Did you see Greg Lambert out there?"

"Outside your front door? Nope. You should join us tomorrow," Jimmy said, in his fake newscaster's voice. "We're picketing the polling places."

"End the war while voting?" Ivy shook her head. "I'm gonna pass midterms. Then I'll work on the Revolution."

"You're studying," Jimmy said, as though he were surprised. "That means you're not getting jerked around by Bert and Tessa."

"No one jerks me around," Ivy said. If Bert and Tessa believed she should quit studying, they hadn't said so.

"If SDS had some discipline and a coherent platform..." Jimmy put his arm around Gail, who set her face on neutral and clutched her teacup.

"I'm not a Trotskyist, just anti-war," Gail had insisted, days ago. "And I'm only dating Jimmy till Joe comes home."

"I liked SDS," Jimmy said. "Stuck with 'em right through August. Then in Chicago I went to the Student Mobe conference and saw how an effective organization works."

"A democratic organization doesn't set itself up as a front for an old Socialist Party." Strut your masculinity, Ivy thought: flex those gorgeous shoulders, hug the girl who's not your girl yet. "You know your party won't win on a Trotskyist platform, so you shout 'Support the Troops—Bring Them Home.' No fair."

"A democratic organization works for what the people want," Gail interjected, moving out from under Jimmy's arm. "People want that war *over*. No one's forcing anyone to vote for Halstead."

"After I graduate," Jimmy said, ignoring the women, "I plan to enlist to organize the armed forces."

"You think they'll let you in?"

"Why not? I wouldn't be dumb enough to tell them my plans."

"I guess you wouldn't," Ivy said. What a cool, confident mask he'd adopted. She could barely put this unflappable Party operative together with the young man who'd resembled a classical David, who'd had his arm busted by Black militants, who'd romanced Jane and followed Bert around.

"I just wish we were coordinating our efforts," Jimmy said, smiling. "Like we did at the Dow protests. Man, we had a big crowd."

"Those protests were *fucked up*," Shelly said from the kitchen doorway. Still in her apron, she leaned against the frame with her arms across her chest. "Once it was over, no one understood why we chose to picket Dow Corning recruiters when we could have gone straight for the military, or the weapons manufacturers in the flats, or the campus security police who've been attacking people they don't recognize and kicking them off campus when they don't have ID cards." She was flushed and breathing hard. Ivy had decided Shelly was right, after all, and felt a rush of affection for her.

Jimmy turned his head as though he was mildly interested in the noise by the kitchen door. "Get real, Shelly," he said. "You're hung up on the Revolution because it's sexy—way more sexy than digging in and working step by step."

Grow your hair, Ivy thought. She'd hoped he could be honest, at least.

"What I'm saying is," he went on. "If you're serious about revolution, you join the party that's organized to do it."

"Not necessarily," Ivy said. Was that an echo of *vote for the winning team*? Oh, this discussion was a waste of her time. Jimmy was rattling off a string of numbers: registered YSA members, circulation of *The Militant,* committees against the war..." Stop it!" she said. "I'm not listening!"

He stopped. "No," he said. "you're not listening." For a split second he looked desperately sad. "When you want to listen, let me know." His teacup clattered lightly but definitely into his saucer.

Ivy lunged for the stairs. "I'll be in my room," she said. Biology would calm her down. She lit a cigarette, breathed in good smoke with the Krebs cycle equations, blew out emotions she couldn't name. Downstairs, voices rose and she felt guilty for leaving Shelly to defend SDS without her. She thought of the men under the street lamp. Then she remembered: blond hair, pink glasses, dark blue polo shirt. Her Big Penny customer: the chicken salad sandwich she'd had to pay for herself. And Greg, if that was Greg, had vanished quickly. She bent over Helena Curtis's pages and gradually the first chemical exchange made sense, then the next one. Downstairs the voices softened; eventually the front door closed.

It was deep night when the whole Krebs cycle fell elegantly together; all its terms had meaning. Ivy went downstairs, hungry and eager to tell someone. But no one was there; evidently, Shelly and Gail had left along with Jimmy. The tuna fish casserole was still warm, so Ivy filled her plate and set it on the kitchen table. She could read the paper while she ate: for Issue III they'd changed the name from *Underground News* to *The Steam Tunnel Express*. Smart.

Knocking at the front door. Maybe Gail had gone with Jimmy, and Shelly had forgotten her key.

It was Chuck, his ears red with cold. "I'm looking for Shelly," he said quickly.

"She's not here," Ivy said. "Come in anyway." He stepped across the threshold—nervously, Ivy thought. Since the break-up, they'd seen each other at meetings, but this was the first time they'd been alone in a room. "Gail isn't here either," she said. "I've been reading your article on the Milwaukee 14. It's good."

"Thanks," Chuck said, looking around. He stayed a yard away from her and kept his hands in his pockets, his scarf around his neck. "I thought Shelly could help me locate Bert Augustin."

"Haven't seen him," Ivy said. "I'm out of touch. Been studying for midterm exams like crazy. I heard Bert was in the steam tunnels a lot. Or with Angela. You know her?"

Chuck nodded, already backing toward the door. "Well, I just happened to be in the neighborhood, as they say." He stopped. "Maybe I could use your phone to call Greg? He's been running around with Bert."

"I think I saw Greg in front of this house about 5:30," Ivy said, "talking to a man wearing pink plastic glasses, a Big Penny customer I recognized."

"Pink glasses?" Chuck turned slowly. "How old?"

Ivy shrugged. "Thirty-some. Blondish. Obnoxious. Last summer I served him a chicken salad sandwich and he didn't pay for it."

"Oh shit," Chuck said. "I gotta find Bert *now*." He yanked at the door.

"I only saw the chicken-salad man's face," Ivy said. "So I'm not sure that was Greg talking to him."

"It's worth telling Bert anyway," Chuck said. "Steam tunnels next."

"There's an entrance in front of the nursing school," Ivy said. "Right across from the Church of the Covenant. You want me to show you?"

"I know where it is," Chuck said. "See you later." He trotted down the porch steps. Ivy returned to the kitchen and told herself she was glad not to be out in the cold with Chuck. Awkward having him here, discovering that easy familiarity returned automatically—and was out of line. She should just eat her casserole and settle down to art history. Breathe deep and there'd be no need to cry at all.

A deep *boom*, like nothing she'd ever heard, rattled the teacups on the counter. The rickety table trembled. A bomb? No, an earthquake. Did Cleveland *have* earthquakes? She tried to take a bite, but her mouth didn't work. Too dry. Glass of water. Nothing came out of the tap. Okay, there was still tea in the pot. The teapot rattled against the glass as she poured. Little shreds of tea leaf floated in the pale-brown liquid. Another one: *boom.*

Whom could she call? Where could she go? She put on her sneakers and was sitting on the stairs tying the laces when Shelly and Gail burst in the door. "Big underground explosion," Shelly said. "The parking lot by the Church of the Covenant has a huge crack in it."

"More like a crater," Gail said. "We were at Dean's Diner when we heard it. We got to the church just as the police arrived."

"They said a steam-pipe burst," Shelly said. "They shooed us away."

"Damaged our water system," Ivy told them. "I can't get the tap to work."

"Let me see," Gail went to the kitchen. They heard her say "Oh shit!"

"We went out for a beer and some analysis of Jimmy Fulero," Shelly said.

"So is he counter-revolutionary or not?" Ivy asked.

"Not that kind of analysis," Shelly said. One of Shelly's assets was that she didn't judge people on their politics, the way Jimmy did. If Gail decided to join SDS, for instance, he'd drop her fast. If Gail became a YSA member tomorrow, Shelly would remain her friend.

Gail came back. "I'll call the landlord and tell him. I was counting on a shower tonight. And, Dear God, how are we gonna flush the toilet? Shit shit shit!"

Ivy started to laugh.

"We've got to figure out what happened." Shelly picked up the phone. "Dial tone. At least this works. What are you laughing about?"

"What Gail said—can't flush the toilet, shit shit shit!" It was a silly joke, but Ivy could barely stop laughing enough to talk.

"Look at her," Gail said. "Biology's addled her head. We should've brought this girl some beer." She started laughing, too.

"We'll use the big cooking pot," Shelly said. "Dump it in the bushes, then scrub it out real good." She started to wipe out the pot she'd boiled macaroni in, banging in the sink.

"I knew I should buy that chamber pot." Ivy tried to explain about the china chamber pot at the house sale where she'd bought her dresser, but she was laughing too hard to make sense.

Gail reached the landlord and learned that pipes had burst all over the area. "He'll get to us when he can," she said to Ivy. "Can you imagine Guilford? All those nursing students must be going nuts. *Oh no! Can't set my hair! Can't put on makeup! Haven't showered for three whole hours!*"

Shelly laughed as though she were sobbing. "The Revolution is here! No more plumbing!" Gail lay on the floor, pounding the rug with fists and heels. Ivy laughed with them, though another part of her mind calculated Chuck's running speed to be sure he hadn't reached the parking lot before...no, of course he hadn't.

Chuck was jogging round the corner of Ford and Euclid when the boom shook the ground, knocking him to his knees. He got up unsteadily. Either the sidewalk was shaking or he was. Sirens and lights converged on Euclid Avenue ahead of him. By the time he got to the church parking lot, police were putting up barrier tape. Chuck looked at the cracked, sunken asphalt thinking of the "stuff" Bert and Greg had probably put in the steam tunnels. He still didn't know what "stuff" it was, but with those two, that night, he figured it almost had to be explosives. He crossed the street and was stopped by a policeman. "It's not safe," the cop said. "We're closing off this whole area."

"What happened?" Chuck looked over the uniformed shoulder at the dark lawn in front of the nursing school. The entrance was beyond a hedge.

"Burst steam pipe," the policeman said. "You better move along now."

Chuck moved along. Bert had shown up for only one meeting since that trip to Greg's garage, that night he was so crazed with lack of sleep. Chuck had seen him in the Student Union with Angela, now his girlfriend. Ivy's guess was reasonable: Bert was probably sleeping in Angela's dorm room. Chuck was writing the article about the Boulder convention, and now, after Tessa had given him her version of events, he wanted to talk to Bert again. Tessa's version was limited to three committee meetings and two friends from New York. Not enough to make sense of what was apparently a huge gathering. Chuck wanted to know more about the National Caucus; he wasn't sure he trusted it. He set off toward the girls' dorms.

He would try being friends with Bert again. Working on the Revolution together, you had flares of hostility and craziness. You had to put personal feelings behind you. Right now, his thoughts about the man smoldered in a dark, small place in his psyche, but he could wall that place off.

Ivy wasn't sure she'd seen Greg. And Chuck wasn't sure he'd seen Greg on television in Chicago. But he wasn't the only one who thought he'd glimpsed the guy who'd said he was busy at the steel mills. And Ivy's customer with the pink glasses was almost certainly a plainclothesman he'd seen at the Wallace march, when Greg had started to throw that half-brick. The pink-glasses man had showed up again at the new campus coffee house called the Olive Tree, and then again, sitting outside the Monmouth in the pale blue car. He never made eye contact. Did he think Chuck wouldn't recognize him, or didn't he care? If Greg was their informer—and the pieces were fitting together in Chuck's mind saying YES—Bert needed to know that.

Chapter 25

November 7, 1968
Coventry Road

Light peered around the edges of the window shade, turning the humped gray shadows into furniture—a stuffed chair, a lamp—and Chuck recognized he was in Jane's fold-out bed, naked and chilly. He pulled at the sheet and blanket that had slithered away, but the covers were wrapped around Jane, who curled with her back to him. He reached for her shoulder. In his arms last night she'd felt small and bony, except for the soft globes of her breasts, nipples growing firm in his mouth. He thought of her tawny-beige skin, the sharpness of her hips, the soft concavity of her stomach, and rolled to her, reaching for the blanket and sheet. He kissed her cheek, felt her curls against his ear. She squeezed her eyes tight and shook her head as if to get a fly off.

They'd brushed against each other yesterday in the office, moving between the typewriter and the layout table. Soon they were rubbing against each other, as if to satisfy an itch. Desire had come like smoke from new-lit tinder and Chuck's sense of purpose vanished in the flame. They made love right on the table. Then they picked the papers off the floor, put the work away, and unbuttoned each other's shirts. The second time they were on the office couch. The third time, after they'd cooked and eaten supper together, they were on the couch in her apartment. She was fierce, scratching, biting, then slippery and laughing; he chased her around, picked her up and held her like a fireman rescuing a child. The couch unfolded and became her bed. The fourth time, in the middle of the night, they grappled sleepily and then blended together in darkness—hours ago, he thought, but he wasn't sure.

Now Jane's back and neck were warm; Chuck palmed her breasts and reached for the damp forest between her legs. She clamped her thighs together and reared away, groaning "Leave me alone," digging her elbow into his stomach. He let go.

She rolled over, loosing the covers he'd wanted in the first place. He pulled them over his chest, settling into the warm hollow she'd vacated, happy, ready for more sleep.

Jane Revard. "Olive complexion," she'd said of her skin. "French trait, like the name." Her grandparents had come from Quebec. Chuck would like to visit France, where the Revolution had flared in May with a blue flame. *Bleu*. He couldn't pronounce the word; it came out *bluh* or *blur*. He could get along in Spanish; he'd rather visit Mexico, Cuba, or South America, where the Revolution burned like beacons in scattered rubble heaps. The oppressors used buckets, fire hoses, and asbestos blankets, came down hard with clubs and guns, but they could not quench all the flames. Like magma bubbling from the core of the earth, the people would assert their rights. "Freedom. Dignity." Chuck tongued the words like food. The Doors' "Light My Fire" was not about sex; it was about revolution. He needed to write his vision; maybe his notebook was under the clothes that filled the stuffed chair by the window. *Set the night on fire*, he thought, rearing up into cold air. With the soles of his feet on the chilly boards, he came awake, and the troublesome details returned.

He hadn't found Bert that night. Angela was in her dorm studying for midterms, but she hadn't seen Bert. "Not since Halloween," she'd called, gripping the rail of a third-floor balcony. "He was gonna go to Ann Arbor," she shouted down to him. "Maybe he's there now." On the sidewalk below, trying not to shout outside a girls' dormitory in the middle of the night, Chuck couldn't raise the questions and alarms that banged around his head. In order to sleep, he'd decided Bert must be in Ann Arbor, and the next day Tessa had reassured him further.

"He should be coming back tonight," she said. "Or tomorrow. He's gonna love that steam tunnel explosion." She grinned, and Chuck wondered what she meant. He had so little information—a conversation between Greg and Bert, another between someone who might not be Greg and the plainclothesman in pink plastic glasses. Glimpses, hunches. Still a terrifying story formed in his mind.

He'd found Jane and Marvin in the office and confided in them, but they were obsessed with planning the Charity Lunch Invasion, urging him to hurry the next issue of *The Steam Tunnel Express* so they could sell copies at the action. "You don't need to hear more from Bert about Boulder," Jane had said. "Here's a plan: I'll work with you to get that issue out in a hurry." She'd been with Chuck ever since, talking, writing, typing. Making love. The paper needed only one more article.

Bert could be here now, asleep in Tessa's bed. Good. Chuck would tell him what Ivy had seen, and the whirlwind in his head would stop.

A door opened and closed: Tessa emerging. Chuck threw the bedclothes over his lap and watched her; she was too sleepy to notice. Her bathrobe hung open; he glimpsed her breasts, her belly, pubic hair and thighs—just a glimpse, but he stiffened; then she'd gone into the bathroom. Damn. He needed the toilet.

"Hi, Chuck." Jane was awake, her curly head sticking out of the covers.

"Hi." He dropped to one elbow to kiss her, but she stopped his lips with her hand.

"Don't," she said. "My mouth tastes awful—kind of like the way your feet smell."

"Thanks a lot," he said, sitting up again. "You sure know how to squash a guy." Just like that: flaccid again.

"Yeah," Jane agreed, stretching her arms overhead, rotating her neck. Her underarms were as furry as her crotch. "Is Tessa here?"

The toilet flushed. "I'm next in the john," Chuck said. "Gotta wash my feet."

"Don't take it personally," Jane said. "I need autonomy in the morning. And we did enough last night to take care of our sexual urges for…"

"I could do it again," Chuck said. "In a few minutes." He climbed into his shorts and jeans, zipping carefully. The jeans were loose; he was getting thinner.

"We need to finish the paper." Jane sat up, her skin goose-bumped, her little brown nipples erect with cold. For a painful second Chuck thought of Ivy's peachy-pink body, her way of cuddling up to him in the morning, ready for soft, blowsy sex. He shivered and reached for his shirt. Standing with Ivy in her living room that night, he'd been alarmed by the waves of affection flowing between them. She'd almost hugged him, he was sure, but pulled back at the last instant. He'd left dizzy and raw. The explosion a few minutes later seemed to echo his own state of mind. Maybe that was why he'd felt such fear and urgency.

The bathroom door opened. "Hi there," Tessa said. She held the halves of her robe overlapped at her waist. "Do we have coffee?" she asked Jane, who bent naked over a laundry basket.

"Yeah," Jane said. "Make some for Chuck and me too, okay?" Tessa grunted, and Chuck claimed the bathroom.

He took his time relieving himself and studied his chin in the mirror. Bristly, but not uncomfortable yet. He wet-combed his hair to get rid of the fuzz around the tops of his ears, doused his face and wiped it dry. He tucked in his shirt and buckled his belt. Twenty-four hours ago, he hadn't suspected he would have wild sex with Jane Revard. Four times. If she had sex with someone else tomorrow, that would be just fine with Chuck. He would not compare himself with that other person—Marvin, for example, or even Bert. His mind was free of jealousy. His feelings were finally aligning with his politics.

Jane was pounding on the door. "Let me in, I got to pee!"

He turned the latch, and she rushed for the toilet, still naked, sitting and peeing before he closed the door behind him. Should he have left the door open? Did more equality mean less privacy? Tying his sneakers, Chuck thought about the politics of bathrooms and bodies. What if he had sex with Tessa? Would Jane mind? Probably not.

In the kitchen, coffee perked on the stove. Tessa was moving from the fridge to the counter; the robe parted to show her upper thigh. "Is Bert here?" he asked.

"No," Tessa said. She handed him an empty cup. "I thought he might come last night, but he's erratic, you know that. I haven't seen Bert since..." She thought, calculating. "Last Saturday. Coffee's not quite ready. I suppose I should get dressed."

"Not if you don't feel like it," Chuck said, nonchalantly; with practice, he could learn to not be aroused near a half-naked woman. He looked out the window at bare branches against a leaden sky, and thought how he'd once glimpsed the bump of his mother's nipple beneath her thin nightgown when her robe opened as she leaned forward. Just once. It was her birthday, the only day in the year besides Christmas when she came downstairs in nightgown, robe and slippers, to show that she was taking it easy while Father made pancakes. He couldn't remember seeing his sister's body, ever; by the time he was seven or eight she was locking herself in the bathroom. Both Mom and Bonnie seemed far away now, in a foreign land with strange rituals.

"It's cold," Tessa said. "My feet are freezing. I'm using a pair of your socks." The last remark was to Jane, who'd come in wearing jeans, a high-neck sweater, and fleece-lined moccasins.

"Wait, I need them," Jane said. But Tessa had hurried out of range. "Now Tessa's got my last pair of clean knee-socks." Jane poured coffee for herself. "I was saving them for the Charity Lunch Invasion. Day after tomorrow. We'll be able to put *The Steam Tunnel Express* in print, won't we? How much time, do you think?"

"We have one column to fill," Chuck said. "But the name sounds wrong now." When Tessa came back and they'd had coffee, all three of them, he'd tell about the last time he saw Bert with Greg. He'd ask, *What if Bert was in that tunnel?* so Tessa could give him the information that would prove his fears wrong. He thought of her bare legs last summer on the Severance Hall steps.

"Okay, we'll fill that column today." Jane tilted the coffee cup against her lips, sipped, and set it down.

"Maybe Tessa would write an article about the symphony," Chuck said.

"Ask her." Jane picked up *The Plain Dealer*. "She doesn't go to concerts any more. She thinks it's culturally elitist."

"So she could write about why. Sounds interesting." Chuck watched her eyes dart around the newspaper, not reading, not even scanning. He opened his notebook and took out his pen. Before Tessa returned he needed to know how Jane felt about last night, to understand how the sleepy, naked girl in bed with him could be the same person as this woman across the table, sweatered from neck to wrists, avoiding his eyes. He touched her hand, one thumb-stroke on the knuckle of her first finger. "I had a great time last night. How about you?"

"Mmm," she said. "Hey woops, that wasn't a steam pipe that blew up. It was a bomb." She spread the paper on the table, and Chuck stood to read over her shoulder. Investigators had discovered remnants of what they called a bomb factory. "'Believed to be the work of New Left Extremists,'" Jane read. "You're right, we need another title for our paper."

"Big trouble." Chuck studied the photo of people picking their way around the asphalt crater in the church parking lot. "They'll be questioning us."

"Look at the editorial page," Jane said, spreading the paper wide and refolding it. In an effort to be hip, the editors praised certain "responsible critics" of society. "They're citing the Beatles, as if the Revolution could be accomplished without destruction." She was indignant. "As if the government and the corporations weren't bombing the hell out of... I hope they do come talk to me. I could tell them a few things."

But the hip editorial writer wasn't going to talk to them. Chuck could almost hear the revving engine of the pale blue car. Ungvary, like J. Edgar Hoover and Curtis LeMay, had no interest in rethinking small explosions as symbolic acts of protest against much bigger, vastly more damaging moves of the U.S. Government. "They already know Communists are responsible," Chuck said. "Bert could give them the analysis in elegant, damning detail, if they asked."

"They won't ask," Jane said. "And we have no idea who might have planted a bomb down there. Do we?" Her eyes were blue-gray and fearful. "Stupid place for a bomb," she said.

She knew Chuck's thoughts, then. His mind began to whirl, this time about Greg's role in the "bomb factory." Lambert was excited by explosives, certainly. It was harder to imagine him playing double agent—the guy was such a lunkhead.

Tessa came in wearing a tight red sweater. "How's the coffee?" she asked and saw they were both staring at her. "What?"

"Here." Jane gave Tessa *The Plain Dealer*. "Article page one. Editorial further in."

Tessa read for ten seconds. Then she closed her eyes and took a long slow drink of coffee, holding it in her mouth, swallowing before she opened her eyes. "Let's unplug the phone," she said, "and find Bert." She headed to the front room where the phone was.

"I thought you were with him last night," Jane called.

"I haven't seen him in five days!" Tessa called back.

"Do you have a phone number we can call in Ann Arbor?" Jane asked, when Tessa appeared in the doorway. "We'll have to call from a pay phone, but…"

"I don't even know for sure he *got* to Ann Arbor," Tessa said. "But I know where he'd stay. I can phone them." She sat down at the table holding her coffee-cup with both hands as if all other sources of warmth had failed. Even her hair, rippling to her shoulder blades, seemed frozen. "He has *never* mentioned plans to blow up anything," Tessa said, her voice firm and icy. "Much less the church parking lot."

"I'm wondering where Greg Lambert is," Chuck said. "About a month ago—no, less than that—Greg came into the office with a television and told Bert about stuff he'd brought from Republic Steel. That was his word: *stuff*. I didn't ask what it was, but they were both pretty turned on."

"Marvin told me Bert had been making bottle-bombs in the apartment," Jane said. "He was so pissed he told Bert to leave."

"And Ivy thought she saw Greg hours before the explosion," Chuck added. "She could have been wrong, but she got a clear look at the guy he was talking to. You remember that plainclothes detective who wears pink plastic glasses?"

"Bad haircut," Jane said. "Doughy face. I saw him at the Wallace rally, standing at the back of the balcony. You've got Greg's phone number, right?"

Chuck nodded. "It's his mother's house," he said. "But what do I say? *Your cover's blown, man?*"

"Give him a chance to explain," Jane said. "No, wait. We've got to think this through."

"Fuck fuck *fuck* you, Augustin!" Tessa yanked her purse off the back of Jane's chair and looped it over one shoulder. "I'm going to hunt that fucker down." She rushed out. The door banged.

"She didn't even put on a coat," Jane said.

"That *stuff* conversation was right after Boulder," Chuck said. "Bert was crazy from frustration and lack of sleep. I could see him heading over some kind of a cliff. And Greg, he's always been loony."

"I'm thinking about the Hour's Late manifesto," Jane said. "It's all over town."

"But neither Tessa's nor Bert's name's on it." Chuck had read the manifesto twice. Get with the working class, it said, or languish among the bourgeoisie. It quoted Cleaver: *If you're not part of the solution, you're part of the problem.* Join the international struggle against American imperialism. Follow the lead of the Black militants. Prepare for armed struggle. Most of the argument was borrowed from a century of Marxist intellectuals, and most of it was abstract jargon. What bothered Chuck more was the incendiary language. SDS had *blown up* rather than increased in number. The U.S. Army was *a time bomb* of the ruling class. "What I don't understand is how Tessa Buchanan..." he mused.

"She believes what that manifesto says," Jane said. "She identified the symptoms, diagnosed the illness, and prescribed the solution. She used the textbooks: Fanon, DeBray, Mao, Guevara and the rest." Jane seemed to shrink into herself, staring into a crevasse Chuck couldn't see. Thoughts of an hour ago, with Jane's body next to him and Tessa stumbling past in her half-open bathrobe, no longer belonged in these rooms.

He studied the newspaper's photograph of the asphalt crater, roped off, with the church in the background. Maybe Ivy was there, among the tiny blurred people. No, she had midterms. He felt reassured to know she was deep in her books and papers.

"We should get with Marvin," Jane said, businesslike. "He may want to cancel the Charity Lunch Invasion, but I don't think we should."

"Canceling would connect us with the bomb factory— if that's what it was." Chuck picked up his pen and opened his notebook. "The last article," he wrote, and wondered what they could put in the empty column. He'd planned to skip the Charity Lunch thing, since Ivy was involved. Silly, he thought, now that he'd been cleansed of all possessiveness. He pictured Ivy in her summer dress, kissing Bert on the cheek. He heard in his mind Bert's voice singing with Sidney Poitier. "Bowling green, sewing machine," he sang softly.

"Are you going to write something?" Jane bowed over the splintery table; all he could see was the top of her head, fingers in her hair.

"A disclaimer? We know nothing about any plans to bomb any part of Cleveland by anyone affiliated with *The Steam Tunnel Express*?" Chuck smiled, but Jane didn't look up.

"We'll think of something better than that." She sipped coffee and put the cup down, looking into it as though it were a mirror. "I liked having sex with you," she said to the coffee. "I might want to do it again sometime. But I don't want you to expect it. Do you understand? We have a good working relationship. I want *that* to stay. Do you understand?"

She'd asked twice, so Chuck had to say yes, of course. But a little while ago he'd thought he understood a bunch of things he no longer felt sure of.

"I'm going to write something now," Jane said. "You can write too, or you can go do something else. Just don't talk to me till I'm ready."

"Any clue when that might be?" Chuck didn't think he could sit still, not right now.

"No clue," Jane said. Chuck pictured Tessa raging through the streets without her coat. Jane was intensely quiet, taking a yellow pad and a pen from the shelf below the dishes. He realized he loved her in an odd way he'd never felt before. He gathered his things and left the apartment. He would walk for awhile. Then he'd write.

Chapter 26

November 11, 1968
The Movement Office & Coventry Road

"Have we found Bert?" Jane called to whoever was in the office before she stepped in the door. She hoped it was Bert. But there was only Marvin hunched in the desk chair, twirling a pencil like a miniature baton between his fingers. "I'm waiting for a call," he said. They had decided to answer the phone only if they knew exactly who was calling.

When reporters converged after the Charity Lunch Invasion, Marvin had expressed deep regret and total ignorance about the "bomb factory" under the church parking lot. It was impossible to tell from *The Plain Dealer* what had been found or what the police actually knew. Yesterday's editorial assured Clevelanders that Communists were known to be advising New Left youth.

"Tessa's gone through more rolls of quarters than I want to add up," Marvin said now, "calling around the country from pay phones. He can't be far away. Look." He cocked his head toward a sleeping bag wadded at one end of the couch. Books and magazines were piled on the floor next to Bert's cowboy boots.

"What's he wearing on his feet?" Jane asked. She meant, *Where's he hiding?*

"Moccasins?" Marvin stared at the phone as if willing it to ring. Then he stood and walked to the front window. Cold afternoon rain blurred the street, hissed and wept under the traffic noise.

Jane shook out the sleeping bag, a brown khaki mummy-shape stuffed with down and decorated with a faded Boy Scout *Fleur de lis*. She rolled it up as best she could. Then she stacked the papers and arranged the books by size. Here was Bert's notebook, a cheap cardboard stenographer's pad. She sat on the couch to look at it.

"Tessa got names and numbers out of that book," Marvin said. The phone rang and he leapt for the desk. Then he stood and let it ring two more times. *Bert*, Jane thought. Marvin picked it up. "Oh, hi!" His voice was eager. "Yes, of course we are. Yes, bring it. But don't use this number, okay?"

It was just Eleanor. Jane had met her briefly at the Charity Lunch Invasion—a nice woman with thin brown hair and glasses. Jane had expected someone more dramatic, perhaps with a deep resonant voice, draped in bright shawls. Eleanor seemed sensible, friendly, and shy.

They should get rid of Bert's notebook. He'd actually made diagrams of bomb-construction. He'd also written doggerel: "Oh, Nixon's such a hog/he'd starve a collie dog" and "I would pay a lot to own a/share of Ivy Barcelona." He'd played tic-tac-toe with himself. There were dates, times, and lists of names. In meetings he'd scribbled a few notes and some long frustrated rants.

Marvin was talking with Eleanor as if they'd had fun at an innocent free-speech event, as if no one had meant to cause trouble, as if he weren't scared of what would come next. Then Jane remembered: he knew he was talking to the police as well as his girlfriend.

Policemen disguised in suits had arrived at the Sheraton with the news reporters, and for a few minutes it looked like the Movement people—nicely dressed, all 25 of them—wouldn't be allowed in. But Mayor Stokes had intervened, welcoming them as the People's Contingent, so they'd filed in with their protest signs.

Not that they were exactly welcome. During Stokes's opening speech, Roldo Bartimole, the maverick journalist, made a megaphone of his hands and called, "If you're so glad to have us, Carl, how come your undercover police are here?"

"Are they?" Stokes flashed his dimples. "I didn't know." The newspaper and television journalists looked eagerly around.

"There!" Marvin pointed at one of the men who stood in a silent row against the back wall, their suits so smooth they could have been made of plastic.

"Go ahead—take their pictures!" Roldo yelled. As the news cameras whirled, the undercover agents scattered like cockroaches, and Ungvary backed through a door.

Later, while the charitable donors and United Way officials ate chicken croquettes and green beans almandine, Jane walked around the dining room offering "Welfare Lunches" for thirty-seven cents each, exactly what a welfare budget would allow: bologna, white bread, and Kool-Aid. She carried a sign: "Our bologna is more nutritious than your baloney!" The dressed-up welfare administrators smiled nervously, as if they approved of the invaders' message. Twenty of them paid thirty-seven cents each, but only three accepted the sandwiches. Jane had been tense the whole time, as if she were longing for someone to get hostile.

A dozen people bought copies of *The Steam Tunnel Express*. Chuck had produced an explanation of the title ("a conduit for hot news that travels underground") that revealed how puzzled the editors were about the steam tunnel explosion. Jane had written a long response to The Beatles' "Revolution". Those who knew could see it was also a response to "The Hour's Late."

"No, the cops didn't force us to leave," Marvin said to Eleanor along with the police on the phone. "The dining service union had a rule against outsiders' selling food in the Sheraton. Yeah." He listened for a minute. "We don't know anything...if there even *was* a bomb factory...Yes, really. See you." He hung up.

"Keeping up the pretense?" Jane flipped the pages of Bert's notebook, bothered. Not because Marvin was lying by omission but because he was so damned calm. "The Subversive Squad's almost certainly preparing a warrant to invade this office, you know." She turned the page and saw *Marvin Kaminsky Marvin Kaminsky Marvin Kaminsky*...Bert had written it over and over, all down one side of the center line. And down the other side: *Dare to Struggle Dare to Win! Dare to Struggle Dare to Win!* Every line was full.

"The trouble is," Marvin broke off and slouched toward the window again. Jane put the notebook down and came next to him. He had both hands in his pockets. "I am *furious* at Bert," he said. "He's acting out the enemy's worst fantasies about us. And to run around with Greg Lambert...he knew that was reckless, even if we didn't suspect Greg of informing."

Jane leaned against him. His thick wool sweater scratched her cheek. "Do you know if Chuck found Greg?" she asked.

"Couldn't reach him on the phone," Marvin said. "He planned to invite him over to the office; then he and I would grill Greg with questions. I don't think we'll get to do that—unless Greg's completely innocent, in which case we'll just hurt his feelings. For now, I don't want to think about it."

"How come the Movement's splitting apart?" Jane asked. "Did it start when so many of us gave up on nonviolence? Did the informer plant distrust? Maybe some people are intrinsically attracted to violence. Maybe we're all too hung up on theory."

"And there's the imperfectly understood nature of being human. I don't know." Marvin clasped his hands together, thumbs up, and moved them forward through space; when his arms were extended, the hands came apart. He stared at the void he'd made in the air. "Bert denounced me for not owning a gun." His voice thickened. "He thought all Jews should have guns to protect themselves, just like all Blacks should. If we'd had guns in Europe 35 years ago, millions of people would have been saved." Marvin pulled on his mustache and covered his mouth with his hand.

"How do I respond to that? He's only 22, and look at the mess he's made. That damned manifesto," he added.

"'Make the mostly-white Movement into a disciplined fighting force'," Jane quoted. "If we did that, we'd be wiped out by the National Guard in a few minutes. 'Become intimate with the true struggles of working class youth'? So we go to Little Italy and make friends with the restaurant workers and car mechanics?"

"It worked in Cuba and Algiers, and it's working all over China," Tessa had said, when Jane asked her that question. "You're stuck in outdated bourgeois liberalism, Jane. I've finally, slowly come unstuck. I've repudiated white privilege. We must change ourselves deep down."

Across the street, an aqua Corvair parked at the derelict gas station. A woman got out, tying a plastic rain hat under her chin, squinting and wincing when raindrops hit her face. She walked toward the corner, high heels wobbling as she tried to avoid puddles. "Those are working class shoes." Jane pointed. "What if Tessa and Bert are right? Are we getting soft and liberal? Look at this." Jane opened Bert's notebook to the *Marvin Kaminsky/Dare to Struggle Dare to win!* page. "Unhinged."

Marvin saw the page and closed his eyes. "Oh God." Then he peered out the window. "Who's that?"

A short figure crossed the street wearing a cap, jeans tucked into knee-high boots, a newspaper rolled under one arm. "Angela," Jane told Marvin. "Bert's newest girl."

She came through the door. "Hi there," Jane said.

Angela took off her cap and shook water onto the cement floor. "Is Ivy here? Or Shelly?" she asked. "They're not at the Hessler apartment." She seemed gaunt, with gray skin around her eyes, her teeth too big for her mouth. "Bert's dead." She gave them *The Cleveland Press.*

"No he's not." Jane felt the room darken as Marvin spread out the paper. "Remains" had been found in the rubble, identified with fingerprints, confirmed with dental records—and for a second Jane could have sworn Bert was reading over her shoulder. Robert Joseph Augustin, of Trenton, New Jersey. The family had been informed. "I didn't know he's from Trenton," she said. It was troublesome to read while she felt Bert's presence—contentious, difficult, essential. She swallowed and felt the void Marvin had created when he'd pantomimed their Movement's split with his hands.

"His parents live in Trenton." Marvin steered Angela to the couch and urged her to sit. She pulled Bert's sleeping bag into her lap and rocked forward and back, forward and back.

"Let me get you a drink of water," Jane said. She had to move and wanted to be useful.

"No," Angela said. "I'm fine." Then she bent over the sleeping bag with noisy gasps and sniffles. Jane had wept like this at Che's death, thirteen months ago, in what now seemed another era. How could she tell Angela that Bert Augustin was not at all like Che, when he himself had wanted so much to be so?

Marvin sank into the desk chair and sat with his back to the room, elbows on the desk, forehead resting on his crossed arms.

Maybe Bert *wasn't* so different from Che, Jane thought. He was just in different circumstances. She would cry soon— or howl with rage. For now she just felt strange.

"He didn't *mean* to blow up a goddamn parking lot," Angela cried, from the folds of the sleeping bag. "It was a fucking accident, that's what it was."

Jane sat cautiously next to her. "He told you about his plans? *Only* you?"

"He wanted to tell Tessa," Angela pulled a shredded bit of Kleenex from her pocket to wipe her nose. "He only told me because I said I wouldn't fuck him till he did. But he knew I was *with* him all the way. The Hour's Late. It is *so* right on."

The phone rang. They let it ring.

Angela sat straight. "I haven't eaten or slept since the parking lot. I *knew* in my gut, but I couldn't say so till the paper came out. I couldn't tell Chuck." Her fists were clenched on her knees. "Now we must move ahead. That's what Bert would want: Dare to struggle, dare to win."

The parking lot had exploded a week ago. No food or sleep? Of course the girl was haggard. Jane counted phone rings. Five, six, seven, eight. "Let's not rush anything," she said. "What exactly were his plans?" Nine rings. Ten.

Too quick for Marvin to stop her, Angela had picked up the phone: "Hello...Ivy!" Jane heard Marvin breathe in. "Yes. No. Yes, they know...Hold on." She put one hand over the receiver and looked at Jane. "Do you have a car? We need to go quick."

Jane nodded, glad to help the phone call end before Ivy or Angela said something the listening police would twist. "Round the corner. White, with a red door." She pointed the way to Angela and gave her the keys. "I'll be there in a second." The young woman left, and as Jane stood up Marvin held out his arms. She walked into the space between them and they embraced. Jane felt his shoulders shake.

"It's fucking *hard*," he said into her shoulder, "when you hate someone and love him at the same time."

"You're so honest, Kaminsky," Jane said. "Hold together for me, okay?"

"Okay," Marvin said. The Valiant stopped in front of the office door. "Keep Augustin's notebook," he said, putting it into her hands. "Don't let it out of your possession."

"I won't." She slipped into her jacket and shoved the notebook into her leather purse. Then she went to the car and got in.

Angela drove jerkily, but the midday traffic was light on Euclid. Rain fell in cold silver streams. Jane tried another approach. "Do you know Greg Lambert?"

"Sure," Angela said, her mouth twisted to one side. "He's annoying, but he's good for some things, Bert says. Said," she corrected herself. "He brought some excellent industrial metal boxes he got from his job. They were air tight, could hold anything forever, keep it dry, like..."

"Like ammunition?"

"I don't think it was ammunition," Angela said. "Bert said he wasn't ready for guns. But they probably did hold ammunition, once."

She was guarded even with Jane. What hell had Bert been cooking? They stopped at the curb and Angela ran up the porch steps. Ivy opened the door, and they stood, Ivy in and Angela out, as Jane approached. Ivy had been crying, but her voice was firm. "Tessa needs you and the Valiant in the apartment on Coventry. I couldn't explain over the phone. Do you see anyone out on the street, any cars?" Jane looked at the empty sidewalks, empty curbs, and shook her head. It was the middle of a workday. Veterans Day, Jane realized. Nixon had been elected president. Everyone in the Movement could be rounded up on suspicion of some kind of subversion.

"Angela should stay here," Ivy said to Jane. "I'm making pea soup," she said to Angela.

So Jane understood, even before she got to the apartment on Coventry, that she was needed to help Tessa leave town, and that no one else must know when or how.

In the apartment, Tessa pulled clothes out of drawers and sorted them into piles on her bed. "I'll wait till I get to New York to understand Bert's gone," she said. The police had not come here, but they soon would. "The bus to Port Authority leaves in an hour."

Watching her, Jane could see: Tessa had no choice but to leave without mourning. Jane's grief—or so she named the hard ball pounding inside her head—must wait, as well.

"I can stand the family for about 24 hours; then I'm in the City," Tessa said. "I'll keep in touch. Everybody in the Movement's in touch." She pawed through socks, rolling each pair into a firm little ball.

Jane held the duffel bag open while Tessa dumped in pants, sweaters, socks, and shoes. This was what to do for a friend in a time of such confusion: help her pack. Then drive her to the bus station without expecting her to say how she felt or what she thought. Tessa loaded her cream-colored vanity case with books, a wad of paper, a handful of pencils and pens. In the top tray she put her toothbrush, toothpaste, hairbrush, Noxzema, and her packet of birth control pills. In spite of Angela, Bert and Tessa had not stopped being lovers. She latched the little case shut, stretched with her arms over her head, and said, "Let's go."

They lugged the duffel downstairs and stowed it in the Valiant's trunk. Jane backed them down the driveway. "So you'll see Bert's friends in New York?" she asked. "You'll contact me with an address and phone number?"

"I won't have one for awhile. I'll be *gone*." Tessa narrowed her eyes. "I couldn't say that in a room that could be bugged. Take care of the Valiant, okay?" Tessa patted the dashboard. "I'll continue the struggle. That's what Bert would do, if he were the survivor." She stared out the window at the city in the rain. Her voice reminded Jane of flat metal. "I'm sick of being a white person," Tessa said suddenly. They were driving through the Black neighborhood near the Greyhound Station. "Look at me. Tonight I'll be in Long Island having dinner with the Buchanans. I don't think I can stand it."

"You can't exactly turn back," Jane said. "I mean *Black*." Two months ago in Long Island, Jane had watched as Tessa transformed into a darling, fixing her parents perfect martinis, listening to them chat about their summer tennis tournament and their vacation on the Cape. The attentive daughter was nowhere inside this impersonal woman in Army pants. Jane parked the Valiant.

"You were right the first time," Tessa said. "I thought I'd completely repudiated my background, but I have to go further."

"So what does it mean to *repudiate* further?"

"I'm not sure. The first step is to kiss Marjorie, Tom, and Long Island good-bye." Just this precipitously, Tessa had quit medical school to work full-time on the Revolution.

"How will they take it?"

"They'll assume I'm just visiting friends," Tessa said. "I hope they'll understand eventually. But they're not easily disturbed, you know."

Marjorie and Tom had taught Tessa to wear the impermeable coating she was using now, Jane realized. "What about the rent?" she asked. They'd relied on the Buchanans for that—and the phone, and the heat.

"We're paid up till the end of the year. By then you shouldn't need the apartment anymore."

"Why not?" Jane hauled the duffel bag out of the trunk.

"The Revolution will blow."

"What exactly do you imagine?" Jane demanded. She helped balance the duffel bag while Tessa slid her shoulder under the strap.

"I'm past imagining, Jane. I'm planning." Tessa flexed her legs to center the load and picked up the vanity case. Maybe she could somehow force the Revolution to start next week— or next month.

Their hug was perfunctory. Tessa walked across the parking lot to the terminal, swinging her vanity case in one hand. Her other hand clutched the strap of her duffel packed with all the clothes she'd need for a long time. Big enough to contain another person, it barely slowed her down.

Tessa could only *repudiate* so much, Jane thought. She could avoid gallery openings and live performances of classical music, but she'd listen to the radio with an ear that loved Beethoven and choose revolutionary posters with an eye that knew art. She couldn't quit being upper class any more than she could quit being white. But Jane would have to go on without her. Tessa would tell her not to cry. She started the car, weary and weak with fear.

Cleveland's damp air chilled more thoroughly than if it were freezing. The Valiant chugged up Cedar Hill, the first foothill of the Alleghenies, the entrance to Cleveland Heights. When the Revolution came, these venerable ivy-covered buildings and their genteel white occupants would be doomed. For the first time, Jane knew, down deep, that the Revolution would not be what she had imagined it was. She'd been told many times: *Revolution is not a dinner party*. This time she felt the slogan as truth. No matter who was leading, there would be damage. Maybe to her.

In the apartment, the radiators clanked and stayed lukewarm; Jane could rest her hand comfortably on the metal. She turned on the kitchen light and watched cockroaches stream away. No, she couldn't stay here. She started the Valiant again and drove back down the hill.

Chuck's Pontiac sat against the curb in front of The Monmouth. Jane parked behind it. She would not fall in love with Chuck, though he was a genuinely nice guy. She liked the companionable craftsmanship working with him on *The Steam Tunnel Express*. When she got up to his apartment, they could talk about the paper's new name. *Augustin's Rag*? No.

Maybe Chuck's sexual over-eagerness came from missing Ivy. And Jane knew she herself had been uptight since Chicago. No wonder it had felt natural—good, even—to sprawl on the layout table with her shirt up and her pants down, slamming into each other as the table legs screeched on the cement floor. Chuck's mouth was voracious, his cock enormous, and the sex was delicious, there on the table, and later on the couch. She kept wanting more. The third time, though, she forced herself because he was so eager, and the fourth she was too sleepy to resist. She liked sleeping with him afterward. She'd felt safe and held his hand.

In the morning her vagina burned and she was disgusted. Chuck kept saying, "Four times!" as though that were important, as though he expected her to say *it was fabulous, let's do it again right now*. All that sexual energy could have come from anger. She thought of his resentment pouring into her body, her own long-brewed ferocity responding.

Now she needed a friend. The front door's metal tooth had not quite caught; she heaved and it lurched open. Jane climbed the three flights, walked to Chuck's door, tapped. Then she knocked. Then she pounded three times. He wasn't home.

Who else could she visit? Ivy was with Angela, and Shelly was probably there too. They'd all practiced *Female in America* together; the reading was scheduled for next week in the church basement. The play showed women's *lack* of liberation, Jane thought now. She had thought of a second act, about Welfare Mothers, and a third that showed what a liberated woman would be like. She imagined a national women's basketball league. But she didn't want to talk about that now, and on Hessler Road she would not be able to avoid the subject, unless she wanted to slake their curiosity about Tessa, which she couldn't do.

Dora would scorn what Bert had done. She'd say, "Fool! Why didn't he make himself useful, take care of the babies like he used to do?" Bert had loved the tiny kids in the Community Nursery. Tears came hot now, a good feeling in the cold car, softening and loosening. She let them come for a while and thought of Marvin. She hoped he could cry with Eleanor. Their experiments had brought them from bourbon to marijuana. Maybe getting stoned would be good for him. She wished...

Patricia. Her letter was among the papers in Jane's purse. Sitting in the car, she read it again. "The real Revolution has already started, and armed struggle is *not* where it's at," Patricia had written. "Even Che knew that armed struggle was a last resort, not a strategy." She added that she was eager to see Jane at the Women's Conference—something to look forward to. She would write to Patricia soon.

Now she was growing hungry. She had one dollar left till Thursday. She knew how to eat for nearly nothing, but it would be better to wait for Chuck. He was the one. She could lie comfortably by his side, her head on his shoulder, her eyes closed. *Friendliness, tenderness, togetherness...* But then she was imagining her father's arms, and herself small enough to be held with her legs wrapped around Dad's waist, her head on his shoulder, before the Rosenberg execution, when he crumpled, shrank, and grew cold. "Love Hurts" played its weeping chords in Jane's mind, in time with her sobs.

She was wakened by pounding and a shout. "Jane! Jane!" In the gloom on the other side of the window she saw Chuck's face, fierce and terrified. She'd fallen sideways on the seat, and he was pounding on the window near her shoes. Scrambling up, she hit the horn. It squawked, and she saw Chuck relax as she rolled down the window. Cold air poured over her.

"Are you all right?" he asked.

"Let me out." She shivered and pulled the halves of her jacket across each other. Chuck opened the door, and she stood next to him, wondering how to explain.

"Let's go eat at The Big Penny," he said.

In the booth, Jane stirred three packs of sugar into a cup of coffee, sipped it, and filled the cup to the brim with milk. She would buy rice and lentils later, or eggs and a few potatoes; then she'd have plenty to eat right through Wednesday.

"I've seen Ivy," Chuck said. "She was with Angela at the Student Union."

"Was it hard?" Jane asked. "Talking with Ivy, I mean."

"Yup," he said. He stroked his mustache, as if pondering which thought to share. "Tessa's giving up the symphony has inspired Ivy to give up the Art Museum. She said the lines had hardened."

Neither renunciation would work, Jane thought. "Tessa's on the way to New York," she said softly. "She had to get out of town. She may be gone for good."

"Of course." Chuck picked up his coffee cup, looked into it, put it down. "I couldn't listen very well, when Ivy was there."

"You were just..." Something so kind about Chuck: he approached the world tenderly when it hurt. "I like that you were willing to sit down with her," she said.

"A great thing about spending a night with you," he said, "was feeling the hook come loose."

"Glad to be of service," Jane said.

"I didn't mean that like it sounded," Chuck said. His sandwich arrived, warm and fragrant with bacon. He asked for more coffee. "Ivy says, 'it's time to commit,'" he said. "And I kind of lose it—because she means the Revolution, but of course I was ready to commit in another way, not so long ago, and she knew that. I don't like hearing them talk about the international struggle against U.S. imperialism when they don't understand what that means. Here we are, shell-shocked because Bert's been blown to pieces, and Ivy and Angela try to talk like Bobby Seale." He cut his sandwich into two triangles. "Movement people sure love the word *struggle*."

"Most struggles are internal," Jane said. "Maybe all of them."

"Here." Chuck put one triangle on his saucer and passed it across the table. "I think *struggle* probably means too many things."

"Tessa accuses me of navel-gazing," Jane said. "She says the problems are always in the objective conditions, never internal." The BLT felt wonderful in her mouth. Tessa was partly right: Jane felt remarkably more cheerful with food.

"Objective conditions: that's another mind-boggler," Chuck said, chewing. "I was going to ask if I could come home with you tonight."

"Want to sleep in Tessa's room?" Jane asked.

"I suppose," he said.

She wanted to explain that she didn't want sex right now. Why did that seem like a big deal? Couldn't a couple sleep together for comfort without the sex? She'd talk with him when they got there. At least she wouldn't be alone.

He was incredulous that she really did not want sex, even after he'd given her a tumbler full of wine. He simply did not *get* that she could let him hold her while they talked on the couch but could push him away when he started to unbutton her jeans.

"What am I doing wrong?" he asked.

"Nothing," she said. She didn't have words.

"Maybe if I'm really, really gentle?" He poked her shirt out of the way and kissed her collarbone softly.

She exploded from the couch. "Goddamn it, Chuck, I like you. Don't spoil it." She shut herself in Tessa's room, heard him in the kitchen washing dishes, singing "Rainy Day Woman" off-key. She liked having him here, but sex kept rearing its ugly head. The penis *did* have an ugly head, all blind, gooey mouth. Jane tried to get rid of that abnormal thought, but it wouldn't go away.

Tessa had left behind her stereo and her records, filling both shelves of an orange crate. Che and Beethoven glared from the walls. On the dresser was a jewelry box: Jane opened it and a dancer began to twirl to a tinkly phrase. On the tray inside lay a circle pin and a pair of pearl earrings. The room was colder than the rest of the apartment. Jane climbed into the bed and tried to sleep. Still half awake, she heard a tap on the door.

"What is it?" She propped herself on one elbow.

He peeked in. "I need company a lot more than I need sex. Really."

"I need sleep," she said. "But it's cold in here. Company would be nice."

He'd made toast and buttered it right to the edge. They ate it with hot tea and returned to the unfolded couch. Jane wore her pajamas and socks, and to keep warm she lay close to him, their legs and arms touching. After a while, he kissed her. She kissed back, and his kisses grew hungry. His hand came under her shirt. She shook her head, *no*, but he pulled her close and held her tightly, fumbling with her pajama strings. She pushed him away with both arms and climbed off the bed.

He caught up with her at the door to Tessa's room and picked her up, laughing, carried her back to the bed. He pulled down her pants and climbed on top of her. She could not stop him.

Afterward, she wept on his chest, his arm around her. "What's wrong? Why are you so upset?" he asked.

"I'm sad," she said. "About Bert and...oh, Chuck. I didn't want you to force me."

"But you wanted it. I know you did."

"No," she said. "I really didn't." She could not look at him. She curled into the far corner of the couch and pulled the covers over herself.

After a few ominous minutes she heard him whisper "I'm sorry." She did not respond. Eventually he left the bed. Then she heard the shower running. She did not move. She would not give up her bed, could not let him near her. Chuck's footsteps made the apartment floor creak. After awhile Jane heard him leave.

Chapter 27

November 14, 1968
The Movement Office & Case Western Campus

Chuck pulled "Good bye, Bert" out of the typewriter: 400 words, the best he could do using one quote from Marvin Kaminsky ("a passionate, committed revolutionary activist") and another from Shelly Kaplan ("Robbie accomplished more in 22 years than my grandpa did in four times that many").

"Can't you think of something that won't apply to most men in the Movement?" Chuck had asked Shelly.

"Sure," she said, "but not something I'd tell you. Or put in the paper."

"What do you want me to say?" Marvin had responded to the same question. "First he was my surrogate younger brother and then he loused up my Movement? I'm a slow-to-anger guy, so it took a while to get up a full head of steam against Bert Augustin. Now it's here, and I'm not ready to give it up."

The page and a half had taken eight hours and a full wastebasket. Now Chuck understood why most obituaries were so dull: the writers were choked on what couldn't be said. He'd written "dramatic, attractive, infuriating, brilliant, and certainly unlike anyone else"—all true, yet none of those qualities would stick to the page. If he wrote about Bert's attraction to guns and explosives, that would lead straight to home-made dynamite in the steam tunnels. Tactical and political differences seemed beside the point—which was that Bert had captured Ivy's affection and maybe her permanent allegiance.

All day Chuck had been taking coffee breaks to swallow the anger back down. Wasn't he sorry that Bert was dead?

Yes, because so much was still unresolved. Unsolved. Unfinished. Chuck rolled the desk chair with his heels, up and down the layout table. The folding chairs had been moved out. The phone had been disconnected. In sixteen days the lease would expire, and everything else would have to go, too. Today was the 14th; hadn't Sheldon promised him the Ahmed Evans interview by the tenth? In losing Bert—and any sense of safety, and a kind of innocence—Chuck had almost forgotten about Ahmed Evans, soon to be on trial for his life.

Sheldon didn't want to be visited at work unless there was an emergency. Okay, this was an emergency; Chuck felt entitled. He locked the office and walked to campus.

In a basement under one of the Case engineering buildings, Sheldon was a keypuncher; he typed with extreme accuracy into a machine that produced cards with little holes in them. The cards could be fed into a computer that occupied a room at the end of the hall. Chuck stood outside the door and watched through the glass as Sheldon's hands flew over the keys. *This is the new proletarian production line*, said a part of Chuck's mind. But there was no production line; Sheldon was alone in the room and wore an alligator sport shirt and loafers rather than a blue-collared work shirt. Chuck tapped on the glass, then knocked. Sheldon couldn't hear him. Chuck pounded. No response. Finally Sheldon picked up the stack of cards his machine had spit out and came toward the door. Then he saw Chuck.

"I couldn't finish that article," Sheldon said. "I was hoping you wouldn't notice." They walked a long hall tiled with beige linoleum, lined with beige walls. How did Sheldon tolerate this basement for eight hours every day?

"I need something for the next issue," Chuck said. "Just tell me how the interview went." They came to a beige door, and Sheldon knocked.

"I'm waiting here for Rhonda to take these cards and give me more data," Sheldon said. "Data are currency here, food for the System. Did you know data are plural? One datum, two data. Maybe it'd be better if..."

"What does all that stuff say?" Chuck indicated the stack of cards.

"Each card," Sheldon said, "carries a little bit of information that someone upstairs will use to plot into curves that predict a trend. I can't tell you any more than that. None of my business anyway. If you'd been polite enough to come at lunchtime we could've gone out. Howard Johnson's would've been nice, especially the breaded clams. I was about to suggest that you disappear for a minute, but it's too late now."

A woman opened the top half of the door and traded Sheldon's cards for a few pages. She had very dark skin, a short Afro and big gold hoop earrings. "Howard Johnson's would be outasight," she said. "What do you know good?"

"Just lovely," Sheldon said, beaming at Rhonda. His expression went blank as he leafed through the pages of new data to be keypunched in.

Their little exchange apparently was not about the work; it was probably a street-talk ritual. Chuck felt excluded.

"All copacetic," Sheldon said to Rhonda. "Back at you later." He and Chuck walked down the hall again.

Chuck knew he'd better leave. "Just give me your notes on Ahmed," he suggested. "I'll type them up."

"The problem is," Sheldon said. He unlocked his door, opened it, beckoned Chuck to follow him in, and shut them into the sound-proof room. "I talked to Brother Ahk-med—listened to him, mostly. I'd ask half a question and get a long response. I wrote as fast as I could. The notes are here, but..." He took his jacket off a hook on the door and pulled a roll of notebook paper from the pocket.

"What's he like—Ahmed Evans?" Chuck held out his hand, and Sheldon hesitated. Then he laid the roll across Chuck's palm.

"He's tall. Six-five, six-six maybe, with a deep voice—wonderful preacher's voice. Dark skinned. And he's nice. Sweet, even. We're sitting on either side of a table in the jail, bulletproof glass between us, guards standing by. The brother's polite to the guards. Asked after my mother."

"He knows your mother?"

"Everybody knows my mother. That's the way she is."

"I don't know her," Chuck said. "I want to. Then I can be like everybody."

"You're a conformist at heart," Sheldon said. "I knew that. Listen, I got no time to be rapping with you; I got to punch keys. The thing is," he flushed and moved to a corner of the room, his voice an urgent whisper, "I'm not writing that article, and you shouldn't publish it."

"Why not?" Chuck thumbed through the pages—twelve of them, close-written, two sided. "You got plenty."

"Yes indeed, stuff galore," Sheldon said. "Nothing about the shoot-out, of course, or the Republic of New Libya; the guard was listening."

"That's okay. We have other sources for that information. Is that the problem?"

"No," Sheldon said. "It's this: the brother makes no sense. We can't write an article that says Ahmed Evans is crazy."

Chuck looked through the notes. "Golden rule," he read, "Supremacy of Allah, the merciful, blessed be his name. Shining beauty of Malcolm X." He imagined the words in a deep preacher's voice raining down from a height of six-five or six-six.

"Look at the part about the UFO." Sheldon found the page and read, booming his voice: "Space creatures from another planet—they say my brothers and I, we beautiful, that the continuance of life on earth is in our hands. Beware of the gun, they say." He cocked an eyebrow at Chuck. "He met that flying saucer in 1962."

"Interesting," Chuck said. "But it rings true enough—except for the part about the space creatures. We could just write that he had an encounter with a UFO."

"Then he tells me the future," Sheldon went on. "He's got it all figured out astrologically: huge earthquakes, floods, massive upheavals in major cities throughout America. All the prison doors wrenched open. Fire and rain pummeling Cleveland. Next summer, or maybe not till fall."

"Some version of the Revolution," Chuck said. But he was beginning to see the problem. The stuff had a kind of zaney beauty, but how could he edit it? Where was the hard information?

"Sitting in the jail, listening to Brother Ahmed, I didn't know what to think," Sheldon said. "Maybe he killed those pigs after all."

"But we know he was inside an attic when the police got killed," Chuck said. "Don't we? And he wouldn't have killed his own people."

"Things are getting dangerous," Sheldon said. "It's not a good idea for me to be writing for you. My boss..." (he glanced out the window into the hallway) "did not appreciate the fact that I was at the Wallace demonstration with people who call policemen pigs."

"You let him intimidate you?"

"Yes," said Sheldon. "I do. Some of these data"—he riffled the pages Rhonda had given him—"are for police departments. I didn't tell you that earlier. Do you see what's happening? Keep out the way of that window, okay?"

"You're in line for a promotion," Chuck said. He found a place to stand behind a closet's open door.

"I want it, too," Sheldon said. "You're a good fellow, Mr. Chuck Leggit. I hope to see you around, but I'm not going to jeopardize my livelihood. Dig? Better give me those notes."

Chuck handed him the roll of pages. Sheldon started to tear them, then stopped. "I'll destroy these at home. Don't want anybody finding this stuff in my wastebasket." He practically pushed Chuck out the door.

So Sheldon thought things were dangerous. Chuck crossed the campus looking for Ungvary's pale blue sedan. Whoever had said *When people are threatened by us, we're getting somewhere* hadn't mentioned how sad that was.

By the time he got to The Monmouth, he'd thought of an editorial about how Movement people should learn to live with increased danger. *Eyes on the prize, hold on.* That would be the title.

Chapter 28

November 21, 1968
The Cleveland Museum of Art

Ivy held the bomb in both hands: a nine-inch lead pipe stuffed full of explosives and attached on one end to a long braided fuse soaked in gunpowder paste. She'd expected a bundle of dynamite sticks or something with wires, screws, and a clock attached, but Angela had assured her this would work. Ivy tucked it carefully into a paper bag and picked up the message-slips:

"Rulers know who they are, and they can no longer deny they are complicit in the oppression of a majority of people throughout the world. The Art Museum, its very size and shape based on centuries of European imperialism, its marble walls, staircases, and statues asserting the insidious principle of white supremacy and the power of the ruling classes, can no longer pretend to be benign. We repudiate cultural elitism."

She'd typed the sentences three times using carbon paper to make six copies, then cut them apart. Each was the same size as the slips of paper Bert had attached to balloons half a year ago. "Put them under rocks on the path around the lagoon." she said.

"Good idea," said Angela. "If we can find 24 rocks fast enough. Let's go."

It was deep night. Ivy wrapped her scarf over her nose and mouth; the cold made her eyebrows ache. They walked down Bellflower, past the big fraternities and the small Humanities departments, single file with Angela in front carrying the paper bag. The street lights made pale glowing pools of slate on the sidewalk.

Bronchitis: that's why Ivy's lungs felt as though they were full of kindergarten paste. She pushed herself forward. They rounded the corner where Severance Hall loomed, spot lit to emphasize its precious dominance, then crossed to the Museum grounds.

Angela twirled to walk next to Ivy, whispering *Dare to struggle dare to win* over and over. Her pea jacket was open; she practically danced. Ivy didn't have enough breath to chant. The scarf kept cold air from stiffening her lungs further, but it muffled her nose and mouth and grew damp, then froze. There was no going back.

One symbolic explosion—that's what Bert and Angela had planned. They hadn't settled on a target, but Ivy agreed Bert would approve of something at the Art Museum. Angela climbed the marble steps and stopped. Ivy followed, her heart slamming against her ribs.

The fountain wore a canvas hood for winter. The white marble oversized lovers writhed in each other's arms next to the dry pool. Between the gods and nymphs, naked children sat on little art-deco thrones, their smooth marble legs covering their genitals, their faces bent solemnly toward the ground, their arms outstretched. They looked as if they'd been pinned by the wrists to their thrones. In the dim light the tableau looked ghostly and obscene.

Angela was singing "All Along the Watchtower" in a breathy voice. "Let us not talk falsely now..." She clutched the paper bag, wide-eyed—high on something, Ivy realized. The streets were empty. They had only to place the pipe, light the fuse, and run for home.

"Let's put it in the fountain," Ivy said to Angela. "Those are odious statues."

She thought of Bert, that warm day on the grass near Koscuiszko, his hands on her skin, fingers tracing the bumps of her ribs. "You have a barrel chest," he'd said, and kissed her again.

"I'm an asthmatic," she'd told him. For the first time she had confessed asthma outright, admitting to herself the condition was permanent.

Bert had laughed, kissing her again. "Like Che."

That moment came into her mind, followed immediately by the picture of Che's corpse, laid on a table, his naked sprung ribs arched like a cliff over his concave belly. She'd seen the photograph in *Ramparts*, and now she realized she was putting Bert's face, his long straight nose and strong cheekbones, on Che's body.

Angela, who'd been staying in the Hessler Road apartment, adored Bert as if he really were Che. For weeks she'd sneaked him into her dorm room and fed him with what she could liberate from the cafeteria. "It's up to us," she'd said to Ivy, when they learned Tessa had left town. "Shelly's too materialistic, Gail's joined the Trots, and Jane's into feminism, which is not revolutionary all by itself."

Now she stood on the steps, her eyes enormous under the beak of her cap. "Not the fountain," she announced. "We're going to the *center*." She turned and ran up the next flight.

Ivy forced her feet to make the climb, her chest a fragile vessel about to burst. She envied Angela, who stomped and whirled like an Indian. Ivy wished she could have taken whatever it was—acid or mushrooms or speed. She'd forced down all the aminophyllin she could stand and now in the cold she felt nauseated, her senses dulled. But she was here.

"We're revolutionaries!" Angela spoke loudly, raising her arms high; Ivy thought of a Caryatid holding up a heavy roof. "*We hate* the *ruling class*" (four fist-punches into the air) "and *we love* the *people!*" Three more punches. She screamed the last sentence into the night. A police car tore up Euclid Avenue, its siren blaring. When it was gone, Angela took Ivy by the hand. "The museum's the center," she said. "Let's go."

On his pedestal, The Thinker brooded under his big eyebrows. "Help me up." Angela wanted to climb on Ivy's back; she wanted to reach The Thinker's feet, tuck the bomb behind the big knobby toes. He looked utterly vulnerable.

"I can't," Ivy said. She couldn't take the weight on her back. But she also didn't want to.

"We should've brought a ladder."

"Put it somewhere else. If not the fountain, then those 19th Century stiffs near the side entrance, the ones with pious American faces." Ivy tried to shout through her scarf. "Indian slaughterers, slave owners. And it's not a good piece of sculpture. Deserves to be blown up more than..."

"This is the symbolic center of the Museum," Angela said firmly. "Bert deserves nothing less."

"I can't blow up The Thinker." Suddenly Ivy felt like a killer. The statue was *he*, not it. He'd pondered with her through centuries of art and literature. He'd showed her how to ponder—naked, acknowledging both dark and light, paradise and inferno. *Phaeton* tumbled through her mind.

Limited, counter-revolutionary thinking, Bert would say. She knew the correct line: *attack the entire institution, challenge its purpose and its right to exist.* They had discussed the possibility that Bert planned to blow up the Administration Building or the chapel. Logical targets, but Ivy didn't like the idea. There was a risk of killing someone, for one thing. *The Plain Dealer* had reported an investigator's guess that Bert had simply lit a cigarette too close to some dynamite mixture. "We haven't strategized enough," Ivy said.

But Angela was past strategizing. With a fierce look at Ivy, she pulled the pipe out of the paper bag, bent her knees, threw up her arms and jumped. For a long second she seemed to soar, and the bomb flew into the air. Then it landed, neatly, in the crack between the bronze ankles, its fuse dangling down the pedestal. Angela took a Zippo lighter out of her coat pocket. "Run!" she hissed as the fuse caught.

Ivy ran. She let gravity propel her down the steps, then jogged along the walk by the lagoon's rim, her shoes ringing on the pavement. She had come almost to the far side when she heard the dynamite explode. The great choking balloon in her chest forced tears into her eyes. She could not hear Angela, neither her breathing nor any footsteps at all. She couldn't see anyone in the winter-barren garden. The Thinker's pedestal was empty. Sirens began.

They had forgotten the typed explanations, forgotten to find rocks to hold them on the paths. Ivy took them out of her pocket and threw them into the lagoon. They floated like trash on the surface. *There must be some way out of here.* She had to walk as fast and firmly as she could, as if she'd decided to take a brisk walk in the middle of the night because...because, she'd say if she was asked, she couldn't sleep. That would not be a lie.

She made it to the staircase that would take her up to Euclid Avenue. Clutching the iron banister, she pulled herself forward, eighteen, nineteen, twenty steps. Stop: no breath at all.

Angela would be loping across the lawn in front of Guilford by now; another minute and she'd be in her dorm room. The girl was utterly fierce, burning from within. In the Hessler apartment she'd gone foodless and sleepless, reading and scribbling in her notebook. Finally she'd let Ivy feed her Cream of Wheat and hot chocolate. One morning she had decided to quit school. Two days later she'd decided to major in physics.

It must be 4:00 in the morning by now. Pulling herself up another step, then another, Ivy saw the silhouette of a man in a long coat standing at the head of the staircase. "Miss?" said a voice. "You stop there, okay?"

She couldn't answer; not enough breath. He descended toward her, three steps, seven. "I'm with the Police Department," he said. "And you'd better tell me what you're doing here in the middle of the night."

Ivy shook her head. It was almost more than she could do, to shake her head. "Can't talk." She lowered her scarf and mouthed the words. His coat fit too smoothly over his shoulders. His shoes gleamed in the streetlight. He was a plainclothesman, wearing a private eye's fedora hat. He wasn't wearing glasses.

"Do you have an ID?" he asked. She shook her head. As soon as she could breathe again, she'd ask to see his. "Then I'll have to ask you to come with me." He held out his arm to indicate the direction.

Ivy shook her head; she couldn't move, and when he took her arm firmly she leaned on him, letting him practically carry her up the last ten steps. "You can't breathe, can you?" His voice turned suddenly human. "You're stuck out here having an asthma attack. I recognize that." He pointed to the base of Ivy's throat, where the skin moved as she forced air in, out. "We're going to the Emergency Room."

No. She had a flash of alarm. She would get home on her own if it took all night. She pulled away from his hand. "I'm okay," she said. Then she recognized his car, a pale unmarked sedan. "You work for Ungvary." Her voice sounded loud.

"And you're a friend of those subversives. I'll need you to tell me what you know about the explosion you couldn't have missed." In the distance, beyond the lagoon, police cars had gathered, their lights spinning red and white. "But right now I'm going to keep you alive."

Ivy turned toward the curb, ran three steps, and fell into a sort of blur.

She woke in a wheelchair that rushed down a corridor. Then came a bed, curtains, needles, an oxygen tent.

Slowly Ivy's head cleared in a mist-filled plastic-walled cell. Her hand was pierced, taped, and fastened to an IV. Her back muscles hurt from pulling the ribs open, pushing them closed. If she sat still, she could breathe using the very tops of her lungs. She peed whenever she coughed. As dawn came, she saw through the plastic a faraway room with a window and a framed print of blotchy flowers. A nurse came to check the bottle that fed the tube and inject it with medication. She pulled back the plastic curtain and said, "Okay, hon?"

There was no sign of Ungvary's deputy.

Ivy dozed and waked, half-dozed and half-waked. Sometimes the room was light; sometimes it was dark. She lost her ability to imagine the world outside the oxygen tent; reality was mist and the harsh jerk of her own breath coming into the little space at the top of her lungs, leaking slowly out again.

Through the mist she saw Chuck with daisies in his hands. Love and sadness rose in her chest like foam; she coughed and coughed, filling tissues with mucus, dropping them into a pile on the bed. When she could see again, Chuck was standing next to Aunt Peg, who was fumbling at the tent wall to find the nurse-call button. Ivy's heart squeezed. Why did her visitor have to be Chuck? Where were the others—Jane? Tessa? Angela? Shelly? The Movement was full of comrades who hadn't come. Then Chuck spoke to Aunt Peg, and she understood why.

"The police stopped me on the way in," he said. "The flowers helped convince them I was Ivy's brother. It was the only thing I could think to say."

I tried to stop from blowing up The Thinker, Ivy wanted to tell Chuck. *At the last minute I said...*What had she said? Probably nothing. She was as complicit as she could possibly have been. The Thinker was off his pedestal, and she'd been picked up by the police. They'd be back. She felt a wave of sleepiness she knew came from the medication snaking into her arm.

Aunt Peg poked her head through the plastic curtain. "Shall I tell Chuck to come another time?" she asked. "You'll be out of that tent in a few days."

"Tell him not to come back," Ivy whispered, teary from coughing and sadness, barely able to keep her eyes open.

"Your parents will be here tomorrow," Peg said.

"I don't want to see them," Ivy whispered. She meant *I don't want them to see me*. Before she could correct the wording, she passed out.

They came anyway, John and Hetty Barcelona, appearing in the room, then disappearing, then re-appearing, peering at her through the plastic of the oxygen tent, squeezing her hand—the one that wasn't needled and tubed. Days went by; Ivy didn't know how many. "We've been talking with the medical staff," Hetty said. "Your father's been dealing with the doctors and the billing department. So all your business is settled. You'll get better care now."

Ivy hadn't realized there was anything wrong with the care she was getting. She was still alive, and she might not have been. The space at the tops of her lungs was a little clearer. Her reasoning came back one morning, so she knew she'd been irrational. "How long have I been here?" she asked a nurse.

"Three days, so far," the nurse said. Reason told Ivy that Chuck, Peg, and her parents all knew she'd been found, *status asthmaticus*, on the steps to the Cleveland Museum of Art lagoon shortly after the blow-up of The Thinker with a scarf half over her face. If you were that cop, Reason said, you'd be talking to all four people, finding out about Ivy's subversive tendencies. And Chuck at least would have figured out exactly what she'd done.

But no policeman came the next day when they removed the oxygen tent. The space in the room felt luxurious. Ivy admired her bare foot on top of the blanket. It looked healthy, rotated hopefully on its ankle bones, wiggled its toes. Marvelous creature, that foot. She wanted very much to live. If she had to fight to breathe, if she had to be fat, if she had to go to prison for blowing up a priceless statue, if she failed the Revolution, if she had to be sorry the rest of her life for breaking Chuck's heart, if her parents hated her—even then, she wanted to go on living.

When the police arrived, she almost wanted the oxygen tent back, because she recognized him: the man with pink glasses who collected information from Greg Lambert and owed her $2.50 for his sandwich. He acted like he'd never seen her before, keeping his eyes on his clipboard-list of questions. "Your parents say you're a good student, been spending some time with the wrong people, like that fellow Leggit."

"We broke up," Ivy said. "Am I charged with anything?"

"Not yet," the policeman said. "We're still investigating. It's a slow process, but you could speed it up with information about the vandalism at the Museum of Art."

So Chuck hadn't mentioned Angela. Okay. Ivy wouldn't either. "Sorry," she said. "I took a walk that night. I'd been having bronchitis. I left my inhaler at home." That much was true. He didn't need to know she'd over-used the inhaler. "Are you the man who brought me here?"

"Not me." He shook his head. Then he asked a few more questions, looking at his clipboard, listening to her answers, this man who had ogled her in the waitress dress. Yes, of course, she'd heard the bomb go off. No, she hadn't seen anyone, not a soul. Well, sure, she was emotionally distressed, who wouldn't be, with explosions right next to her own campus, not to mention that it's distressing to be unable to breathe? He took her parents' address and warned her not to run away. Then he left.

Two days later Ivy left the hospital feeling scoured, inside and out. Aunt Peg hovered as she packed shoes, clothes, and books. No chance to be alone, to make phone calls, to talk with Shelly. Her parents had gone home, so now Peg drove her to Bloomington, grousing. "And this Thanksgiving I *needed* to stay in Cleveland!" She was managing Welfare Food Budget Week, planning a final shoestring dinner with all twenty volunteer families. "I wanted to help you, make things easier," Peg scolded, "but you've made it difficult. Every step of the way. You know that?"

"I'm sorry," Ivy said. She stared out the window at the bleached fields, the bony woods, the sky spitting gray snow. "I fucked up, Aunt Peg. I may have to go to prison." She tried to explain to Aunt Peg what she'd been so sure of, how the Museum symbolized imperialism and so on. "I don't think we were successful in raising anyone's consciousness," she said.

"Mmmm," Peg said. "Seems to me bombs are bombs. At least *you* didn't kill anybody."

"I think Bert Augustin had an accident," Ivy said. "Let's not talk about this with my parents, okay?" They didn't. Conversation over Thanksgiving dinner was cautious and light, floating on the surface of everything Ivy couldn't say. She stayed in her room most of the weekend with the excuse that she needed to rest.

Back in Cleveland, the antibiotics finished their work. Ivy went to classes and felt energetic. On Hessler Road, Gail fixed omelets as Jimmy complained about extremists who hurt the cause. Angela had gone home to Baltimore. So far as Gail or Shelly knew, she had not come back. "She must have dropped out," Gail said.

Shelly had attended Bert's memorial. "It was like you'd expect," she said. "Full of singing and revolutionary statements. I wept." But even Shelly couldn't or wouldn't tell Ivy what she needed to know, and Ivy would not talk about having become a midnight bomber.

Jimmy was busy promoting the demonstration planned in Washington for Nixon's inauguration. "With responsible demonstrators," he said. "You coming, Gail? I think these eggs need to be a little harder."

"I don't know, Jimmy," Gail sai,"whether I'm coming— or demonstrating responsibly. Fix your own eggs, next time, okay?" She went upstairs. Joe was coming home from Vietnam for Christmas.

Ivy dug through the newspapers and found a three-day old article that said the investigation was ongoing. A photo showed the toppled *Thinker* with his forehead pressed against the ground. Where his feet had been was a curve of bronze, like a huge ragged fin. She wished she could see him, tell him she was sorry. *Bombs are bombs*, she thought. Matter converts to energy, which in this case had dispersed into the cold. Last winter she'd seen The Thinker with snow on his head and his naked shoulders. Frozen in his own mind, she'd thought then.

On Marvin's kitchen table, Chuck lined up the next issue of *The Steam Tunnel Express*—still under its old name, which he didn't regret nearly as much as the missing articles. With Marvin's help, he'd written up the Charity Lunch invasion. He'd managed a brief story on Evans. The explosions couldn't be written about while investigations were "ongoing." No word on how long they'd on-go. Jane had not turned in the article about Welfare Budget Month, intended to run before Peggy Barcelona's chirpy story of the low-budget Thanksgiving dinner. But here was Aunt Peg's article, and Jane was gone—to an International Feminist Conference, she'd said. If that was all, why was the Coventry Road apartment up for rent? He had no way of finding out when she'd come back. He missed her. He missed Ivy worse. What a fool he'd been, standing there holding a bouquet of daisies, unable to touch her or talk with her, barely able to *see* her floating in that misty tent.

Between customers at the bookstore, he'd begun writing letters to an imaginary Communist advisor. "Dear Vlad, All these years I been waiting for you to come out of the woodwork, but no. You left us to make this Revolution in our own way. No wonder we fuck up! What's the correct party line on a Thinker who's lost his standing?"

Someday when he knew more, Chuck would have a lot to say about the steam tunnel explosion; *fuck-up* would surely be among the terms. "A regrettable accident," Marvin had written, in the editorial Chuck had demanded. "But Clevelanders' fear of Communist-inspired revolutionary vandals is ill-placed when the Establishment is the biggest vandal of them all."

Marvin stared into space these days. His girlfriend Eleanor was spacey too, Chuck had discovered last night when Eleanor shared marijuana with both of them. Marvin had sat cross-legged in silence, his eyes bright and unfocused (no glasses; perhaps everything was blurring together). Then he'd said, like a film narrator with a profound discovery. "Right...now...I can feel how everything's connected." Grass, it turned out, mostly made Chuck hungry. Marvin's undercooked spaghetti tasted wonderful; the long loaf of Italian bread was better; and the chocolate—oh, the chocolate cake!

No wonder Chuck felt dull and sleepy now, though it was the middle of the day. He sat at the table and began again. "Dear Vlad, Is marijuana a bourgeois thing or a potential leveler of masses? What about red wine?" He would have written more but someone was pounding on the door.

A man in a big coat stood outside Marvin's apartment. "You're Chuck Leggit."

"Yes, and you're...?"

"Detective Raymond Ford, Cleveland Police. I'm investigating a couple of explosions."

"Am I charged with anything?"

"Not yet," Detective Ford said. "But you're up for induction soon, are you not? If you're working with us, we can arrange a sort of delay..." He gave a little speech combining patriotism and bureaucracy. "This could be a great opportunity," he said, "to do yourself and your country a favor."

"No, thank you," said Chuck. "I have nothing to tell you."

"We have reason to believe that you were involved. I wanted to ask you before charges were filed."

"Fine. I still have nothing to tell you," Chuck said. He wished he could say, 'Let's go talk about things for a few days; then maybe we'd both understand why I studied pacifism while Bert played with dynamite and why a girl put a pipe-bomb between The Thinker's legs as a warped expression of loyalty.' I'd like to talk about what the American government is doing in Vietnam. We could try thinking how each bomb in Southeast Asia sends out shock waves that travel in concentric circles, further and further until *boom!* a crater forms in the Church of the Covenant parking lot and The Thinker topples. Was such a conversation possible? "I guess you'll have to file charges, when it comes to that."

"If you're sure," Ford said. "I can't be too much plainer."

"I'm not going to turn informant to escape induction, if that's what you're suggesting," Chuck said. "The truth is, if I could help you and the community settle your questions, I would. But I don't think I can, not the way you want me to."

"You edit the underground paper," Ford said. "You know a lot."

"Not about those explosions," Chuck said. Ford wanted names, that was all. *HUAC*, whispered Vlad the imaginary Communist. *Witch hunts.* "I'm very sorry."

"Me too," said Detective Ford.

Chuck locked the door, returned to the kitchen, and put on the water for instant coffee. He had things to write.

Chapter 29

December 27, 1968
Ann Arbor

From the Ann Arbor bus station, Ivy walked directly to the university and the SDS conference: Black fists on white paper were taped to the doors. Inside, a leather-jacketed man with a sandy beard sat behind a pile of literature. "I'm James," he said, "Marxist activist from Penn State."

"Ivy Barcelona," she said. "Case Western Reserve."

"No kidding," he said. "Where Bert Augustin got wiped out trying to blow up The Thinker?" He had a dry, sandy voice to go with his beard.

"Something like that," Ivy said, collecting an agenda, pamphlets, a position paper. James wouldn't care for details; he was already flirting with a woman whose head was wrapped with a paisley scarf. All over the room people were greeting each other with glad cries, hugs, and kisses.

"We've got the place to stand," she heard someone say. "Locate the lever, and we'll roll the whole capitalist-imperialist stone off its cliff into oblivion." Ivy shoved her suitcase and sleeping bag behind a turquoise couch.

"I'm going to Washington," a woman's voice said, "'Cause Nixon *sucks*."

"How are things in Bloomington?" Marvin Kaminsky sat down beside Ivy on the couch. Finally, a friend.

"The Barcelona household rang like a bell with its clapper muffled in felt," Ivy told him. The metaphor had come to her on the bus humming its way north. Her parents were worried about Glen who had not even sent a postcard from

India. "We had one pleasant conversation—me, my parents, my brother Randy—about the people who'd sent us Christmas cards. And Aunt Peg showed up with *The Cleveland Press*." So Ivy had learned that investigations had been called off.

Marvin listened. He'd bought Ivy a Black Russian on her 21st birthday, and they'd talked for hours about things like how the negative income tax could work and what a university might be like in the year 2000. He seemed to understand in a way Ivy could not imagine that there would indeed be a year 2000. He wondered if she'd like to drop acid. "It's an amazing experience," he'd said. "Extends the boundaries of reality." He described an acid trip's wild colors and images, and she'd said she might try it, someday. At the end of the evening he'd kissed her politely.

Now he rose from the turquoise couch. "Let's go to the Midwest Caucus," he said. "Tessa might be there." Tessa! Ivy was in the right place.

The caucus met in a classroom, and Tessa was there, in the teacher's spot, standing on one leg and twisting a lock of hair as she spoke. "Classical music was created by lackeys for the European nobility," she said. "We learn from Mao that *There is in fact no such thing as art for art's sake.* It's always political. Don't be fooled by special concerts for school kids. The whole point of giving kids the bourgeois experience is to show them that's what they should aspire to. It stops fundamental change."

"Whoop!" Angela jumped up from her seat, waving her Greek fisherman's cap at Ivy. Her cheeks were pink and round. Apparently she'd had sleep and food.

Tessa gave the podium to James, who quoted Mao: "If you want to know the taste of a pear, you must change the pear by eating it yourself. That's direct experience." When he moved his arms, the fringes on his leather sleeves swung dramatically. Ivy thought back to the darkness near the Art Museum, the *boom*, the adrenaline that made it possible for her to run without breath. Direct experience. Of what? Had she eaten the pear?

"I heard you were in the hospital," Angela said. "What the fuck happened?"

Ivy explained. "The police never really interrogated me," she said. "Now the investigation's been called off. I don't know why."

Angela shrugged, arms swinging from her shoulders. "I was in Baltimore," she said. "Some police came to the house, and my father threatened them. You know, police just aren't the brightest people. This guy really turned Dad off. Then the next day, Dad said, 'Okay, young lady, I've settled some things. Better tell me what you've done.' So I did."

"Just like that? What did he think?"

"He thought I'd been involved in the kind of prank he used to do with his fraternity at Williams. I just let him think that." Angela was too cheerful. Ivy felt the need to get away. She'd stepped across that hard line, turned against the Museum, and participated in a bombing. It was necessary and horrible. She'd thought Angela knew that.

A dozen cigarettes sent up filaments of smoke that collected in clouds on the ceiling. The alveoli in Ivy's lungs began to swell; she'd learned that's what the "tightening" was. She went out for a pill. In the hall she found a new steel drinking fountain with very cold water. Chin dripping, she looked up to see Chuck standing at the lit table, leafing through *New Left Notes*. Maybe he wouldn't notice her.

But he sauntered over. "How *are* you?" he said. "Besides thinner."

"Couldn't eat while not breathing," Ivy said. He was studying her face. "I'm fine," she said. To show him she took a breath and blew it out. Then she turned to go. He followed her.

"How's the Midwest Caucus?" he asked.

"Tessa's there," she said. "So's Marvin, Angela, and Mao Tse-tung. Also, too much cigarette smoke. I'm going outside."

"Do you mind if I come along?"

Of course she minded. But she didn't want to be alone. "Okay," she said. It was a bright, cold day, with almost a foot of snow carved into paths across the campus. Ivy wrapped her scarf around her mouth and nose. "I liked your editorial in the December issue," she told Chuck. "About the reverberations traveling from Pleiku to the steam tunnels." For a minute, reading his editorial, she'd felt the Movement was sane and whole again.

"How's Jane?" She hoped they'd been sleeping together; she didn't like to think of Chuck forlornly holding flowers on the other side of her plastic tent. "I missed the reading of *Female in America*, so I haven't seen her."

"She's in Minneapolis with her folks," Chuck said. "In a few weeks she's moving to Boston. She won't be back to Cleveland."

"Those Boston women she met? She's *moving* to be with them?" Ivy felt a pang. She liked Jane. Admired Jane. Would she ever see her again? "Are you sad about that?" she asked. They had left the campus and were walking past shops— a restaurant, a bookstore, a place full of leather-and-bead stuff.

"We weren't all that compatible," he said.

"Oh." There was a lot she couldn't ask. Yet Chuck was familiar in a way nobody else could be, walking slightly behind her, chopping and stirring the air with his hands as he talked. A long time ago she'd adored him without question, could not have imagined herself without him. Now the boyfriend-girlfriend almost-married thing was far behind, on the other side of October. They were just comrades, walking along. "Companionable silence," she muttered.

"What?" he asked.

"Nothing. Have you got CO status?"

"No," Chuck said. "I'm being inducted."

"Oh Chuck, why?" She stopped. They stood near a filling station with Christmas lights in its window. Chuck took a few steps and faced her.

"I'm not really a pacifist," he said. "So I'm resisting the Selective Service System."

"Maybe they won't induct you."

"They already have," Chuck said. "I got the notice before I left Cleveland."

"What will you do?"

"Go to prison for a year or so. Write a lot. Read a lot." His face looked healthy, his voice was strong. "A lot of men are doing it, and they've survived," he said. "Do you still plan to go around the world?" He had not said anything about the police investigations.

"Eventually," Ivy said. "I wish there were a way to just study things I'm curious about. Revolutions in China and Cuba. American Indians and slavery. How women came to be dominated by men."

"I'm not convinced women *are* dominated by men," Chuck said. They had walked a loop of some sort; the campus lay ahead of them. "Well, I guess I'll be seeing you." He turned to go down a side street full of houses.

"You won't be seeing me," Ivy said. "That's what you mean."

"Yeah, you're right. I won't see you." He took three steps. "Good to talk."

"Yes," she said. She held out her hand to him.

He looked at her hand curiously, then pulled at his mustache. "I'm staying with a friend I met yesterday," he said. "You want to come inside and get warm?"

"For a little while." There would be time, later, for a discussion with Tessa, who would know why the Subversive Squad's investigation had been stopped. She might know how Angela's father had "settled" with the police. And living among the vanguard in New York, Tessa would know the way forward.

The house was a block down. Inside was a Movement living space: posters, bookshelves made of cement blocks and used boards, a couch draped with an India-print bedspread. No one was home. "I think I saw some tea in here," Chuck said.

While he rattled in the kitchen, Ivy browsed the bookshelves. These people had art history books and poetry. One cup of tea; then she'd go back. They sat at the kitchen table looking at the yard, where a snow-mounded tire hung from a tree. "New snow looks so clean," Chuck said. He took her hand. "You've changed," he said, "in a good way, I think."

He still didn't hate her. She couldn't not love him. "You wrote a nice eulogy for Bert," she said.

"It was crap, nothing like what Bert deserved," he said. "Oh shit, Ivy, if you stay here another five seconds I'll have to kiss you. So if that's out of bounds, just go now, and maybe someday I'll write to you from prison."

"It's not out of bounds," she said. They kissed in the kitchen and she thought, he's gotten better at this. She didn't want to let go of him. And then he was helping her off with her sweater, leading her to the bedroom where he was staying, a tiny space off the kitchen. "Um. I've gone off the pill," Ivy said.

"I think I have a condom somewhere," Chuck said.

"Never mind, I'm having my period." It was good to feel his hands on her shoulders, to wrap her arms around his torso and move in close, close.

"You're lovely," he whispered.

For months, it seemed, she'd lived in pain and suffocation, her body a container of sticky phlegm, urine, and bitter chemicals. She hadn't felt lovely till now, sliding into his arms and onto the bed. They made love more gently than ever before, knowing this was the last time.

Afterward she rushed to the bathroom to avoid getting blood on the bed. The house was cold; she had goose bumps, and her feet were frozen from the ankles down. "Do you think it'd be all right if I took a shower?" she called. Chuck didn't answer. Maybe he'd gone out for a minute. She should have stayed in bed longer.

She shouldn't have gone to bed with him at all.

She stepped into the tub and turned on the water; it gushed out cold, sluicing over her, drenching her hair, pouring down her back. She rubbed soap on her thighs and between them, making herself withstand the ice on her skin, gasping and shivering as blood washed down the drain. She was too cold to move toward the cheap shampoo on the shelf behind the cold waterfall. Then she got used to it, or perhaps the shower was becoming tepid. It was. The water grew lukewarm, then warm, then hot, and Ivy began to weep. She didn't deserve a hot shower, and she loved it so. She shampooed her hair and scrubbed the rest of her body. She shampooed again.

Chuck was writing in a notebook at the kitchen table when she came out, her body pink and strong, as if it were pleased with her. "This was a note for you," he said. "I gotta get back to the meeting. You took a long time. Are you okay?"

"I washed my hair," she said. "I better stay indoors till it dries, or I'll catch cold. Can't do that anymore. You go on back. I'll read something."

"I will go," he said. "I don't want to make a habit of you. I think that was my big mistake: you were a habit." He was putting on his jacket as he talked, tucking his pen into his pocket, his notebook under his arm. "Well, good bye." He reached out his arms. Then he tucked one hand in his pocket and shook hers with the other. The warmth of his familiar fingers made her feel like weeping.

"Bye," she said. "See y... Have a good meeting." He would be an imprisoned draft resister. She could suggest they write, but what if he didn't? What if he did, and she didn't write back? What if he sent impassioned letters "how sincerely I do love"? No. Better this way. Except that it wasn't better: she was crying alone on the lumpy couch in a stranger's house. Chuck was beside the point, wasn't he? She was committed to the Revolution, and there was a long road ahead. Hadn't she glimpsed Brecht on a shelf here? Ivy trolled the spines, found the book and read "To Posterity" again, carefully, in both languages. The translation was not quite right. "In the dark ages" was not about an era, it was just "in dark times." And "Do not judge us/too harshly" was more like "Think of us with patience" in German.

She paged through, sinking into Europe of 30 years ago. "Children's Crusade" was not about medieval children trying to save Jerusalem, but about a band of children in Poland, 1939, fleeing their burned-out villages. Brecht made them a teeny society; they took care of each other, cooked, made music, taught each other to write, acquired a dog. They made love, fought a short war, held a funeral. Winter came, and the children began to starve. Then they disappeared. The dog showed up in a strange village with a note: "Please send help! We don't know where we are!" But no one looked for the children, and the dog starved to death.

It could have happened. In a house lived in by people she'd never know, Ivy sat on the couch, holding *Selected Poems of Brecht* and weeping as, outside the window, afternoon shadows crept across the winter landscape, bounded by pines and birches. Broken sunflower stalks stuck up through the snow. Someone had painted a peace sign on the garage, with a dove and clasped hands, one black, one white. The paint was peeling, and the garage roof sagged. She was not weeping for Brecht's lost children. She did not regret having sex with Chuck. She would not try to find him back at the conference.

She found Angela and Tessa in the meeting of the whole. A skinny, blond man with deep eye-sockets wielded a microphone on a platform in the center. "Klonsky," Tessa whispered. "National Secretary."

"What have I missed?" Ivy asked.

"A *lot* of talk," Angela said.

"We're aligning ourselves with the working classes," Tessa said, vaguely. She was paying close attention to the speakers, each introducing himself by political position:

"I'm Ed Waverley, Maoist anti-imperialist from San Francisco State!"

"I am Gene Bazarov, independent radical!"

Following Tessa's example, Ivy listened carefully; the issue seemed to be who was most oppressed. Someone thought the Chinese peasants had been more oppressed than American Blacks. Another said the American Blacks were more oppressed, because land reform had succeeded in China. A few women pointed out that women were most oppressed of all. Wrong. A wealthy woman—Jackie Kennedy—could not be said to be oppressed, under any circumstances. Fred Holt, Marxist from Illinois, yelled, "Students are an oppressed group by definition!"

Not all students. Not by definition. Three people took turns explaining which students could be called oppressed and which could not. James took the microphone and looked severely out at the crowd as he delivered a class analysis of American students. He must be too hot in that fringed jacket, Ivy thought. She'd removed her coat and she was still too warm. James was just swinging his fringes. She couldn't follow what he was saying.

Then a passionate student accused James of being an old-line Communist. "I'm oppressed, and I go to Columbia!" His point was that students lacked control over the means of production. "John-John Kennedy is oppressed!" he cried, listing John-John's constraints: no choice of school or playmates; couldn't go anywhere without the Secret Service; couldn't *play*— "not even a fucking simple game of stickball!"

Competition, Ivy realized. They want to be Black, but they can't, so they'll try to be Algerian and Russian. The winner gets to be an honorary Chinese peasant. There were no Chinese peasants in the room to judge, though there were plenty of quotes from Mao.

A Black man took the mic and tried to summarize what he'd heard; it sounded even crazier through his mouth. "If any of you people come down to my community and try to organize me," he said. "I'll blow your fuckin head off!" Then he left the hall.

There were a few seconds of silence. Klonsky came back to the microphone and said, "John-John is *not* oppressed, people. Get your heads out of your asses."

Angela whooped approval. Tessa looked stoney.

The discussion went on; Ivy lost any ability to pay attention. What the hell did *oppression* mean anyway? Had she ever known? She went out to the lobby and realized she didn't care, any longer, to question Tessa. She hadn't eaten all day. Maybe there was a place on campus to buy a sandwich.

Angela found her. "Marvin says they put The Thinker back."

"Without his feet? Why? What does that mean?"

Angela shrugged. "You have to ask him. I just thought you'd like to know it's back up. You liked it."

"I did. Do. Can't wait to see him without his feet, staring into chaos." How fitting. And the missing feet somehow echoed Brecht's lost children: *We don't know where we are.*

"Listen," Ivy said. "I'm sorry I…"

"You were pretty sick," Angela said. "I figured that out after."

Inside the meeting Tessa yelled, "Extermination of the ruling class and seizure of state power is the only demand that is not co-optable!"

"These meetings make me dizzy," Angela said.

"They're boxing themselves into corners that don't fit the real world," Ivy said. She thought of the cop in the winter coat who'd put her into his car and driven her to the emergency room. The possibility of a kind policeman didn't fit in that room full of independent radicals, Maoist-pacifists, and unrequited lovers of the working classes.

"You and I both loved Bert, didn't we?" Angela said.

"So did Tessa, even more than we did," Ivy said. "If he was here now, he'd probably be telling us all to get guns."

"Well of course," Angela said. "That's the next step."

"Who would you kill first?" Ivy asked her. "If you don't plan to kill anyone, you don't need a gun." Somewhere in the last week, or the last hour, she'd come to that.

"The next step after symbolic bombing," Angela said. "You watch, they'll come after us as soon as school starts again in January. We should prepare to defend ourselves."

"Maybe so," Ivy said, telling herself that if Chuck could go to prison, she could, too. Nixon would be president. Suddenly she was frightened.

Back in the meeting, James had the microphone again. "I think we can all agree that all nationalism—Black nationalism, too—is basically reactionary," he said. He didn't know about the Glenville kids in their bandoliers, Ivy thought. Dying. She fled the hall.

Marvin stood by the lit table fastening the toggles on his duffel coat. "Where are you going?" she asked. Maybe he would say *Out for a drink*.

But he said something better: "Cleveland."

"Will you take...I mean, do you have room in the car for me?" she asked.

He smiled. She retrieved her sleeping bag and suitcase from behind the couch. "So how did they decide to prop up The Thinker?" Ivy asked as they crossed the parking lot.

"Sherman Lee," Marvin said. "He said it was historical— a sign of the times. A repair job couldn't do it justice."

"Is that why they called off the investigation?"

"Hell, I don't know. Here, get in." He opened the car door. Red. The Valiant had made the trip. "Doesn't have much oomph, but if we take it slow," he said, sliding into the driver's seat, "we'll get there."

He drove through Ann Arbor, pretty with its snow cover. "Here's what I know about the investigation: I was interviewed by two guys who didn't seem to like each other."

"Did one have pinkish frames on his glasses?"

"Yeah, that was one. The other was tall and non-descript, but thoughtful. You could tell he had a mind."

"And they didn't get along?" Ivy could see puzzle pieces come together.

"They seemed at odds. They didn't play good cop/bad cop. They just got in each other's way. I think the dumb one was the supervisor. He couldn't stand having a subordinate brighter than he was. But listen, I could be completely wrong."

Tessa would never say that: *I could be completely wrong.* Neither would Bert. They would be scared to say that, Ivy thought. "What about Greg Lambert?" she asked.

"He's back at Cleveland State," Marvin shrugged. "I saw him there the other day. I waved. He got a little pinker in the face, but he waved back."

"Wow," Ivy said. She told how Angela's father had "settled" with the police. "I guess he paid them?"

"I guess so," Marvin said. "I don't even know Angela's last name."

"Neither do I," Ivy sighed. "Maybe she's another informant."

"She's too young," Marvin said. "And I don't want to even think about another informant—not yet."

"Do you think there's a need for symbolic bombing?" Ivy asked. She wanted to keep Marvin talking. Would The Thinker be as symbolic as Angela had meant it to be?

"I think it's like this," Marvin said. "When something— a police station, bank, school administration office, cultural warehouse—when it symbolizes a kind of power that makes you feel small and scared, and it then explodes, you get a burst of courage and wild joy."

"That's oppression, isn't it? Feeling small and scared?" Ivy thought of the oxygen tent.

"Yes, and there's also not having any money, not having enough to eat, getting kicked out of your apartment, getting shot at by police..."

"Objective conditions, Tessa would say."

"Right," Marvin said. "And some people are just *good* at destruction."

"Bert?" Ivy thought of Bert at the dinner table on the night of the Columbia Takeover, moving bowls and silverware around to show the location of Morningside and the gym—and then looking longingly at Tessa. Ivy thought of his demolished baby finger, his balloon-drop, his sexiness. He was good at a lot; destruction was the least of it.

"Maybe if Bert had another life, he'd go in for demolition work," Marvin said. "You know what? I was relieved when he was gone. It was an ugly feeling—bothered me. Now I think some destruction's necessary."

"Just for that burst of courage and wild joy?"

Marvin laughed, almost choking. "Don't underestimate courage and wild joy. No. Maybe it's like this: some of us destroy, others build, and we need each other."

"Oh," Ivy said. "And some of us try to understand what's going on underneath. Jane did that."

"I'm going east to visit her," Marvin said. "Then I'll go west."

"You're not staying in Cleveland? Why not?"

"I want to see California."

Ivy considered saying, *Take me with you. I want to visit Jane. And then I want to go west.* But she wanted to graduate. She wanted to see what could be done next in Cleveland: building, not destroying.

After they crossed the Ohio border they bought hamburgers and kept talking.

"You know, it's a shame," Marvin said. "A couple of months ago, SDS had more influence than we knew what to do with. But that was just it: we didn't know what to do. We'll have to start over."

"That's not how they were talking at the conference," Ivy said. She took another bite of hamburger and chewed. They were in darkness now, traveling east.

"I think I saw at that conference how insignificant a Movement could make itself."

Ivy slumped, surprised. SDS was the vanguard, the crest of the wave. Marvin didn't even seem to be angry when he said "insignificant." She'd come today hungry for clarity and comradeship because confusion was so painful, because she'd missed that lively warm wave of the Movement, and now? *Splat.* Ideas had deteriorated into theories which had frozen into hard lines. "But Marvin—we're going to make the Revolution, aren't we?" She was frightened. She didn't want to lose that future she carried, sometimes like a torch, other times like a magic stone in her pocket.

"Well," Marvin said. He took his glasses off and wiped them with his handkerchief, one hand at a time. Then he put them back on and squinted over the steering wheel into the snowy waste. "We can try," he said. "That's all we can do: figure out one thing and do it. Then figure out the next thing, and do it. Then the next."

AFTERWARD

But you, when at last it comes to pass
That man can help his fellow man,
Do not judge us
Too harshly.
from "To Posterity" by Bertolt Brecht

Late in 1968 the Selective Service raised its quota to 3,000 new draftees per month. By the end of that year, 14,589 American soldiers had been killed in Vietnam. The war would drag on seven more years.

Into the future Ivy would carry the kaleidoscope Chuck had given her, its patterns dissolving and forming, each a microcosm of the luminous world. She noticed her memories acted like its colored glass bits, finding new places to fit in the circle, shifting every time she tried to talk about what had happened that year.

Chuck took his notebooks into draft-resisters' prison, filled them and brought them out again a year later. He wrote himself from 1968 into the future, struggling to understand what was happening and what he thought about it all, filling notebook after notebook, publishing in newspapers and magazines and later on the Internet.

Jane carried nothing to Boston, where she settled with Patricia in a collective of women, learned to build furniture, and wrote handbooks on women's health and Welfare rights. She developed a habit of writing what she called love letters to Dora and the three children, to Ivy, and to Marvin. She wrote love letters to Tessa as well, but couldn't sent them, as the address had been lost.

Acknowledgments (continued)

Susan Streeter Carpenter grew up in Cleveland, roaming Cleveland Heights, University Circle and Liberty Boulevard (now Martin Luther King, Jr. Parkway). She graduated from Case-Western Reserve and eventually she settled in Yellow Springs, working as an alternative school teacher, anti-poverty worker, home health care administrator, independent radio producer, free lance writer, and teacher of writing. For twenty years she was involved with the Antioch Writers' Workshop.

"Writing this book has been a long process of coming to terms with the cataclysmic events of those years," the author says, "events at once personal and national."

She is now assistant professor of English at Bluffton University, specializing in fiction writing. For her fiction Carpenter has received an Ohio Arts Council Fellowship, a Pushcart Prize nomination, and two first-place Westheimer awards from the University of Cincinnati, as well as a Distinguished Dissertation Fellowship in the Humanities. She has published essays, poetry, and short stories in magazines such as *Snake Nation Review*, *The Beloit Fiction Journal*, *Crab Orchard*, and the anthology *Best of the West 2009*.

Susan Streeter Carpenter, Washington, D. C. 1969
(Photo by Berch Carpenter)

LaVergne, TN USA
30 October 2010
202884LV00002B/6/P